Win a Cherry on Top

LETIZIA LORINI

To the girls who are too much
and the boys who wouldn't take any less.

Author's Note

This book contains on-page intimate scenes and mature content and is intended for mature audiences only. For more details on the content warnings for this novel, please visit: www.letizialorini.com

Tease

CHAPTER 1
Recipe For Change

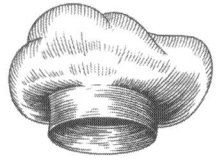

Everyone in the kitchen, stat," Ian calls as he comes out the back of the restaurant. Chefs and busboys around me begin to stub out their cigarettes, and I wait for Oliver as he takes one last puff.

This is weird. Ian and Amelie usually keep their businesses separate, yet today, the private chefs from Chef & Tell have been asked to Daisy, her restaurant. And her staff is here too—every single one of them.

"Must be big news," Oliver says as he walks through the open door. His tired eyes meet my gaze over his shoulder. "Everyone's here."

We join everyone else in the crammed kitchen—though the dining room would be a more spacious setting, the lunch service is about to start, and the waitstaff just finished setting tables.

"All right," Ian says, adjusting the cuffs of his black shirt as he turns to his wife. He rubs his hands together, and in the silent exchange between them, I sense a sizzling nervousness. Considering it's Ian and Amelie, I wouldn't be surprised if they announced they're retiring and moving to South Africa or relocating to build houses in Haiti.

1

"We have some personal news we'd like to share with you."

"Oh! Should we expect a mini-Ian?"

Amelie's bobbed hair shifts as she tilts her head. "Because every woman my age with a piece of news must be pregnant?"

Ian's eyes widen as he holds a hand up. "No guesses, please. And no, we're not expecting." He clears his throat. "As you all know, Chef & Tell, my venture of private chefs, is turning one year old soon." There's a general swell of excitement, and Ian placates the group with a wave. "Thank you, thank you. We're still new, but things are going well. We have thirty chefs working with us and a long waitlist of clients." Another round of applause, then, "So when a new opportunity presented itself, I figured . . . I think the restaurant and the company can both survive our absence for a while."

Their *absence*?

"Amelie was asked to join the judges' panel of The Silver Spoon."

A series of *Ooh* and *Aah* rises from the crowd, and after a fresh round of applause, Amelie takes a step forward.

"Thank you so much. For those of you who don't know, The Silver Spoon is a competitive cooking show. Filming lasts about a month, and I'll need to be in Mayfield a week from today."

"And I'm going with her," Ian adds.

Oh. She's leaving. They both are.

That effectively creates a wave of panic, and as a low murmur spreads, Oliver turns to me. "No head chef and no manager? It'll be *epic*, man."

I give him an indifferent shrug. Maybe he feels that way because he works here at Amelie's restaurant, but as one of Ian's private chefs, I work alone.

Well, I *will* work alone once they assign me my first client. As of now, all I've done is meet Amelie after hours almost every day to build my cooking skills, and take the course they asked me to ace: Cooking Techniques 101.

Gotta say, there's nothing quite as humbling as twenty-year-old brats who can't even tie their shoelaces helping me through a course I'm too old to take anyway.

But I guess that's the price to pay for starting a new career at the age of thirty-seven. Raw talent, as Amelie describes it, but no basic training.

"Wait, so what's going to happen with the restaurant?"

"Barbara Wilkow will step in and cover for me," Amelie says. "She's the head chef of La Brasserie, back in Creswell, so you'll be in perfectly capable hands."

"And who's going to crack jokes and pretend to be working hard?" one of the line cooks asks Ian.

The crowd chuckles.

"You're fired," he deadpans, which causes everyone to burst into even more laughter. "Shane will help with management, and I'll still work with all of you from Mayfield." He points his finger at the line cook. "You're not getting rid of me yet."

"Shane?" Oliver whispers.

Weed has *fried* his brain cells. "Hassholm. The owner of the bakery out front. Desserts for Stressed People?"

He recoils. "A *baker*?"

I hold back an eye roll. The one perk of not having spent half my life in the kitchen is that I'm not nearly as arrogant as some of these people.

"He's a baker, yes," Ian says. When Oliver realizes Ian's heard him, he awkwardly crosses his arms. "But if I were you, I'd focus on his reputation rather than his cooking skills. He's managed events for years, where he's been lovingly referred to as Mr. Asshole."

Oliver swallows.

"Clever," I comment, enjoying his sudden tension. "Because Hassholm sounds like ass—"

"Yeah, I get it," he mumbles.

With a satisfied smirk, I focus on Ian and Amelie.

"Guys, I promise, I wouldn't have signed off on the opportunity if I wasn't sure the restaurant would be in the best hands." Amelie's usual patient smile is accompanied by a slight tension at the corners of her brown eyes. "This is really important to me. My father was a judge on the show, and you might remember him as—"

"*Le dictateur*," someone says.

"Exactly." Amelie's shoulders stiffen. "I'd like to leave another sort of legacy. I want to be part of helping a new generation of cooks, and guarantee at least one of them a really bright future." She looks around. "You all know how much I love my kitchen. This wasn't an easy decision."

Some of the crowd settles, but there are still plenty of worried faces. I can't begin to imagine what the head chef leaving must mean for the restaurant cooks, but it's probably like a captain abandoning the ship.

Sure, she's getting them another captain, but things will be weird for a while.

"Okay, well, that's it from us. We're happy to take any questions, and the door to my office is always open, okay?" Ian's lips bend in a dashing grin. "Now, back to work. Or go home—whichever applies."

As everyone begins dispersing, Oliver jerks his chin at me. "I'm off until dinner service. Want to go grab a beer?"

A beer? "It's midday."

"So?"

Oh to be twenty-four.

I open my mouth to tell him I have a daughter who'll be out of school in a few hours when Ian calls my name.

"Coming." I walk toward him, patting Oliver's shoulder. "Rain check on that beer."

Ian gestures at me to follow him into the office and once I close the door behind me, he drops on the chair. "How's it going?"

"Good. You?"

He shrugs. "A little worried those people will burn down my wife's restaurant."

I take a seat opposite the desk. "This is a great opportunity for Amelie."

"It is. And with her family history . . . you know." He brushes a hand through his dark blond hair, his muscles shifting with the movement.

The complicated relationship with her cold, stern father who died almost a year ago and the non-existent relationship with her absent mother? Yeah, I'm aware.

Amelie and I have spent what must be hundreds of hours over the last year in the kitchen, just the two of us, cooking. Prepping. Studying recipes. And talking, for hours and hours.

She's basically family at this point.

Ian waves the thought off. "Anyway, I really think it's the right decision."

"I'm sure it is. And it's only for a month."

He hums, then laces his fingers together over the desk. "Which brings me to today's order of business." He grabs a folder then hands it over. "Your first client."

My first . . . *what*?

I stare at him, gobsmacked, until he gestures at me to open the folder.

I do, my heartbeat increasing steadily.

Beatrice Arnault.

"*Reaaaally* rich woman," Ian comments as I read through the first page. Lunch, and dinner, five days a week. "Really arrogant too. She *demanded* we send Amelie."

"Amelie?"

"Yeah. I guess she thought she worked for me." Ian huffs out a half-laugh. "Anyway, I told her we'd send the next best thing."

Me? *I'm* the next best thing? The guy who just got his Cooking Techniques 101 diploma? What about Howard, a seasoned chef with traditional Italian training? Or Robbie, who's worked in some of the best restaurants in the country?

"Ian, maybe I should start with some low-profile client. This feels . . ." I tap my foot against the floor in a restless rhythm. "Above my pay grade."

"Aaron, Amelie has been mentoring you. She's taken you under her wing. She wouldn't have done that if she didn't believe you were worth investing in." He narrows his eyes at me. "You know, you've been eating up a lot of our private moments."

"And I'm incredibly grateful, but—"

"No 'but.' My wife thinks you're ready, so I think you're ready." He taps the folder. "Allergies and preferences are there. Mrs. Arnault wants to meet you before giving you a key, and after that, she'll share with you her calendar so that you know when she'll be home for meals."

"Okay, so when she's not home . . ."

"Her kid still needs to eat."

Her kid. Of course. "No husband?"

"Nope. Divorced." He widens his eyes. "We spoke for less than five minutes on the phone and I can confidently say I'd divorce her too if I could."

With a thoughtful nod, I read through the list. Apparently, someone's allergic to pineapple, and they refuse to eat pork.

"You'll start in two weeks, which unfortunately means we won't be here. But I'll be available if you have any questions, and Robbie has agreed to help you out should you need it." He claps. "You're good, Aaron. You'll do great."

Sounds like I don't have much of a choice.

"Okay. Thank you." I set the folder down. "Do you think Amelie would be open to—"

"Concocting a menu with you?" He smacks his lips. "She knew you'd ask that, because *she* would ask that. And the answer is yes."

I rub the five o'clock shadow on my jaw. Maybe they're right.

Maybe I'm ready, and I'm just freaking out. I've been dying for an actual client for months—I just didn't expect it to be the queen of England or something.

"Maybe I should talk to her. See if—"

"Aaron," he interrupts. "I get it. You and Amelie, besties forever. But *I'm* your boss, and I'm telling you this is your assignment. What say you?"

I clear my throat. "Yes, boss."

"There ya go." He shuts the folder, and his relaxed demeanor is back. "Now that work's covered . . ." He reaches into one of the desk drawers and takes out a small card. "I've got something for you."

"What's that?"

He smirks. "One of the other chefs, Jerry, is working for the owner of TOP, and they sent us a few gift cards. I've got about fifteen of them."

"TOP?" I look down at the metallic card, then turn it around and notice the words engraved in the back.

Tease. Obsess. Play.

"What the hell is this for?"

"It's for a . . ." He tilts his head. "A subscription service."

"To . . ." I look down at the card again. Cherry red, sleek, and somewhat cryptic. With how vague Ian is being, this can only be about one thing. "Erotic content?"

"Bingo."

Jesus Christ. "What—Are you giving me a jerk-off gift?"

"Well, it's not like I'm handing you lube or anything."

"There's plenty of free stuff I have access to," I say as I hold the card out. "Give this to one of the younger people who actually have the energy to jerk off."

"See, that's just proof of how much you need it." He shakes his head firmly. "Take the card. How about Sadie sleeps over tonight? Last time she did my nails, and you know I'm overdue for a mani."

Half the time I talk to Ian, I actually can't believe what I'm hearing. "You want to babysit so I can masturbate."

"Uh-huh." He bites his bottom lip to hide a chuckle. "I'd offer to babysit so you can take an actual woman out, but—"

"I'm not ready for dating."

"So take the card."

I hesitate, then with a nod I tuck the card in my pocket, my face flushing. Though I have every intention of throwing it out, I could use a night by myself. The house is a disaster, and the meal prep schedule I came up with has gone to hell already. "Sure, okay. I'll drop her off after dinner."

"Great. See you later."

He waves, the same cheeky smile on his face. As if it wasn't weird enough that he gave me a gift card for an erotic subscription service, the thought of him knowing I'm jerking off as I do it has killed any possibility of it actually happening.

But he doesn't need to know that, so I slip out of the restaurant and into my car.

Looks like I have a date with myself tonight.

"Did Mom call?"

Sadie has been buckled into her booster seat in the back of the car for three minutes, which is two more than she usually lasts before asking about Josie. Though I can't blame her for it, a new part of me gets ripped out every day. "Yes, baby," I lie. "She said she loves you and she misses you a lot."

"Is she coming back?"

Another hit. Another morsel ripping away. "Of course she is, just not now. She needs some more time to feel better."

Sadie looks out the car window. I can't pinpoint how exactly, but she seems older. I see it in the sharpness of her eyes and the set of her jaw. And the fact that she stopped smiling six months ago, when her mom last committed herself to rehab.

"How was school today?"

"We learned about colors. Did you know that blue and yellow make green?"

"I did, yes. What do blue and red make?" Through the rearview mirror, her wide eyes stare at me. "Purple, your favorite color."

Jaw dropping, she grabs her backpack and takes out her notepad and markers. I assume she has to see for herself, and I'm proven right when she strikes a blue patch of color with her red marker and holds it up for me to see. "Daddy, you're right!"

I nod, grateful for her short attention span. "You can keep trying more combinations at home. Are you hungry? We're having meatballs."

"Yes." She falls into silence again, and though I've had months to get used to this new version of Sadie, I still haven't. Before Josie left, she spent more time talking than thinking. She looked forward to everything. Now with every little change I see, I can't help but wonder . . . is it growth? Is it trauma? Should I push her or let her be?

"Are you and Mom getting divorced?"

My shoulders tense and when I check the rearview mirror, I find her studying me.

Fuck my life.

I get that Josie is sick, and she needs help before she can come back and care for her daughter, but I'm so fucking mad at her. I can't help it. She left me here to deal with the aftermath of our relationship failing. With our daughter wondering where her mom is. It's been two years of this—of her jumping from rehab to rehab, relapse after relapse.

"Why—er, why did you ask me that?"

"Dalton's mom says you're divorced and Mom left us behind."

Dalton's mom, whoever she is, should chew glass. "Oh, really? Do you know what divorce means?"

When she nods, I do too. "Okay, well . . . first of all, Mom didn't leave us behind. She's not well, and she's in a place that'll help her so she can come back to us. But she wishes she could be with you every day."

We come to a red light and I twist in my seat, turning my focus on Sadie. "But yes, Mommy and I are divorcing." A light in her eyes dims. "It's not your fault, and it doesn't mean we don't love you or each other. We do, so much."

"Then why are you not together anymore?"

"Because sometimes you can love someone a lot, but they're still not good for you."

Sniffling, she looks down at her lap. "Is Mom sick because you're not good for her?"

This question is *loaded*. I take the honest approach with Sadie whenever possible, but how do I explain that, yes, I'm partially responsible for my wife's drinking, seeing as I unknowingly took her from the love of her life—my *little brother*—and got her pregnant, effectively trapping her in a relationship she didn't want in the first place?

"You know how Uncle Logan is allergic to strawberries?"

"Uh-huh."

"It's just fruit. And it's delicious, right? You love strawberries." I get a nod. "But they hurt him anyway. It's like that with me and Mom. Nothing wrong with us, and we love each other. But we don't want to make each other unwell."

This time, without any sign of acknowledgment, she turns to the window. Someone behind me presses on the horn, and noticing the light is green, I drive.

I need to change the topic. It feels like that's all I've been doing for months.

"Ian and Amelie invited you to a pajama party."

She straightens at the news, eyes lighting up in the mirror. "Really? At their house?"

"Yep."

"Can I take Mollie?"

Mollie. Also known as the worst mistake of the last month. I figured, Sadie has been asking about a pet for as long as I can remember, and what better moment than when she desperately needs a distraction? So I got her the gray-and-brown cat the lady at the local animal shelter swore was "cute as a button." Instead, I got a demonic beast who wishes upon the destruction of every material good I own.

"No, I think Mollie should stay." It's one thing she's ruining our house, but I can't let that feral creature loose in someone else's apartment.

"*Pleeeease*," she insists.

"No Mollie, sorry. She'll keep me company tonight."

A few minutes of silence go by. I'm about to ask if she wants to put some music on when her small hand reaches forward and squeezes the top of my arm from the back seat.

"You're not bad, Daddy. Even if you're like strawberries for Mom. Strawberries are my favorite."

I swallow down a sob. Dealing with Sadie as a single parent on and off for the past two years has been impossibly hard, but sometimes, she'll say stuff like this and all the worries and concerns I have over not doing a good job by myself vanish into thin air.

"I love you, baby," I say as her hand squeezes. "Daddy's not going anywhere, okay?"

CHAPTER 2
Cherry Mis-Chief

I glance down at my list and cross off another item. Groceries are done, the kitchen is clean, and the garbage has been dealt with. There's still a disgusting amount of chores I should take care of, so I check the time and walk to my entryway. I'll have to stop by the dry cleaner tomorrow, and I should add my coat to the pile.

Emptying the pockets, I feel something metallic. The TOP gift card.

I pause, turning it back and forth and watching the gloss shine red as it's hit by the hallway light.

No. I'm not going to jerk off. Ian expects me to, and it's just too fucking weird.

But he has a point. With all my cooking sessions with Amelie, the course I've been taking, and caring for Sadie full time, I haven't had a whole lot of time for myself. And I guess it'd be nice not to do it silently in the shower for once.

"Fuck me." I abandon my coat and step into the living room, moving past the couch and the small dining area. The kitchen is tucked away just out of sight, hidden behind a narrow corridor. I walk through it until I reach the kitchen island, its surface scattered with papers and a couple of mugs that haven't been put away.

I grab the laptop and walk back, then settle at the dining table.

There's nothing to be ashamed of, right? Even though I have a daughter, and technically, a wife, it doesn't mean I'm not a man. A human being. I shouldn't have to stop living just because we're all hurting. And besides, it's not like I don't watch porn. This is the same, except . . . *live.*

But as I type in the URL, I feel dirty. It still doesn't seem right.

For months, I've put my needs on hold for Sadie and Josie. As ugly a thought as it may be, I feel like a grieving husband. Except it isn't my wife who died, but the concept of family I've known for the past five years.

I stare at the red screen, the small text box asking me to create an account, then press my tongue against my molars. There's no way I'd enjoy any of it, not with the sense of guilt already washing over me.

"What's even the point," I say to myself as I drop the card.

When the doorbell rings, I check the time. Nine thirty. Who could it be?

I don't have a chance to be curious though because a moment later, I'm met with my brother's broad shoulders and blue-green eyes. Kyle, standing next to him on my welcome mat, jerks his head forward and moves past me. "Hey. Where's Sadie?"

I glance at the box he's holding against his tank top as he heads for the living room, then focus on Logan. "Amelie and Ian are babysitting. Why?"

Logan shrugs. "He got her some dollhouse. I don't know."

"I told you guys you have to stop buying her shit. She'll become spoiled."

"She didn't *ask* for it!" Kyle calls from the living room. "And besides, her mom is a—"

"*Kyle,*" Logan interrupts, then turns to me with a resigned shrug as he enters the house. "Not that he's wrong."

I step aside and ask, "How are the twins? Primrose?"

"Everyone's fine. And sleep deprived. And sleep deprived—wait, did I say that already?"

"It's been happening all day," I hear Kyle say. "He also tripped on a watermelon on the farm. It was awesome."

"Newborns are fun, aren't they?" I ask, thinking of Sadie at that age. And he has *two* of them—two beautiful girls, Harper and Maeve.

"Yeah." There isn't an ounce of sarcasm in his voice. "They're really fun."

"Well, I'm always happy to babysit. You guys want a beer or something?"

I follow him into the living room where he kneels next to the couch, opens the box, and takes out the dollhouse. Kyle returns from the kitchen, holding up two beers and pushing back a lock of his chocolate brown hair. "Way ahead of you, buddy."

"Get me a screwdriver," my brother says, and before I can tell him the toolbox is in the walk-in closet, Kyle lets out a loud "Ooh."

Holding the TOP gift card, he gasps. "TOP, huh? Nice. I thought you were a step away from joining a monastery."

"TOP? What's TOP?"

Ignoring Logan, I walk toward Kyle. "I don't know why everyone keeps saying shit like that. The divorce isn't even official yet."

"But you filed two *years* ago."

Yes, and since then, Josie has been in and out of rehab more times than I can keep track of. It's not easy to navigate the logistics around that, especially if you have a young child and a new career. "Two years is not that long."

"What's TOP?" Logan presses.

"Noth—"

"It's jerk-off capital, boss," Kyle explains. "You can join streams and watch girls do—well, basically *anything*. Or you can have one-on-ones. Personal calls. Those are . . ." He rolls his eyes suggestively. "Fuck me."

"Seriously? You do this shit?" Logan asks. I'm not sure who the question is for, but I shake my head.

"Hell yeah," Kyle chirps. "Remember last year, when I had chickenpox? I couldn't leave the house for a month. Trust me, TOP saved my life." He points at the laptop. "Need help setting up an account?"

"No. I just got a gift card for it, and—"

Kyle sits at the living room table, laptop open in front of him, card still clutched in his hand.

"Why am I not surprised you would do something like that," Logan says with a glare my way before turning to the dollhouse.

I open my mouth, then close it. Though Logan and I officially cleared the air over what happened with Josie around the time I asked for a divorce, we've made no progress since. He won't admit it, won't even let me broach the topic, but he still holds a grudge after all these years.

I get it. I'm his brother. I slept with his girlfriend. But for some reason, I naively thought that once he moved on from Josie, things would be okay between us too. Lately though I worry that'll never be the case, no matter how much I try.

"You're a father, Aaron," he spews. "To a little *girl*. The porn industry is a sexist, abusive, and—"

"Oh, lighten up," Kyle says as he begins tapping keys on my laptop. "It's not porn—it's camming. Trust me, these women make more than you or I cver will selling vegetables. Not to mention they have all the control." He nods at me, then, "Username?"

"No username, Kyle."

"*Chef*, uh . . . *728*."

I don't even want to ask what the numbers represent. "Look, my brother has a point, and—"

"No, he doesn't." He types something. "Are you straight?"

I huff out a breath. What kind of question is that? "You've met my wife."

"Ex-wife."

"Whatev—"

"And you *could* be bi."

"You've known me since you were five, Kyle. I think you'd know if I were bisexual."

Logan asks about the screwdriver again, and once I point him to the walk-in closet, he disappears.

"So there are men on the platform?" I ask, walking closer.

"There's everything. Trans, drag queens, couples. Proper porn stars and influencers. You have masochists, subs and doms, and any kink you could possibly be looking for." He points at the screen. "See? You select what you like here."

Beneath a circle meant to host a profile pic, there is a series of categories that can be selected.

Orgy, cum play, threesomes. And the list goes on.

"And all of this is strictly online?"

"Uh-huh. Creators upload videos, and the algorithm will only show you shit you're into. Either you join a public live stream, or have a one-on-one with a girl."

Yeah, this feels like way too much commitment.

"Is this my account?" I ask as I point at the page.

"Yep."

"Cool," I say flatly. "Delete it."

"What? No!" Kyle turns to me. "Do you know what 728 stands for?"

I wait for the inevitable answer.

"The approximate number of days since you had sex. Makes you think, doesn't it?"

No, not really. Sex might be a big part of his life, but it's not hugely relevant to me. I'm much more concerned about the number of days since my daughter last saw her mom, which is skirting dangerously close to two hundred. "Delete it."

"Wait—wait." He holds on to my sleeve when I motion to leave. "Look, she's my favorite creator. I had to stop seeing her because, I swear to god, I was falling in love."

He taps on the keyboard, pulling up the profile of a blonde woman with the largest breasts I've ever seen. So large, in fact, that in her picture, she's biting her own nipple.

"Jesus, Kyle."

"What? She's really smart."

"Yeah. I'm sure that's why you kept going back."

He holds up the card. "This will cover a one-on-one. I strongly recommend stocking up on tissues and contacting Jewel."

"*Ugh.*" Logan emerges from the hall with a nauseated expression. "Why do you always need to be so fucking gross?"

"Oh, I don't know. Remember that time I caught your soon-to-be wife sucking you off in the stables?" At Logan's glare, Kyle shrugs and stands. "Come on, let's get out of here and leave him to it."

"N-no." I try to stop them as Logan drops the screwdriver on the carpet and stands. Now *three* people will know I'm masturbating? "No thank you. Really—"

I follow them through the house until they pull open the front door. Kyle flashes me a playful finger gun. "Enjoy, okay? And tell Jewel *PussyAssassin* sends his regards."

On the echo of a groan from my brother, the door closes.

PussyAssassin? That's a whole new level of unsettling.

My shoulders drop as I wander back to the living room, the princess castle box open and the pieces scattered on the carpet.

One more thing for me to do.

I crouch down and grab the instruction manual. It's several pages long and I'm already fucking tired, but thinking of Sadie's face seeing it all done gives me the push I need.

I sort through the pieces then begin reading, but halfway through the second page, my eyes dart to Jewel. To the obscene picture staring back at me.

I need to delete that account.

I stand and walk to the laptop, venturing out of Jewel's profile and back to my own. I tap on "Delete your account," and patiently wait for the page to load. A pop-up asking me if I'm sure appears, but before I can tap on the trackpad, Mollie lands on the keyboard.

"*Holy crap.* Where did you fall from?" I look around, then grab the little shit and pull her off my laptop. "Sorry, this is a *different* type of pussy."

I turn to the screen, horrified to see that she's led me onto some other woman's profile.

Horrified for all of a second, before my shoulders drop and my mouth snaps open.

This woman . . . wow.

She's stunning—well, whatever I can see of her is. Her face is not visible but I think she's a redhead, though her hair is different in a few of the pictures in her carousel. A short black bob in the shot where she's wearing a leather corset, blonde waves in the picture of her lying down on her stomach. Wigs, maybe.

As for the rest . . . My eyes bounce across the screen. Most of this must be photoshopped—or AI or something. Nobody real is that hot.

Her ass, two perfect, swollen circles; her tits, definitely smaller than that other woman Kyle is obsessed with but otherwise ample sized. Her freckled skin, her hips, her endless fucking legs.

Damn, I miss women.

I miss sex. The smell of it, the sound of it, the ego boost of making someone feel good enough that their world tips over. And I miss intimacy. Kissing, hugging. Knowing someone's ready to pick up the slack if I need it. Talking for hours on end about nothing and everything.

But I certainly won't find any of it with this woman, no matter how devastatingly attractive she is.

I won't find any of it on TOP.

I tap to return to my profile, but Mollie seems to think my

fingers are her personal playthings. Her paws latch onto my hand, sharp nails sinking into my skin.

"Son of a—"

A ping cuts me off, and my eyes snap to the screen where a call window has popped up. The ringing continues as I hover over the keyboard, frantically pressing the *Esc* key over and over.

"No, no, no—"

I grab the edge of the laptop, ready to slam it shut, but before I can, the black square vanishes and a woman appears in its place.

She's kneeling on a bed, eyes locked on the camera, lips curved seductively.

My heart stops.

Mollie is still mauling my fingers, but I barely feel it.

It's her. The goddess. She's fucking stunning.

"Hello?" she drawls.

Hair as red as fire, fair skin, and adorable freckles that pepper her cheeks and nose and chest.

"Holy shit."

Her eyes are a dark, muted green, and her smile is contained, until it stretches and she says, "Why, thank you."

"N-no, that's not what I meant." Can she see me? She can definitely hear me, but I don't see my face on the screen.

"Oh? You don't think I'm holy-shit beautiful?"

She is. Absolutely. She's also young. Far too young to appreciate the see-through pink nightgown she's wearing. The way it dips down her chest and rests on her skin like liquid silk. "No—I mean, yes. I just . . . I didn't mean to start the call. My cat—" Noticing Mollie is still wrestling with my hand and making my fingertip bleed, I shake her off. "My cat hates me. She, um, called you."

"Your cat called me?"

Even if I wasn't seeing her narrowed eyes, her voice is doubtful enough to tell me she doesn't believe it for a second. Why would she? I sound insane.

"Yes. My cat called you."

"Okay." She leans forward, resting her chin on her hand. "Meow, then."

I huff out a single breath, watching her tits press together in the new position.

"Are you new, Chief?"

"Chief?" I echo.

"Your username."

Chief? That fucking idiot can't even spell, can he?

"Yeah. I am. That obvious?"

She chuckles under her breath. "Seasoned users know they don't need to scapegoat their cat to call."

"I'm not . . ." Throwing a glare at Mollie, who's currently sprawled over the table and playing with a wad of balled up paper, I roll my eyes. "Anyway, I should—"

"Let me guess," she says, settling on one hip and looking at the camera. Her long, wavy red hair slips down one shoulder and onto the white duvet. I don't think it's a wig, but what do I know. "You're too old for me. You're a good guy, and you can't fathom paying for someone to get you off. Or you're married, and your wife would kill you if she found out you called. Or maybe it's that you have a little girl and you can't help but picture her here instead of me, a testament to where you went wrong raising her."

Damn. Am I that predictable?

"Uhhh . . ."

"Which one is it?"

"A little bit of everything, actually," I admit.

"Ah, yes. The three-for-one guilt combo." Her nose wrinkles at the tip. "I love older men. Most women do, you see, because men our own age are several years behind us in maturity. As for your wife, well, you wouldn't be here if you could get what you need from her." She seems thoughtful for a moment. "And your little girl . . . if she, all grown up, told you she wanted to work in the adult entertainment industry—that it's her dream and what makes her happy—would you stop her?"

Well, I would fucking try.

"Is there anything wrong with enjoying performing for others?" she asks as she lowers one strap of her nightgown, baring her shoulder. The movement is hypnotic, my eyes following every inch of its descent. "Anything wrong with enjoying money? Fame? Sex? Desire?"

"No, of course not."

"If you knew that she was perfectly safe," she continues as she lowers the other strap, revealing another freckled shoulder, "and that she was thriving, would you stop her?"

Sadie's defeated expression earlier today in the car comes back to me. "No. I'd do anything to see her happy."

The woman grins. "Let me ease your concerns then. There's a button on my screen. It reads 'Leave.' If I should click that, the call would end instantly, no questions asked. I'd be given a chance to file a report on you, and you wouldn't be able to rate my performance or get your money back."

I listen with rapt attention. Her voice is sultry, sexy. Low, like she's whispering straight into my ear.

"And if you were found to be in violation of the Terms and Conditions—trust me, it's easier than you think—you'd be kicked off the platform. If you weren't, I'd be able to block you and never see you again."

She straightens, gripping the edge of the mattress. "TOP values its performers more than its customers."

"G-good." Even so, I'm not sure I can go through with this. Maybe I could donate the money on my card to her—or would she interpret that as an act of pity?

"And as you can see," she says as she turns the camera around and shows me her room. "I'm not exactly strapped for cash. I'm not here because I don't have a choice. Hell, I still live at home."

She shows me the flatscreen TV mounted on the wall and the

thick, expensive-looking carpet under her California king bed. But what really catches my eye are the sketchbooks stacked on the desk, a half mannequin draped in fabric, and colored pencils and markers spilling out of a container.

She must be an artist.

An artist who, judging on the dexterity with which she goes through her speech, has given it many times before. With the easy confidence she emits, it doesn't feel like I'm talking to a full-blown pornstar like Jewel. Just a . . . woman.

But none of it really matters, does it? She's *young*. Barely legal, I assume. "How old are you?"

"How old do you want me to be, Chief?" she says with a sneaky little smile before tucking a lock of hair behind her ear.

"Please, don't—don't call me that."

"What should I call you?"

"Aa—" Nope, not a smart idea. "I'm not sure."

"How about I tell you my age, and you tell me what I should call you?"

I hesitate, but with a twinkle in her eyes, she says, "I'm twenty-three," then lets the nightgown drop until it pools around her hips, uncovering the most perfect, heavy set of tits I've ever seen. Freckled. Freckled tits with beautiful pink nipples.

I have no idea how old she is.

"Call me . . ." I think of my nickname throughout high school. "Cole."

"Hmm. That's one sexy fake name."

"Nickname, actually," I say distractedly. I don't even know *her* sexy fake name, and, dead serious, right now I'd tell her my name's Aaron Coleman, I'm thirty-seven, and I live at 23 Mapleview Ave, Roseberg. My social security number too.

"Thank you for sharing that with me, Cole." One hand rises to the side of her neck, then trails down in between her tits and down her flat stomach. "I like your voice, you know?"

"Do you?"

"Oh, yeah. It's raspy, dark. I bet I'd like it mumbling dirty words in my ear. Or . . ." She hums. "Or whimpering, moaning as you come deep inside me."

"*Hmmsf.*" I cringe instantly, holding a hand to my crotch as if it'll stop me from getting hard. *What kind of noise was that?*

"Tell me, Cole. What do you need?"

"Need?" I echo, my chest rising and falling quickly as my eyes flick between her tits and those beautiful green eyes.

"Yes, need. What can I do for you, baby?"

Holy hell. The *things* I'd do to this woman. What does it say about me? I'm over a decade older than her, yet I don't think I could control myself if she were naked in front of me, asking me what I *need*.

Actually, I don't think I can control myself now either. "I . . . I need . . ."

She grins, shifting to all fours on the bed. Her tits bounce with the movement as the nightgown drops to her knees. "Yes?"

Fuck, look at those pink lace panties. She's so sexy.

"I need—" The phone rings, startling me back to reality. My heart is galloping, my forehead covered in a thin layer of sweat. "—to go. I have to . . ."

Shaking my head, I press on the red button, and once the call ends, I land on her profile again, my heart pounding in my ears.

Cherry.

That's *her* sexy fake name.

CHAPTER 3
The Béchamel Redemption

C ome on!" I snap, shoving the pot down onto the stove. This should be easy. I've made béchamel hundreds of times, but tonight the flour keeps clumping, the butter is burning—everything is off.

"Aaron," Amelie calls from the other side of the stainless steel counter, her voice bouncing off the walls of the empty kitchen at Daisy.

Before she can say more, I drop the pot in the sink and grab another one. "It's fine. I just need to—"

"No, hey, please." She gestures toward the graveyard of pots I've already abandoned. "At this point, we're just wasting ingredients. I know what's happening."

"You do?"

"Of course."

For a moment, I wonder how she could possibly know my mind has been consumed by the only tits I've seen in two years. How she could have figured out that I almost jerked off to a cam girl whose voice won't leave my head.

What do you need?

"You need to relax, Aaron." Amelie walks around the counter

to join me. "You're tense about your first client, but you're ready for this. I know you are, because I personally made sure of it. Almost every day. For a year."

She playfully glares, but instead of putting me at ease, it just makes me more nervous.

"And I have to prove that your time wasn't wasted, that your trust wasn't misplaced. I have to show Ian his insane choice of hiring me instead of the much more experienced candidates wasn't a giant mistake. Oh, and let's not forget that Ian never would've hired me if it weren't for his friendship with Logan."

Amelie clicks her tongue. "His *fear* of Logan."

"And my brother does *not* need more reasons to hate me."

"I see." Her eyes narrow. "And your parents have expectations too. Plus there's Sadie."

"Right! Yes!"

Her smile turns mocking.

"You don't get it, Ames. You weren't there."

"When you knocked up your brother's girlfriend?"

I glare. "Yes. I have a lot to prove—to everyone. That I'm not a heartless monster who prioritizes his dick over his closest family member, that I can parent my daughter alone, and that the career change from accounting to cooking wasn't a financial sinkhole." I wave a hand around. "Among other things."

"Jeez, Aaron. You run on coffee, guilt, and a crushing sense of responsibility, don't you?"

I reach for the butter, but Amelie snatches it out of my hands before I can grab it. "I can't believe *I'm* saying this, but enough with the butter already." She sets it down with a huff. "Aaron, trust me, I understand the need to prove yourself more than anyone. But you've gotta relax, man. You're going to give yourself chest pains."

"It's just really important that I don't mess this up. I'm on a path to redemption."

At this point, I'm clinging to the desperate hope that any of this will end my probation. That Logan will stop looking at me like something disgusting is stuck to my face. And like he wants to remove it with his fist.

"You won't mess it up. You know why?"

"Because I had the best teacher ever?" I mock.

"Exactly." She wags a finger at me. "But I don't appreciate the tone."

When I manage a half-hearted smile, she steps away, only to return with a bottle of wine and two glasses.

"I think it's one of those nights."

Not every night we spent in Daisy's kitchen over the past year was dedicated to cooking. Most were, but some were wine-and-talking only.

I grab two stools and pull them closer. Once we're settled, Amelie pours us each a glass and takes a sip. "Aaron, look. The last year hasn't been easy for you. If this is too much—"

"Do you think it's too much? Because if you're not sure I can handle it, then—"

"Woah." She widens her eyes dramatically. "You *are* ready. But if you need more time, you can take it."

And continue being nothing but an expense for her husband? No, I can't. Ian paid for my course and all he's gotten in return is less of his wife, who's spent a good chunk of her free time helping me improve my technique and babying me through my tantrums.

It's time I actually made him some money.

"No. I need to do this."

Amelie pats my hand. "I agree. This is just nerves. They'll fall away the second you start cooking. But you need to ease up on the pressure."

"How are *you* handling the pressure?" I ask, steering the conversation away from me.

She shrugs. "Me? Pressure's my middle name."

I tilt my head, watching her as her shoulders drop.

"Fine. I'm scared, obviously. Leaving Daisy to work on this

show . . ." She traces the rim of the glass with her finger. "I just hope it's a good decision."

"Well, I'm obviously biased, but I think you're a great teacher. I'm not eager to share you, but as long as you promise I'll remain your favorite student . . ."

"Top three, for sure."

"Hilarious. The point is, those contestants are lucky to get mentored by you."

She grins, but then, as if a dark thought flickers through her mind, her expression dims. "I was planning to have a ceremony."

"A ceremony?"

"For . . . the first anniversary."

Her father's death. Of course. "You can do it in Mayfield. Or when you come back, if that's—"

"Nobody was willing to come," she interjects. She swirls the wine in her glass, staring into it. "Dad had a couple of brothers he wasn't close to, but that's it. All he left behind is a lot of frenemies."

In a year of friendship, Amelie has only mentioned her mother once to say they barely speak. But the woman was married to her father at some point. That has to count for something, right? "What about your mom?"

"My mom, not that she'd ever bother to visit, would probably dance on his grave." She exhales, shaking the thought away. "I decided I'll just . . . remember him. By myself. Or, well, with Ian. He grew to like my dad, but let's be real, he likes everyone."

I turn on my stool to face her. "I will too. While I didn't know him, I'll remember him as the man responsible for a lot of this. Of you."

She squeezes my hand, grief shadowing her face. I've seen this play out enough times to know that cooking gets her out of this mental space, so I smack the counter and stand.

"You know what? Hand me the butter."

"Aaron—"

"This will be great, okay? We'll both do great. I'll be the best private chef this woman could ever dream of, and you'll come back in a month happy you took this chance. You need it, after the year you had. And it all starts now—with a perfect béchamel sauce."

Clicking her tongue, she stands too. "As most redemption stories do."

I grab a clean pot, then turn to Amelie and hold my hand out. Time for the best French sauce to ever grace this kitchen. "Hand me the *fucking* butter."

I STEP into the preschool classroom, scanning the low tables until I spot Sadie at the coloring station, her tiny fingers gripping a crayon as she concentrates. When she looks up and sees me, her face lights up, and she jumps off her chair. But before she can run over, her teacher, Miss Delaney, gently places a hand on her shoulder.

"Sadie, sweetheart, go get your things in the other room?" she tells her. "I need to talk to your dad."

Sadie hesitates, looking between us, then drags her feet to the cubby area. A prickle of unease creeps up as Miss Delaney gestures for me to follow her. Impromptu conversations with teachers are never a good sign.

We step into the small office next to the classroom, and she shuts the door behind us. She crosses her arms, her long honey-blonde hair swaying with the motion and her hazel eyes sharp with concern.

"Aaron, I wanted to touch base with you about Sadie," she begins. "She's been having a tough time of it lately."

"What's going on?" I ask, as if I didn't know this was coming.

"We've noticed she's been pulling away from group activities more than usual. She's not talking much, and she doesn't seem to socialize the way she used to."

I run a hand through my hair. "Yeah . . . things have been hard at home."

"I'm aware of your wife's . . . *situation*. I can only imagine how difficult this must be for the both of you. Sadie's still very young, but kids are perceptive. She's feeling the shift, even if she doesn't have the words to express it."

"I just . . . I don't know what to do," I confess. "I try to be there for her, keep things normal, but she just . . . she misses her mom."

"I know," she says kindly. "But I do think Sadie could benefit from a little extra support. We have a school counselor who works with under-eights. It might help for her to have another trusted adult to confide in."

"Oh—kay." I take a deep breath, feeling the weight of it all. She's six, and she needs a *shrink*? Jesus fucking Christ. "I'll think about it, Miss Delaney."

"Please, call me Penny." She gives me a small smile, the kind that lingers just a second too long. Her lips are painted pink, the only pop of color against her light blue overalls. "I can tell you're trying, Aaron. She's lucky to have a dad who cares so much."

I nod, pressing my lips together. "Thanks. I appreciate you looking out for her."

"Always." She steps closer and gives me a curious look. "And if you ever need to talk, I'm here," she says, her voice dipping. "For Sadie . . . or for you."

I glance down at her fingers gripping my shoulder, then back at her hopeful expression. "Yeah. Sure—thank you."

"Should I give you my number?"

"I, uh . . . I think I have your . . ." I point at the office phone. "That should be fine."

Hand retreating, she nods. "All right." She leads me back to the classroom and Sadie looks up as we enter, her big brown eyes full of curiosity.

I kneel down to her level. "Ready to go, kiddo?"

"Look, lady, I don't give a fuck if she's in the middle of Pilates or a silent retreat or fucking therapy. I need to talk to my wife *right now*," I bark into the phone.

"Mr. Coleman, as I said several times, Mrs. Coleman wishes not to be disturbed until the end of her program."

The fading sunlight casts long shadows across the backyard, the last streaks of orange and pink stretching over the wooden fence. I smack my fist against the outdoor grill, the side of my hand throbbing immediately, and a few birds flutter from the trees, startled by the sound.

I turn around to make sure Sadie didn't hear anything, but she's still watching TV, Mollie curled up in her lap. "And how long exactly is this program? Because your website says four weeks, and she's been there for six months," I hiss through my teeth.

"However long our patients believe—"

"Look." I grip my hair at the roots, closing my eyes. I need to calm down, to not antagonize this woman, but I'm this close to getting into my car and driving there. "It's important I speak to her, okay? Tell her it's an emergency."

"I'm sorry, but—"

"Tell her it's about her daughter. Her *six-year-old* daughter."

"Mr. Coleman, I truly wish I could help you, but—"

"No, trust *me*, you'll wish you'd helped me if you don't put her on the phone *right this fucking minute.*"

There's silence on the other end of the line, so I try a different approach. "I'm sorry. Really, I am. But please, put yourself in my position. I want nothing more than for Josie to be healthy, but her daughter needs her. I don't know what else to do."

"I understand, but—"

"*Please,*" I insist, my voice shaking. "I'm begging you, okay? Just one minute of her time, and I'll take all the responsibility."

With a sigh, the woman on the line says, "Give me a moment, please."

"Yes. Yes, of course." I raise my fist in the air as the annoying hold music starts. This has never happened before. Despite my numerous attempts, no facility staff ever got close to letting me talk to Josie. Shit, I hope they will this time.

The door to the backyard opens, and Sadie sticks her head out. "Daddy, I'm hungry."

"Yes, baby. I'll make you a PB&J—give me just a minute."

She nods and returns to her spot on the couch.

"Hello?"

My body tenses, my eyes going wide. Is that . . . that sounds like Josie.

"Aaron? Are you there?"

"Y-yes." Holy *shit*. We haven't talked since she last disappeared, leaving only a note behind. Took me months to get over that and start worrying about her prolonged absence. "I'm here."

"I told you not to call."

My chest heaves, the pain digging deeper and deeper. That's all she has to say? You know what—Kyle's right about her. "Your daughter is alive. Thank you for asking."

"I know Sadie is okay. I talked to your parents."

She what? "When?"

"Every week. Don't be mad at them—I asked them not to say anything. It's better for my sobriety if we keep some distance from each other."

I slump onto a patio chair. "No, I'm not mad at *them*. I don't have any room for more anger, honestly."

"Why are you calling?"

"When are you coming back?"

"*Why* are you calling, Aaron?"

"That's why I'm fucking calling, Josie. You've been gone for six months, and I know your sobriety is important, but if you don't give a shit about leaving *me* stranded, come back for your daughter. She needs you."

She sniffles. "I can't come back until I'm better."

"Maybe you won't get better until you come back home."

"And how could you possibly know that?"

I look up at the sky, letting the orange and pink hues ground me as the sun sets on another day. "I don't, actually. And to be honest with you, I don't *care*. Not right now. Not when my daughter is saying her mom left her behind."

"I hope you told her that's not true."

"No, Josie. I told her you liked another child better. What the fuck do you think I said?"

"See—this is why I can't come back yet. I've been talking to you for one whole minute and I already want to drink."

Lips pursing, I try to summon all the calm I can harness. "*I'm* the problem, Josie? Well, fine. You'll never have to see me. You can have the house, the car. Fuck, you can have everything, and we'll only cross paths when I pick up or drop off Sadie. But you need to come back. It's been six months. You don't get to abandon your kid indefinitely."

"Aaron, I have to go."

"Her teacher wants her to see a counselor," I rush out, standing. My heart is pounding, because if I don't convince her now, I might not get another chance to talk to her.

"What? Why?"

"Because she's struggling. She's closed off, and she's not socializing. I see it at home too. She's sad, lost in her thoughts. She needs you, Josie."

She's silent for a long while—so long that I check if the call disconnected. Eventually, she says, "Have you considered that my being there might make things worse? That if I come back before I'm ready, I might stumble again? Do you think that'd be good for her?"

"No, of course not."

"I'm a mom, and I'm a cop, Aaron. When I come back home, come back to work—I need to be sure I'm ready to face the challenges and responsibilities that—"

"I *get* it," I insist.

"Then let me go, Aaron. I'll be back when I'm ready."

I squeeze my eyes shut, trying hard not to cry. But the stress is creating a fire-hot ball in my chest, and I'm so fucking tired. Exhausted from being worried. Worried Sadie can see how exhausted I am.

What if she never gets better? What if she never comes back?

"Talk to her at least," I try. "Please, Josie. Just talk to your daughter for five minutes. Tell her you miss her, that you love her and you'll come back to her. *Please.*"

She hesitates and I hold my breath, waiting.

Until the signal tells me she hung up.

She hung up.

On me—on her daughter.

"Daddy! Can I have the PB&J now?"

My chin is shaking, my eyes burning so much I can barely keep them open, and I'm pretty sure if I hold on to this phone any longer, I'll crack it.

But I'm all Sadie has. For now, and maybe forever. So I force a smile on my face and get up to take care of my kid.

CHAPTER 4
Emotional Support Orgasm

I tap my fingers on the edge of the nightstand, eyes are glued to my laptop screen—specifically, to TOP's homepage.

I don't know why I'm back here. Hell, I even had to add money to my account because I used the gift card already. And it's not like seeing some stranger's naked body will help in any way at all—maybe at the moment, but it'll wear down quickly.

So why am I here?

I should just clean up the mess of clothes piling up in the corner next to the big wardrobe, but after straining my ear to make sure there's no noise coming from Sadie's bedroom, I adjust the laptop on my lap and type her username in the search bar.

Cherry.

She's the first result that shows up, that shot of her in a pink bra and thong bringing back the familiar pang of want.

I peruse her profile, my brows shooting up my forehead when I see she has dozens of thousands of followers—not that I'm surprised. The world is full of losers like myself, and she's more beautiful than beauty.

Under her username there's a list of the things she's comfortable doing—though by the length of it, I suspect it'd be easier to list what she *doesn't* consent to. And besides, another field reads "On a call."

Of course.

What did I expect?

There must be a line to get some one-on-one time with her.

Slumping back against the wicker headboard, I keep scrolling through her profile. Photos of her nearly naked and bent in every sort of position litter my screen, and I can distinctly feel my mouth watering. My erection stiffening.

There's content I could pay for—explicit, it says, as if the rest is PG-13—and though I can't deny how badly I want to see those tits again, I don't click on it.

It wouldn't be the same, would it?

I scroll back up, briefly considering checking out other profiles, then realizing I've got no drive to. I'm hovering over the *X* to close the page when her status changes from orange to green. From "On a call" to "Taking calls."

Nausea grips me and before I can make a fully conscious decision, I'm pressing on the call button.

"Fucking hell," I breathe out as the call screen appears and the rings accumulate.

Maybe she's not going to answer. There must be a lot of people calling her, right? Shit, maybe I don't *want* her to answer.

The screen buffers, the ringing subsides, and my heart leaps in my throat as she appears, as beautiful as ever.

"Cole," she says, and I detect surprise in her voice. "I didn't think you'd come back."

She remembers me. I mean—it's only been twenty-four hours, but she must talk to loads of men in that timeframe, and she remembers *me*.

I really am a loser, because the awareness warms me up instantly.

Ugh. Now I sound like Kyle.

"H-hey."

"Let me guess." She leans forward and the black minidress she's wearing inches up her thigh. "Another feline setup?"

I adjust the volume to make sure I won't wake Sadie up, then remind myself that I've locked the door so she won't accidentally stumble into whatever is about to happen.

"Actually, I've abandoned the cat at the closest dumpster."

Cherry's smile falls.

"Just—just a joke. The cat's fine. Sleeping, at least until I go to sleep. Then she'll start playing whack-a-mole with my face."

She giggles. "I'm happy you called back."

"Yeah?" I ask. She likely tells that to everyone, but I don't care. My almost-ex-wife doesn't want to talk to me—or her daughter. Sadie is hurting and there's nothing I can do about it. But for the next ten minutes, I can pretend this woman was waiting for my call. I can pretend *someone* was.

"Absolutely. You left in such a rush yesterday. I didn't even get to hear your voice do all those fun things we talked about."

I breathe out, her words sinking deep into my stomach and taking hold of my common sense. "So how . . . how does this work?"

"It works however you want it to." She rises to her knees, then takes a box and drags it to the center of the bed. "You want me to play with toys? I'll even let you choose the size. You want me to deny myself orgasms? I'll wither for you. I'll dance for you, or talk you through the best handjob of your life. I'll tell you every single thing I'd let you do to me if you were here."

I shift on the white sheets, my erection straining against my jeans. Most of that seems . . . too complicated. Too rehearsed, even, when all I truly want right now is for this to feel real.

When all I want is to feel like someone out there wants me to give them pleasure.

"Could we just . . ."

She tilts her head. "Yes, baby?"

"Could you . . . come? For me?"

She blinks and for a second seems taken aback. Maybe it's a weird thing to ask, but before I can take it back, she plasters the usual flirty smile on her face. "How would you like me to do that?"

I open my mouth, then close it. It's my personal experience that a woman knows exactly what's going to make her come. "Any way that *actually* makes you come."

Her bottom lip disappears under the top one. "That's it? You just want me to orgasm?"

"Yeah."

"No show?"

"No show."

She laughs for a brief moment. "I gotta tell you, Cole. It's not going to be all that interesting."

Seeing a woman as beautiful as Cherry bring herself to climax? Agree to disagree.

"But, hey, it's your money." She pulls at the sides of her dress and drops it beside her. She's not wearing a bra, only see-through black underwear. "Can I take these off?" she continues as she fits a thumb under the side of her panties.

"Y-yes. Of course."

Underwear out of the way, she spreads her legs and looks straight at the camera. I don't know what to focus on first. Her eyes, green and staring straight into mine, or her tightly pebbled nipples. Maybe her pussy. Shaven, pink, freckled.

Perfect.

I might be flatlining, flashes of my cock sinking into her chased by her sexy voice calling my name, her red nails scraping my back.

Fuck, I'm lightheaded.

"Your turn now, Cole."

"Wh-what?"

"Unbutton your pants, baby."

My fingers move to my zipper, and the second I pull it down, I exhale in relief.

"Hmm." Her fingers swipe through her pussy as she licks her lips. "Better, isn't it? Take it out now."

What am I doing? Am I cheating on my wife? I mean—we've been in the process of divorcing for two years, but the whole thing is still not finalized.

"Stop spiraling, Cole." She parts her lips with her fingers, showing me her hole, her clit—everything wet and ready. "I'm horny, and I need you."

That effectively snaps me out of my guilt trip and, equally motivated by anger and need, I pull my boxers down. "I'm . . . I've done it."

"Are you hard for me?"

"*So* hard."

"Yeah?" She teases her clit, head tilting back as she looks up at the ceiling. "Is it wet at the tip?"

Fuck. It is *now*.

"Spread it all over for me, then spit in your hand and grip that hard cock in your fist."

Shivers run down my spine as I tease the head with my fingers. Then I spit and wrap my fingers around it. "Oh fuck," I drawl as I give it a stroke.

Forget about one-pump chump. I won't even get there—not with this orgasm threatening to explode.

"Want me to let you in on a little secret?"

"Yes," I breathe.

Her fingers circle her swollen clit as she opens her eyes again and looks straight at the camera. "The only way a man has ever made me come is by eating me."

"Oh?"

She nods, sliding two fingers inside, and in response, I give my cock a tug. "And not just . . . a half-hearted attempt. You'd have to eat it like a man starved."

"I would," I say in a shaky, raspy voice. No hesitation because it's the simple truth, and I'm too fucking turned on to try to hold it back.

"Hmm. I know you would, baby." She reaches into the box by her side and takes out a small blue toy. "This—this is the closest thing there is to having your pussy eaten. There isn't all that fun stuff like tongue-fucking and desperate lapping, but . . ."

Fuck, the way she speaks. Like none of this fazes her in the slightest. Like she's completely comfortable.

"It gets the job done. At the right setting, it feels like a very talented tongue flicking my clit, and . . ." She rolls her head back dramatically before looking back at me. "It's the only way I've been able to squirt. Just once, but it was . . . unforgettable."

I force myself to speak, though there's nothing but noise inside my brain right now. "Can I watch you use it?"

She turns it on then clicks the button three times, the buzzing increasing. "You can do whatever you want with me, Cole."

She brings the toy to her clit, and immediately, her body jerks, her muscles tensing up. Her eyes roll to the back of her head as she whimpers, and I swear I see her clench again and again.

The noise of her pleasure is addicting. Her voice is much softer than when she speaks, but I can hear it perfectly over the wet buzzing.

"I'm thinking about you, Cole," she says, her eyes finding the camera again. They're half-lidded now, the green nearly swallowed by the black of her pupils. "About your tongue exploring every inch of my cunt."

"*Yes*," I grit out. I stroke myself increasingly faster, my breaths coming out in frantic, hot puffs. Fuck, what I wouldn't give to lick it clean. To watch her squirm, to fuck her hard and raw while I hold that blue vibrator on her clit until she squirts all over my lap.

"Fuck, fuck, fuck," I sputter, letting go of my cock when tension starts forming at the base of my spine.

"Not yet, baby," she says back. Her legs clench around the toy, and with a deeper, louder whine, she turns around on all fours, ass in the air and facing the camera.

She finds her clit again and her back arches, her legs shaking. I watch, unable to look away, as moisture runs down her thighs, making her skin slick.

I'm not going to last another second, but I also can't wait any longer, so I continue fucking my hand, picturing it's her hot pussy instead. Warm, tight, spasming around me and sucking an orgasm straight out of my balls.

"I knew I'd love your moans," she says.

I hadn't even realized I *was* moaning, but I can't help it as she rolls her hips, chasing her orgasm.

I think she's close because her legs tremble hard, and so does the one arm holding her up. Though the view is spectacular, I want to watch this orgasm play out on her face.

"Turn around," I bark, devoid of any self-control. My first instinct is to apologize, but she flips on her back, watching the camera with a predatory glint in her eyes.

She likes it.

And I definitely can't regret it now that I'm looking at her messy hair, the red hue over her cheeks.

Her chest rises and drops sharply, and when she moans, her lips twist, like she's stuck between agony and ecstasy.

I get it, because I'm right there with her.

"Cole . . . *Cole*—oh my god." She throws her head back, then forces herself to lock eyes with the camera again. "Say my name. Moan it."

"*Cherry*," I groan. "Cherry, Cherry, Ch—"

She gasps, then her whole body is shaking. She's mumbling unintelligible words, whimpers cascading out of her lips like the sweetest symphony.

Before I know it, an orgasm is rushing up my spine and spilling into my hand, again and again, until I've made a mess of my pants and stomach.

"Ah, *fuck* . . ." I grunt, stroking myself and getting every drop out. She's riding the wave of her orgasm too, her body rising and falling against the mattress as she struggles to keep her head up.

When my hand abandons my cock, my whole body is tingling. I think this orgasm just extended my lifespan. It was the most intense pleasure I've felt in . . . shit, maybe ever.

She turns the vibrator off then drops against the mattress with an exuberant laugh, knees bending to one side. "Holy shit, Cole. I knew I liked you, but this? This was *good*. Really, really good." She grins up at me, then licks her lips. "You sound *so* pretty when you come."

Pride swells in my chest, but it lasts only a moment. Then, it all comes rushing back. The stress, the anxiety, the terror. Sadie, and Josie, the teacher at school, tonight's phone call.

It's all so heavy, it feels like the walls are closing in around me.

"Cole? Are you still there?"

"I—yes. Sorry, I . . ."

"You have to go?" she suggests, throwing an amused glance at the camera. "You don't need to apologize, baby. That's how it works—you can hang up now."

"No, I know." I watch her grab a folded cloth from beside her and use it to wipe up her thighs and pussy. I don't want to go. I don't want to hang up, but I think I'm supposed to.

Now clean, she fits back into her dress. Then, probably weirded out by my silence, she asks, "Are you okay?"

Am I okay?

No.

I'm not even remotely okay.

I shake my head, knowing she can't see me, and before I can hope to control it, a sob bursts past my lips, then another, and another. Within a second I'm crying uncontrollably, and fuck me, I doubt she's ever witnessed something more disgustingly pathetic, doubt that anyone's ever made her more uncomfortable.

Being the weirdest guy on a platform like TOP? Not a great fucking feeling.

"I'm—I'm sorry." Fuck, I can't control myself. I can barely keep my eyes open with how desperately I'm sobbing, and the more I try to stop, the more I replay that conversation with Josie. The more I replay what Sadie's teacher said today.

My baby—my six-year-old princess—needs a shrink. We fucked her up *that* bad, and Josie has no intention to help me remedy any of it.

It's all on me, and I want to fix it more than anything else, but I don't know what to do.

"That's okay, Cole," Cherry whispers. She doesn't look shocked or annoyed. There's a little pout on her face, her eyes squinted as she patiently waits for my hysterics to subside. "I asked you what you needed."

I nod, hiding my face in my hand.

"Maybe you just need someone to sit with you and let you cry."

CHAPTER 5

The Omelette Test

I've got big news."

I smack the car door shut and wait, the chirping of birds filling the silence as I squeeze the phone in my hand. I know Ian's voice well enough to anticipate *good* news, but tension coils through me anyway. "Yeah? What's up?"

"We have a menu."

"Holy shit." I tilt my head up, personally thanking every star in the dark sky. "We do?"

"We fucking do, Aaron. Wait—"

There's a shuffling noise, then I hear Amelie's giggles. "You finally have an approved menu," she cheers, the joyful sound ripping a smile out of me too. Fucking Beatrice must be the pickiest eater ever, because it took five attempts before she agreed to a menu for the next two weeks.

"Anything in there I don't know how to do?"

"Nah. Well . . . your mac and cheese could use some fine-tuning, but—"

"My *what*?" When she laughs, I roll my eyes. I walk around the car and help Sadie remove her seat belt, and then she's hopping down and running toward my parents' house. "Funny."

"You'll do just fine, Aaron. Ian is saying that he'll email you the finalized menu, okay? Give it a read."

"Thank you. I will."

"One more thing."

I watch as Mom opens the door and picks Sadie up. They're both smiling, which immediately lightens the weight on my chest. "What's up?"

"Yes, I know it'd be easier if I just gave you the phone," I hear her tell Ian, "but he's *my* friend first and I won't see him for a month. What am I supposed to say?" Ian's muffled voice, then Amelie continues, "The client wants to meet you."

"Yeah, all right—"

"Today."

Oh. I'm not supposed to start for another week, but seeing how anal this woman was with the menu, I'm not particularly surprised. "Sure, okay."

"Ian says he'd come with you, but . . ."

"Don't even think about it. You guys are leaving tonight, aren't you?"

"Yes. And I'm already trying as hard as I can not to call Barbara and check on Daisy. My husband says I'm not being helpful at all with packing."

I lock the car and walk toward the front door. "You said Barbara is the best chef you've ever worked with."

"I did."

"And La Brasserie is one of the most successful restaurants in the country."

"Uh-huh."

"But if it'll make you feel better, I'll keep an eye out, okay? Maybe stop there for some takeout."

"Would you? I really need all my best people on this."

"You got it. Now, focus on The Silver Spoon. And try to keep the cameras on your right—Ian says it's your best side."

She gasps, then I hear a smacking noise and Ian's voice says, "Ow—what the hell?"

With a chuckle, I rush out a "Bye!" and hang up.

I slip my phone into my pocket and step up to the front door, the familiar scent of rosemary and garlic wafting from the kitchen before I even knock. My mom has always been big on home-cooked meals, and if there's one thing that never changes, it's the fact that dinner at the Colemans' will always smell incredible.

The door is already open a crack and as I step inside, I call, "Sadie?"

"In here with Grandpa!" her small voice chimes from the living room.

I find her perched on Darren's recliner, legs swinging as she listens intently to whatever story he's telling her. He glances up when he sees me. "There he is," he says, giving Sadie's back a light pat. "Sadie was just telling me about school. Is Miss Nieves a new teacher?"

Well, fuck. I barely stepped inside. "Uh . . . no. No, she's a . . ."

Sadie perks up. "A *counselor*."

Darren tilts his head in question, but I give him a look that I hope he reads as *Not now* and duck away to the kitchen.

I find Ma stirring her Marinara sauce on the stove. Logan's favorite. The wooden spoon in her hands trembles slightly, clinking against the pot as she looks up at me, but before I can ask if she's okay, she squeezes my hand. "You two eat yet?"

"No. Figured I'd mooch off you."

She huffs, waving the wooden spoon at me. "*Mooch* my ass. You barely come by, so sit down and eat."

I smirk, grabbing a chair. "Good to see you too, Ma."

"Yeah, yeah. Smart-mouth." She huffs, joining me at the table. "How are you—*really*?"

"I'm . . ." I'm okay, I guess. Since my meltdown on TOP a week ago, I decided it was time to stop *waiting*. It's what I've been doing since Josie left and I think it's hurting Sadie. Living in this sort of limbo. "Fine. I'm done wallowing."

She begins slicing a loaf of bread. "I wasn't aware you were *wallowing*. Does that mean you're ready to try again?"

"Try?"

"With love, Aaron. You know, sharing your life with someone? Not growing old alone? You're not a kid anymore."

From the other room, Darren says, "You gotta give me and your ma more grandkids to fuss over."

Yeah, right. I'm glad Darren's around for my kid even though we're not related by blood. Hell, he's so important to me I took his last name when he formally adopted me. But one thing's for sure: I'm not planning to give them any more grandchildren.

"I already have my plate full with Sadie." I lower my voice and throw a look at the living room to make sure she's where I left her. "Her teacher at school wants her to see a counselor. And I said I'd think about it, but what I meant was I need Josie to make this decision with me."

She hums, crossing her arms.

"But it may be months before she comes back—if she ever does. So . . . I went ahead. And Sadie seems to like her. I'm sure it'll be good for her."

Ma nods, watching me with that expression like she's reading through me. "That's good. Real good."

I hold her gaze. "You've been talking to Josie."

"Did she say?"

I nod. "Right before she refused to even say hello to her daughter on the phone. And basically blamed her drinking on me."

"Aaron, you know I'm not Josie's biggest fan. She broke both my boys' hearts. So much chaos for our family." She shakes her head with a frown. "But she's still Sadie's mother—"

I pick at a loose thread on the table cloth. "Is she?"

She looks down for a moment as though weighing her words

carefully. "She hasn't been the greatest co-parent, I'll give you that. But for what it's worth, she cares. I've heard her. She cries over Sadie. She misses her. More than you might realize."

I swallow hard, my throat tight.

"Your anger is justified—believe me, I get it. I see how much you do for Sadie. But Josie is Sadie's mother, and whether we like it or not, that'll never change. For Sadie's sake, we have to support her, encourage her, and give her a chance to come back."

My shoulders sag as the weight of it settles in, and Ma reaches over, gently patting my hand. "It's not easy. But you're strong, and you're doing the right thing for Sadie. Just remember, you don't have to carry all of this alone. Whatever you need, you call *me*, okay?"

"Hmm."

"Hmm?" She gently slaps the back of my head. "Want to try again with your mouth open?"

"Okay," I grumble.

"Okay what?"

"Okay, whatever I need, I'll call you."

"Good. Now take the trash out, please."

I stand, grabbing both bags. They're unexpectedly heavy and as I open the door, something inside clanks loudly.

"That's your ma's doing," Darren says as he trails after Sadie down the hall. "Four glasses, two plates, and one vase. She says they were accidents, but I have a strong suspicion she's been getting rid of whatever she doesn't like around the house."

I huff out a laugh on my way out, still thinking of my mom's words. Maybe I *have* been harsh on Josie, and whether she deserves it or not, hostility won't make her come back any sooner.

I'm taking the last step back up the porch when I hear the phone ring inside. My mom's voice comes next as she says, "Hello?" Then, "Oh, hi. Yes. Okay."

I enter the kitchen and she covers the phone with one hand. "Call Sadie, please?"

Sadie?

I walk to the living room and tell Sadie someone's on the phone for her. It must be Logan—he's the only one who knows we're here every Friday night.

"Hello?" Sadie grips the phone and brings it to her ear, her face splitting in a wide smile before she bursts into tears. "Mom! Mom, is that you? Daddy, it's Mom!"

What?

Mouth wide, I turn to Ma, who gives me a silent *I told you so*.

I can't believe Josie called. I can't believe she's talking to Sadie.

I walk to my beautiful, crying daughter and sit next to her on the floor, dragging her onto my lap. As she mumbles a few yeses and noes, I pull her hair back and dry her tears.

Now I'm really, actually fine.

"WOAH." I look up at the towering building in front of me, making sure the address I have is right. Josie and I moved to Roseberg after we got married, and this is the first I'm finding out this apartment complex even exists. It's definitely the fanciest place in a fifty-mile radius.

So naturally, Mrs. Arnault lives on the top floor. The penthouse.

I straighten my jacket and take a deep breath, reminding myself I've done harder things than this. I've cooked for Amelie, and as patient a teacher she is, she demands perfection. I've consistently delivered perfection. It'll be fine.

I ring the buzzer and the door swings open before I even hear the chime. A sharply dressed usher stands in the doorway, looking me up and down with a quick, impersonal glance. "I . . . I'm Aaron. Coleman. Mrs. Arnault's private chef."

He blinks. "Mrs. Arnault?"

"Yes, hmm . . . Beatrice."

He hums. "Montgomery."

Are we just throwing out random names? "What?"

"Come in," the man says, stepping aside.

I follow him into a sleek, marble-floored hallway, my shoes clicking sharply against the polished surface. He doesn't speak as he leads me to the elevator and presses the button for the top floor. The doors close with a low hiss, and we ascend in silence.

When we arrive, the usher steps out first and opens the only door on the floor. "Mrs. Arnault is expecting you."

I nod, crossing the threshold out into the expansive penthouse. The air smells faintly of expensive flowers, and a long corridor extends in front of me. There's an arch to the left and I see a living room through it.

"Come in," a clipped, cold voice calls, and with my heart pounding, I follow the sound until I step into the kitchen/living room space that must be as wide as my two-story townhouse.

Then I see her.

Mrs. Arnault sits poised on an elegant chaise lounge, one leg crossed over the other, a crystal glass resting between her manicured fingers.

She's older—mid-fifties, maybe—but the kind of woman who's only grown more striking with time. Her cheekbones are sharp and her jawline defined, her skin smooth with just the faintest traces of age around her piercing brown eyes. They flick over me with calculated interest. Assessing, measuring.

"You're not Amelie," she says.

I blink. "No, ma'am. I'm—"

She smooths her silver hair with one hand. "I expected Amelie."

"Amelie's out of town for the next month. She—"

"Where?"

"Mayfield. She's working a temporary gig. And . . . and besides, she doesn't work for Chef & Tell—that's her husband's venture. She owns a restaurant downtown. Daisy?"

She doesn't respond right away. Her gaze drifts over me and I try not to squirm as I feel her sizing me up. Finally she lets out a curt sigh, as if her day has been one long series of minor disappointments. "Fine. I suppose you'll have to do."

She sips the dark amber liquid from her glass and stands. Assuming she wants me to go with, I follow her to the kitchen area, which is as immaculate as I imagined—black marble countertops, gleaming appliances. When she turns to me, as if expecting something, my heartbeat picks up.

"Shouldn't you be looking around? See if anything's missing? Or are you as useless as the half dozen chefs I've gone through in the last year?"

"No, I'm . . ." I glance around and spot a sous-vide machine, a blowtorch, and even a truffle shaver sitting neatly on the counter.

I open each drawer and cabinet, half hoping I'll find something missing—something, *anything* that would make me feel useful. But no. Every possible tool, gadget, and high-end appliance is accounted for, arranged perfectly, and has clearly never been used before.

"Everything looks—"

"Make me an omelette."

I glance at her. "Excuse me?"

"An omelette," she says, taking a seat at the island. "You know? With eggs? Make it for two people."

I swallow. *An omelette?*

She's testing me. There's no way Ian knew I'd be expected to cook or he would have told me. I don't even have her list of their allergies and no-go ingredients with me. "Do you have a preference? Anything you'd like or—"

When she looks away, I nod, heart racing. I can't screw this up. I just can't.

I open the fridge, scanning the contents. Eggs, butter, maybe some herbs . . . there's not a lot to go on. Will she expect something fancy? Is the point of this to see me tackle the simplest of recipes? Does she like mushrooms?

I grab a few items and walk to the counter. Once I crack the fourth egg, she clears her throat. "Four eggs?"

"Uh . . ." I look down. "I can add more—"

"It's too much."

I watch her, unsure what to do, until she points at the sink. "Start over."

Seriously? She wants me to toss these perfectly good eggs just to crack two more? "I could set half away—"

"Start over," she repeats, her gaze unwavering.

I turn around and empty the contents of the bowl into the sink, watching the eggs slosh down the drain. Anticipating her reaction if any of the old eggs came into contact with the new eggs, I wash the bowl, the sink, and walk back to the counter.

Two eggs cracked, I begin whisking. "I normally add a splash of cream—"

"We don't eat cream."

"Or milk."

Her lips purse, which I assume is a "No" on the milk too. I grab some mushrooms, cut them up and add cheese, then a little bit of chives.

"You know what cheese is?" she asks. I glance dumbly up at her. "Flavored fat."

I look down at the mixture, jaw tensing. She saw me pull the cheese from the fridge. She watched me grate it—why is she only saying this now?

"Start over?" I guess.

She grabs a magazine from the pile and begins lazily flipping through pages. I walk to the garbage bin and throw everything away, then start again. Crack, whip, mushrooms, chives, salt.

"Start over."

She can't be serious. What did I do now?

"We don't want anyone to feel bloated, do we?"

Bloated? "It was just a pinch of salt—really, just for flavor."

It's like I'm speaking a language she doesn't understand, so without further argument, I walk to the bin and throw out this mix too.

This *must* be a twisted way for her to see how much she can push me before I crack; otherwise, she would have given me instructions before I started.

But Mrs. Arnault has met her match, because I'd sooner spend thirty-six hours making this omelette than raise my voice at her. Or rightfully tell her to go fuck herself.

I'm not going to disappoint Ian and Amelie. And I'm definitely not quitting on my first client.

I grab two more eggs. Crack. Whisk. Mushrooms, chives. This will be the shittiest omelette ever, but there's only so much I can do with these ingredients.

I move a pan to the stove, flick on the burner. I reach for the butter, then turn to her. She's glaring at it so hard it's already melting, so I set it away. I add a bit of oil, then pour the mixture into the heated pan.

The omelette comes together—fluffy, delicate. I take the spatula and gently flip it. If I'm being honest, I'm impressed I managed to make something halfway decent under such a rigid microscope.

I slide it onto a plate and turn to her, trying not to look too hopeful.

She eyes it for a long moment, then picks up her fork and takes the tiniest bite. I hold my breath, but her face doesn't give anything away.

She chews, swallows, then puts the fork down.

"Here's your copy of the keys." She holds out a small envelope. "Inside, you'll also find my phone number, my daughter's phone number, and Katia's—that's the maid. Our schedule is also in there, so you can prepare the correct portions."

"Uh-huh." She must be pleased. I've made it through the first hurdle, and I get to tackle the second one. "Sure, yes."

"Come and go however you please during the day, but I expect you here to serve lunch and dinner. Noon and five o'clock. Bring the ingredients with you, take leftovers when you go. Nothing should be left in the fridge."

"O-okay." It's . . . weird, but great, honestly. My mom would have watched Sadie regardless, but with this schedule I'll be able to have dinner with my daughter every night.

"And one more thing." A powerful glare. "In this house, we eat no more than twelve hundred calories per day. I expect you to respect that."

One thousand two hundred calories. For an entire day. For a *grown woman*. I school my expression, but internally, I'm screaming. That's barely enough for a sedentary teenager, let alone a woman who—presumably—functions in society.

Mrs. Arnault taps a manicured nail against the island. "That includes breakfast, lunch, dinner. There shouldn't be any indulgences in between meals." It sounds like a warning. "Understood?"

I nod, gripping the envelope. "Crystal clear."

She points toward the archway. "Down the hall—first door's a bathroom, second is my daughter's room, and straight ahead, there's another bathroom." She pauses for a breath. "Around the corner is my area. Home office, bedroom, the works. And if you've made it that far, you've gone too far."

"All I need is here," I reassure her, gesturing at the kitchen.

"Wonderful. My daughter isn't home, so you'll meet her next week. She struggles with her weight, so you're going to follow my instructions and ignore hers." Her worried gaze runs over me. "She can be quite . . . persuasive."

Oh, well, *that* makes me feel better. I'm not just denying food to a client who doesn't want it; I'm also keeping it from her overweight child.

Does her kid even *want* to lose weight?

Does this woman understand that a hypocaloric diet doesn't need to mean food deprivation?

"Is there a problem?"

I wear my most disingenuous smile. "None. Twelve hundred calories a day, no bribes accepted."

She opens her mouth to say something, but a sound at the front entrance steals her attention. "Looks like you'll get to meet her tonight."

Someone—I assume it's her daughter, walks past the kitchen. I don't see much of her, but it's enough to know I've grossly misunderstood her, because that woman is *thin*. Probably thinner than she should be. And she's not a child.

"Charlotte?"

"What?" she says flatly from the corridor.

"Can you come in here, please?"

There's a mumbled curse and some shuffling, then she enters the kitchen.

Instinctively, I take a step back, knocking into the counter. I brace myself on it as if it's the only thing keeping me upright.

Because holy *shit*.

Charlotte—Mrs. Arnault's daughter—is Cherry.

As in *Cherry*, the cam girl. Cherry, with the sharp green eyes, the sultry voice, the way-too-intense stare that made it feel like she was looking right at me through the screen.

No way. No *fucking* way.

She crosses her arms, her weight shifting to one hip as she studies me with mild interest. A fitted black top clings to her frame and exposes one of her toned shoulders. With it, she wears a high-waisted denim skirt, fitted through the hips and flaring slightly toward the hem, almost brushing the marble floor. A slit in the front offers a glimpse of the tall, black leather boots at her feet, and there's a black belt cinching her waist, a subtle gold buckle catching the light.

She looks different than the dreamy, sexy woman in the pink nightgown.

For a moment, I almost expect a flicker of recognition in her gaze, but then I realize . . . she's never seen me. She doesn't know who I am.

I feel like I've been dunked in ice water.

"Well?" Charlotte says, tapping her foot on the floor. Her voice—it's different now. Less of that smooth, practiced purr from her streams and more . . . dry, unimpressed.

"This is Chef Coleman," Mrs. Arnault says. "He'll be working for us."

Crap! I gave her the name *Cole*. What if she figures it out?

I fucking came in my hand in her presence. Then I burst out crying and continued for a good fifteen minutes. Don't get me wrong, it was the most liberating cry of my life—and the most expensive one too—but I don't need to relive the humiliation.

Charlotte's expression doesn't change as her lips press together slightly, like she's biting back a reaction. Then, she sniffs. "Great. Hope you love making salads, *Chef*."

"Chef Coleman is a professional," her mother says smoothly. "He knows exactly what you need."

What do you need?

You're so *pretty when you come.*

I hook a finger in the collar of my shirt, desperate to loosen it. Her voice has been haunting me for a week. It echoes through my thoughts when I open my eyes in the morning. I hear it before I fall asleep, in the silence, and when there's chaos around me. Her voice whispers to me in the shower as I fist my cock.

What if she recognizes my voice?

Charlotte's eyes flick back to me. "That so?"

I still haven't said a word, and I'm probably looking like a clueless idiot. This is so much worse than just cooking for some overbearing, calorie-obsessed socialite. Her daughter, fourteen years younger than me, was sprawled on silk sheets a week ago, moaning my name through a screen.

I clear my throat, gripping the envelope tighter. "Yeah. That . . . that's so."

She remains motionless, save for the barest hint of amusement in her expression. I think she'd look more shocked than this if she recognized me—she must talk to dozens of people every day after all.

"Well then. I guess you're perfect for the job." She takes a step closer, eyes still set on mine as one corner of her lips curl up, then purrs, "Almost . . . Cherry-picked, huh?"

CHAPTER 6

Pasta Problems

Day one and I already wish I could go back in time and tell Ian he should assign this job to Robbie. I probably should have. Hell, I spent the last week contemplating my resignation. It's not my fault the cam girl I contacted after he *roped me* into trying TOP ended up being the daughter of my first client.

But she's fourteen years younger than me. *Fourteen.* That fact alone makes what happened between us so beyond inappropriate that I couldn't bear to witness his reaction. Amelie's reaction.

Plus, I didn't know what he'd say to Mrs. Arnault. What if he told her about Charlotte being on TOP? I seriously doubt her mom knows about her side-gig.

But now that I'm standing outside of the apartment complex, I wonder . . . What if it were my daughter? I'd like to know, wouldn't I?

I'm a fucking father. Maybe that's where my loyalties should lie.

And she must have worked out who I am. That comment—*cherry-picked*—couldn't have been by chance. At the very least, she's aware that I *know* she moonlights as Cherry. And what is someone that rich doing on a platform like TOP anyway?

I'll just have to ignore her. I need to keep this job, prove myself. I'll cook. Be in, be out. That simple.

With a headache forming in my temples, I enter the hall and walk by the glaring usher.

Inside the elevator, I catch my reflection, looking into my hazel eyes as I tuck back a few loose strands of hair and give myself an encouraging nod. This'll be fine. According to the schedule, neither Charlotte nor her mom will be home for another hour, so I'll have time to get settled. To cook without that harpy watching over my shoulder.

The elevator dings and the second I step onto the penthouse floor, I tense. Music. Definitely not the type of music I expect Mrs. Arnault to listen to—some type of rap on a techno base that immediately makes my lips twitch.

I open the door and enter the foyer, and through the gap that leads into the living room, I see women. Several women—all of whom wearing next to no clothes. They're all in shorts or bikinis, walking around the living room with red drinks in their hands. Chatting, laughing.

What the fuck am I supposed to do?

I take a step back, suddenly awkward. My first thought is to call Amelie, but to say what? It feels awfully close to clinging to Mommy's skirt on the first day of school. And all Beatrice said is that I'm not supposed to feed her daughter more than one thousand two hundred calories a day. If she's drinking and partying when she's not even supposed to be home, it's none of my business. She's an adult.

"I knew I heard something."

I look up, meeting a woman's gaze. She's Black, with tight curls cascading down her shoulders. She's wearing a light-blue bikini and a bright smile that I immediately try to reciprocate. "H-hello, I'm . . ."

"Who is it, Bonnie?" Charlotte joins her friend, eyes running over me. "Oh, it's our new chef."

"You have a *private chef*?" Bonnie tsks. "Seriously, you won the life lottery, Char."

I swallow, uncomfortable under their scrutiny. I refuse to let my eyes dip past Charlotte's neck, but even from my periphery, she's impossible to ignore. The shorts she's wearing cut so high on her thighs they might as well be lingerie, the frayed edges teasing at her skin, drawing attention to the dip where her waist curves in.

And then there's the top. Blood-red silk, with thin straps holding it up precariously over her shoulders. It hangs loose in all the right places, draping over her breasts just enough to suggest more than it hides. Like it has a mind of its own, like it's begging for attention.

And those freckles everywhere.

"Yeah. Lucky me," Charlotte says unconvincingly before plastering a smirk on her face. "He's pretty too, isn't he? Look at that thick brown hair."

Bonnie hums. "Messy in a hot way."

"And those long lashes? Those hazelnut eyes?"

Bonnie crosses her arms. "I love tall, strong men with a little beard."

They both stare at me, which I take to assume they expect an answer.

Ignoring the sweat dampening my back, I mumble, "Thank you. You're both . . . beautiful." *What the fuck, Aaron?* "Not—not *beautiful*," I say, bringing a hand to the back of my neck. "I mean, you *are*, but not in a weird, uh . . ." I blow out a sharp breath. "Okay. I don't think I'm supposed to say any of that, so I won't. But thank you."

Bonnie turns to Charlotte, who, with a tilt of her head, studies me thoughtfully. "Really pretty."

"Thank you."

Stop thanking her!

"Give us a second?" Charlotte says, turning to Bonnie. With a long, meaningful look, her friend walks away.

Shit.

Teeth sinking into her plump lip, Charlotte waits a moment before she says, "You look nervous, Chef."

She steps forward and I stumble back, hitting the door I just shut behind me. Noticing, she stops and chuckles. "Wow. You *are* nervous."

"First day," I stutter.

"Uh-huh." She walks forward slowly, as if afraid I'll bolt, which I just might. When she's in front of me, chin lifted slightly to look into my eyes, she says, "I think the two of us need to have a talk, don't we?"

Christ, that voice.

What do you need?

You sound so *pretty when you come.*

I press my eyes closed for a moment, conjuring the thought away. "Not—not really. I'm just here to cook. Cook and clean, then leave. That's it."

"Except that's not it," she insists. "We've met on TOP."

A trickle of sweat runs down my temple.

"Don't deny it, Chef. I know that look. And besides, I don't mind. In fact, I love it. Thank you for your business."

I open my mouth only to quickly close it. Her voice is back to that same sultry tone she uses on TOP.

"Did we ever have the pleasure of getting on a call, just you and me?"

"Um . . ." She doesn't know who I am. Has no clue that I'm the guy she's probably been referring to as the Weepy Wanker. *Thank god.* "N-no. Just a regular, public live," I lie.

She clicks her tongue, fingers reaching for the top button of my shirt. "Too bad. Maybe we should, huh? I could give you a promo code." She worries at her bottom lip suggestively, flirty olive-green eyes scouring mine. "We could spend some time together. On the house."

This is madness. *Madness,* and I need it to stop right now.

I reach for her hand, wanting to gently move it away from me, then drop my arm down my side before I can touch her. Touching her *isn't* a good idea.

"I appreciate the offer, really—"

"Of course, it'd have to stay between the two of us," she interrupts, tracing a finger down my chest. Shivers rain down my spine, raising the hairs on my arms. "If Beatrice knew about my side-gig, I'd have to leave the platform."

She calls her mom by her first name?

With an exaggerated pout, she adds, "And we wouldn't get to hang out anymore."

Oh. *Oh.* Of course. She's scared I'll tell her mom. That's why she's . . . *flirting* with me. I doubted whether this could get more inappropriate, yet here we are. She's trying to buy my silence.

"Look . . ." I glance at the living room, making sure no one's around. "I have no idea what you're talking about. So there's nothing I could tell your mother." I say the next word slowly. "All right, *Cherry*?"

She narrows her eyes at me. "Are you sure about that?"

"Yes. Positive."

She holds my gaze for a moment longer. "Okay." Her hand grazes the back of mine, gently tugging at my wedding band. "'Cause I'd *hate* for your wife to find out what you do in your free time. Wouldn't you?"

My hand clenches in a fist as she walks away, and the second she disappears into the living room, I let out a heavy exhale.

I didn't even make it into the kitchen before being blackmailed.

Wiping my forehead, I enter the open space. The women—four in total—are tall, leggy, and radiant, their bodies sculpted to perfection—the kind of women you see gracing billboards or magazine covers. Two of them, Bonnie and a brunette in a pink bikini, are out on the terrace, lounging on sunbeds, and their laughter carries over the music that's blaring from the living room speakers.

Charlotte struts toward them, and with her freckled skin, the sunlight catching in her hair, the sway of her hips—she moves like she owns the world. For all I know, maybe she does.

The last woman, a blonde with icy blue eyes, is curled up on the couch, engrossed in her phone. She's wearing a white bikini that contrasts against her tan, and her legs, long and toned, stretch out lazily.

I clear my throat, trying to focus on the task at hand. The counter in front of me is littered with empty glasses, some crumbs, a half-drunk pitcher of something vibrant and fruity.

Not my problem.

I'm not supposed to feed Mrs. Arnault's daughter more than 1,200 calories a day. If she gets extras elsewhere . . . well, quite frankly, good for her. I'm here to cook, and that's all I'll do. But as I gather the ingredients for the meal, I can't help but overhear bits of their conversation—stories about wild parties, the places they've traveled, the men they've met.

Who are these people? Seriously, I need to google this family.

The blonde on the couch looks up, her eyes landing on me for a brief second. Uninterested, she turns back at her phone.

I follow her example and focus on the eggs, cracking them into a mound of flour on the counter. Today's menu includes a fresh seafood pasta, tossed with a lemon-basil sauce. I'm using my fingers to mix the eggs in, the dough forming as I work it together, when Charlotte's voice carries over.

"Peter. Again," she says, holding her phone up with a bored expression.

"You *have* to go out with him, Charlotte. Are you kidding? A photographer like him?"

I eye them while I knead the dough, pressing the heel of my palm into it, stretching and folding until it's smooth and elastic, and catch Charlotte rolling her eyes as she takes a sip of her drink.

"He's such a douche," she whines.

Bonnie hums. "But he's got a Ferrari."

The brunette holds up a finger. "A Maserati."

Bonnie rolls her eyes. "Who cares? The point is he'll probably take you to Paris on his private jet."

"And book you for *anything* you wanted."

Dragging my eyes away, I focus on the task.

Book her? I *seriously* need to find out more about these people.

"For some pussy, Peter will probably *give* me his private jet," Charlotte deadpans, causing the other two to burst into laughter.

I should mind my business, but I can't look away as Charlotte tilts her glass back and empties it in two sips. I zero in on the curve of her neck, the parting of her lips after she swallows, and I have every impure thought that's ever occurred to man.

"Hey, Charlotte," the blonde woman says from the couch. I find her gaze on me and quickly turn to the dough, smoothing my palm over it before wrapping it in plastic to rest. "It looks like your *cook* wants some pussy too."

Her voice is sharp and mocking, like she's daring me to react, making no effort to hide her disdain. Though I feel heat rise up my cheeks, I refuse to acknowledge her.

"Maybe he's fantasizing about touching someone *important* for once," Bonnie adds.

The brunette snorts. "You sure you can handle all this, Chef? You look a little out of your depth here."

I hate myself for the way my cheeks flare up. They're fucking kids. Pretty, spoiled twenty-something-year-olds trying to get a kick out of humiliating someone for *working*.

It's not worth getting flustered about.

"Hey, maybe you could keep him as your sidepiece," Bonnie insists. "Men who can't afford you try much harder in bed."

They all giggle, and in the silence that follows, I meet Charlotte's gaze.

She hesitates for a moment, drink halfway lifted to her mouth.

Then with a shrug, she turns away. "Afraid he's going to have to keep dreaming. I don't fuck the *help*."

MY EYES DON'T STRAY from the counter. I keep my hands busy —kneading the last bit of pasta dough until it's smooth, dusting the surface with flour, rolling and cutting it into delicate ribbons. Then it's the sauce's turn—a drizzle of olive oil, fragrant garlic sizzling until golden, white wine to deglaze the pan. Fresh basil, a whisper of lemon zest, and the seafood goes in last.

For forty-five minutes, I listen to their frivolous chatter without a peep. My head doesn't lift when the girls check the time and decide to leave before Beatrice arrives. Not when they move past me in a cloud of perfume and giggles. Not even when Charlotte lingers, coming back alone to gather their glasses and set them in the sink with a muted *clink*.

I'm not offended, of course. A twenty-three-year-old calling me *the help* like I should be ashamed of having an honest-to-god job reflects worse on her. But the implication that I *want* Charlotte? That sticks. That needles under my skin in a way I can't shake.

Because she knows it's true.

I wouldn't have ended up on her page if it wasn't.

"It's too much food."

Charlotte's voice jolts me out of my thoughts. I flinch, glancing behind me at the sink where she's rinsing the glasses.

"It's about two ounces of pasta each."

She nods. "Too much food."

I glance down at the pan, at the child-sized portion of pasta cooling in the sauce. My jaw clenches. When I turn back to her, she's still at the sink, scrubbing away any evidence of her friends' presence.

"Sorry. About what I said."

"Huh?" I frown. "It's fine."

"No, it's not *fine*." She sets a glass down. "I want those girls to like me so much I don't even bother to question whether I like *myself* when I'm with them." A humorless chuckle escapes her. "Trust me, I don't judge people based on their money or their job."

I watch her for a moment, her delicate hands wiping down the counter, then flick the burner off.

"I mean it," she says with a slight shrug. "I'm a whore after all."

I freeze, my grip tightening on the handle of the pan.

"That's not true." The words tumble out instinctively, my throat tightening around them. "You're not a whore."

"Sure I am." Charlotte wipes a glass, her movements steady. She sets it on the counter then lifts her chin, meeting my eyes. "I take my clothes off for money. I make men orgasm, do whatever they ask me to. I'm not ashamed of it."

Silence stretches between us.

"At least I make my own money. Like you." She nods toward the hallway. "Those girls? Daughters of rich people. They'll never get it."

So *that's* why she moonlights on TOP. She wants her own money. "Is that what you want to do for the rest of your life?"

Her glare is murderous. "Is cooking for my mom what *you* want to do for the rest of *your* life?"

I shake my head. "I didn't mean—"

"No, no." She lifts a hand, mockingly polite. "Please, I insist, *save me* from this terrible cycle of prostitution I'm stuck in." Her eyes harden as she grabs the glasses and shoves them back into the cabinet.

"That's not what I meant," I reaffirm. "I just . . ."

One of her brows arches, daring me to continue.

"I saw the art equipment in your room."

"You did?" Her eyes narrow. "I hardly move my camera around during lives."

Shit, shit, shit.

She seems to shake the thought away with a shrug. "Well, it's a hobby." Her lips purse. "You know . . . things you do because they're fun?"

"Got it." She wipes the counter once more, ensuring not a single crumb remains, while I dish the pasta onto the plates, glancing at her for approval. She assesses the portions, then reluctantly nods.

That has to be . . . three ounces for two people.

It's despicable.

I shouldn't push. I shouldn't care. But for some reason, I do.

"Why do you want to be friends with those girls?" I shrug. "I mean, if you don't like them."

"Because," she says as she drops the cloth on the counter, "when you're starving, even poison is better than nothing."

The words settle like a stone in my chest, cold and sharp. She's not just talking about food, I know that. The way she says it, like she's too used to taking whatever scraps are left and pretending they're enough, makes my heart clench.

What the hell is going on in this household?

Before I can dig for answers, the door swings open and Beatrice breezes in, barely lifting her gaze off her phone. She sheds her coat in one fluid motion, tossing it over the back of the couch along with her bag. "Lunch should be ready."

"It is." I set the plates on the table, forcing my expression into something neutral.

Her sharp gaze flicks to the food, assessing it with the precision of someone who measures worth in calories. Straightening her white blouse, she nods once before turning to her daughter. "Charlotte. Time to eat."

She moves toward the counter, but stops suddenly. Her eyes narrow.

"What—" Her voice is clipped, suspicious, as she peers at something near the fruit bowl.

A crumb.

A fucking crumb.

Charlotte's entire body stiffens.

"What is that?" When Charlotte doesn't say a word, Beatrice strikes her with a glare. "I asked you a question."

I turn my back on them, heart racing.

"How am I supposed to know? I don't cook."

"Chef Coleman?"

Oh, for fuck's sake.

I twist, pan in hand. "Yes?"

"Was Charlotte eating something when you got here?"

I flick my gaze to Charlotte. She's standing there with her arms crossed, but her eyes—her eyes are screaming at me.

Lie.

I glance back at Beatrice. "Excuse me?"

"My daughter," she says sharply. "What was she doing when you came in?"

My gut twists. I'm a father—I should take the mother's side. But this? This woman is *starving* her child, picking apart every single morsel of food she eats like it's a crime. And Charlotte—she's obviously terrified of her.

But what if she finds out anyway?

I can't be fired.

I *can't* be fired.

"Answer my question, Chef." Beatrice's voice sharpens. "The food's getting cold."

I inhale deeply. "She was on her phone, and I didn't see her eat anything. The crumb must be from the pasta dough."

She steps closer—maybe to taste the crumb to see if I'm lying?—and I casually wipe it away with my cloth, then meet her infuriated gaze. "It won't happen again."

Beatrice must be happy with my response, because she pulls out a chair and sits at the table. I watch Charlotte out of the corner of my eye as she joins her mother, a mix of gratitude and amusement playing on her features. Then she lifts her fork and takes a bite. Her lashes flutter.

She likes it.

She likes my food.

When she looks at me again, there's something in her gaze that feels just for me.

Like a window cracked open after years of stale air.

CHAPTER 7

Preheat the Drama

Everything is clean and in order, and my first day is officially over. It seems that Beatrice appreciated lunch *and* dinner—braised lamb shanks slow-cooked until tender and served over creamy-sans-the-cream mashed potatoes, with roasted carrots glazed in honey and thyme. She made a polite comment about the flavors, nothing overly enthusiastic but enough to let me know she enjoyed it. Charlotte, on the other hand, barely said a word. She picked at her plate, eating in small bites.

When dinner was over, the women went their separate ways. At some point while I was cleaning, I heard the front door open and close, but I have no idea who left.

I glance around the kitchen for the millionth time, making sure everything is back in its place and spotless. Satisfied, I grab my bag and head for the door.

Who would've expected this job to be so emotionally taxing?

It should be simple—cook, clean up, get paid. But something about this house, about the way Beatrice and Charlotte barely interact, how meals feel more like obligations than moments to enjoy—it's all very unsettling.

And then there's Charlotte.

Gorgeous, mysterious Charlotte who I should stop thinking about.

I take the stairs down, figuring I could use the workout. The usher at the front gives me his usual glare as I pass and I nod at him, adjusting my grip on my bag, then stepping outside.

Pulling my phone from my pocket, I open my texts and tap on Amelie's name.

> **AARON**
> Tell your husband dinner went by smoothly. I'm off.

> **AMELIE**
> Congratulations on a successful first day.

> **AARON**
> How was yours?

> **AMELIE**
> The producer asked me to "raise my voice if I feel the need to."

> **AARON**
> Did you?

> **AMELIE**
> Please. By the end of this, the Preston name will no longer be associated with culinary dictatorship. Maybe puppies and rainbows.

> **AARON**
> Good for you. Say hi to Ian.

"Texting your wife?"

I look up, and there she is—Charlotte, perched on the steps, knees pulled to her chest, a cigarette dangling lazily between her fingers. A faint ember burns at the tip as she takes a drag, and the the late afternoon sun casts a warm, honeyed light across the curl of her lips.

So she's the one who left the house.

"I . . ." I clear my throat, slipping my phone into my pocket. How come whenever she's around I'm tenser than I've ever been? "A friend, actually."

"Those are nice too," she says, exhaling a thin stream of smoke into the sun-warmed air. Her gaze flicks over me before she adds, "Dinner was delicious."

"Yeah?" I step closer, curious. "You didn't eat all of it."

She shrugs, taking another drag. "I get extra points when I don't finish my meals, and I *need* extra points for this Friday."

I frown. "Extra points?"

"For a concert I want Beatrice to let me go to."

Excuse the fuck out of me?

I watch her, unable to disguise my shock but not knowing what to say. I should probably keep my mouth shut, but the way she said it—so casual, like it's normal to starve oneself for rewards—has my stomach clenching hard.

"You and your mom, you . . ." I hesitate, choosing my words carefully. "You eat very little."

"Uh-huh."

I wait, expecting her to elaborate. She doesn't.

"Any specific . . . reason for that?"

She bursts into laughter, her head tipping back slightly. There are butterflies in my stomach at the light, airy sound. "I have a show soon."

I tilt my head in a silent question.

"I'm a model. Beatrice is my mom *and* my agent."

"Oh." Of course. With that body, I should have figured. Those girls from today must be models too. Is that why she calls her mom by her first name? Because they work together? Hell, maybe it's just because Beatrice is utterly despicable and she needs to distance herself from the woman. "When—when's the show?"

She chuckles again, bringing the cigarette to her lips and inhaling. "Saturday."

Jesus. That's five days away. Maybe I can ask what her favorite meal is and cook it for her on Monday, like a little celebration.

"Of course, there's a shoot next week," she adds.

I frown. "There is?"

"And the week after that."

She must be popular, then. Maybe even famous, if she books that many shows. How does that work with her being on TOP? She has tens of thousands of followers on there. "Aren't you . . . worried?"

"Like in life? Not really," she says with a playful smirk.

"About someone figuring out who you are," I clarify. "Would the people you model for be okay with you camming?"

"Oh, absolutely not." She blows out smoke. "It's only a matter of time before one of my viewers rats me out. My days are numbered."

I expect her to say more, but she just shrugs, unbothered.

"What do I have to lose?" She taps her cigarette, watching the ash fall in a drift. "I'll celebrate unemployment with a cheeseburger."

My jaw tightens as I glance back at the building. "It's not healthy to eat twelve hundred calories a day. You're still young. Developing. Your body needs—"

"Oh, I have lots of *needs*, Chef."

She pulls her shoulders inwardly as if to highlight her cleavage, and my jaw locks. She's so sexy—*no, Aaron. Focus.* She's *deflecting.*

"I'm serious."

Dropping the act, she says, "Fine, you look like a big turkey leg to me right now. Happy? But I'm still not the one in charge, in case you haven't noticed."

Yeah, I *have* noticed. Unfortunately, I doubt Beatrice wants my input on her daughter's diet.

"I could give you more food," I say, before I can think better of it. The second she looks back at me, I know I said the *one* thing I shouldn't have. "Secretly."

Bad, bad move.

Okay, there are worse things I could have said. Things I thought of *many* times since that night on our call—like how I'd love to feed her something other than food. But Beatrice gave me one rule, and I just broke it. Although "Don't fantasize about my daughter" was probably implied.

"Beatrice would kill you."

"She'd have to find out first."

Her head angles back, like she's wondering why the hell I'd put myself in that position. For a second, I wonder the same thing. But the answer is simple: I want to keep my job, but not more than I think Charlotte a right to basic nutrition.

"She'd find out once she weighs me," she says.

"Once she . . ." I trail off, blinking.

She stands, stubbing out her cigarette against the step. When she walks closer, eyes sweeping over me, I catch a hint of perfume beneath the stale scent of smoke—something floral and subtle.

"You're new here," she says, almost like it's an explanation. Then, after a beat, she pulls at the sleeve of her sweater. "But . . . thanks for earlier. For covering for me."

She walks up the steps, leaving me standing there, hands clenched into fists.

"Hey, Chef?"

She's paused in the doorway, one hand braced against the frame. Sunlight spills in behind her, casting a soft glow along the curve of her hip and lighting up the sharp angles of her collarbone where her sweater slips wide at the neck. Her head is tilted slightly, eyes locked onto mine like she's daring me to look away first.

"I'll be online tonight."

Heat coils in my chest, rising to my face, and I swallow thickly. "Yeah?"

My voice comes out rougher than I intend, like the single syllable got caught in my throat on the way out.

Charlotte hums in confirmation. "Will you?"

My mouth opens, but my brain refuses to cooperate.

Does she . . . *want* me to be online?

It can't be about the money, right? She must have plenty of other dudes who'd love to watch her get naked for them. Guys who probably send tips just for the chance to hear their name from her lips, who flood her chat with requests, who would kill for even a fraction of the attention she's giving me right now.

And yet, here she is.

Asking *me*.

It shouldn't matter. It *doesn't* matter, because there's no possible version of this where I say yes.

I shift my weight and glance toward the street, willing for something to save me. "I don't think so." I point vaguely at the building behind her. "It wouldn't be . . . appropriate."

She drags her teeth over her lower lip, the corner of her mouth lifting in a tease. Not a nervous gesture—no, this is calculated. Meant to make me *think* about her mouth. About what she does with it.

"I know," she says, eyes hooded. "That's what makes it fun."

Jesus fucking Christ.

She's still watching me, waiting, like she knows exactly how much of a mess she's making of my brain right now.

And she *is*.

Because as much as I tell myself I won't, as much as I *know* I shouldn't . . . fuck yes I'll be online tonight.

I PULL INTO MY DRIVEWAY, cutting the engine with a yawn. The late afternoon sun casts long shadows across the pavement, warm and golden, and there—planted right on my front steps like he owns the place—is Logan.

He's impossible to miss—broad-shouldered and scowling. The sunlight skims the sharp angles of his face, catching on the scruff lining his jaw and the loose tie of dark waves at the nape of his neck. He's in his usual leather jacket, jeans stretched tight over his massive thighs.

What's he doing here? I don't dare hope he's decided we should actually *talk*, so . . . is he here to see Sadie?

When I open my door, he lifts a hand in a lazy salute. "Where's my favorite niece?"

I grab my bag and step out of the car. "With Josie's parents. They should be dropping her off soon." I say, climbing the steps.

He rises to his full height—taller than me by a few inches, built like he wrestles grizzlies for fun. My little brother who's not so little. He nods at my bag. "How was it?"

Oh, so *that's* why he's here.

To check on me, on the job. To make sure I don't fuck up and create problems for him.

"It was . . ." I think of Charlotte's snobby friends, the weird dynamic between Beatrice and her daughter, the fact that I'm counting down the seconds before I get to visit her page on TOP. Words like *concerning* and *intoxicating* roam through my mind, but I shove them down. "Good, good."

He doesn't look convinced.

"Were you waiting long?"

"Five minutes."

I unlock the door and push it open, gesturing for him to come inside. He follows me in, shutting the door behind us as I toe off my shoes and shrug out of my jacket.

"You sure today was good?" he asks, his eyes sharp on me.

I hang my bag on a hook and make my way into the living room, then walk through the small corridor to the kitchen. "Yeah, why?"

"I don't know. You have that face."

I pause, squinting. "Face?"

"Yeah." He runs his tongue over his teeth. "A face like you did some shit."

I grab a water from the fridge and twist the cap off, drinking deeply. He doesn't say anything, just leans a shoulder against the counter and waits with his arms crossed.

"Nah. No shit was done."

Some shit was done.

"Look, I don't need to tell you that Ian and Amelie are very dear to Primrose. And whatever is important to her is important to me."

My grip tightens slightly on the bottle, but I cover the ripple of unease with a chuckle.

"What's funny?"

"The way you talk about them. Like they're just Primrose's friends."

"They are."

He can't be for real. "They only gave me a shot at the job because of *you*, Logan. And besides, you spend all your time with them. Or Shane and Heaven from the bakery."

Logan just shrugs, ever the unreadable fortress of a man.

"Right. I forgot—you don't care about anything."

"Fine. I guess I like them." Then, after a beat, he adds, "Not Ian. He's an insufferable man-child who can't appreciate a second of silence."

A laugh escapes me before I can stop it.

"But I like the rest of them, so . . ." He tilts his head. "Try not to screw this up?"

"You got it."

He watches me for a moment longer, like he's waiting for further reassurance. When I hold his gaze, he grabs a beer from the fridge, and we head to the dining area.

He sits next to me, and I raise an eyebrow. He delivered his message; this is usually the part where he leaves. Because he has no real interest in being here. So why is he staying?

He doesn't speak right away, just reaches into the back pocket of his jeans and pulls out a crumpled envelope. Immediately, a knot tightens low in my gut. Something about the way he holds it tells me this isn't good news.

"What's that?"

His eyes turn dark. "Just open it, please."

A beat of hesitation. Then I take the envelope from him and slip my fingers under the flap, tearing it open. I slide the documents out, familiar words jumping out at me as I scan the lines. Legal jargon I've read before, but it's different this time—the finality of it. It's no longer a hypothetical or a process in motion but a decision made, an ending sealed.

My breath catches as I see the judge's signature at the bottom.

It's done.

I'm officially divorced.

For a moment, I simply exist. Stare at the paper. Really let myself *feel*. Then I set the papers down and look up at Logan. "Wow."

He stares down at his beer, rolling the bottle between his palms.

"Why are you—"

"The court sent both copies to Josie by mistake."

So she sent her ex—my *brother*—to give me mine.

"This must feel nice for you, huh?" I say, forcing something light into my voice. "Karma or something."

Immediately, his glare strikes me. "It doesn't, actually."

"I know, I know." I raise a hand, already regretting my words.

"No, *do* you?" He flicks the papers with the backs of his fingers. "Because if you think I want any part in this, you're out of your mind."

I bite my bottom lip until it stings. "I can't believe she sent *you* to give me these."

"She said she didn't want to make Mom do it. So . . ." He points a thumb at himself with a humorless smirk. "I got the honor."

I take another sip of water, letting the silence stretch between us. The kind of silence that's full of things unsaid and regrets not expressed. Sometimes I think it's the only silence we'll ever be capable of.

"Any news on when Josie might come back or . . ."

"Nope." Not one single peep from her since the call at Mom's house, though it must be a step in the right direction. A sign that things are improving. I hope so anyway.

After a long moment, I say, "You ever wonder what would've happened if Josie and I didn't . . ." The words lodge in my throat, so I try again. "I mean, not that I regret Sadie in any way, but . . . if she'd stuck with you, would Josie be in rehab right now? I don't think so."

He leans back in his chair. "Her drinking isn't your fault."

"Isn't it?"

"Of course not." His voice is steady, certain. "Divorce doesn't make you drink. Unhappiness doesn't make you drink. Alcoholism does."

"But she might have never developed a problem if—"

"If she'd never been unhappy?" he offers before a grimace. "Maybe not. But that's a part of life, Aaron. It's not something you can control." He fidgets with the beer label. "You know, toward the end of our relationship, when it was mostly fights . . . I remember her partying a lot. I was never really concerned—at that age, everyone drank—but now . . . it makes me think."

I drum my fingers against the table. At least this got Logan talking a little more than usual. I should try to push him while I have the chance, right?

"Logan, look. Can we—"

"You been by Mom's lately?" he cuts me off, looking away uncomfortably.

I pause. "Yeah. Last week. Why?"

"She came with us to the girls' pediatrician appointment yesterday, and . . ." He shrugs. "She seemed off, I guess."

"Off how?"

Another shrug, but this one is tighter, less casual. "I don't know. She went to put on her cardigan and was taking forever. When I went to check on her, she was . . . there. Staring down at it. She almost looked confused, or . . . I don't know. Then she got weird about it, like she didn't want me making a thing of it. Said she was tired."

Confused? Mom?

Mom's never been confused a day in her life.

"Maybe she was distracted, or . . ." I wave a hand around. "Worried about the appointment."

He nods, though he doesn't look convinced. "Yeah. You're probably right."

Sure I'm right. If Mom wasn't fine, she would tell us.

But now that he's brought it up . . . there was that tremor in her hands. I didn't get the chance to ask, but Darren mentioned she kept dropping kitchen utensils. Does that count as confusion?

He studies me for a moment, then says, "To answer your question—no, I don't wonder. I'm much happier with Primrose than I ever was with Josie. So I don't wonder—*ever*."

I raise my water in mock salute. "Glad to be of service then."

His lips twitch, but his gaze doesn't waver. "What I mean is . . ." He pulls his beer closer, fingers tracing the condensation. "Maybe there's a woman out there who you'll be happier with than you were with Josie. Who'll make you stop wondering and silence all those questions. A woman who'll consume your mind."

I swallow, my throat suddenly dry.

A particular freckled face flashes before my eyes. The face of a stranger, but one who for some reason *is* consuming my mind.

One who has no business being there.

CHAPTER 8

Duck Confits and Ego Trips

By the time I close Sadie's door for the fifth time tonight, my whole body feels heavy with exhaustion. It's nearly two a.m., and I should get some sleep. Instead, I find myself grabbing my laptop and migrating to the bedroom.

The house is quiet, save for the muted hum of the occasional car passing by. I settle onto the bed and open the laptop, the dark screen waiting.

I shouldn't. I *really* shouldn't. But I tap the trackpad, heartbeat quickening.

The screen flickers to life and my fingers hover over the keyboard, hesitation curling in my gut. My inbox is full of unread emails, including one from Ian that I *should* answer.

I don't.

Instead, I type *TOP* into the navigation bar.

The homepage loads instantly, a carousel of faces smiling seductively at the camera. I ignore them all and type her username, finding her immediately.

On a public live feed.

The thumbnail is small, but even in the still image, she looks like trouble. She's sitting on the edge of her bed, hair loose around her shoulders, lips slightly parted like she's just uttered something sinful.

I shouldn't click.

I *should not* click.

But I do.

The screen buffers, the little loading icon spinning for a few seconds before the image clears.

Charlotte's face comes into focus—dimly lit and framed by the cascade of her scarlet hair. She looks tired, but not in a bad way. Cozy, wrapped in a loose sweater that's slipping off one shoulder.

Her eyes are warm as they land on the chat, her lips curving just a little more than usual.

"Cole," she says almost fondly, "You're back."

"Yes. How—how are you?" I say. Should I try to mask my voice? I guess the laptop microphone doesn't modify it enough for her not to recognize it, so I probably should—

"Microphones and cameras are not allowed during lives, only one-on-ones. You'll have to write for me, baby."

Oh. I glance at the chat box, fingers hesitating for a second before typing.

CHIEF.728

> I couldn't sleep. I figured I'd check to see if you were still up.

She grins, tucking a strand of hair behind her ear. "I was about to call it a night, actually. There's hardly anyone at this hour."

That makes sense. The chat box is empty, save for my message. No flood of donations, no names popping in and out.

It's just us.

CHIEF.728

> Don't let me keep you up. It was nice to see you.

I throw my head back. "Jeez, why not write her a love letter?"

But she reads the message, and the way she blushes makes it impossible to regret sending it. "Leaving already? Did you change your mind about wanting to hang out?"

Why would I, when you look like that?

She shifts to get more comfortable, her legs kicking lazily behind her. "Have you ever been in a live feed on TOP?"

Not really. Give me the tour?

"You got it." She points one long, manicured finger at the camera. "There should be a few buttons on your screen. Each of those corresponds to a donation."

I glance at the panel and locate the buttons lined up in a neat row beneath the feed, each one labeled with an action and a price tag. Twenty dollars to lift her top. Fifty to remove her bra. A hundred for her to touch herself.

My stomach feels weird—tight, like I swallowed something too big to go down.

It's not that I didn't know what TOP was. But seeing it like this? With *her*?

It feels too fucking wrong.

She's watching the camera, probably waiting for a response, so I force my fingers to move.

What about the last button? "Custom request"?

A smirk tugs at her lips. "Straight for the gold, huh? That costs two hundred dollars. I get loads of those during lives, so I pick the ones I'm comfortable with, and anyone who wants to see it happen will donate too."

I swallow.

I don't know why I ask the next question. Maybe I shouldn't.

What's a popular one?

"Um . . ." She taps her lip, considering. "Butt plugs are a big hit. Lots of fake blowjobs, foot shots. Some people want to watch me try on clothes, others want me to put makeup on."

I rest my fingers on the keyboard, my pulse thick and slow.

I should *definitely* say something, but my mind is stuck, tangled up in the image of her on all fours with a butt plug in her beautiful hole. Of blowjobs, and messy sex, and loud orgasms.

I close my eyes for a moment, trying to breathe through the arousal.

"Did you fall asleep on me, Cole?"

No, sorry. What's a fake blowjob?

"Ah, yes," she says, shifting slightly to the side before reappearing fully in the frame. "The demonstration is complimentary."

She picks up a long purple dildo and kneels down. Locking eyes with the camera, she grins then extends her tongue to glide it across the smooth surface, all the way up to the tip. Taking just the end into her mouth, she moves her lips, and the sucking sound sends a wave of shivers down my spine.

"Oh, fuck." I press a fist against my mouth. I was already turned on from just thinking about her, which intensified upon seeing her, but now the surge of desire is so intense that my balls tighten.

This has no business being so fucking hot, but holy shit, watching her service a silicone dick through a screen feels as good as sex.

Head rising, she winks. "What do you think?"

That there is no way in hell I can justify making her do this, even though the whole thing would be over in two minutes, judging by the stiffness between my legs. I *can't*.

CHIEF.728

I think I'll pass.

"Shit, you really can't convey tone via chat," I mutter when her smile dampens.

"You didn't like it?"

I rush to type.

CHIEF.728

I got so hard so fast, my dick might turn into a missile and shoot into space.

Just not tonight.

Charlotte laughs, the sound loud and genuine, and quickly covers her mouth with her fingers. Her eyes dart toward the door, then back to me. "I can't make too much noise. Don't be funny."

I lean back against the headboard, one corner of my lips pulling up. "All right," I say, even though she can't hear me.

I need to wipe this idiot smile off my face. The only problem is that I enjoy watching her laugh more than I enjoy watching her orgasm. And I *do* love watching that.

She's just . . . so different on TOP. Less restrained, polished. More like herself.

I'm obsessed with it.

"So . . ." She shifts, propping herself up on one elbow, her cheek resting on her palm. Loose strands of hair tumble across her face, and she brushes them away absentmindedly. "What do you want to do tonight?"

I glance at the screen, my fingers hesitating for just a second before I move to the fourth box.

Custom request.

A lump forms in my throat as I type, then press enter.

Her eyes narrow slightly, then she drags her cursor across the screen. "Hmm. A custom request, huh? Let's see."

There's a *click* as she selects it, then she blinks.

"'Let's keep talking'?" she reads aloud, her voice lilting with curiosity.

Shit. Did I make it weird?

I can request a variety of explicit things and she wouldn't judge me, but I just want to hear her voice. No fake-blowjobs or foot pics —that's not my thing anyway. But is this even *allowed*?

She blinks, watching the camera, watching *me*.

"You don't have to pay me to talk to you, Cole."

CHIEF.728

Well, you're still on the clock, aren't you?

"Yeah." She presses her lips together for just a second before she leans toward her laptop. "Then . . . click on the first button. That's too much money for just talking."

CHIEF.728

You're not a great haggler.

She chuckles, the sound hushed and warm, and shifts again, curling into her pillow. The glow of the screen makes her look even cozier, and it's easy to fool myself into thinking this isn't just a job for her, but a late-night conversation between two people who should be asleep but aren't.

"I'm not taking this much money to just talk to you while I'm half asleep," she murmurs.

I tap on the third button, 100 dollars' worth, then type.

CHIEF.728

Meet me halfway?

She considers that for a moment, biting her lip, then nods. Once she accepts my donation, her eyes flicker back to the screen.

"Okay, Cole." She tucks her arm beneath her cheek. "Let's talk."

THE APARTMENT IS EMPTY, the hum of the fridge the only sound as I set my bag down and pull out the ingredients I brought: duck, oranges, fennel, shallots, fresh thyme, and a head of garlic.

I'm making duck confit, which means hours of prep before it even touches the oven. The legs need to be trimmed, salted, and cured with aromatics before they cook in their own fat. While that's happening, I'll prep an orange-fennel sauce and a crisp salad to cut through the richness.

I'm excited to be here early, and while I tell myself it's just because I like having enough time to cook, to do things right, that's not the whole truth.

I'm looking forward to seeing her.

Charlotte.

The way the air shifts around her, like she drags in electricity without even trying. It's ridiculous, really. We spent several hours chatting last night. About her favorite song, "Dreams" by Midnight Reckless, and about the best trip she ever went on—a getaway to a small Italian island where she saw the most beautiful sunsets of her life. She asked about my demonic cat, and about my daughter.

She shouldn't be this interesting—she's too young for that. And it shouldn't feel so easy to talk to her, but it does. It's not like talking to a friend, but neither is it like getting to know a stranger. It's a feeling I can't compare to anything I've ever experienced before.

I begin seasoning the duck legs with crushed garlic, fresh thyme, and a touch of orange zest, and when I hear the door opening, my heartbeat kicks into overdrive. There's a low murmur, a breathy laugh. It's Charlotte, definitely, but not just her. There's a man's voice too.

I freeze, listening. The footsteps are unhurried as they move through the house, and I catch a glimpse of them when they reach the arch that leads into the corridor.

They're pressed together, her back against the wall, his hands on her hips. His mouth on her neck.

I don't know what I expected, but it wasn't this.

Something in my chest twists, sharp and sudden, before I can shove it down.

I don't move. I should make a sound, announce myself, *something*. Instead, I stand there like an idiot, stuck between wanting to make them stop and wanting to disappear.

They're too lost in each other to notice me, her fingers tangled in his hair, his hands roaming her waist. She snickers again and something dangerously close to jealousy coils in my gut.

I've *got* to make it stop.

I clear my throat, and in the silence, it lands like a drop of ink in water—small, but impossible to ignore.

Charlotte startles, her head snapping up, while the man's hands drop from her body like he just realized it's on fire.

"You're here," she says tentatively.

"Yeah." I arrange the duck legs on a tray, covering them with plastic wrap. The last thing I need is for her to see something in my face that I shouldn't be feeling.

Her *companion* steps forward, hands tucked in his pockets. Blond, clean-shaven, expensive-looking sweater draped over his shoulders. He studies the kitchen with casual disinterest before settling his attention on me.

"Your mom got a chef?" he asks, then nods to Charlotte. "Good for you."

"Let's go to my room, Peter. We have an hour before Beatrice comes back home."

One hour.

Her. With him. In her room.

A sour twist tightens inside me. I shouldn't care—I *know* I shouldn't—but the thought makes me nauseous, a bitter taste creeping up the back of my throat.

He doesn't move right away. Instead he steps closer to the counter, eyes shifting to the food I'm preparing. "One sec," he tells her before pointing a finger at me. "Mind making us some snacks?"

Do I mind making Peter some snacks? I do, actually.

"He's not going to cook for you," Charlotte says, rolling her eyes.

"Why not?"

"Because my mom has given him very clear instructions, and your *snacks* aren't part of that."

He snorts. "Models, am I right?"

The way he says it. Like he's bored of fucking models left and right, and I'm supposed to somehow relate to that. Like Charlotte is just another body he's entertaining himself with, and he assumes I think the same way.

This is the guy Charlotte was talking about with her friends, isn't it? The Maserati owner with a jet who's an important photographer. He looks to be in his early thirties.

I tighten my grip on the wooden spoon in my hand, imagining how satisfying it would be to shove it straight into his smug mouth.

"How about you make us some drinks, then?" he tries, and Charlotte lifts her arms in exasperation before she heads toward the hallway.

He leans in, lowering his voice. "Make them extra heavy, all right? I could use some help getting her loosened up."

What did he just say?

Anger unfurls in my gut. Of course he's one of those pricks. Guys who think alcohol is a shortcut to consent, who believe women are just obstacles to maneuver around rather than people with agency.

I set another pan on the fire. "Well, that changes everything," I say, my tone light. Let him think I'm going along with it for just a second.

He waits, but when I don't move from the stove, he scoffs and extracts a fifty-dollar bill from his wallet. "Come on. Man to man."

I let out a sardonic laugh. *Man to man*.

I finally meet his gaze head-on, leaning with both hands against the counter. "You're not a man," I say. "You're a boy."

His features pinch, lips parting in stunned offense. "The fuck is your problem?"

"A *man* doesn't ply women with alcohol so they'll sleep with him. A *man* respects their partner enough to let them choose what they want, without manipulation or games. He knows that true intimacy is built on mutual respect, not pressure."

Peter's jaw tightens, his entitled little brain slow on the uptake. He straightens, puffing his chest slightly.

"You know, I could get you fired," he finally says.

I smirk. "Could you?"

Somehow I really doubt that if he relayed this conversation to Beatrice, I'd come out a loser.

I push away from the counter. "I suggest you get out of my face and go entertain Charlotte however *she* wants you to."

He shifts his weight, swallowing. I can tell he's used to people deferring to him, to women bending under the weight of his charm, to men nodding along to whatever bullshit he spews. But I'm not one of his frat buddies. I don't owe him anything.

"And I recommend you don't take it a single step further than what she's comfortable with." My voice drops lower. "Because, *man to man*, your last name or your money won't help you if you do."

His nostrils flare, but he says nothing.

"Peter?" Charlotte calls, her voice cutting through the tension.

We both turn where she's standing by the entrance, arms crossed and gaze flicking between us. I don't know how much of this she's heard, but I hope it's a lot.

"Are you coming?"

He scoffs, swallowing whatever he was about to say. "I am." He winks at me. "And so is she, *buddy*."

Fuck me. There is absolutely no way I'll stand here while he does whatever he's planning to do in that room. Not after what he said.

"Afraid Beatrice is on her way," I say as he steps toward her. Charlotte's reluctant gaze is on me as I raise my phone. "She just texted."

"Really?" she asks. How do I just know she doesn't believe me for a second?

"Yep. Just a minute ago." I focus on Peter. "So you should go. Now."

He clicks his tongue then turns back to Charlotte, whose eyes stick to me.

"I'll see you later, okay?" she says.

"Seriously?"

She nods, and then he's storming away, mumbling curses under his breath.

Though I don't dare to look up, I can feel her gaze burning on the side of my face until she disappears again.

CHAPTER 9
More Than Just a Slice

C an we get pepperoni?"

The sidewalk glows under the amber haze of street-lights, the scent of melted cheese and dough drifting from the pizzeria up ahead as Sadie tugs at my hand.

I look down at her. "*And* cheese?"

"So we have breakfast pizza tomorrow!"

"Fine." I ruffle her hair before she swats my hand away, her giggles bubbling through the air like shaken soda. We usually get pizzas on Friday, but she insisted she wanted it a day earlier, and I'm too tired to cook dinner anyway.

"Dad! Stop it." She pushes at the door with all the might her little body can muster, and when it's still too heavy, I step in to nudge it open for her. She struts past me like she owns the place, chin high, pigtails bouncing. "Hi, Dave!"

"Hello, angel." Dave, the grizzled owner behind the counter, looks up from where he's stretching dough, flour dusting his fore-arms. His eyes shift to me, a knowing grin already forming. "Hey, Aaron. The usual?"

"And a pepperoni, apparently."

Dave lets out a low whistle and grabs a notepad. "Wow. Trying something new today, huh?"

Sadie nods solemnly, proud of her major life decision. He jots it down, winks, and calls into the kitchen, "One cheese, one pepperoni!"

At the sound of clattering pans and Italian words drifting from the back, Sadie fists her hands in my jeans and tugs. "Daddy, sodas?"

"Go get them—hey," I call when she starts hopping toward the fridge, already too excited. "*Two* sodas."

She rushes off, her sneakers squeaking against the tiles as she pulls the fridge open with both hands. I glance her way—until something red catches my eye.

At the last table on the right, half hidden in the corner, sits Charlotte.

My stomach tightens.

She's bent over a notebook, one hand gripping a pencil and the other resting on the page as she sketches. Headphones cover her ears, and she's completely lost in whatever she's creating.

I should look away. I should turn back toward the counter, keep my distance.

After what happened with her *friend* two days ago, we've barely interacted. I didn't see her at all today, and Beatrice didn't seem remotely worried about her daughter skipping lunch and dinner. She ate, complained about the chicken being overcooked, and retreated to her office.

But I've been thinking about Charlotte nonstop. Wondering if she's upset I ruined her "date." If she'll see Peter again.

My gaze flicks to the notebook, curiosity getting the better of me.

What's she drawing?

I can't see.

God, she's so fucking intriguing.

Before I can take a step closer, Sadie's small voice rings out.

"My mommy has red hair like yours."

Shit.

I snap my head toward her just in time to see her tiny fingers reach out, gently brushing the strands of Charlotte's long, thick hair.

She flinches, her shoulders tensing, but when she turns and sees Sadie, she relaxes instantly. With an easy smile, she pulls her headphones off and hangs them around her neck. "Hey, you."

Sadie grins, bouncing slightly. "Your hair . . . I love it."

"You do?" Charlotte asks, voice playful.

Seriously, Sadie knows better than to talk to strangers. Of course, Charlotte *isn't* a stranger, at least to me. And she's smiling —smiling at my daughter, warm and unguarded. And I thought she was beautiful before.

She nods toward Sadie's messy pigtails. "I like yours too."

Sadie beams and does a little twirl, clearly pleased. Then, as if deciding she's had enough attention, she points at me.

"My daddy was looking at you."

Great.

My body locks up as Charlotte's eyes flick to me, then narrow with curiosity.

I step closer, and before I can decide what to say, she leans back in her chair. "A chef walks into a pizzeria and says . . ."

I sigh, relieved at her playful tone. "Hi, Charlotte."

She clicks her tongue. "Where's the punchline?"

"Daddy, she's funny," Sadie announces.

I gently pull her against my hip. "Sorry about that. Sadie knows better than to approach strangers."

"But you were smiling at her, Daddy!"

Good lord.

Charlotte's smirk deepens, her eyes alight.

"No, I wasn't," I protest, but Sadie isn't done.

She wiggles out of my hold and steps up to Charlotte's table.

After peering down at the open notebook, she gasps. "This looks like my Daddy."

Shit, Sadie—*Wait, what?*

Charlotte lets out a low, satisfied laugh. Closing her notebook, she picks up her pencil, twirling it between her fingers. "Wow. You're a little snitch, aren't you?"

"What's a snitch?"

"O-kay," I interject, my pulse a little too quick. "We should let Charlotte draw. Right, baby?"

Sadie ignores me. "Do you like pepperoni pizza?"

What is with her sudden obsession with pepperoni?

"I love it," Charlotte says. "Do you?"

"I think so. I'm eating it for the first time tonight." She leans against the table on both arms, her little feet swinging inches off the floor. Then, with all the casual ease of someone who hasn't yet learned the concept of social boundaries, she asks, "Do you want to eat pizza with me and my daddy?"

"Sadie," I scold, keeping my voice gentle but firm.

She turns, wide-eyed, like she has no idea what she's done wrong. But she does. She knows she's not supposed to invite strangers over. That applies especially to women her father should stay far, far away from.

"Why don't you bring those sodas to Dave so Daddy can pay?" I suggest, nudging her along.

She pouts but obeys, skipping off toward the counter.

After watching her go, Charlotte turns her attention back to me, a smug smile on her lips. "Hi, Daddy."

I blow out a breath, looking around to make sure nobody heard that.

"I'm not sure what's gotten into her. Sorry."

She props her chin on her hand, studying me. "From the sound of it . . . you were smiling at me."

"And from the looks of it, you were drawing me."

Her teeth sink into her bottom lip. "Right."

"Right."

For a long moment, we watch each other—long enough for me to regret my words. That was flirty, wasn't it? Why is it so fun to flirt with her?

No, Aaron. Don't.

She taps her pencil against the notebook—the one Sadie so helpfully pointed out might contain a drawing with my face in it. I have no idea what she's actually drawing, but I know one thing: I need to get my pizzas and leave.

Though I am curious to know why she's having nothing but a coffee at Tony's.

"Are you getting a pizza?"

"Me?" She snorts. "Pizza?"

Yes, it goes against every one of her mother's rules, but she skipped both main meals today.

"Beatrice has a date over," she explains, not quite meeting my eyes. "And I can't go back home until she's done with him."

She's banished from her own house?

A low simmer of anger stirs in my bones. What kind of mother kicks her daughter out every time she brings a man home? Where the hell is Charlotte supposed to go?

I glance at Sadie who's at the counter, bouncing on her toes as she watches the big oven with barely concealed excitement. Then back at Charlotte, picking at the corner of her sketchpad, her fingers smudged with graphite.

"Did you eat anything today?"

She blinks, as if the question takes her by surprise. "Uh . . . no."

No? *Nothing?* Since this morning? Last night?

I rake a hand through my hair, studying her. She looks fine, but now that I'm paying attention, there's a sluggishness to her movements. A dullness in her expression. How the hell is she still standing if she hasn't eaten all day?

"Daddy!" Sadie's voice breaks through my thoughts, and I

turn just in time to see Dave setting the pizza boxes on the counter. "The pizzas are ready!"

"Coming, sweetheart." I shift my gaze back to Charlotte, who's already looking back at the sketchpad, shoulders tense.

I can't leave her here. Tony's will close up soon, and I'll worry all night long that she passed out from hunger or wandered the streets for hours until her mom let her come back home.

I also can't invite her over, though. Can I? It'd be unprofessional, and I've already crossed more lines than I care to admit.

Fuck me, I know which of the two arguments feels weaker in my mind.

"You should come over."

Her eyes lift. "What?"

"Come over," I repeat. "Sadie would love to have company."

At that, the corner of her mouth twitches into a tired half smile. Maybe it's because we both know Sadie won't enjoy her company as much as I will. "Are you sure?"

"Yeah, of course. I'll give you a ride back home."

"Oh, well." She gathers up her things. "As long as I get a *ride*."

She can't help herself, can she?

"Sweetheart," I say as I join Sadie's side. "Charlotte is a friend of Daddy's from work."

"Like Auntie Amelie?"

"Yes, and she's coming over to eat pizza. All right?"

She nods frantically. "Yes!

I hold the door open as Sadie asks her about her clothes, her favorite animal, and more I miss because all I can see is Charlotte stepping past me.

There's no way this ends well. But right now, I'm not sure I care.

"Aren't you going to eat?" Sadie asks, watching Charlotte as she stares at the pizzas laid out before us.

Her lips part slightly. "Uh . . ."

"You said you liked pepperoni," Sadie insists, pointing at the untouched pizza.

Charlotte narrows her eyes playfully. "*You* said you'd try it, and you're eating cheese pizza."

"I'll try it after!"

"Sadie," I say gently, cutting in before Charlotte can retort. "We don't insist when people don't feel like eating. They might have allergies or dietary restrictions or . . ." I trail off as she watches me with a puzzled expression. I reach out and tuck a stray strand of hair behind her ear. "It's impolite, love."

"Sorry, Charlotte."

"That's okay." Charlotte hesitates for a moment, then inhales as if gathering courage. "Maybe . . . maybe I'll have a slice."

Her gaze lingers on the pepperoni pizza, almost reverently, like it's something forbidden. But then, I see it—the way her eyes flicker up and away. She's counting calories. Debating the extra fat, the indulgence, the guilt.

"You know," I rush out, "meat has wonderful nutritional value."

Her eyes fill with cautious hope.

"Proteins," I add. "Cheese . . . it's mostly fat."

Charlotte's lips quirk. "Pepperoni has cheese too."

"Yeah." I scramble for something better. "But if you're going to eat junk food, you might as well get some nutrients out of it."

She remains tense, and I know it's because Beatrice's obsession has settled so deeply in her mind that she can't even enjoy a slice of pizza without guilt clawing at her.

I brush my hands together then reach for a slice of pepperoni pizza and set it in front of Charlotte, who stares at it like it's a loaded weapon.

Sadie's been oddly quiet. When I glance at her, I notice she's watching Charlotte in pretty much the same way she watches animals at the zoo.

That can't be helping.

"So, how was school today?" I ask quickly.

Sadie's face lights up. "Good! We're studying shapes. I like triangles. Duncan didn't come to school today. Frances said he has head lice."

I tune out the rest of her story when I see Charlotte finally lift her slice. She gives it a tentative bite, and the second she begins chewing, she lets out a groan—loud, unfiltered, and utterly obscene.

Sadie's eyes widen before she bursts into giggles so honest and unrestrained that I can't help but chuckle too.

"Oh, this is so good," Charlotte says, tapping her feet under the table in excitement. She laughs along with us before taking another, much bigger bite. "I forgot how much I fuck—*freaking* love pizza."

"Daddy, she said a bad word!" Sadie gasps.

"She did, baby."

"When I do, Daddy takes away my favorite toy."

"Yeah?" Charlotte smirks, eyes twinkling. "Are you going to punish me, Daddy?"

A flush creeps up my neck, and I shift in my chair. I can still picture *her* toy, picture her playing with herself and moaning my name. And now she's flirting with me—here. In front of my kid.

"Daddy, can I get Mollie?"

Fuuuuck, I forgot about the fucking cat. I never mentioned her name to Charlotte, but if she learns I have one, she'll figure out I'm Cole-slash-Weepy Wanker, that we have been on a call together. That I spent most of it crying.

"Not now, sweetheart."

"Who's Mo—"

"Are you a chef too, Charlotte?" Sadie asks suddenly.

For once thankful she still has this bad habit of interrupting people, I answer, "No, sweetheart. I work for her mom," before Charlotte can. Who knows what *she'd* say.

Sadie gasps. "He cooks for you?"

"Yes, he does. He's really good too."

The simple compliment warms me in a way I don't expect. I've always loved when people enjoy my food, but watching Charlotte eat what I cook feels different. Feels personal. Primal.

Her leg presses against mine under the table, and heat shoots straight up my spine, curling around my resolve. I flinch back on instinct, but she follows, dragging the side of her foot against my hamstring.

I'm painfully aware of every inch of space between us—mostly because she's taking all of it.

I need to stop. All of this needs to *stop.*

I stand, my chair scraping against the floor, and Charlotte looks up, biting her bottom lip. "Water. I need—these sodas are way too sweet."

I walk through the small hallway that leads into the kitchen, open the fridge, and grab two water bottles. Then, making sure I'm out of Charlotte's and Sadie's field of vision, I breathe out.

Why is she flirting with me? I thought she was just trying to buy my silence. But now? Now it feels like she enjoys watching me squirm. And apparently, she has no problem doing it in front of Sadie.

But does she mean it? Or is this revenge for driving Peter out of the house?

I shut my eyes, jaw tightening as I remember her with him only two days ago. The way she let him pull her close, kiss her neck, their bodies fitting together. She's obviously dating anyone she wants and just messing with me because she can. Because it's fun for her. Because she knows I won't do a damn thing about it.

It's not like she's actually interested in me.

Come on, Aaron. Why are you thinking about this?

The sudden ring of the landline phone cuts through my spiraling thoughts. I pick it up. "Hello?"

"Hey, Aaron."

Is that . . . *Josie?*

"Hi—hey. Hello."

"I was wondering if I could talk to Sadie."

"Of course," I say quickly. Is this becoming a regular thing? Could it be that she's going to start calling now? "One second."

"Aaron?" she says before I can call Sadie over.

"Yeah?"

"I'll call again around this time tomorrow. And the day after tomorrow. Would that be okay?"

I can feel my shoulders relax, like turning from marble to clay. "You can always call, Josie."

"Okay. Just checking."

I rejoin the table, catching the tail end of Charlotte and Sadie's conversation. They must be talking about Sadie's favorite show, *Bluey*, because she's rambling about Bingo and Bandit.

"Mom wants to talk to you," I say, handing her the phone.

Sadie tears it from my hand. "Mom? Hi! Yes, we got pizzas."

I meet Charlotte's gaze as I sit back down.

"And pepperoni! I'm trying that too."

I squeeze Sadie's shoulder, gesturing toward the stairs so she can have some privacy. She stands and trails away, asking, "Is it really spicy?"

Silence drapes around Charlotte and me as she takes another bite of her slice. "This is the best fucking pizza I've ever eaten—and I've been to Italy several times."

Her eyes flutter shut as she chews. Her lips glisten with oil, a strand of melted cheese stretching between her mouth and the slice. She catches it with her tongue, and I lean back against the chair, watching her with a smile.

"I think you're just hungry."

"Maybe," she concedes, swallowing. "Fifty percent hunger, fifty percent this is a *really* good pizza."

Her long fingers tear off the edge of the crust before popping it into her mouth. She's eating like someone who actually enjoys food—not delicately, not self-consciously, but *fully*.

She's just a girl enjoying a meal. It feels like my biggest victory in a while.

"I can't believe you've never eaten at Tony's," I say, shaking my head. "It's by far the best pizza in Roseberg."

She shrugs, licking a smudge of tomato sauce off her thumb. "We just moved here."

I pause mid-sip of my water. "You did?"

It's a genuine surprise. Their penthouse is fully furnished, has that lived-in feel.

"Where did you live before?"

"Europe, for the most part. Sydney for a while, and . . . lots of other places."

"And now, Roseberg."

"Yeah. I've got quite a few projects lined up, so, if everything goes well, we'll stay a while." She bats her lashes. "Roseberg might be my new home."

Roseberg might be her new home.

I don't know why it hits me like that—maybe because I hadn't considered it before. That this sharp, teasing, impossible girl isn't just passing through my life but *rooting* herself into it.

I barely know her, but she's in my mind. In my house. She's met my kid too.

I nod, my fingers tightening around my water. "Guess I'll have to start saving you a seat at Tony's then."

CHAPTER 10
Finger Lickin' Good

Charlotte ate three slices, then stopped herself from reaching for a fourth. She almost looks drunk with food, her body sinking deeper into the chair, lips parted in a lazy kind of satisfaction. I doubt she ever feels this way—full, content, at peace with her stomach. A selfish part of me wishes I had been the one to feed her, to be the reason for this rare kind of bliss. But I can't bring myself to be sad when she looks this happy.

From upstairs, Sadie's voice carries over, her excited chatter echoing against the walls.

"So . . ." Charlotte's gaze flicks to my left hand. "Your wife doesn't live here."

The words barely register before I correct her automatically. "Ex-wife."

"Really?" She points at my hand, at the ring that still sits there. "So what's with that?"

My fingers flex on instinct. I *should* take it off, but every time I try, it feels too final, like pulling out the last thread holding something fragile together. The final step toward admitting my biggest failure.

Now, for the first time, I *really* wish I had.

"Uh . . . I don't know. The divorce only became official this week, and Sadie just found out."

"But she knows now, right?"

I reach for my water, the condensation slick against my fingers. "My ex-wife . . . she's in rehab. So the whole divorce thing has been complicated."

"I'm sorry."

I nod once and look away, my jaw tight.

"That must be hard for Sadie," she adds after a beat.

"It is."

She hesitates, then, "And for you."

I glance at her. Most people don't say that. They focus on Sadie, or on Josie, or on the logistics of it all. But *me*? I'm the one who fucked up. The one who caused this situation. I'm the one who was in love with Josie when she belonged to someone else.

"Losing your wife and your co-parent at once . . . it can't be easy."

I clear my throat. "No," I admit quietly. "No, it's not."

She doesn't respond right away, just watches me, her gaze steady, and I offer a small smile, trying to defuse the sudden tension. "Don't feel too bad for me. This is kind of . . . my fault. All of it."

She stills, thoughtful. "Really? *All* of it?"

"Uh-huh."

"So you cheated."

I huff out a laugh, shaking my head. The answer isn't a simple *yes* or *no*, and I don't think the truth paints me in a much better light.

"You could say I cheated, yes, but not on my wife." Her forehead creases, and I continue. "I fell in love with Josie when we were kids, but I never did anything about it. My brother, on the other hand, isn't as slow as me. And he didn't know about my feelings."

Charlotte's lips part slightly. "Uh-oh."

"Yeah." I stare at Tony's logo on the pizza box. "They started dating, grew up, and, of course, they had issues. Mid-twenties, figuring out their lives. Normal stuff."

She wiggles her eyebrows. "Is that when you swooped in?"

My eyes dart to her as she masks her amusement with a sip of water.

"Hey, I'm not judging," she says, setting the bottle down. "Brothers fighting over the same girl? A *classic*. I love the drama."

"Oh, it was *some* drama all right," I muse. "Because when I . . . *swooped in*, Josie got pregnant with Sadie."

Charlotte gasps, her eyes widening. If this wasn't one of the most painful chapters of my life, I'd almost enjoy her reaction.

"You're kidding."

"I'm not." I take a deep breath. "And . . . Josie decided to stick with me. I guess my little brother seemed like the least smart decision. Kind of a hothead, that one. Which turned out to be wrong, since he's successful, just had twins, and is getting married in a month."

She hums, tilting her head like she's piecing together a puzzle. "As opposed to . . ."

I shrug, pointing a thumb at myself. "Uh . . . a single father and divorcé with an alcoholic ex who's restarting his career from scratch and is approaching his forties?"

Who visits an erotic website to jerk off to a cam girl fourteen years his junior?

Her grin spreads, bright and genuine, like seeing what a mess I am somehow makes me more interesting. "You know," she says, tearing off a piece of crust, "I think having your life together is grossly overrated."

"Really?"

"Yes. All the best people only figured it out later in life. They explored, made mistakes, hit a wall a million times before they found their thing."

"Yeah? Like who?"

She waves a hand dramatically. "Vera Wang didn't design her

first dress until she was forty. Christian Dior was an art dealer before he even *thought* about fashion. And Anna Wintour got fired before she became the editor-in-chief of *Vogue*."

I smirk. "So modeling's your true calling."

For a moment, she hesitates. Then she shifts in her chair, arching her back just enough to be provocative, her eyes locked onto mine. "What do you think, *Chef*?"

My throat goes dry.

Jesus.

I look away, pretending to study the corkboard hanging crooked on the wall that leads to the kitchen—pinned with old to-do lists, postcards, and a couple of sun-bleached Polaroids. "Yeah, no. Absolutely."

She laughs, delighted. "Stop getting all squirmy."

"I'm not—"

"Oh, *please*." She grins. "Seriously, if you want to pretend you're not ridiculously attracted to me, you'll need a better poker face."

I press my palm against the back of my neck. "I'm not . . ." My fingers feel damp. *Great.* My hands are actually *sweating*. "A better poker face, huh?"

"Yes." She gestures between us. "Do you think *I'm* attracted to *you*?"

I study her, my head shaking. "You called me pretty but . . . did you mean it? Or were you fucking with my head? No idea."

"Exactly." She looks entirely too pleased with herself. "Poker face."

Does that mean she is attracted to me? Or does it work both ways? A poker face to *hide* attraction and one to fake it? "So if I have no poker face, does it mean that on Tuesday, uh, you . . ."

"Did I know you were lying when you said Beatrice texted you that she was on her way?" I swear her eyes sparkle. "Yes. And I don't appreciate a man trying to dictate who should or shouldn't enter my bedroom, but, if I'm being honest, you kinda did me a favor. Peter is . . ."

"The worst?" I offer. Not the kind of man she should let into her bedroom—or her bed? Someone who undoubtedly doesn't deserve her? "I can't say that I regret it, but . . . I *am* sorry I over-stepped."

She grins, shrugging. "I have to say, now that you told me your whole . . . situation," she says, wiping her fingers on a napkin, "it makes more sense."

"What does?"

"How you ended up on TOP."

"Oh, that." I blush, staring at a faded scratch on the wooden table, suddenly the most interesting thing in the room.

"Freshly divorced, probably haven't so much as touched a woman in months, maybe years?" Charlotte muses, her voice low, teasing. I can feel her watching me, waiting for a reaction. When I continue avoiding her gaze, her fingers find my chin, the warmth of her skin a slow burn against mine as she tilts my face up.

My breath stutters.

Her touch is featherlight, her fingertips pressing just enough to send a current of heat rolling down my body, making every nerve hyperaware of her.

"How long, Chef?" she purrs, her eyes sharp on me.

"I . . ." My throat is suddenly too dry, my voice hoarse as I force the words out. "A couple of years."

"*Oof.* That's a long time." Her finger drags over my bottom lip, the kind of touch that teases more than it soothes. My lips part involuntarily, my body betraying me, craving more.

Her eyes flick down to my mouth just as the tip of my tongue slips out, brushing the pad of her finger.

"Careful," she says, like it's a game she *wants* me to lose. "You keep doing that, you'll crave an actual bite."

Fuck me, I do. I want a whole meal. The appetizer, the main

course, the decadent dessert. I want slow tastes and fast bites. I can't. I *absolutely* can't, but I'm past hungry.

I'm ravenous.

"Did I make you come? When you visited me on TOP?"

Heat rushes south, so tight and insistent that it fucking hurts.

"Yes," I rasp.

What the fuck is happening to me?

She's got me spilling my guts like she pressed some cheat code. One touch and I'm in full confession mode.

"Good."

"*Charlotte . . .*" I warn.

"*Aaron . . .*" she murmurs, leaning forward just enough that her arms press against the swell of her tits, pushing them up. My eyes drop of their own accord, and her lips twitch in amusement.

Fuck.

"We can't."

With a giggle, she lets my chin go. I mourn the loss of her touch instantly. "Oh, come on. We're just talking."

"We can't talk about this stuff."

She shrugs. "*I* can. If you can't, just listen."

"I can't listen either."

She rolls her eyes. "All right then." Tugging at my hand, she says, "No more talking."

I tense, but she pulls gently, coaxing my arm to relax until she holds it in front of her on the table.

Her head tilts forward, her lips parting ever so slightly. A flicker of mischief lights up her eyes, and she takes my finger into her mouth.

Heat shoots through me, pooling low in my stomach as her plump lips wrap around my digit, a warm, wet slide that weakens my knees.

My world narrows to this single point of contact, to her mouth tightening around my knuckle before she slides back up with a languid pull, and a guttural sound rumbles in my throat, something between a groan and a plea.

She hums, her tongue flicking ever so slightly as she releases me. Still watching me, she lifts her hand to her mouth and, with a deliberate motion, removes my wedding band from between her lips. My breath catches as she holds it up for a moment, her gaze locked onto mine.

Did she suck it off my finger?

"Feels lighter, doesn't it?" She slips it into the front pocket of my jeans, fingers tracing down my thigh. "Maybe you should leave it in the past."

"Mommy says hi!"

The moment shatters like glass as Sadie bursts down the stairs, her little socked feet pattering against the hardwood floor as she practically throws herself into the living room.

Charlotte leans back, and I try to shake off the heat clinging to my skin, then turn to my daughter as she climbs onto the chair.

"No pepperoni?" I ask when she grabs a slice of cheese pizza from the open box.

She shrugs, taking a big bite. "Maybe later."

Charlotte's lips curl up, and it feels like my ring's digging a hole in my pocket. There's a part of me that's still pretending this can stop. That it *has to* stop. But, fuck me, it's getting quieter by the second.

"Daddy! *Daddy!*"

The frantic cry jolts me awake, yanking me from the depths of sleep into a disorienting blur of darkness and Sadie's trembling voice.

My heart pounds as my eyes snap open, zeroing in on her tear-streaked face beside me. Her hair is a tangle of curls, her chest rising and falling too fast, her wide eyes brimming with fear.

I push up on my elbow and croak, "What is it, baby?"

She hiccups as she wipes her wet cheeks with the sleeve of her pajama shirt. "There was a monster," she sobs, her voice wobbly. "And it took Mom, and—and it was gonna take you next, and—"

"Shh. Come here."

I shift, making space for her in the bed, and the second I do, she scrambles up, burrowing into my side like she's afraid something might snatch me away.

I pull the blanket over her, cocooning her in warmth. "It was just a dream, love," I murmur, pressing my lips to the crown of her head. Her curls tickle my nose, smelling faintly of the strawberry-scented shampoo she insisted on picking out last week. "A nightmare. It's not real."

Her sobs shake her small frame, but as I rub soothing circles on her back, her fear starts to dull, and her fingers let go of my shirt. She sniffles, shifting just enough to peek up at me. Her lashes are clumped together with tears, her lips quivering as she hesitates. "Can we call Mom?"

I glance at the alarm clock on the nightstand. The numbers glow 3:58 a.m.

"No, baby," I say gently. "She's sleeping right now, and so should we. But she'll call tomorrow night, just like she did today."

Sadie doesn't answer, the rise and fall of her body growing steadier. I almost drift off, thinking she's asleep, when she says, "Mom doesn't love me anymore."

The exhaustion that had been dragging me under vanishes in an instant, replaced by a sharp, sinking weight in my chest.

"Of course she does, Sadie. She loves you more than anything in the world."

She stares at the fabric of my shirt as she picks at it with fidgeting fingers. "What if you stop loving me too?"

A knot forms in my throat.

"Hey." I tilt her chin up, forcing her to look at me. Her big, tearful eyes meet mine, desperate for reassurance. "You listen to me right now," I say, my voice firm and sure. "I will *always* love you. *Always.* And so will Mom. She can't wait to come back to you."

Sadie sniffles again, her bottom lip wobbling. "She didn't want to talk to me," she whines. "I heard you."

My mind races back to my phone call to Josie's rehab—I stepped out to the backyard, lowered my voice so Sadie wouldn't hear the clipped tension in my words. But she heard.

Fuck.

"N-no, you misunderstood," I try, but the damage is already done.

Sadie pulls the blanket higher, burying half her face in it. "What if she left us forever? Willow's daddy never came back."

I blink hard, forcing down the lump in my throat.

She's six. She shouldn't have to worry about shit like this. She shouldn't have to lie awake at night, wondering if her mother will come back to her.

I cup her cheek, my thumb brushing away a stray tear. "Do you trust me?"

She hesitates before she nods.

"Do I ever lie to you?"

She shakes her head.

"Then please believe me when I tell you Mom loves you. She *will* come back to you, and nothing's going to stop her."

A long, shaky breath escapes her, then she tucks her head under my chin. "Daddy?"

"Yeah, love?"

"We started practicing for Mom Day."

I pause. "Mom Day?"

She nods against my chest. "At school. Mommies are supposed to come. We're making a show for them."

Fucking hell—*Mother's Day.* Mother's Day is less than three weeks away.

"Willow's mommy and Jason's mommy and Lisa's mommy are coming," she stutters. "But . . . what if mine doesn't?"

I close my eyes for a second, trying to claw myself out of the helplessness that comes with knowing I can't give her what she wants most. "I could come."

"You?"

"Uh-huh."

"But you're not a mommy."

Hard to argue with that. I think for a few seconds. "What about Auntie Primrose? I'm sure she'd love to come."

"But she's not my mommy."

"You really want Mom to come, huh?"

She nods, snuggling closer, then pops her thumb in her mouth.

"I'll talk to her," I murmur.

And just like that, she finally drifts off while I stare at the ceiling, wondering how the hell I'm supposed to keep my promise.

CHAPTER 11

Sicilian Sake Roll

The fridge hums as I close it, the dim kitchen light casting long shadows across the floor. I was going to drink some water, but I might brew some coffee instead—it's not like I'm going to sleep tonight.

It'd been such a good night. Sadie had the best time with Charlotte, who even agreed to stay through *Willy Wonka & the Chocolate Factory*. Once she insisted she'd get an Uber back and left, I really thought Sadie's joy over having her over would translate into a full night of sleep.

I obviously didn't factor in Mother's Day.

My phone screen lights up on the counter with an email from Amelie. At this hour?

I scoff, swiping it open, but instead of reading, I hit call. She picks up after two rings.

"Hello?"

"What the hell are you doing awake?" I ask as I lean back against the counter.

She lets out a breathy chuckle. "I could ask you the same thing."

I walk to the couch, sinking into the cushions. "You first."

"Ugh . . . can't sleep. New pillow, new mattress. Remember being young and able to sleep anywhere, even on a park bench?"

"Can't say I slept on a lot of park benches, actually."

She giggles again, the sound familiar. I've missed this—missed her. Cooking together in quiet understanding, chatting about nothing, Ian glaring at me every time I made her laugh.

"Is Ian staring ugly at the phone right now?"

"Ian's asleep," she replies, her voice tired. "He's still young on the inside."

"Ah, yes. Good for him."

"You didn't tell me why you're awake at . . . what is it, four twenty in the morning?"

"Uh . . ." I tilt my head back, staring at the ceiling. "Did you know Mother's Day is in three weeks?"

"I didn't know that, no."

"Well, Sadie does."

"Oh." Her voice loses its teasing edge. "Had a bad night, then, did you?"

A bad night? My teeth sink into my bottom lip as I'm reminded of the feeling of Charlotte's mouth around my finger. Not exactly.

"Yeah," I lie, rubbing my eyes. "Apparently, they're putting together a show for the moms at school."

She clicks her tongue. "That doesn't sound very inclusive."

"It's not. I mean, there are two kids from gay couples in her class. And I'm pretty sure one of her classmates lost his mom last year. And Sadie . . . well, you know."

"Yeah." A pause. "I know."

She doesn't say anything for a moment, and neither do I. "So what are you going to do?" she asks finally.

No fucking clue.

Sadie doesn't want me there. She doesn't want Primrose either. She wants Josie. And Josie is the one person I can't get to go.

"Aaron, did I ever tell you about my mom?"

I frown. "Hm, no. I know you're not close. That she lives abroad."

"She left my dad when I was six," Amelie says, voice quieter now. "Just like you and Sadie."

I sit up a little, giving her my full attention.

"She says he was toxic," she continues, "that she needed to get away. And on some level, I understand that. My dad wasn't the easiest person."

"But she left you too."

"Uh-huh." There's no bitterness in her voice. "And that? That, I'll never get. Sometimes love ends. Marriages crash and burn—it happens. But my mom wasn't content moving to another house. To another town, even. She left the country and never looked back. I've seen her three times since."

"Jesus."

"Yeah. And she's been trying lately, you know? She wants to see me, wants to meet Ian, visit the restaurant."

"You don't want her to?"

"Not really," she says, and it sounds like she's smiling. "I *chose* my family. I made my own—I don't need her. So I'm quite happy to keep it at one phone call a month."

I hesitate. "Sounds like you won't be celebrating Mother's Day either."

"Haven't celebrated it once in my life since I can remember."

I roll my shoulders. "Not that I don't want to hear about all of this, but . . . Josie *will* come back. She will. Right?"

She's quiet for a beat, then asks, "What do you think of me, Aaron?"

The question catches me off guard. "What do you mean?"

"Would you say I'm . . . a nice person? Well-adjusted? Happy, caring, successful?"

"All of it and more."

"You know Ian's the only one who can give you a raise, right?" she jokes. Then, after a pause, she adds, "I don't know Josie, and I can't say whether she will ever come back. But what I *do* know for a fact is that Sadie will be okay."

My throat tightens.

"It feels like the end of the world right now," she continues. "I get that. And I'm not saying it'll be easy. But us girls . . . we're resilient. We survive—and then we thrive."

I close my eyes, letting her words sink in.

"Mother's Day will be hard," she admits. "Christmas will be horrible. Until Josie comes back—and maybe even past that—things will be rocky. You will make mistakes, because as much as you try, you won't be able to be both parents in one. And Sadie will miss her mom. A lot."

I close my eyes. "Tell me there's a 'but.'"

"*But,*" she says cheerfully, "even with all the mistakes my father's made, he stuck around. He gave it his all, and he worked on himself. Hell, the last words he ever said to me were 'I'm proud of you.'" She pauses, and I can almost see her choking up like whenever she brings up her late father. "Trust me, that makes all the difference."

My throat burns and I scoff, trying to play it off, but my voice betrays me. "I just wanted her to . . ." My jaw clenches. "To have a normal, happy life. She deserves so much better than this."

Amelie hums. "Nobody has a 'normal, happy life.' And you know what? The few people who do—they're boring."

I huff out something that sounds like a laugh.

"One day, Sadie will be an interesting, successful, kind woman. Because her father stuck around and made sure she became one." She sniffles. "For better or worse, I *am* my father's daughter."

I blink up at the ceiling, chest tight, throat thick, emotions threatening to swallow me whole.

"Thanks, Chef," I say, voice raw.

"Anytime, Chef."

BEATRICE

No need to come cook lunch. I'll be out and Charlotte is having a protein shake. See you at dinner.

I READ the message one more time before tucking my phone away and knocking at the door.

This is stupid. So stupid.

I shouldn't be here.

Beatrice said not to come, and she's the one making the rules. But when I read "protein shake," my head started steaming. All Charlotte had yesterday was pizza at my place; she needs actual nutrition today.

So I decided three hours of notice *could* be too little. I *could* just not have looked at my phone. *Could* have just missed the message and showed up anyway.

Anything's possible, right?

I glance back at the stairwell, debating turning around, but the door swings open and there stands Charlotte, her expression shifting from confusion to amusement. "Chef?"

Holy *fuuuuck*.

My gaze falls down her body.

She's wearing a black satin two-piece set that should be illegal. The silky blouse is barely fastened with one single button at the center, dipping low enough to reveal the angles of her collarbone. And the skirt—fuck, the skirt. Short. Dangerously short, clinging to her hips before ending mid-thigh.

She slightly bends one of her legs, like she's posing without meaning to, the back of a black stiletto pressed against her calf. "Chef?"

My eyes snap back up, to the molten-red hair pinned up in a messy twist, stray strands slipping free to frame her face. To the gold hoops in her ears and the gloss on her lips. "Huh?"

She crosses her arms, her lips curving into something wicked. "Do you need a glass of water or something?"

I nod, though I have no idea what she just said. How can someone look so sinful while being dressed? How can someone *real* be this achingly beautiful?

"I . . . I'm here to fill you up."

Her eyes go wide and I suck in a breath.

What the fuck did I just say?

"N-no, your *stomach*." Oh boy, I don't think I'm making this better. "Fill up your stomach."

Stop. Saying. That.

She brushes a speck off my shirt, fingers lingering. "Fill me up, huh?"

I open my mouth, then shut it. My brain is glitching. "I-I meant—"

She leans in just a fraction. "Are you offering to *stuff me*, Chef?"

I make a strangled sound. "That's not—"

She taps her chin, feigning thoughtfulness. "Or were you thinking of something . . . *deeper*?"

My throat goes dry. "Jesus Christ."

She laughs, low and delighted, before stepping back. "Relax, Chef. I'm just hungry." Then, with a teasing glance over her shoulder, "For food."

I watch her go before following her inside the house. I need to get a grip. And a cold shower.

"Didn't Beatrice tell you not to come at lunch?"

I clear my throat. "Did she? I must have missed the message."

"Huh. Interesting."

"What is?"

She smirks. "You don't have a poker face *or* a poker voice."

I look away—plausible deniability and all of that—but she doesn't press. Instead, she pads toward the living room. "So, Chef. Why are you *really* here?"

"To cook for you."

She plucks a sweatshirt out of a tall pile of clothes thrown over the white couch. "Yeah? Or to *fill me up*?"

"I really didn't mean—"

"Come on, Chef. You wanna fuck?" she asks drily.

My skin runs hot. "No. No, I—"

"Is it about TOP?" She glances over her shoulder. "Do you want a free performance?"

"*No.*" I shift my weight from one foot to the other. "Is it *that* impossible to believe I just want to do something nice? No hidden motive?"

"Yes."

She sounds like she's never been more sure of anything, and it's a thorn lodged down my throat. Who taught her that? How many people have used her? How many times has she been made to feel like a transaction instead of a person?

"You think my mom cares about my career out of love?" she asks. "She does *not*. She's my manager. I'm her job."

"I'm sure that's not true," I say, though really I'm not, and I think she can tell by my uncertain voice.

She rolls her eyes, like I'm being naive. "My first boyfriend liked my pool, my second boyfriend liked my mom. My best friends liked my boyfriends, money, or my pool boy." She leans against the back of the couch, her voice almost bored. "Everybody wants something from me—always."

I maintain her gaze. "Not me."

I just want *her*.

She bites the inside of her cheek, looking fascinated rather than annoyed. Eventually, she straightens and shrugs. "All right, Chef."

She turns and slips out of her top, and at the sight of her blue bra, my brain fries out. The fabric of her skirt slides down her body next, pooling at her feet like it was always meant to be there, discarded and forgotten.

I immediately spin around, locking my gaze on the nearest wall and away from her matching blue panties. "Oh—I'll give you a minute."

"Don't worry about it," she says easily. "It's nothing you haven't seen on TOP anyway."

I press my lips together, inhaling through my nose.

Sure, I've seen her naked on TOP, but that doesn't mean she's just an image on a screen. Something for anyone to access at any given moment, as if her body belongs to the world instead of to her.

She's still *her*.

Needing a distraction, I stride to the fridge and pull it open. My gaze sweeps across the contents—or lack thereof—and a hard knot of frustration forms in my gut.

A pear. Two eggs. A single Tupperware filled with plain boiled rice.

That's it.

I shut the fridge with a little too much force.

"Beatrice makes sure I'm not tempted while she's away," she says behind me.

Tempted. Like food is something to resist. Like hunger is a flaw. Like the simple act of eating—of enjoying something indulgent— is a crime.

"Well, what would you like to eat?"

She looses a cackle. "Let's see. A bacon cheeseburger. No, wait, fries. No, mozzarella sticks. Actually . . . scratch that. I'd like a corn dog with a ton of ketchup. No, wait . . ." Her eyes light up like she can already taste whatever she's thinking about. "I want a sundae. A big one. With warm, gooey chocolate sauce dripping down the sides, rainbow sprinkles—like, a *ton* of them—so every bite is crunchy and sweet. And nuts. Oh, and whipped cream piled so high it almost topples over." She presses her hands together, practically bouncing on her toes. "And you know what goes on top, obviously." Her playful gaze flicks up to mine. "How does that sound?"

Like the stuff you eat when you're drunk or aren't familiar with mid-thirties heartburn.

Before I can say anything, her expression shifts. "But ice cream is a curse word in this house," she says. "I can't eat fried food. Or mozzarella. Or bacon. Or salt." She shrugs, forcing another smile that doesn't quite reach her eyes. "I definitely can't have sugar. Or chocolate. Or whipped cream."

It's a joke—she makes it *sound* like a joke. But there's an ache beneath the words, something resigned and weary, as if she's spent years making herself smaller and learning to quiet her wants until they become nothing more than idle fantasies.

"So how about you make that, um"—she waves a hand vaguely in the air—"whatever fancy thing you were about to suggest, and I'll moderately enjoy it because you are, despite this ridiculous diet, a great cook?"

She waits for my nod, then disappears down the hall.

And I stand there, wondering how to give her everything she's not allowed to want.

I ABANDON my tuna roll to cut up the salmon sashimi. I had to drive across town—past three other supermarkets—just to find sashimi-grade fish, wasting nearly an hour in the process.

She looks up from her phone, the glow throwing soft shadows across her cheekbones. After a long look at me, she focuses on the screen again.

I'd pay money I don't have to know what she's thinking.

I press my lips together and refocus on my rolls. The scent of fresh seaweed and sticky rice fills the kitchen, but my mind drifts anyway—back to the first time Amelie and I made sushi together. I couldn't believe she'd never done it. Josie is a big fan, so it was one of my staples at home.

When Amelie found out I was an expert, she made me drop

everything and teach her on the spot. After she'd spent months nitpicking every single dish I made, watching her become annoyed over not getting it right the first time was quite the show.

"What is it?" Charlotte asks from the couch.

"Hm?" I blink, realizing I'm smiling. "Oh, nothing. I was just thinking about . . . I taught my mentor how to make sushi."

Her eyes narrow. "Your *mentor*? Like in a cult?"

"No, like in cooking. My boss's other half is a chef. When I tried out for the job, words like 'incredible raw talent' were thrown around. Apparently, it's 'unfair' and 'basically cheating.'" I swallow against the dryness in my throat, still not sure if Amelie's a visionary or a lunatic. "And a lot of nonsense like that."

"And *you* taught *your mentor* how to make sushi?"

"Yeah." I flip the knife in my palm. "French-training—not a lot of raw fish in those kitchens."

Charlotte makes a thoughtful noise. "How did you learn?"

"I . . ." I wipe my hands on a towel before picking up the bamboo mat again. "I spent a year in Italy in my twenties."

"Ah, yes. The famous Sicilian salmon roll."

I snort, and her smirk widens.

"If you'd let me finish," I tease. "I had a Japanese roommate. His mom used to work in a . . ." I pause, searching for the name of the place, something he used to rave about. "A *konbini* in Tokyo, where apparently you can get the most amazing sushi for next to nothing. He taught me."

Charlotte hums, considering. "The best sushi I ever had was in this tiny, hole-in-the-wall place in Shinsekai."

I look up. "You've been to Japan?"

"I've been everywhere."

Of course she has. Modeling must take her all over the world.

A small pang of something twists in my chest—envy, maybe. Longing. I haven't traveled much since Sadie. And she must sense it because she says, "I haven't seen much of anywhere though. It wasn't *fun*-traveling."

"Sorry."

She shrugs. "But I've eaten enough Michelin-star meals to tell you that your mentor is right. You're talented. Talented like people who've been doing it for decades."

I grin, cheeks heating. "Thank you."

"Where would you go if you could choose?" she asks. "If you could travel anywhere in the world?"

The question makes me pause. The last few years haven't been much about my wants, but more about my responsibilities. I glance up, meeting her gaze. "Shinsekai, maybe," I say. "Try this sushi you love."

Her head sinks into the back of the couch, her loose waves fanning out against the cushions. That same knowing smile lingers on her lips. *Lazy. Amused. Dangerous.*

"Am I invited?"

I scoff, wiping my hands on a kitchen towel. "How else am I gonna find it?"

She giggles, light and airy. "When I was younger, I used to play a game I called 'Where would I be?' I would imagine a scenario where everything was different and picture where I'd be. Like, if my father hadn't left, or if I'd never gone to that first audition, or . . . you get it."

The thought of a younger Charlotte sitting in a Paris hotel room dreaming of being anywhere else makes my heart clench. "Really?"

"Yeah. Sometimes, I'd picture a small town somewhere by the beach. You know, one of those places where people don't bother putting actual clothes on. Just shorts and their bikini tops. And Small Town Charlotte would do something . . . I don't know, low-key. Like work at the local market, or sell flowers."

The thought is utterly ridiculous. She would die of boredom on her second day.

"I'd crochet, maybe. Have a Pinterest board for healthy recipes and cute home DIYs."

My lips bend in a sad smile. I don't like this version of herself she's describing, because it doesn't sound anything like her, but I get it. This isn't just a whimsical fantasy, but a very real urge to escape. A wish for a life where she isn't picked apart, where she belongs to herself.

Why doesn't she do it? Why does she let Beatrice run the show like this?

I dry my hands on a towel, then toss it onto the counter. "You wouldn't last a week."

Her eyes gleam with challenge. "Oh?"

I grab a plate from the cabinet. "You'd get restless." I set it on the counter. "You'd start charming tourists for sport." Setting the sushi on the plate, I insist, "You'd get banned from the market for making inappropriate comments to half the town just to see them blush."

She stays quiet, watching me, waiting.

"How about this game instead?" I ask. "Where would you be if you were a strong, beautiful young woman with the potential to achieve anything you wanted?" I walk to the table and set the sushi down, then spin to face her. "Because that's exactly what you are, and that's exactly where you should be."

She stands and approaches me. Once there's only her chair between us, she looks up at me. "Kinda like how if nothing held you back, you'd be inside me right now?"

She's deflecting, *again*. She keeps doing it, keeps hiding behind her sexuality like she doesn't want anyone to see there's more to her than that. Maybe she doesn't want to see it herself.

"You know, for most of my life, I worked in accounting. I put on a suit every day, and more than that, a *mask*. When my marriage crumbled, I realized I was pretending to be happy in more ways than one, and I knew I had to stop and face my feelings, no matter how inconvenient."

Her smile turns into a thoughtful frown.

"I just wish I didn't wait until I was thirty-six to do it."

"Why did you?"

I shrug. I could tell her that I'd fallen short of too many expectations to launch myself into another potential failure, or that I was too busy trying to keep my marriage together to try to fix myself. All of it is true, but you know what else is? "I needed someone to believe there was something more to me, and Amelie did."

Her lips part for a moment before they bend down at the corners. "*Amelie?*"

"My mentor," I explain, confused when her cheeks darken and she looks away. She looks almost . . . jealous. Did she think it was a man?

It hits me in a strange, warm wave. Because if that's what this is, it means she cares. It means I'm not the only one feeling this thing crackling between us.

And it's reckless, but I don't hate it. I don't want to push it away. I'm not used to being wanted for no reason, just like her. Not without guilt or compromise. So instead of backpedaling, I continue, "Just a friend."

It's a promise I want her to hear.

But I know I lost her when she sits and grabs the chopsticks. "Whatever. I'm happy for you, but my life is fine as it is."

CHAPTER 12
Corn Dog Couture

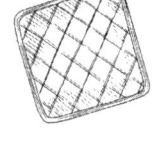

W hy not? It's just a stupid concert!" are the first words I hear when I open the door to Beatrice and Charlotte's penthouse in the afternoon.

Sounds like Charlotte didn't get those extra points. It *also* sounds like her life isn't fine as it is.

"If it's so stupid, then you don't need to go."

"Jesus—I *swear* I'm not going to eat anything. Or drink. I'll just go and listen to the band—"

"Why put yourself through temptation, Charlotte? You're a model. Focus on that. You'll have time for concerts when you're old and your body is worthless."

My mouth falls open, an icy wave rolling down my spine. *Did she really just say that?*

"You dragged me out here," Charlotte spits. "You're using me like you always do. I think at the very least, I deserve to—"

With a clipped voice, Beatrice cuts her off. "Where is your ambition, Charlotte? Is 'having fun' all you care about?"

"Yes. I'm sorry I'm not the daughter you wanted, just a shittier version of her."

Lips pinching, I listen without making a sound.

"If you're so unhappy, then why don't you leave?"

Silence.

I wait, and after a shrill "I hate you," I hear Charlotte stomp closer. When she turns the corner, her teary eyes meet mine. They widen for a moment before she shouts, "*Ugh!* Do you *always* have to be around?" Then she whirls toward the hallway off to the right and storms into her room, slamming the door so hard the walls shake.

Beatrice steps into view, composed as ever, her icy gaze locking onto mine like a sniper's crosshairs. "You're here."

I clear my throat, adjusting the strap of my bag. "I . . . the fish needs time to—"

"Come," she says, turning and heading for the kitchen. "I need to talk to you."

Must be my lucky day.

I hesitate, lingering in the doorway for a second before following. She's already sitting at the island, sifting through a stack of papers.

"Gin and tonic."

Does she want me to make her one?

She turns her head slightly, then gestures toward the bar cart. "*Make me* a gin and tonic. And whatever you're drinking."

Oh, boy. That probably means this will be a long conversation.

I drop my bag onto the counter and make my way over to the bar cart, glancing at the collection of expensive liquors. I make quick work of fixing us both drinks, then slide one of them across the counter.

She takes it without looking up. "I'll be gone this weekend," she says, her tone crisp and business-like. "I know you're off, but I was wondering if you could prep some meals for Charlotte today. She's completely clueless in the kitchen. And everywhere else."

A muscle in my jaw twitches. I can barely move past the insult, but didn't Charlotte say she has a show this weekend? I figured that her agent—her *mom*—would go with her.

When she raises a brow in question, I rush out, "Uh, yeah. Of course."

She pulls a sheet of paper from her stack and pushes it toward me. "Here's what I have in mind."

I scan the list. Grilled chicken breasts, steamed broccoli, brown rice. Dry, plain, joyless. "Uh-huh. All right."

"Keep the portions light. Avoid beans—bloating. No salt, minimal oil. Stick to lemon and herbs. And whatever you do, no butter."

I grip the edge of the paper a little too hard, my knuckles turning white. Jesus. This isn't meal-prepping. This is fucking abuse.

If Charlotte wanted to eat like this, that'd be one thing. But I've seen how she lights up when something actually tastes good. The way she devoured that pizza.

And I've seen how her own mother talks to her.

"Everything clear?" Beatrice asks, her eyes scanning my face.

"Yes." I glance at her drink, almost completely gone. "Another one?"

Beatrice points at my glass—still untouched. "Don't make me feel self-conscious."

I lift the tumbler and bring it to my lips. The gin burns its way down, crisp and bitter, but I barely taste it. I have no interest in drinking with this woman, but if there's even a remote chance I can do something for Charlotte, I need to stay on her good side.

She swirls the ice in her glass, watching the liquid slosh against the sides before speaking again. "Your boss . . . Ian, I think? He said you have a kid."

"He did?"

"I requested service every day of the week, but he said you needed two days off to spend with your child, and I didn't want two different people. Of course, at the time, I thought Amelie would be my chef."

Ian never even brought it up with me, but I guess it just goes to show what a great boss he is.

"I could see if someone else—"

"So *do you* have a kid?"

"Yeah. I do."

"I hope for your sake that it's a boy."

I blink. "A daughter, actually. She's six."

Beatrice scoffs, her gaze dropping to the bottom of her glass as if there's an answer to something in the remnants of her drink. "I was happy at first, you know? When we found out it was going to be a girl. Girls are easier, I thought."

"They're not?"

"Maybe until puberty. You better brace for that. Men, parties, mood swings." She exhales heavily. "Boys are easier."

I take another sip, letting the gin heat my throat.

"I had another daughter before Charlotte."

That gets my attention, and my fingers tighten around the glass.

"I lost her."

There's no hesitation, no trembling in her voice, no moment of silence to prepare for the weight of it. Just a flat, matter-of-fact statement, like she's talking about losing a set of keys and not a living, breathing child.

"I'm so sorry," I murmur.

She doesn't acknowledge me, just looks away. "But she was . . . easier. A hard worker, that's for sure. Ambitious, focused. She knew what she wanted and went for it. Didn't let anything distract her."

Maybe that's where this controlling behavior comes from. Maybe after losing her first daughter, Beatrice became so afraid of losing another that she wrapped Charlotte in an iron grip, trying to mold her into something she could control.

"I thought Charlotte would be my do-over, you know?" Her lips twitch. "But she's nothing like her. *Nothing.*"

Anger flickers in my chest, sharp and instinctual. If I didn't know better, I'd think she was disgusted. But it can't be that, can it? She's a mother, for Christ's sake. A mother who has already lost a child. That kind of pain is not something I can even begin to imagine.

"She was the perfect mix of me and my first husband." A faraway look settles in her eyes. "She took the best from both of us. His stubbornness, his talent. My strength and beauty. She looked just like me." Her voice wavers slightly, and I realize that her eyes are moist.

For the first time, I see something raw in her.

Grief.

And yet, I can't ignore the bitter aftertaste of her words. She's punishing Charlotte for not being the daughter she lost. For not being like her mother.

But Charlotte is her own person, and a pretty incredible one at that. She might not be the carbon copy Beatrice wanted, but she's still her daughter.

I swallow, then ask the question that's buzzing underneath my skin. "What about Charlotte?"

Beatrice sniffs. She tilts her glass back and downs the rest of her drink in a single motion. "She's just like her father—my second husband. A lazy but gorgeous man who wanted nothing to do with her." She sets the glass down with a quiet clink and stands. "So here I am. Raising *his* daughter."

"*Your* daughter," I say before I can control myself.

She looks at me, and every single emotion I've seen play out on her face is replaced by cool indifference. "Yes. My daughter. My beautiful but lazy daughter, who disappoints me at the same rate her father did."

I force myself to stay still, to not react. If I open my mouth again, I won't be able to control what comes out.

"I've given up everything for her. For ten years, we haven't had a home. Just moved from hotels to apartments. City to city.

Country to country. All to give her the chance I never had." She turns to the corridor, a sneer on her lips. "And how does she repay me?"

"You've had to sacrifice a lot," I agree. She nods, clearly pleased with my approval. "Both of you," I add then.

With her little spark dimmed, she looks away.

"Are you sure that's still what she wants? Charlotte?" I ask before taking another sip. I'm pretty sure I'm not supposed to engage—that I should act like a wall she bounces her thoughts against, but I can't let this opportunity slip.

"Why wouldn't it be? She's living every woman's dream."

Dreams don't usually come with cages.

Beatrice rises from her seat and starts gathering her stack of papers. "I'll make sure to clear with your boss the extra payment for the weekend meals."

"That's not nece—"

"I won't be here for dinner, so you don't need to cook for me."

She turns, her heels clicking against the polished floor, her back rigid. There likely won't be another moment like this—where she's got her guard down, where she's somewhat vulnerable.

I need to say something.

"For what it's worth," I blurt, losing half of my confidence when her sharp brown eyes pin me on the spot, "I think Charlotte is pretty impressive."

Her sigh is exasperated. "You've known her for *five minutes*. How many words did you exchange—twenty? I just heard ten of them, and they didn't sound impressive."

I think of our nights on TOP. Of her eating pizza at my place, flirting with me, sucking the ring off my finger. Of her laughter, unrestrained and wild, when she lets her guard down.

"I can tell she has your strength. And she's beautiful, that's for sure. But she's smart too. And she might not have the same drive you had at her age, but everyone's different, right? She's still young. She has plenty of time to figure out her future."

Beatrice doesn't say a word.

I know I'm fired. So I might as well finish my thought.

"You've lost a daughter," I continue, mouth dry. "And I can't . . . I can't imagine the constant pain you're in. Nobody can. But there is one daughter you *haven't* lost. One who's still here. And she needs you."

For a long, heavy moment, she says nothing. Then she adjusts the stack of papers in her hands. "You better start cooking," she says before whirling around again and walking away. "It's almost time for Charlotte to eat dinner."

"I WOULDN'T BOTHER with cooking if I were you," Charlotte says, startling me. She's been locked in her room for an hour, and as I glance up from the cutting board, ready to ask why, I do a double take.

She's changed.

Gone are the sweatpants and tank top. Now, she's wrapped in a wine-red satin slip dress, the fabric skimming over her curves and catching the light with every shift of her body. A thigh-high slit flashes glimpses of smooth skin as she moves, and the delicate lace trim along the plunging neckline has me choking on my own saliva.

Holy crap.

Holy crap, please tell me this isn't what I think it is.

She grabs her keys, tossing them into her purse.

"What—where are you going?" My voice comes out gruffer than I intend, my eyes still locked on the dangerous slit along her thigh.

She steps closer, her heels clicking against the floor as she smacks her lips together. "Remember what you said today? About how I should be where I want to be and do what I want to do?"

"Not *exactly* what I said, but yes."

"Well, I want to be at the Silverlight Arena, bouncing up and down to Midnight Reckless."

I set the fish fillet down with a dull thud. "Oh, no. No, no, *no*."

"Yes." She blinks at me, all wide-eyed innocence. "Yes, yes, yes, y—"

"Doing whatever you want regardless of what your mom says isn't what I meant, Charlotte."

She grins. "Isn't it? Then what did you mean?"

I open my mouth, but my brain short-circuits as she bends to catch her reflection in the oven door, then applies cherry-red lipstick in precise strokes. The movement is hypnotic—her mouth parting slightly, the pigment gliding over her lips and making them look even fuller, more kissable.

"I-I don't know, but not *this*." She rolls her eyes. "What if your mom comes back?"

"She won't."

"But what if she does?"

She turns, amusement curling at the edges of her mouth. "She's spending the night with her boyfriend, so you don't need to worry about that."

"But—"

She's suddenly in front of me, tilting my chin up with two fingers. "Chef, I work every day and every night. I'm stressed, and I'm tired, and I'm not going to argue with you. All right? I deserve this, so I'm going." Her voice takes on a teasing lilt. "But your worried face is *adorable*."

She walks away and opens the door, ready to step out of the apartment, but my feet are already moving.

"Wait, wait."

Her shoulders stiffen.

"I get it, okay? But do you really think this is a good idea?" My voice is lower now, and she angles her head to watch me from the corner of her eye. "She makes things hard enough for you, Charlotte."

Her expression flickers, but then she gives a one-shouldered shrug. "Which means I don't have a whole lot to lose."

She presses the elevator button, the numbers steadily rising as it makes its way to our floor. "Who's going with you?"

She taps her chin. "Tens of thousands of fans."

She's going *by herself*? I don't like that. Not one damn bit. The thought of her alone in a crowd, surrounded by strangers, dressed like *that*. I know men too well to be comfortable with it.

She reads my face, because of course she does, and smirks. "I can take care of myself, Chef."

"I know you can. I just . . ."

"I've looked like this since I was fourteen. That's how old I was the first time I got catcalled. You know how many talent managers I've had to put in their place?" Her voice drops to a conspiratorial whisper. "You know how many before I even turned eighteen?"

Eyes bulging, I freeze. "How many?"

"You're missing the point."

"No, I'm pretty sure I'd like an actual number. *And* names."

She hitches her bag higher up her shoulder. "Adorable." She hesitates for a beat, then, "Look, I don't need you. Seriously. But I *do* have an extra ticket."

My lips press together as the implication sinks in.

If she's not going to be here to eat dinner, my job is kind of pointless tonight. I've already prepped her meals for the weekend. And if I were in Beatrice's shoes, I'd sure as hell prefer my daughter not go to a concert alone. At least if I'm there, she'll be safe. She'll be with me, and my intentions are pure.

Mostly pure.

"Assuming Sadie's cared for."

"What?"

She tilts her head. "Sadie? Your daughter? If you can't go, it's fine. She's probably waiting for you, right?"

"She, um . . . she's with her grandma."

She asked about my daughter. It's just the decent thing to do, I guess. But my mind plays an unfair comparison game, and Charlotte *caring* is enough to overwhelm me with gratitude.

She watches my internal war with undisguised amusement, then steps inside the waiting elevator, leans against the back wall, and grins.

"Get a jacket, Chef," she says, voice dripping with satisfaction. "It's chilly out."

THE COOL NIGHT air hits us as we burst out of the stadium, and I can still feel the faint vibrations from the bass in my chest. Charlotte's giddy with energy, her hands flailing in the air as she talks a mile a minute about the show.

"Did you hear that guitar solo?" she shouts. "It was like he was *flying* through the riffs, I swear! And the crowd? Insane! When everyone was jumping, it felt like an earthquake, didn't it?"

She laughs with her whole face, and it lands right in the center of my chest.

I don't think she notices how quiet I've gone. I can't stop staring at her, watching her move. Her eyes are sparkling, her cheeks flushed, and there's this unguarded joy on her face that I rarely see. When I cook for her and her mom, she's always so . . . composed. But tonight, for hours, she's been *free*—her every word, every gesture, so full of life. I can't look away.

She's still talking, but her words are a hum in the background now. I'm thinking about how she looked tonight, dancing and singing, caught up in the music.

"So what did you think?"

"About what?" I ask, jolted back to the present moment as we weave through the lingering crowd.

"The music! The concert—the band?" Charlotte throws her hands up like it should be obvious.

"Oh. Yeah, it was . . . great."

She halts abruptly, making me nearly crash into her. "You hated it!"

"I . . ." Her mouth curves into a contagious smile, and before I know it, I'm smirking too. "Not *hated* it, no. It's just not my style, I guess."

"What's your style then?"

I scratch the back of my neck, suddenly feeling like I'm about to be judged. "Well . . . I like Carnal Sins."

She nods. "Oh, yeah. That band from the 1900s."

Ouch.

"What?" she asks when I fight a chortle. "What did I say?"

"Nothing. You just made me feel a million years old."

She shrugs. "What else?"

"'Let It Go' is a big hit at home."

She gasps dramatically. "'Baby Shark'?"

I throw my head back. "Thank god Sadie's over that shit. Most difficult summer of my life."

Her laughter echoes in the cool night air, and for a second, I let myself enjoy this—the lightness, the easy back and forth. It's rare. Too rare.

We push past a few more people before finally stepping into the parking lot. Before I can point out where I parked, I spot a corn dog stand a few feet away and remember she missed dinner. We both did.

I gesture toward it. "Let's get some food."

She follows my gaze, eyes narrowing slightly. "Corn dogs?"

"Yeah. You know, the gross sausage covered in a greasy crust. You said you wanted one, didn't you?"

She stares at the stand like she's looking at a mirage in the middle of the desert. "I've wanted one for ten years, since I started modeling."

I pause. She started modeling at thirteen? Is that even legal?

Instead of voicing that thought, I nod toward the stand. "You had pizza the other night, and you survived just fine."

She hesitates, and judging by the way she's staring at the stand like it holds some kind of moral dilemma, she might need some encouragement.

I take a step forward, and after a beat, she follows, a little skip in her step. It's such a small thing, but the sight of it tugs at my heart. Excitement over a damn corn dog.

We step into line, sandwiched between loud drunks. One guy in front of us sways slightly, and Charlotte subtly moves closer to me.

"Your runway show is tomorrow, right? Are you nervous?"

She looks at me, expression flattening. "Not really. I'll get poked and prodded by a dozen hands backstage, stand around for hours waiting my turn, wear something ridiculous that no normal person would ever wear in real life, and walk in a straight line." She crosses her arms. "But if it's Paris-themed again, I swear I'll set fire to the Eiffel Tower backdrop myself."

I take my wallet out. "You don't sound enthusiastic."

She shrugs. "It's all the same. You put on the dress, the hair, the makeup, you become this . . . thing for people to look at. And then you go home, scrub it all off, and wonder if you actually exist when no one's looking."

I watch her, my heart in a vise-like grip. Does she truly feel that way? Like she's nothing more than an object? As if her worth is confined solely to what the world can see?

Before I can say anything, the people in front of us get their food, and it's our turn to order. I get two corn dogs and two bottles of water, handing over a few crumpled bills before stepping away from the stand. The scent of fried batter and grilled sausage lingers in the air as we settle on the curb with the food.

She watches her corn dog with a strange expression, twisting it between her fingers like it's something foreign, and in the silence, my mind drifts.

Why does she model? She makes it sound like a punishment. And yet, when she talked about those stylists and that *Vogue* person, there was passion, like she actually gives a shit about the industry.

"Come on, just ask me your question."

"Hm?" I blink, pulled from my thoughts.

She studies the corn dog as if it might talk back to her. "You want to know why I'm on TOP, right? I obviously don't need the money, and if I feel like an . . . *object* when I model, why would I put myself through more of that online?"

"Because when you're on TOP, it's the only part of your life where you're . . . on top." I smirk, watching her lips part in surprise. "It doesn't take a genius to figure it out."

She blinks. "No, it doesn't. It takes someone who pays attention though."

How could I not? She commands it. I couldn't stop if I wanted to. And to be honest, paying attention to her is one of the easiest things I've ever done. Every little movement, every word, it all pulls me in.

"So, um . . ." She brushes the moment away, balancing her food on her knees. "What's your question then?"

I hesitate, not knowing where to start. "You must make a lot of money on TOP, right?"

She looks genuinely surprised as she leans back, her fingers digging into the dewy grass. "Ten thousand on a good month."

Holy shit.

"And modeling . . . that must pay well too."

"Depending on the show," she says. "I can make anywhere from five to fifty grand for a single show or shoot. Before taxes."

Holy shit?

I rest my forearms on my thighs. "So why . . ." I clear my throat, wary of offending her. "I know you said you're happy with your life, but you're old enough to get your own place. To choose what you want to eat."

"Oh. You want to know why I still live with Beatrice."

"Yes, I guess so."

She shrugs. "She keeps the modeling money—that's what we live off."

So *that's* how they afford their lifestyle. Beatrice lives on Charlotte's shoulders.

"Wait, so, technically . . . *you're* paying me?"

"Hmm. Yeah, technically, I am."

Great. Even more reasons for this to be wildly inappropriate.

"Plus, she's my agent. All my connections in the modeling world are her connections first. If I left, I'd lose my job."

"And you *want* to keep modeling?"

"Until someone from TOP narcs on me." She sits up and brushes the dirt off her hands. "I mean, what should I do instead? I don't have a college degree. I'm not smart, or good at *something*. I'm no good for anything except putting my clothes on and taking them off. Performing for people who just want to see my body."

The words feel like they shouldn't belong to her, like they make no sense. But she says them like they're a fact.

"Which is why I probably shouldn't eat this." She takes the untouched corn dog off her lap and offers a small, resigned smile. "Look, Beatrice can be a bit . . . I mean, I hate her half the time. But the bottom line is this is all I know how to do. And if I want to continue modeling, I have to follow her rules."

I stare down at my own corn dog. Now I regret suggesting we get them. The last thing I want is to make things harder for her.

"What about your art?" I ask.

"My art?"

"Yeah. You're always sketching."

"Oh. That's not art, it's just clothes."

Just clothes?

I think of the way she talked about people who got their shit together later in life. I assumed modeling was what she wanted to do because they were big names in the fashion industry. But Vera Wang, Christian Dior, Anna Wintour . . . they're not models—they're stylists, designers, critics.

"You design clothes. That *is* art, Charlotte."

She nods, looking almost shy now. "Well, I don't just design them. I make them."

My brain scrambles. "Wait. You sew and . . . whatever else making clothes entails?"

She laughs. "Yes, Aaron. I sew and whatever else making clothes entails."

"Seriously? Have I ever seen anything you've made?"

"You're looking at it now."

I glance down at her red dress—it looks made for her., because it *is*.

"This? You made this?"

She nods. "Most of the clothes I wear are my own."

My mouth falls open. "Wait—so the black two-piece? The dress with the corset? And the—shit—the jeans skirt? You made those?"

Her smile widens. "You've been noticing my outfits?"

I notice everything about you.

"Hard not to," I murmur. "It's just—the way you dress . . . you're not wearing your clothes. It's like they're a part of you. Which I guess they are."

Her shoulders roll back, like she's standing a little taller despite still sitting on the curb. "What's your favorite?"

Oh, fuck. How am I supposed to pick?

Maybe . . . I glance down at the lace edging her décolletage, at the tiny satin-covered buttons lining the side ."This one. It's really . . ." Hot. Inappropriate. Perfect. " . . . pretty."

She fondly looks down at the dress. "It's my favorite too."

"It shows."

She glances down at her corn dog. "I could make something for you."

"For me?"

"Yeah. Your clothes kind of . . . lack personality. No offense. You're not your clothes—you just wear them."

She's right. I don't give a single shit about what I wear. But if she made something for me, I'd wear it until the seams frayed and the fabric turned to dust.

"Wouldn't you rather work with that instead of modeling?"

She shrugs. "Beatrice always says that it's a horrible waste to hide a body like mine behind the camera."

Oh, wow. She's the actual worst.

"Or," I say, turning to her, "you could just have the body you want, eat corn dogs and pizza until you have love handles and a belly, and do what you love."

Her eyes widen like I've just suggested she jump into traffic naked.

"What? You think you wouldn't still be astonishingly beautiful if you put on some weight?"

She frowns. "I'm not fatphobic or anything. Some of the most beautiful women in the world are curvy. Paloma Elsesser, Nicola Coughlan, Sugar High."

I blink. *Sugar High?* "You're kidding."

"What?"

"Primrose—that's my brother's fiancée."

She gapes at me. "*You're* kidding. Sugar High? She's an icon! Her following is insane, and, oh, she's just so unique. Her outfits, and her confidence. I can't believe you know her."

I laugh, genuinely amused. "Know her? I drove her home from the hospital, watched her pass out with baby spittle on her shirt."

She's still staring at me like I'm riding a unicorn. "Unbelievable."

As our laughter fades, I point at her lap. "You know, she'd eat that corn dog."

She glances at the offending bun again, lips pressing together.

"You don't have to if you don't want to," I add. "But she wouldn't let someone else decide what she should eat. What her body should look like, what she should do with her life, or what she's worth."

For a moment, there's a warm fondness in her eyes. Then, almost too quickly, she brings the corn dog to her lips, takes a huge bite, and moans obscenely. "Oh, fuck." Her head drops onto my shoulder. "Tell me again how beautiful I'd look carrying some extra pounds?"

"*So* beautiful."

She grins, and it takes every ounce of self-control not to lean forward and kiss her.

It takes even more not to admit that if she asked me to, I would.

CHAPTER 13

Sweet Cherries, Sour Rules

I knock lightly on the door before pushing it open, the cries only fully hitting me once I step inside. Logan stands by the old couch, one baby in his arms, the other lying in a car seat. The twins are crying in stereo, their tiny fists waving in the air.

My nose scrunches. Is that smell . . . baby formula and burnt toast? With how late I stayed up with Charlotte last night, this sound-slash-smell combination is giving me a headache.

"Seriously? I told Prim not to call you," Logan says, opening the door wider but not even looking at me. "They're just being fussy—I've got it under control until she's back."

"Oh, yeah. Looks like it."

"Don't you have work?"

"Not on weekends, no."

Sadie walks in after me, dragging her big shopping bag behind her. "Don't worry, Uncle Logan, we're here to help you!"

"Hey, princess." His shoulders relax just a fraction as he sees her. "Did you go shopping?"

"Yes!" She beams, lifting the bag with pride. "Daddy bought me the most beautiful dress for Mommy's Day. It's blue like the sky, and sparkly, and shiny, and—"

142

"They're having some kind of recital for Mother's Day in little over two weeks," I explain.

Logan's gaze lingers on me for a second, his lips pressing into a thin line. I can see his mind racing, thinking about Sadie's situation, about Josie not being here. "Oh."

"Do you want to see it, Uncle Logan?" Sadie asks as she holds the bag up higher.

"Duh! Go change in the bedroom."

"Careful with the zipper," I call after her, but she's already bounding down the hallway.

I turn back to Logan, who's bouncing the baby slightly to calm her down. The other twin's cries only seem to get louder, so I move closer, taking the baby from his arms gently. "I've got her, man. You grab"—I glance down, but they look exactly alike—"the other one."

Logan's tired eyes flick between the baby and me before he exhales sharply and walks away.

I sit on the couch, adjusting the baby in my arms, and rock her, her tiny body warm and solid against my chest. Her cries turn into little hiccups, her face scrunching up like she's trying to decide whether to keep being upset or give in to the comfort. Across the room, Logan is shaking up a bottle, more exhausted than I've ever seen him.

I get it. The farm doesn't wait for anyone, and Primrose has a whole brand to curate—including events on weekends, like today —which means that the two of them haven't stopped working through the pregnancy and the birth. And now they're getting married in three weeks. It's a lot to handle.

"You know," I start, keeping my voice low not to disturb the baby. "This kind of reminds me of when Sadie was a newborn." I adjust her in my arms, rubbing circles on her back. "On my first birthday after she was born, she had a blowout so bad I had to cut her onesie off with scissors. It was either that or risk getting it in her hair."

Logan doesn't react, still focused on testing the milk on his wrist. But I catch the slight twitch of his mouth, the ghost of a smirk trying to break through.

Encouraged, I keep going. "I was half asleep, covered in baby shit, and I remember thinking, 'Man, this would be so much easier if she could just hold her own ass up for a second.'"

He chuckles, but just as quickly as he started, he stops. "I remember your first birthday after you and Josie got together."

Yeah. I know why he's bringing it up.

Since we were teenagers, Logan and I had this birthday tradition: sneaking out behind the house with a beer, sitting on an overturned crate, talking about dumb shit, big dreams, all of it. It started when I turned sixteen, my worst birthday ever—ironically, because I'd found out the younger girl I liked, Josie, had kissed a classmate of mine. I snuck out a beer and Logan, back then an eleven-year-old clingy brother, followed me.

I still remember running from Mom in tears when he vomited the two sips of beer I'd let him drink.

And then, it became our thing.

But the year Logan's talking about—the first one after Josie found out she was pregnant with Sadie—was the first time we missed it. And we've missed every single one since.

Logan shifts, giving the baby her bottle. "Mom made me come over that day. Said she needed help with painting the garage and it *had* to be done that day." He exhales sharply. "By the time I was done, I was wiped."

He doesn't say anything else. But from the way his jaw tightens, from the flicker of something in his eyes, I can tell—he still remembered it was my birthday. He still hurt.

He looks at me then away as his fingers tap absently against the baby's back.

"Josie wasn't there," I mutter.

I don't know why I'm telling him this. Maybe because I want him to know that I wasn't happy either. That I didn't just walk away from our history into some perfect life. Or maybe my desperation to connect is making me fish for pity points.

"She got me a cake from the supermarket and we had lunch together, but that night, she said she needed to go see her mom, help her with some church event. I didn't mind too much because I had Sadie but . . ." I clear my throat, adjusting my hold on the baby. "The morning after, I ran into her mom on my way to work. She mentioned she hadn't seen Josie in a week. That she hoped she would finally make the time for the parish's charity event."

Logan twists his neck, looking at me. "She lied?"

I nod. "I eventually found out she'd gone out with a friend—probably just wanting to avoid me. I never confronted her about it, but I remember *that* was the moment I knew. Somewhere down the road, we were heading for divorce."

Logan studies me, like he's processing. Like maybe—for a second—he sees something in me that isn't just the guy who married his ex. The brother who betrayed him. Then his voice turns flat as he says, "I sat with a beer in the backyard."

What? I meet his gaze, heart twisting.

Does he mean that? I . . . I didn't know that was an option—hell, at that point, we hadn't talked in months.

With a tender gaze on his daughter that doesn't match his clipped voice, he continues. "Sat there for a while. When you didn't show up, I poured it out and went to bed."

I watch him, lips parted, not a clue what to say. After a long moment, he slips away down the hall without another word.

And just like that, the door I thought had cracked open slams shut again.

"PLEASE, DADDY, ONE MORE TIME."

Throwing a glance at the pink clock on Sadie's nightstand, I snap the book closed. I'll shoot myself in the right temple if I have to read *Rapunzel* a third time, but that's beside the point. "No, baby. It's late. Try to sleep, okay?"

"But I don't want to sleep."

I stand and set the book on the small bookshelf. "But if you sleep, it'll be tomorrow in a second. You'll see."

She fits her head against the pillow. "Okay. Good night, Daddy."

"Good night, love."

I leave a sliver of the door open and walk downstairs. The kitchen is still a mess from dinner, and all it takes is one look at the pile of plates to make me feel exhausted. At least, Sadie seems to be doing better. I'm sure the counselor at school is helping, but Josie calling regularly has been a real game changer. Sadie looks forward to it every day.

I slump on the couch, then take out my phone, the slightly paler skin around my ring finger catching my attention. I've kept my wedding band in one of the kitchen drawers since Charlotte sucked it off my finger four days ago.

Sucked it off.

I pinch the bridge of my nose, trying not to relive that moment for the millionth time. I'm pretty sure I owe her royalties for the amount of time I've spent thinking about it.

Fuck me, I miss her. I saw her twenty-four hours ago. I don't even *know* her, not really, or have had enough time to get used to her presence, and still I miss her.

I'm obsessed, and I don't know how to snap out of it.

I unlock my phone and open the browser. My fingers hesitate over the keys, a final moment of restraint, but it shatters the second I type *TOP* into the search bar.

I'm not going to actually contact her. I just want to see if she's online, check her profile—nothing more.

Just one look.

Just a taste to put all my buzzing worries to sleep. To make sure she's okay, that there were no hiccups with her show, that she's doing well at home alone. Then I'll go to sleep.

Once the page loads I see she's uploaded a new picture, and the small preview alone has me sucking in a deep breath, my grip tightening around the phone.

Fuuuuuck.

She's draped over satin black sheets, her body barely covered by a loose robe that's parted just enough to reveal a strip of bare skin leading down her stomach. The lighting is low, warm, her lips slightly open. Her hair tumbles over one shoulder, framing her face in a way that makes her eyes seem sultrier. There's a glossy sheen to her lower lip like she's just licked it, and the thought of her doing exactly that, thinking of me, sends heat coursing through my body.

I swallow hard and swipe to the next image, then the next, hating myself with every move. Hating every man on this site who does the exact same thing. Hating that I miss her presence more with each shot, that she's here but not really here. She's pixels on a screen, a performance, a fantasy that isn't mine to claim.

Then a ping makes my stomach lurch.

I freeze. Did I accidentally click something on her profile? My heart kicks into a sprint as I scan the screen, but the notification isn't from an accidental like or a misplaced tip.

It's a message.

My pulse pounds in my ears. Could it be her? Could another creator have messaged me, even though I haven't interacted with anyone else on here?

I tap the message icon, my breath knocking from my lungs when I see the name.

Cherry.

Cherry texted me.

I rush to open it, my fingers unsteady as I read.

CHERRY

Online and didn't text me? Should I be jealous?

A sharp exhale leaves me, part relief, part something I don't want to name. I press my tongue against the inside of my cheek. *Come on, Aaron.* It's something she says to every customer, a line to make them feel special, to keep them engaged. It's smart, strategic. It's her job.

She probably doesn't even remember me. And if she does, it's just good customer service, not . . . not real.

But still, I smile. Smile like none of that is true.

> **CHIEF.728**
> I was looking through your pictures, actually.

> **CHERRY**
> Do you like the new one?

Fuck yeah, I like it. She couldn't look bad if she tried. In each shot, she's perfect—sexy in a way that throws me completely off balance.

> **CHIEF.728**
> I like all of them.

> **CHERRY**
> Be a good boy and come in your hand for me?

My body responds immediately, a slow pulse of need spreading through me.

I can't. I can't. *I can't.*

> **CHERRY**
> Unless you wanna talk?

My lips curl up. *Talk.* There's nothing wrong with talking, right? Nothing wrong with hearing her voice. In fact, I *should* check on her—something her mom doesn't seem too interested in doing. It's the responsible thing to do.

Oh, who am I kidding.

CHIEF.728

I'd love to.

A call notification pops up on my screen, and I straighten against the couch before answering. As soon as it connects, I mute my mic. There's no doubt in my mind that if I spoke, she'd recognize my voice in an instant.

The screen buffers for a second before she appears, nestled against a mountain of pillows in varying shades of blush and ivory, her bed draped in rumpled cream-colored sheets that look like they've been slept in all day. Her hair is loose in silky waves, and she wears a thin-strapped tank top that clings to her curves.

She's more Charlotte than Cherry. Relaxed, tired, smiling. She's okay.

I feel better already.

"*Aww.* I don't get to hear your voice today?" she teases.

CHIEF.728

Sorry. Is this okay anyway?

"Of course, baby." She leans back against the pale rose, tufted velvet headboard. The golden amber glow of her bedside lamp casts warm shadows across the mauve walls as she shifts so one leg folds beneath her, the other stretching out in front of her. "I just miss the sound of your voice."

You sound so pretty when you come.

I try to shoo the thought away as she asks, "So, how are you feeling?"

She's being polite or actually concerned after my performance a couple of weeks back. Whatever it is, the question forces me to stop and think.

How am I?

Since she's been in my life—better. Hanging by a thread. Sexually frustrated. Split between obsessing over her and obsessing over how obsessed I am with her. Either way, she takes up so much

149

space in my mind that most other thoughts have gone out the window.

Eventually, I settle on:

CHIEF.728

Happy to see you. You?

She places a delicate hand over her chest. "Happy you're here with me. I'm all alone at home." She pinches the fabric of her top. "Do you want me to take my clothes off?"

CHIEF.728

No. Let's just talk.

A surprised laugh escapes her and she props her chin on her hand, eyes glinting with intrigue. "Sounds good. What do you want to talk about?"

Honestly? Her. I want to use this alter ego to ask her all the things I can't ask her in real life. I want to hear her talk without worrying about how I'm looking at her, or what's appropriate to say and what isn't.

CHIEF.728

Tell me about you. If you want.

"About me, huh?" She hums, tapping a manicured finger against her lips. "Let's see. I play the cello, collect postcards, and love vanilla ice cream."

I scratch the side of my head. Cello? Postcards? I mean . . . I guess it's technically possible. I don't know her well enough to say for sure those facts aren't true. But they don't feel like her.

CHIEF.728

How many lies did you just tell?

Her eyes widen in mock innocence before she throws her head back. "Two."

Unbelievable.

CHIEF.728

If I guess the true one, will you answer a
question? For real?

Her lips curl as if she likes the challenge. "You got it."

CHIEF.728

Vanilla ice cream.

A pause. Then her mouth parts before she bursts into laughter,
her whole body shaking with it. "Damn, you're good." She waves
me on. "What's the question?"

CHIEF.728

What happens if you like a guy? If you end up
dating, or he becomes your boyfriend?

As she scans the text, her lips twitch. Her gaze flickers to the
camera as her teeth sink into her bottom lip. "Are you asking
because you're afraid I'll ghost you, or because you want to be my
boyfriend?"

CHIEF.728

Covering all bases.

She shakes her head lightly, teeth sinking into her bottom lip
like she enjoys me flirting with her. It's mesmerizing, how her reactions play out so clearly. No poker face. It makes me ache to see
them in person—to make her smile just like this, to make her feel
as special as she is.

"Well, let's see." She draws her knees up to her chest, wrapping
her arms around them. "I guess I'd stop camming. Of course, I do
this for the money, but also because it's fun. And I don't think I'd
enjoy it if I were committed to someone." She rolls some hair
around her finger. "Luckily for you, I don't have boyfriends."

CHIEF.728

Never?

"Never." She shrugs, like it's no big deal. "I stick by three rules that pretty much make that impossible."

Three rules. I don't know what they are, but I already want to break them.

CHIEF.728

Let's hear them.

"Number one." She playfully widens her eyes. "No kissing."
No kissing. My stomach twists—I hate it.

CHIEF.728

Right, right. I'm familiar with Pretty Woman.

She clicks her tongue. "Of course, that rule does not apply to a young Richard Gere. Or Julia Roberts."

CHIEF.728

Reasonable.

"Rule number two. No sleeping together. Too complicated—cuddles, breakfast, morning breath. *Faaaar* too intimate."

What's wrong with intimacy? My fingers twitch with the urge to type the question, but she keeps going before I can.

"And third rule . . . no sleeping together."

CHIEF.728

You said that one already.

She tucks some hair behind her ear. "No, Cole. No *sleeping* together."

Wait, what?

CHIEF.728

As in . . . sex?

"As in sex."

As in she *never* has sex? My brain short-circuits for a moment, trying to compute this new information.

CHIEF.728

You mean . . . until the right guy comes along?

She cracks a grin. "I'm not waiting for Prince Charming to give my flower to, if that's what you're asking. In fact, my flower's long gone. It's probably flattened out inside a book and dried up, ready to be hung in some old lady's house."

CHIEF.728

So what do you mean?

She hesitates, something shifting in her expression until she looks more vulnerable. For the first time since we got on this call, she seems almost . . . uncertain.

CHIEF.728

You don't have to tell me, Cherry.

"It's not a big deal." She clears her throat, dropping her gaze for a second before looking up again. "It might sound . . . stupid, but sex is really important to me. Not foreplay—I love messing around with men, having fun. But I find the act of penetration to be . . . emotional. The feeling of someone . . . *filling me up*"—she bites her bottom lip, and I wonder if she's thinking about me. About Aaron, not Cole, telling her those exact words just a few days ago—"pushing inside me. Of being completely open and connected to another person. It's not something I can do with just anyone."

It doesn't sound stupid at all. Casual sex has never done much for me. The physical part is easy, but without a deeper connection, it always feels . . . awkward. Empty.

> I get it. There's a lot of vulnerability in sex.

"Exactly. No kissing, no sex, and no sharing the same bed for the night equals no vulnerability." She tips her head back against the pillows. "And therefore, no boyfriends."

I'm oddly comforted by her admission, like she's soothed the jealous part of me that doesn't want to share her with anyone.

But she's in her twenties—these are the years to fall hopelessly in love. To be reckless, to make mistakes, to chase something breathtaking even if it terrifies you. To have nights that mean nothing and mornings that mean everything. To give your heart away, even if you don't know what to do with it afterward.

Fingers hovering over the keys, I wonder for a long moment what to say and watch her nestled in her own space. A painting of a coastal landscape hangs above the bed, a pale blue duvet is bunched on one side, and the nightstand is cluttered with a half-empty glass of water and a closed book. Not the silk sheets from her photos—not the polished persona.

Just Charlotte. Real and unfiltered.

Eventually, I settle on,

CHIEF.728

> Don't you miss it though?

"Miss what?"

CHIEF.728

> You know . . . the stuff people do when they're dating.

She raises a skeptical brow. "Like what? *Cuddling*?" She rolls her big, beautiful eyes. "Slow dancing in the kitchen? Showering together and making dinner after a long day?"

She throw them out like they're ridiculous, but none of that sounds *bad*. In fact, *I* miss it.

> Yeah. Stuff like that.

She snorts, eyes flicking away. "Nope. Don't miss it at all."

It's a lie. I can see it in the way she won't look at the camera. In the quiet ache that slips into her voice despite her best efforts to bury it.

But I can sense it's better to let this go, so I type:

> Maybe the right guy will come along and barrel through your rules.

"Maybe," she says, a grin playing on her lips. "But until then, Cole, this cherry is yours."

CHAPTER 14

Cheer Up! It's Pancake Time

The sizzle of batter fills the kitchen, the scent of butter thick in the air, but it does nothing to settle the anger rolling through me. My grip tightens on the spatula as I flip a pancake, jaw clenched so hard it aches.

Josie was supposed to see Sadie today. We *agreed* we'd go visit, that we'd spend time together—because that's what our kid needs. Stability. A mother who shows up.

After she kept her promise to call every day, I let myself believe I could trust her.

And then, two hours before we were supposed to leave, a nurse called.

"*Josie isn't up for visitors today,*" he'd said.

That was it. That was the explanation. When I pressed for more, all I got was "She's having a bad day."

A bad day.

Does she know how many bad days I've had over the last six months? How many times I wanted to shut down, crawl into bed, pretend the world didn't exist? But I didn't. Because you don't get to tap out when you're a parent. You don't get to decide you're not up for it.

I meant to bring up the Mother's Day recital with her today. I figured I might have a better shot if I didn't try on the phone, and now that's gone to hell too.

Sadie was inconsolable, of course. Tears, shoulders shaking, endless questions I didn't have the answers to. Eventually, she settled when I promised to make pancakes, but this is temporary. It's a distraction, not a fix.

"No, not like that. You said to split it into three, right?" A pause. "Ugh, mine looks dumb."

I frown, lowering the spatula. That doesn't sound like Sadie talking to the cat. That sounds like she's . . . answering someone.

I turn off the burner and step toward the living room, wiping my hands on a dish towel. "Sadie, who are you—"

I stop dead in my tracks.

She's sitting cross-legged on the couch, Mollie draped across her lap, and in her small hands is—my phone, pressed right up to her ear.

"Sadie? What are you doing?"

She barely glances up, as if this is something she does every day. "Talking to Charlotte."

"You—*what*?"

"I called her." She tugs at a section of her hair, frowning. "I wanted to learn how to braid."

A heavy breath pushes through my nose. "Sadie," I say, my voice much sharper this time. "You took my phone without asking?"

She hesitates now, sensing that she might be in trouble. " . . . Yeah."

"And made a phone call?"

She shrinks into the couch, her grip tightening on Mollie. "I just wanted help."

I pinch the bridge of my nose, a mix of frustration and mortification creeping up my spine. I pluck the phone from her hands before she can protest, bringing it to my ear.

"Charlotte, hi. I'm so sorry about this. Trust me, I had no idea—"

"Relax, Chef. I like talking to your daughter."

Damn it. We spent a couple of hours texting-slash-talking last night, and hearing her voice now feels like finding the missing piece of a song stuck in your head.

"Apparently you're a poor braider, huh?"

"That's what Sadie said?"

"I'm paraphrasing. What she said wasn't nearly as nice."

Chuckling, I look back at my smiling daughter. Little troublemaker.

"Might not be my greatest talent."

"Yeah? What *is* your greatest talent?"

I hold my breath, trying not to let my thoughts wander. "How was your show?"

There's a pause before she answers. "It . . . went well, actually. Better than I expected."

"And you're okay home alone?"

Again, she hesitates for a moment. "Yeah? Yes, of course. Why do you ask?"

Because I care. Because I can't help but feel protective of her, even though I'm not supposed to. "Just making sure you're good."

"Thanks, but I'm pretty used to no one checking in on me. I know how to be on my own."

"I know you do," I say. "But it doesn't mean you have to be."

"Dad, can I still learn?" Sadie asks, tugging at my shirt.

Charlotte must hear, because she says, "Put me on speaker."

I hesitate, then press the button. "You're on."

"All right, Sadie," Charlotte says, her voice coming through warm and patient. "Let's start from the beginning. Take three even sections of hair—doesn't have to be perfect, just close enough."

Sadie scrambles up, gathering her hair into clumsy little bunches.

"Make sure they're separate, then take the right section and cross it over the middle."

I tap the correct section, then watch as Sadie follows the instructions, her fingers fumbling as she crosses one chunk over the other. Her eyes quint in deep concentration, the tip of her tongue poking out from the corner of her mouth, like she wants so badly to get this right.

And for a second, I just . . . pause.

Charlotte is teaching my daughter how to braid over the phone. My kid called her for help, and instead of brushing her off, instead of saying she was busy or telling her to ask me, Charlotte is here, guiding Sadie along like this is the most normal thing in the world. Like it's not complicated or messy or blurred at the edges. Like we're not supposed to be keeping our distance.

Something tightens in my chest.

Sadie loops the last section over the first and beams up at me, her dark curls woven into something that barely resembles a braid. A few loose wisps stick out at odd angles, and it's a little uneven, but the pride shining on her face as she ties a scrunchie to the end is enough to make it all irrelevant.

"How does it look?" she asks, tilting her head so I can admire her work.

"Perfect, sweetheart." I brush a stray curl from her face. "You look beautiful."

She hums and presses her lips together, like she's contemplating whether or not to believe me. "I think I need a second opinion. Can we send a picture to Charlotte?"

Charlotte giggles, and before I can answer, Sadie reaches for the phone.

I hand it over, and she immediately scrambles up on the couch, flipping the camera to selfie mode and angling her head just right. She sticks her tongue out, then tries a pout, then finally settles on a wide, toothy grin before snapping the picture.

As she's tapping away, the shrill ring of the landline phone cuts through the air.

"I'll be right back. Don't make her regret answering your call," I warn, ruffling Sadie's hair before heading into the kitchen.

I pick up the phone, still half listening to Sadie telling Charlotte about her upcoming performance for "Mommy Day" in the other room.

"Hello?"

"Aaron—" My mother's voice is tight, pained. "I need you to come over."

A cold chill runs through me. "What happened?"

"I fell in the bathroom," she says, and I hear her hiss through her teeth. "I can't stand up. I think I might have twisted my ankle."

Shit.

I grip the phone tighter, already moving toward the living room. "Is Darren not home?"

"He's out of town."

Shit, shit, shit.

"Can you put weight on it?" I ask as I join Sadie's side.

"I haven't tried," she says, voice strained. "But it hurts like hell."

"Okay, stay put. I'm coming." I hang up, then turn to Sadie. "Baby, Grandma had a little accident. I have to go help her."

Her face scrunches in worry. "Is she okay?"

"She will be." I press a quick kiss to her forehead. "But I need you to be a big girl for me, okay?"

Her bottom lip juts out, her small hands gripping my shirt. "I'll come with you."

I lead her toward the front entrance. "No, I'm gonna drop you off at the Millers' next door and you'll wait for Daddy to be back." I hold out my hand, waiting for her to give me my phone. "Come on. Let's go."

"But I don't like the Millers! Their ugly dog always barks at Mollie!" She stomps a foot against the hardwood.

I don't have time for this. My mother is alone, hurt, and Darren isn't there to help. Every second I waste is another second she's sitting there in pain.

"Sadie—" I reach for the phone, but she yanks it close to her chest, her eyes pleading now.

"Please, Daddy! I want to stay with Charlotte."

There's a rustle on the other end before I can get a word in, then Charlotte's voice comes through the speaker. "Is everything okay?"

"My mom fell." I try to push down the panic pressing against my ribs. "She must have twisted her ankle or something. I need to—"

"I'll be right there."

I blink. Is she . . . "I'm leaving Sadie with the neighbors. You don't have to—"

"No, no! I want to stay with Charlotte." Sadie tugs at my shirt again. "Please, Daddy! Can I? *Please*?"

"Leave Sadie with the neighbors," Charlotte says. "I'll pick her up in ten minutes."

I swallow hard, torn between wanting to argue and knowing I don't have time. "I . . . Charlotte, you don't have to do this. I can manage."

"I know you can." There's a quiet beat. "But you don't have to."

I squeeze my eyes shut. I should tell her this isn't her problem. That she doesn't need to get tangled up in our mess. That Sadie is already attached, and I can't risk this getting any more complicated.

That I'm experiencing the same issue.

But I don't.

"The yellow house across from ours," I say instead. "I'll leave the keys with them so you can come back home with her. There's pancakes in the kitchen and—"

"Go, Chef." Her voice is firm, no room for argument. "I've already booked an Uber."

I hesitate, grip tightening around the phone. "Thank you," I murmur before hanging up.

I crouch in front of Sadie, smoothing a hand over her messy braid. "All right, kiddo. Let's go."

She sniffles but nods, slipping her small hand into mine as we step out the door.

I could lie to myself and say I was too rushed to argue with Charlotte. That Sadie looked so happy at the thought of seeing her that I didn't want to take that away.

But the truth is simpler than that.

There's only one reason I went along with it.

I *need* to see Charlotte today.

THE HOSPITAL ROOM smells like antiseptic and something faintly metallic, and the white lights do nothing to counteract the harsh, sterile feel of the space. Mom looks small in the bed, swallowed by too-white sheets, but she's still putting on a show. Arms crossed, jaw tight, pretending like she's fine. Except that someone *fine* doesn't collapse on their way to the bath.

At least she still had her phone on her.

"You really didn't have to stay," she complains.

"Yeah, well, I don't trust you not to walk out of here the second I turn my back."

She rolls her eyes but doesn't argue, which is in itself another red flag.

Logan telling me how Mom seemed off recently is a brutal reminder of the fact that I've been distracted. So absorbed in my own bullshit that I ignored the signs that something wasn't right. I see them now, though. Clearly.

"Tell me you didn't tattle to your brother, at least."

"Yes, I told Logan." I ignore the disapproving sound she makes. I've asked her in a variety of different ways what's going on, but she keeps saying everything's fine. Load of bullshit, that is. "He's alone with the kids, so I told him to stay home."

"Good, good. Primrose is in Mayfield this weekend?"

I nod distractedly. Where the hell is the doctor? It's been hours since her twisted ankle was examined and bandaged.

"Did the two of you talk?"

"Talk?" I ask. "About what?"

"You know. *Talk*. Properly, like brothers."

Oh. She means are we still pretending everything's okay? "Mostly about the kids. I don't think Logan is interested in much else from me."

"You two just need to—"

"Talk, I get it. But I can't *make* him, Ma. He'll have to decide for himself when he's ready." She mumbles something about us being stubborn, and I cock my head to one side. "Don't you think it's ironic you'd say that when you're not being open with your sons?"

"Oh, that's preposterous, Aaron. You—"

A knock at the door makes me turn as the doctor steps in, a clipboard tucked under his arm. He's younger than me, with sharp eyes that scan the room.

"Mrs. Coleman," he greets. "How are you feeling?"

Mom waves him off. "Fine. Really, I'm good to go home."

I let out a quiet scoff, and she flicks me a look.

The doctor doesn't seem convinced either. He steps closer, flipping through his notes. "We ran your tests, and while everything looks stable, I want to go over a few things." He pauses. "Any dizziness? Loss of balance?"

She hesitates. "Maybe a little."

"Any stiffness or trouble with coordination?"

Her fingers twitch where they rest on the blanket, just barely. It's small, almost nothing. But it's *not* nothing.

The doctor notices too. "Mrs. Coleman, I'll need you to be more forthcoming about your symptoms moving forward. Who's treating you for your condition?"

"Her *what*?" I cut in.

Silence.

Did he say her "condition"? Mom doesn't have a condition—the woman is healthier than me and Logan put together. But she doesn't look at me when I stare at her, waiting for an explanation, and once I direct my panicked gaze at the doctor, he clears his throat.

"I'll give you both a moment," he says. "Be back shortly."

The door clicks shut and I stare at her, waiting, while my heart pounds in my ears. She's supposed to say something, to explain, to tell me this is a misunderstanding.

But she doesn't.

"What the hell was that?" My voice is rough, my chest tight. "What 'condition'?"

"Aaron, it's nothing. I have some vertigo, and—"

"No." I press my fingers against my eyelids. "No, enough bull-shit. Enough lying—*enough*."

She closes her eyes for a moment, and when she opens them, something in her face shifts, like she's finally giving up the fight. "I was diagnosed with Parkinson's."

For a second, I can't move. Can't *think*. Her words echo in my thoughts but make no sense.

Parkinson's? I scramble for every piece of information I know about it. It's a degenerative disease. No cure. It starts with tremors, stiffness, trouble with movement, and gets worse over time. I think of Michael J. Fox and the therapist from that show *Shrinking* I binged this past winter. Medication can help, but it doesn't stop it from chipping away at a person's independence. There's physical therapy, lifestyle changes, ways to manage symptoms, but in the end . . . it only goes in one direction.

And she's been dealing with this alone.

"How long?" I croak.

Her throat bobs. "A little over a year."

A year.

A whole fucking *year*.

I push to my feet, pacing a tight line next to the bed. "And you didn't think to *tell me*?"

"You have enough on your plate, Aaron."

I let out a bitter laugh, dragging my hands through my hair. "Are you kidding me? Mom, you've been—what? Just pretending everything's fine? Letting me think this was nothing?" I scrape my teeth over my bottom lip. "What about Darren? Does he know? And Logan—did you tell him about this?"

Tears well in her eyes, but she doesn't look away. "I didn't want all of you to look at me like that."

Holy crap, she hasn't told a single soul.

"Look at you like what?" I shout.

"Like I'm slipping away. Like I'm not me anymore," she says in a small voice.

I swallow against the agony that's making my chest feel like a prison, my anger deflating in an instant. I hate that she's kept this a secret, but I try to remind myself that she's not just my and Logan's mom, not just Darren's wife either. She's the one who's going through this, the one with the *condition*.

I squeeze her hand and nod, trying to reassure her without words. The second I open my mouth, I'll start bawling. I can feel it.

Mom's sick, and that's terrifying.

But the scarier thing?

Mom's the healthiest she'll ever be again.

CHAPTER 15
The Taste of Almost

AMELIE

Hey, I thought I was supposed to forget my friends once I became famous, not the other way around.

I study the unanswered message, the timestamp from this morning, then the previous green bubbles I haven't responded to. I can't bring myself to. Not when there's nothing I can tell her. I can't tell her about Ma when she hasn't even opened up to Logan, I certainly can't tell her about Charlotte.

And I don't like lying to Amelie.

I slip the phone in my pocket and step up to the porch, exhaustion settling deep in my bones as I fit the key into the lock and open the door. The house is dark except for the glow of the TV, flickering in the living room like a heartbeat. It's later than I wanted it to be, but I made sure my mom was settled at home and waited for Darren to be back.

I made her tell him. I agreed I won't tell Logan for the time being—she says he should enjoy the happiness of being a new parent, though we both know that's bullshit—but Darren needed to know. Someone needs to help her, to keep an eye on her.

When I left them, he was still crying.

I shrug off my jacket and step toward the living room.

And then I stop.

The place is a wreck.

The coffee table is covered in nail polish bottles, cotton balls, cucumber slices, and what looks like a billion different lotions. There are empty chip bags, a bowl of popcorn tipped onto the floor, and half-eaten candy scattered like someone got distracted mid–sugar rush. The remnants of pancakes and their fixings sit abandoned on the dining table, next to an open bag of marsh-mallows.

And in the middle of all the chaos sit Sadie and Charlotte, fast asleep on the couch—Charlotte with her head tilted back, Sadie curled into her side, and the smug gray-and-brown cat stretched across both their laps like she owns the place.

They're both wearing robes, sleeves comically long on Sadie's tiny frame. Towels are wrapped around their heads, slipping slightly from sleep, and their faces look shiny, like they went to town with whatever lotions are spread out on the table. Sadie's head is pressed against Charlotte's shoulder, her little fingers still curled around Charlotte's hand.

I stand there, frozen in the doorway, watching the steady rise and fall of their breaths.

Sadie looks peaceful. Content.

And Charlotte . . .

She's holding my daughter's hand, even in sleep. She must have let her paint her nails, because there's no way Charlotte willingly chose that neon purple polish. And she's here, in my home, like she belongs.

My gaze flickers to the coffee table, to her laptop, still open, the screen dim but not dark. I glance at Charlotte before my curiosity gets the better of me, then I tilt my head, just enough to see what's on the screen.

A job announcement.

It's an entry-level position at a local fashion designer. Office assistant. Is she considering an alternative to modeling? Could she be thinking of pursuing her art?

I *really* hope so. That the conversation we had after the concert struck a chord.

I crouch in front of her and gently tuck some hair behind her ear.

Beatrice has been gone all weekend, but she might be back by now, and it's already so late. I can't risk getting Charlotte in even more trouble. I have to wake her up.

"Charlotte?" I say, shaking her shoulder. She shifts slightly, her hand tightening around Sadie's like she's holding on. "Charlotte," I try again.

She opens her eyes with a little gasp, then blinks quickly as she looks left and right. Once her gaze settles on me, she squints. "Aaron?" She turns to Sadie. "Oh. We must have fallen asleep during our movie marathon."

"Looks like it." I nod toward the door. "Is your mom back? Should I drive you home?"

"She's back." She straightens, her fingers brushing over the hem of the robe. "I . . . I told her I was sleeping at Bonnie's."

Oh.

She lied to stay over at my place, so that line I've been trying not to cross? It's behind us now. A wave of unease washes over me, and I don't know if it's because of the implications or because, deep down, I don't want her to leave.

She swallows, clearly catching on to the tension, then looks down at Sadie's head on her arm, like none of it matters as long as she's happy. As long as my daughter had a good night.

"Thank you for this," I say softly.

Her voice is just as quiet. "How's your mom?"

"She's, uh . . ." I give Sadie a cuddle. "My stepdad's home now, so she's being taken care of."

"Oh, good." She carefully untangles her arm from Sadie, and a tiny, unconscious protest escapes her lips as Charlotte slips free.

I roll the stiffness from my shoulders, the exhaustion of the night settling into my bones. The hospital was a shitshow—overcrowded, understaffed, so chaotic that it drained me even though I wasn't the one in the hospital bed. And the same thought keeps haunting my mind like a wicked lullaby.

Mom has Parkinson's disease. Mom has Parkinson's disease. Mom has Parkinson's disease.

It doesn't feel real.

"You okay, Chef?"

"Huh? I'm . . ." I burrow my face into the palm of my hand, then look at her through the gaps in between my fingers. "Thank you for this, seriously. I had no idea it'd take this long."

Charlotte glances down at me. "That's okay. We had a very successful self-care day." She scratches the back of Mollie's ears. "And I met your cat. You didn't tell me you had one—she's so sweet."

Sweet? Mollie? Did we switch cats while I was out?

The demon beast opens one eye, watching me with cold indifference.

"Yeah, she's the best."

"Sadie mentioned . . . she said you had other plans today."

Oh. Of course, she must have told her about Josie. "Yeah. Not a great day for her. Not until she called you, at least."

"Not a great day for you either from the sound of it."

I shake my head, looking in the distance until her fingers lace with mine.

I shouldn't say anything—this is my mom's secret to tell, and Logan shouldn't find out after Charlotte, someone who's almost a stranger. But I also can't keep it inside for one more second, so I say, "My mom . . . she's been diagnosed with Parkinson's."

Her jaw drops, then silence, her parted lips pressing together as whatever she was going to say dissolves into nothing.

"I'm . . . I'm so sorry, Aaron." Her thumb rubs the back of my hand. "Was it . . . tonight?"

"A year ago, apparently." The words push against my ribs like they're too big for my chest. "But I only found out tonight. That's why she fell," I explain. "Because her muscles aren't responding the way they should anymore. Because her balance is shot, and she's weaker than she lets on. And from now on, it'll only get worse. At some point, she won't be able to walk. She'll struggle to eat. She'll . . ."

My voice breaks, and she squeezes just enough to remind me I'm not alone.

"I got so mad at her."

"Because she kept it a secret?"

"Not just from me," I say with a click of my tongue. "From my stepdad. My brother. She didn't tell a single person."

Her fingers sweep over my knuckles. "That's dangerous."

"And irresponsible."

"And . . . understandable, maybe?"

My eyes snap to hers, and the muted green has an immediate calming effect on the raging storm in my mind.

"She probably didn't want her family to think of her as a sick woman. Needed time to come to terms with it herself before letting the rest of the world in."

I tip my head back. "That's exactly what she said."

"I get it. Don't you?"

Yeah. I *do* fucking get it. I just wish I didn't react the way I did.

"I should have gotten it before I shouted at her while she was lying in a hospital bed."

"Aaron," she gently scolds. "You're the one she called when she needed help. She told *you*. I'm pretty sure a love like that can survive a bad fight."

The tension in my chest loosens, just enough to let me breathe, as I look up at her. "You're sensitive."

She blinks. "Excuse me?"

"You keep surprising me with something new every day. How smart you are, how mature despite your age. How passionate, how impulsive. It's your sensitivity today. Your emotional intelligence."

She toys with the robe's belt. "Yeah? I'm not just a pretty girl?"

"You're beautiful, not pretty." My gaze drifts to her lips, and the ache of wanting to taste them nearly stops my heart. "And no, you're not."

Her smile grows, as though she's savoring the moment. Her eyes lock with mine, head tilting just a little. "You've got a big ol' crush on me, Chef."

"Yeah, no kidding."

I don't know how it happened—if I'm just that lonely or that stupid—but I *do* have a crush on her. A big, consuming thing that catches in my chest every time she's near. The kind of crush that could turn into something more, something deeper. If only everything about it—about *us*—was different.

Infusing my voice with a lightness I don't really feel, I ask, "Are you going to break my heart, Cherry?"

She leans forward with a suggestive expression. "Definitely."

A grin tugs at my lips, my eyes dropping to her mouth for a beat before I meet her gaze again. "Looking forward to it."

Her thumb is still tracing the top of my hand, featherlight but devastating, and I swear I can feel it everywhere.

This is the moment. This is the second where I either let this slip away, or give in to the fire that's been burning between us since the beginning.

From my crouch, I lean forward slightly and land on my knees, her legs parting slightly to make space for me. Letting me in. I lift my free hand, brushing my knuckles down the slope of her cheek. She leans into it, just slightly, her lashes lowering. The room feels too small. The air too thick.

Her hand moves from the top of mine, tracing the inside of my wrist, dragging up my forearm as she reaches down, nails just barely scratching. It's nothing, really. Just the softest touch. But then she shifts closer, sitting on the edge of the couch, knees brushing my chest.

I know what I should do. I should thank her for today, tell her to take my bed while I crash on the couch, make this less than what it is.

But why should *I* be the one doing the right thing?

I throw a glance at Sadie's sleeping form. Josie should be here, but she's not. My mom should be healthy, or at the very least, honest. My brother should talk to me instead of pretending things are fine between us. No one does what they should. No one acts their age. Nothing's going the way it's supposed to.

And I *really* need to talk to the one person who's been a constant in my life over the last year, but I can't tell Amelie any of this.

So why should I be better? Why should I be the one keeping it together when all I want is to fall apart?

The thought burns through me, hollowing out my insides like a slow-spreading flame. Tonight, I don't want to be strong. Wise. The kind of person who takes the high road, makes the responsible choices. Someone his daughter should look up to.

Tonight, I just want Charlotte.

I lift my hand from where it rests on my thigh, hovering just above hers. I hesitate briefly, but then my fingers find the edge of her robe. The terrycloth bunches under my touch as I toy with the fabric, lightly pulling it to the side.

Charlotte doesn't stop me.

She doesn't shift away or clear her throat or make some joke to ease the tension.

She just watches as I trail my fingers along the seam of the robe, feeling the fine hairs on her skin rise under my touch.

I don't know what I'm doing. Or maybe I do. Maybe I've known for a while now, and this was inevitable.

WITH A CHERRY ON TOP

Her breath hitches, barely audible, but I hear it over the low hum of the TV. Like a spark catching on dry kindling, ready to set everything ablaze.

Her hand travels up to meet mine. She reaches down, cups my fingers with hers, and guides them up her leg, her skin warm and smooth beneath my palm. When she drags my hand to the curve of her outer thigh, I squeeze instinctively, my fingers sinking into her flesh.

A sharp inhale. Hers or mine—I'm not sure.

When she leans down, bridging the gap between us, every part of me tightens in anticipation.

"I won't take advantage of this. Of you."

What?

She traces the back of her fingers along my neck, holding my gaze again. "You're safe to have a bad day around me, Chef."

Disappointment settles in my stomach. I thought . . . I thought this was happening. I thought I could finally stop pretending that I don't *need* her, that I don't want to drown in her. That I have the strength to resist her.

I'm ready to accept that I'm too weak. I want the escape she promises.

But her fingers slip into my hair and twist gently, grounding me before I can spiral further.

I stay there for a moment, forehead nearly dropping to her lap, breathing her in. Trying to commit this feeling to memory. Then, finally, I let my hand slip from her thigh, push myself up, and move to sit next to Sadie.

She rolls onto her side, her legs stretching out over mine and her head settling on Charlotte's lap.

After settling a blanket over the two of them, I meet Charlotte's gaze.

Neither of us speaks. Tonight was hell on earth, but with Sadie tucked between us and Charlotte's warmth just within reach, something eases inside me.

She watches me for a while in the near dark of my living room, her lips curving in a small, knowing grin. The corners of my mouth lift before I can stop them.

And I can't help but picture a version of my life where I fall asleep to her smile every night.

CHAPTER 16
Hot & Microwaved

This morning I stood at the stove for what felt like hours, hands braced on the counter, staring at the empty coffee cup Charlotte had placed in front of me earlier.

I should've said something before she got into that Uber. Should have insisted more about giving her a ride after I dropped Sadie off at school. Should've talked about last night, acknowledged what we almost did. How we fell asleep looking into each other's eyes. But instead, I let her go without a word. I drove Sadie to school with my mind stuck on the way Charlotte had looked in my shirt after her shower this morning. How my couch probably still smelled like her. How she braided Sadie's hair much better than I ever could.

I didn't think I'd manage to sleep last night, not with everything going on, but I did. I slept like a fucking baby. Maybe I was just exhausted, but I have a strong feeling Charlotte being within arm's reach had something to do with that.

Which is why, after staring at that mug for far too long, I decided.

This has to stop.

There's no other choice.

It's not about wanting to fuck her senseless anymore—Charlotte affects me. Whenever she's around, whenever her eyes are on me. I miss her touch, the way I feel like I have nothing to prove with her. She's become addictive, and with my family falling apart, I can't afford to lose everything.

I can't afford another mistake.

Groceries in hand, I peak my head through the archway. The penthouse is silent, probably empty. All doors along the corridor are closed, including the second one, leading to Charlotte's room.

I settle the groceries on the kitchen island, moving a stack of mail to one side, but my eyes snag on the name written on it. *Beatrice Montgomery.* Must be her maiden name. Unable to help myself, I check the rest, noticing that there's an unusual amount of cooking magazines for someone who hates food as much as she does. But on every single piece of mail, Beatrice Montgomery is the addressee. It's the same name the usher gave me on my first day, isn't it?

I briefly wonder why she'd give me her daughter's surname if that's not what she goes by, but shove the thought away when the front door opens.

My heart jumpstarts, kicking into gear again as Charlotte enters the living room, a tote full of fabric looped over her shoulder. "Hey." She lets the bag fall with a dull thud on the floor, eyes filled with worry. "Any news from your mom?"

"Not since this morning, no." But when I talked to Darren, he said she was resting. "I'll probably go see her tonight."

She nods. "She must be sleeping last night off."

"Yeah."

She stands there for a beat longer than necessary, then leans down to grab her tote again. The tension is palpable, thick as molasses.

I need to say something, and I need to do it *now.*

"Last night—" I rush out when she's almost cleared the room. She watches me, expectant, and every thought in my head is gone.

"It would have been a disaster. If we'd . . ." I gesture between us, watching her brows descend over her eyes. She did not like that. "I just mean, because of my job and our age difference . . ."

Now her jaw is taut, her eyes two cruel slits.

"I just—I was obviously out of it, after everything. You know, Josie blowing Sadie off, then my mom . . ."

She blinks.

"Anyway, saying no was the right choice. I wasn't in the right state of mind to make it, so . . . thank you for doing it for me."

With a scoff, she looks away, then back at me. "Yeah. You're super welcome."

Woah-oh. Why do I have a feeling she's mad? I quickly go through my speech, trying to figure out which part pissed her off, but she's already strutting away.

"Charlotte, I didn't mean to—"

"No, I get it. If we'd slept together last night, it would have been a mistake, right?"

"Yes! That's all I'm saying."

She laughs bitterly, shaking her head. "Because you're attracted to me. My body. You want to *fuck me*—that's it. And if you did, then I'd just be another mistake you can torture yourself with." She shrugs like she's brushing it off, but her eyes tell another story. "That's what I'm good for, right? That's all I'll ever be good for, even to you."

My teeth grind together so hard they might crack. "No. No, Charlotte. That's what your mom thinks. Maybe what you think, but it doesn't even come close to what I see when I look at you."

She scoffs, but I press on.

"I see you curled up next to Sadie after your spa day, the two of you passed out with glitter face masks and half-eaten gummy bears between you. I see the way you eat pizza like it's a five-star experience, your talent in every outfit you wear. How you light up when you leave me speechless, like your goal in life is to be disruptive."

She's still. Quiet.

"You think I just want your body?" I shake my head. "It's the last thing I see, Charlotte. Everything else about you keeps getting in the way. *That's* the problem."

Her eyes soften a fraction. "Right. Because Aaron Coleman isn't allowed to make mistakes."

I open my mouth, then quickly close it, not sure what to say.

"Am I wrong? Your mom didn't tell you about her condition for a whole year, and you stood by her side all night. Your wife left your daughter behind, yet she's welcome to call. Hell, she blew you off yesterday, and if she asked you to bring Sadie over today, you'd do it without batting an eye. And your brother—he keeps you at a distance for *years*, and you're still here trying to fix your relationship."

"What's your point?"

"Why is everyone else allowed to make mistakes but you? You're here, punishing yourself because . . . what? You had sex with the wrong person one time?"

"Not just the wrong person, Charlotte," I say quietly. "My brother's girlfriend."

"Okay. Sure," she says. "But can you honestly tell me you regret it? That you wish it never happened?"

"No. Of course not," I admit. "Sadie—"

"Forget Sadie for a second," Charlotte cuts in, eyes blazing. "You've loved Josie since you were a kid."

"I have."

"Do you still love her?"

There's no hesitation this time. "No. We tried. It didn't work."

"Right," she says, like she's unveiling something I've refused to see. "And you wouldn't have known that if you hadn't slept with her. If you hadn't married her. You'd still be chasing the idea of her. And meanwhile, your brother would've married her instead of Primrose. Do you think he'd prefer that?"

"No, he's happier than he's ever been. But—"

"So what you're saying," she says, stepping toward me, "is that everyone ended up better off because of what happened."

"It still doesn't mean it wasn't a mistake."

"Maybe not." She stops in front of me, close enough that I can see the anger tightening in her jaw. "But here's the thing: some mistakes you *have* to make. Because that's the only way to know they were mistakes in the first place. And sometimes, the bigger mistake is not doing anything at all. Because then you're just stuck. Wondering *what if* for the rest of your life."

I blink at her.

"You keep crucifying yourself over the same thing, like if you punish yourself enough, you'll never screw up again. Like you can earn some kind of immunity to being human."

I don't get it. Why is she so angry? "If that's how you feel, then why did you shut me down last night?"

Her chin tilts up with pride. "Because I don't want you to hide behind the shitty day you had, the hard time you're going through. I want you to make a choice, even if it's a mistake."

I can't afford making a mistake so bad it hurts everyone around me. Losing the respect of everyone who means something to me. Of myself.

"You don't get it. I have responsibilities, people who count on me. Sadie, and—"

"You're living your life like your only job is damage control, Aaron," she insists. "Like if you collect enough points, you'll finally earn everyone's forgiveness. Everyone's love."

I swallow hard, my head pounding. She's wrong. She has to be.

"You know what I think?" she says quietly. "I think your brother moved on, Josie moved on, and yet you're still there, waiting for everyone's permission to do the same."

My breaths fan out fast, my chest tight. "Enough, Charlotte."

"I think you're so scared of being the villain in someone else's story that you forgot how to be the hero in your own."

She doesn't understand. People love to romanticize unconditional love, but that's just a Hollywood fantasy. Real relationships aren't about blind devotion; they're about balance. A constant give-and-take where both people show up, put in the effort, and work through the hard parts together. Love isn't a promise—it's a choice, made over and over again.

And now it's my time to choose Logan. Amelie. Ian.

Not myself.

"If you were living life for yourself, you'd slam me against that counter, wouldn't you?" Her nose almost brushes mine, lips breathing on my skin. "You'd show me how much you want me, and there would be no second-guessing. No mistakes, no regrets. Would there?"

My fingers twitch, aching to touch her, but I stop myself. My heart thuds harder, faster. It feels like I'm suffocating. I want her, and it scares the hell out of me. I breathe in, but the air feels too thick, like I'm trapped in some kind of fucked-up loop I can't escape.

"But you won't," she says, voice cold. "Because that would mean accepting you're *not* perfect. That you never will be, and if the people around you can't get on board with that, then they don't deserve to be in your life."

"Enough," I grind out. "Please, just . . . stop talking."

"You—"

"Shut up, Charlotte," I snap, hating the words as they come out.

She lifts onto her toes, and for a breath—just one—I think she's going to kiss me. Or smack me. Instead, her grin turns lethal, her chin jerking up in a dare. "Make me."

Fuck.

Something inside me snaps. Maybe it's the way she challenges me, the way she's been pushing and pushing, teasing me for weeks with every word, every glance. Maybe it's the fact that she's right; I want her, and I'd rather regret her than never know how she feels.

Before I can stop myself, my hands are on her, grabbing her by the arms, walking back until her ass hits the counter. The sharp sound of her gasp echoes through the kitchen, and her breath comes in quick, shallow bursts as she stares up at me, a defiant glint in her eyes.

The now small, feeble voice of reason reminds me that this is a choice I can't come back from, a path I've already walked and brought me to my demise. But Charlotte is right—maybe this is a mistake I have to make. Maybe life isn't worth living without those.

I'm so fucking close I can taste her, my hands gripping the counter beside her as I lean in, and every instinct in me screams to kiss her, to press my lips to hers until neither of us can breathe. Maybe she'd let me—she hasn't pulled back. But I don't want to ignore her *no kissing* rule, so my lips find her neck instead.

The first touch is tentative, just the barest graze of my mouth against her skin, but it's enough to wipe any doubt. Enough for me to know that mistake or not, I'm never regretting this. The pulse under my lips, the warmth, the soft, flowery edge of her scent—I can't stop.

My hands roam over her body. I kiss her harder, more urgently, my mouth leaving a wet trail across her skin as I move from her neck to her collarbone, then lower. I follow the curve of her chest, her ragged breath matching mine, my hands sliding down her sides then gripping her hips.

The hem of her dress brushes against my face as I drop to my knees, until my hands lift it higher, exposing the slope of her thighs. My breath catches in my throat when I look up at her, my fingers trembling as I push the fabric higher inch by inch.

Dark green eyes are on me, lips parted and gasping for air.

"Tell me to stop," I growl as I notice the wet patch on her see-through pink panties, fingers hooking at the sides.

"No."

Fuck, fuck, fuck.

I slide her panties down her legs, the scent of her arousal the only thing I can focus on. That is until I hook one of her legs over my shoulder and I'm faced with her pussy, bare and glistening.

She's breathtaking. All freckled skin, her chest rising and falling rapidly, her nipples straining against the fabric of her dress.

Her thighs part a little wider, so open, so inviting . . .

And I can barely *breathe*.

My lips graze her inner thigh first, just the lightest brush, and Charlotte gasps, her fingers diving into my hair, tugging, guiding. I don't give in yet. Instead, I take my time, dragging my mouth higher, closer, teasing her with featherlight kisses and warm exhales.

Her whimper nearly breaks me.

Some part of me thought I'd never get to do this. I certainly thought so on our first night together on TOP. I watched her come thinking that's all I'd get from her. And now she's here, dying for me to eat her out.

Maybe the last two years weren't a punishment—just a test, and this is my fucking prize.

Her hips lift off the counter, desperate for more, but I press a firm hand to her stomach, holding her down. When I glance up, her eyes are heavy-lidded, pupils blown wide, cheeks flushed. She looks . . . ruined. *Destroyed*. And I haven't even started yet.

"Please," she slurs, breaths shaking out of her lips.

"Yes, baby." I lower my mouth to her center, the first swipe of my tongue making her cry out. "I need it too."

She tastes sweet and tangy, fucking perfect. I groan into her, my brain in a frenzy as I lap at her folds, circling her clit and drinking in every gasp and broken plea she gives me.

She tastes better than every fantasy I've had rolled into one. Like this pussy is fucking *mine*.

"Fuck, I love older men," she says in a breathy laugh as she angles her hips toward me, holding on to the microwave handle behind her for balance.

Relentless, I drag my tongue over her, savoring the way she

writhes against my mouth. Her fingers twist in my hair, tugging, trying to get me to go faster, then trying to pace herself, like she's afraid of coming apart too soon.

But I don't want her afraid. I want her lost. I want her fucking ruined.

I slide two fingers inside her, coaxing, stretching. Then deeper, curling upward, searching until she gasps sharply. Her whole body tenses as I stroke that spot again and again—right there—my tongue working her clit in tandem. Her moans turn frantic, breathy, her hand tugging at my hair harder.

I remember what she told me on TOP—that the only way a man has ever made her come is by going down on her. If I'm not mistaken, her exact words were "like a man starved."

Which works out just fine, because it's exactly what I am.

I flick my tongue and press until she's right there, until she's trembling on the edge, her breath catching in her throat.

Eyes widening, she tenses up, then she shatters.

Her body jerks and she tightens her thighs around my head as pleasure crashes over her in waves. I don't stop. I keep stroking, licking, drawing out every last tremor.

"Breathe for me, baby," I say when I realize she's pressing her lips tight.

She opens her mouth, her cry echoing off the kitchen walls, wild and raw.

Fuck, watching her come might be worth everything that's coming my way. Everything I undoubtedly deserve. So I don't stop. I work her through it until she's nothing but a shaking, writhing mess. Until she's limp and panting, her chest heaving, her body shuddering with the aftershocks. Then, still not ready to let her go, I suck on her clit one more time.

With a loud cry, she flinches, and through the haze, I hear the sharp pop of plastic and metal giving way.

I look up, confused, and my eyes go wide as I spot the source.

You must be *fucking* kidding me.

"HELLO?" Logan says as he picks up, the whirring of tractors unmistakable in the background.

I squeeze the microwave door in my hand, then look up at the rest of the built-in appliance, hinges dangling uselessly at either side. My throat is dry, my hands clammy, and my heart pounds so hard against my ribs it feels like it's trying to escape. "I messed up," I rasp.

There's a moment of silence, followed by an unimpressed "For fuck's sake. Who did you screw *now*?"

My heart stops for what feels like an entire minute. The scent of her is still clinging to me, a mix of jasmine and something warmer. I can feel her—her thighs trembling against the sides of my face, the way her fingers gripped my hair, the breathy moans that still echo in my ears. The taste of her lingers on my tongue, absolutely sinful. I can hear the microwave door she ripped off the hinges hitting the floor with a loud clunk before she mumbled a "Thank you, Chef" and walked away without hesitation.

"N-no one," I rush out. Technically not a lie. "I need help."

"Where are you?"

"At work."

Logan speaks to someone else, probably Kyle, then his voice comes back clearer. "Okay. Address?"

"No, wait. I need you to . . ." I stare at the detached microwave door clutched in my shaking hands, and my reflection stares back at me in the shiny metal, wild-eyed and pale. "Pick up some, uh, pieces."

Another long silence. "Look, if you killed someone—"

"A microwave," I blurt. "I killed a microwave."

"Okay. And you want me to . . ."

"*Fix it*," I shriek. My skin is damp, and I can't breathe. I fucked up so bad I can't fucking breathe.

There's a shuffle on the other end of the line, then a new voice. Kyle's voice. "Aaron?"

I squeeze my eyes shut. "Yeah."

"You broke a microwave?"

"Yes."

"How?"

Charlotte's lips parting in the most beautiful O flash through my mind. Her body arching, her eyes glazing over as she reached for something—anything—to hold on to. The microwave handle, apparently.

"I . . . pulled it too hard."

He snorts. "Is the door ripped off?"

"Yes," I whine, pinching the bridge of my nose. "What the fuck do I do?"

Kyle's laughter only makes the panic tighten in my chest. "I don't know, man. Open a beer and relax? It's just a fucking microwave."

"You don't understand." I pace the kitchen, sweat dampening the skin of my neck. "This is my second week, okay? And this woman is—she's a fucking nightmare. If she finds out . . ."

If she finds out that her daughter was standing against the counter, gasping in pleasure while I buried my face between her legs . . . *Oh my god. What have I done?*

"Amelie and Ian. They're counting on me—on Logan. I can't lose this job. I can't fuck up something else, Kyle, I—"

"Whoa, okay." Kyle's voice is less amused now. "Look, hold the door against the microwave and give it a strong push."

"Wait." I put him on speaker and do as asked, relieved when the door clicks into place. "Holy shit, it actually worked."

"Wonderful," he mocks.

"What next?"

"Open that beer."

Seriously?! "How's *that* a solution?"

"My cousin should be able to fix it properly, all right? I'll bring him over tomorrow."

I palm my forehead before barking my next words into the phone. "And what do I do until tomorrow? What if she tries to use it and it fucking falls on her head?"

"Really?" he says, his voice unbothered. "The woman with a private chef using the microwave? For what?"

My mouth opens, then closes. Shit. He's right. She doesn't approve of eating between meals. It could work.

"Okay. Yes. Okay. Call your cousin, please."

I hang up and look toward the potted fiddle-leaf fig by the archway, where I last saw Charlotte disappear. I just have to make it through lunch.

Yes, this was a mistake.

But this time, I'll take consequences over regrets.

Obsess

CHAPTER 17
Chef's Special

"How long until you're done?" I ask Roman, Kyle's cousin.

He glares at me, the kind of look that says I've asked one too many times, so I hold up my hands in surrender and turn back to the stove. The oil in the pan crackles as I let a drop of water test its heat, and when I lay the salmon down, the satisfying sizzle fills the kitchen. The rich scent of searing seafood rises, mingling with the citrus tang as I squeeze a lemon over the fish, the juice hissing.

I check my phone for the time and notice a missed call from Amelie. Especially after what Charlotte and I did yesterday, I'm desperate to confide in someone, but I can't talk to her about this. She'd tell Ian, and I'd lose my job.

"A lot more?"

"Jeez, Aaron. Let him work," Kyle says from the couch.

I fucking *told* him not to sit on the couch.

I check the time again. Charlotte isn't home yet but she could be any minute, and the last thing I want is to explain that the two guys in her kitchen are fixing the microwave door she ripped off when I was eating her pussy.

She hasn't brought any of it up since—in fact, she hasn't spoken to me at all, or even looked at me all of yesterday, for that matter. Maybe the second she got what she wanted I became old news. Boring. Maybe she's on to the next target and nothing will ever come out of what happened here yesterday. Hell, in the blur of my paranoia, I even visited her profile on TOP, but she wasn't there.

But hey, if she *did* move on, it's good, right? I mean, the thought of not touching her ever again feels like a lion is feasting on my innards, but it's *good*. Or at least that's what I'll keep telling myself.

"Okay, it's fixed."

"Seriously?"

Roman opens and closes the microwave door with exaggerated care, proving that it no longer hangs loose. "Seriously."

"Oh, thank fuck. How much do I owe you?"

He makes a *pfft* noise. "You're Kyle's friend."

"No, I insist." I tap my foot. "Send me an invoice. Kyle will give you my email. Now, please leave."

He gathers his tools, waves, and finally, *finally*, walks out. I turn back to the salmon just in time to stop it from burning, and when I look over my shoulder, Kyle is still lounging on the couch, watching me with a curious expression.

"Get the fuck out before they come back home, Kyle."

"Are you okay, man?"

Why is he still here? "Yes."

"Really? 'Cause you look like shit."

"Sadie is struggling to sleep through the night." Not a lie, but also not completely true. If Sadie weren't keeping me up with her nightmares, my own would.

"Okay. Well—"

The door opens, and my blood pressure spikes. I can feel it— blood pumping harder, sweat gathering on the back of my neck.

Kyle moves fast, ducking behind the couch like a reflex just as Charlotte steps into the kitchen. She crosses the room without hesitation and stops in front of me, close enough that the scent of her skin and the heat of her body scramble every coherent thought in my brain.

I have no idea what to expect. Did she tell her mom? Is she upset? Is she here to end whatever this is before it fully begins? Will she destroy more appliances?

"I need an orgasm," she says, voice casual. "And not just any orgasm—I need one of yours. One that makes me forget to breathe, that hits even harder because you talk me through it using a corny pet name. I need the Chef's Special. I need *you*." She runs her finger from my throat to the tip of my chin, tilting it slightly. "So come to my bedroom and get on your knees for me, Chef."

My heart flatlines.

She turns and walks away, her white sundress swaying with every step.

I'm still frozen in place when Kyle's head pops up from behind the couch, eyes wide with disbelief and just a hint of amusement.

"I—" My throat is dry. Holy shit, I can't believe he just heard all of that.

Kyle nods, biting back a grin. "Dude."

I scrub a hand down my apron. "I have no idea why—what—"

"Yeah. Sure you don't."

"She's . . ." His brows rise. "She's very, um, wild."

Wrong choice of words.

"Oh, yes she *is*."

"Shh, lower your voice," I whisper. "Not wild—what's the word . . ." I turn to the salmon, but it's well and truly smoking. With a curse, I turn off the stove. "Unpredictable," I finish as I turn to him. "That's the word. She's unpredictable."

Kyle's smile widens. "So you're not—"

"No," I say far too quickly. "No, I'm not," I try again. "I would never. That would be unprofessional—and she's *really* young."

He pauses. "How young?"

"No, she's . . ." Jesus, I can't even say it out loud. "Twenty . . . three."

"Huh." Kyle's silence is unnerving. I've never been a skilled liar, and it's obvious he doesn't believe me. What is it that Charlotte said? No poker face and no poker voice. Kyle points at the microwave. "Interesting."

I let out a short, disbelieving huff. "Kyle, you're wrong."

"Am I?"

"Yes, of course. She's . . ." I breathe out, then laugh. It comes out all high pitched, so I quickly stop. "You could say she's been flirting."

"You could."

"And—and she's been . . . after me, I guess?" I'm sweating. "But I would never . . ."

I watch his expression and know there is just no fucking way he's ever going to buy any of this.

Shoulders deflating, I admit, "It happened once."

He holds up a hand with a revering smile. "Respect, Coleman."

"I'm not going to *high-five* you, Kyle." I dry the sweat off my forehead. "We just . . . fooled around. Once. And it'll never happen again."

"Of course, because that'd be really wrong, and *nobody* likes forbidden sex. Yuck." He tucks his hand into his pocket, pointing at the corridor with the other. "You know what you should do? You should go tell her. Right now."

Though there's something in his tone that makes me nervous, I nod. He's right, I have to tell her. Especially after what she just said. I need her to understand that though I don't regret it, what we did yesterday can never happen again.

My heart hurts at the thought.

"Yeah. Yeah, I'll talk to her." He pats my shoulder, and it looks like he's smothering a grin. "Kyle, you can't—"

"I won't tell a soul." He walks toward the foyer. "Have fun."

"What?"

"I said 'Good luck,'" he calls as he closes the door behind him.

That's definitely *not* what he said, but it doesn't matter. I take my apron off and drop it on the counter, then walk to Charlotte's room. The hallway is long and sleek, lined with polished wood floors and abstract art that probably cost more than my car. This is the first time I've ventured this far into the penthouse, and I really hope Beatrice doesn't come back in time to see it.

I knock at the door, then feel like an idiot and open it. I immediately recognize the dimly lit room from our calls, catching new details, like the floor-to-ceiling windows draped in beige curtains. A velvet chaise lounge sits in the corner beside a cluttered vanity, and the air smells faintly of her perfume—sweet and heady.

Charlotte's lying in bed, scrolling on her phone. Meeting my gaze, she drops it beside her. "Finally."

She reaches under her dress and pulls her underwear down, and I get lost in the movement for a second—on the green silk sliding down her perfect thighs.

Quickly, I recover. "N-no, don't—don't take off, uh, anything."

She stops, panties halfway down her legs. "Why not?"

"Because . . ." *Focus, Aaron.* "Because everything I said is still true. I still work for your mom, and if this were to come out—"

She waves me off. "I won't say anything."

"And I'm so much older than you, Charlotte."

"Trust me, experience plays in your favor. I don't wreck appliances every time I orgasm."

I smile, then inwardly curse myself and stop. Her words feed my ego in a way I wasn't prepared to sustain. It's like she's fucking healing me, telling me that I *can* make sex pleasurable for someone. That it's not entirely my fault my wife refused to touch me for years. That I'm not completely broken.

She slides her underwear down to her ankles. "Remind me to breathe, Chef."

Though it's hidden by her dress, I can see her pussy as if it's engraved in my brain. I can smell her, taste her. I'm hard before I can shake my head again.

"My brother, Charlotte. My boss is counting on me, and I—" Her legs spread. "You're off-limits."

She pulls her dress up to her hips, uncovering her glistening pink pussy. "Good thing I'm not one to follow recipes."

I groan into my hand, my erection straining against my jeans and painfully pulsating.

What was I saying? I'm sure it was important.

"Your reluctance has been noted, Chef." Her hair is like a fiery halo on the pillow as her legs spread wider and her dress bunches at her hips. I can smell her—sweet, musky, fucking intoxicating. Her lips are wet, swollen, and begging for attention, with a single bead of arousal clinging to her slit, daring me to taste it. "You're a Good Guy. Capital Gs. Now, should I start without you?"

My breath comes in shallow gasps as I watch her tease herself, her hips rocking into her own touch. She's a fucking goddess, and I *need* to worship her.

Just once more. Seriously, what's one more time? It won't change a thing.

She must see the decision forming in my mind, because with a commanding voice, she says, "Close the door."

As if in a trance, I slam the door shut, then cross the room.

"On your knees, Chef."

I drop my knees to the floor, a roaring sound coming out of my throat.

"Now make me come on your tongue."

I dive forward and waste no time, burying my face between her legs. My beard is drenched even before I open my mouth and begin lapping at her.

"Oh, fuck," she whimpers, her thighs clamping around my

head as I work her clit with my tongue. "This is perfect, Chef. Perfect."

Wrong.

She's perfect.

The most perfect mistake.

I ROUND the corner at the apple orchard and find Kyle, shirtless and sweating, surrounded by a graveyard of chopped logs. He pulls out his headphones and grins. "Yo, Coleman!"

"Jesus," I say, eyeing the destruction. "How long have you been at this?"

"Couple of hours." He flexes, still gripping the axe. "But look at this. Huh? The ladies are going to love it this summer."

"Lucky them."

His grin turns coy. "*Soooo*, whatcha doing here?"

Immediately, I know he *knows*. Still, I stall. "Oh . . . I'm still waiting for your cousin's invoice. I figured I'd come remind you."

"Ah." He grabs a bottle of water, taking a long swig. "That's the best you got? Kinda sad."

"I mean it, I—"

"So how are things going with Charlotte?"

"Shhh," I hiss, glancing over my shoulder.

He raises both hands. "Dude, your brother has big ears, but he can't hear through walls."

I cross my arms, staring at the dirt beneath my boots. Kyle hit the nail on the head—I *am* here to talk about Charlotte. About what's been happening *daily* between us. But now that I'm looking into his eyes, I don't know what to say.

How are things going with Charlotte?

Hot. So incredibly hot. And so unbelievably complicated.

"We . . . we keep doing it."

"Oh, so you didn't end things with her, huh?" His crooked grin widens. "What a *shocking* plot twist on your part."

"Forget about it," I say, raising a hand and turning.

"Come on!" He throws a glove at me. "How's the sex?"

"We're not . . . not, uh . . . we only . . ."

"Show me with your hands."

Jesus. "Just oral sex." I step closer. "She texts me, asks me to come over earlier, and every single day, I do. Then I drop to my knees, and I . . ." I gesture vaguely at my mouth.

Kyle stares. "Every day?"

"Every day this week."

"But she doesn't—"

"Nope." I finally meet his gaze, immediately regretting it when I see the laugh he's fighting to hold back.

"So . . . you're her vibrator."

I roll my eyes. "Basically. But that's not the problem. I mean, it's . . ." My hand will probably start to cramp soon enough. "The point is, we don't kiss. We don't do anything else. There's nothing but *that* between us."

Now it sounds like I want a relationship with her. Which I don't—I obviously couldn't even if I did.

"Sounds like your tongue is the only thing between you two."

Ignoring him, I power on. "I just don't know what to do. Maybe I should resign—but I'd put Ian in a shitty position. He'd have to come back, find someone else to send in my place. So then . . . should I wait for him and Amelie to be back? And do I come clean then? And if not, how will I justify quitting? And what does that mean for Charlotte and me?"

"I'm sorry, *every day*? You just eat her up, then . . .?" He cackles. "Hey, it's still better than all talk and no sex, right? At least you get *something*."

Why am I here? Seriously . . . Kyle? *Kyle?*

I make a show of turning around and walking away, but he calls after me. "Where the hell are you going?"

"To talk to someone older than four."

"Like who?" He waits for me to turn before he says, "Not your bestie, since she's married to your boss. Not your brother, since he's the one who got you the job. Would your ex-wife have anything insightful to say?"

My jaw clenches. "I get it."

He steps closer, slapping a hand on my shoulder. "Look, I love this. *Love* it. It's so fucking messy—I'm having the time of my life. But I gotta say, man, it's good that you're getting used to shit exploding in your face."

My shoulders tighten. "This isn't going to end well, is it?"

"Nope. Eventually, her mom's going to find out she's been paying you to tongue-fuck her daughter."

I glare at him.

He widens his eyes dramatically. "*Ooh.* The vibrator's protective of his human." His voice takes on a more serious timbre. "Dude, Logan's not going to give you another chance. He's just not. And you worked too hard to find your footing after Josie."

I *know*. I *fucking know*. But she's a siren, and I'm lost at sea. All I hear is her call. All I can do is respond.

"She makes me feel alive." Besides Sadie, I've been so miserable. "My life has been a seven-year-long funeral. And now I feel like I'm back. Like I'm myself."

He studies me, for once serious. He doesn't have an answer—because there isn't one. Either I keep going and let this inevitable train wreck hit me at full speed, or I end it and return to existing in a lifeless limbo.

I don't know what's worse.

"Hey, maybe you'll meet someone else at the bachelor party."

I blink at him. "Bachelor party?"

"Yeah. For Logan."

Oh boy. "Let me stop you right there, Kyle. He's not going to want that. And if he does, it'll be at the farm. Us and the cows."

"Or he doesn't know that what he actually wants is a party. In a strip club. With lap dances, and drinks." He wiggles his eyebrows. "Huh?"

"He's going to make you wear your ass like a hat."

Kyle sighs dramatically. "What did you do for your bachelor party?"

My *what?* Josie and I got married in a rush after we found out about Sadie, not because we wanted to, but because her ultra-religious and old-fashioned family wouldn't accept her having a child out of wedlock. "I didn't have a bachelor party."

"*Seriously?*" he screeches.

I flinch, bringing a hand to my chest. "Jesus Christ. You raise your voice like that only if there's someone holding a gun to the back of my head."

"What do you mean you didn't have one?"

"I mean, my girlfriend was seven months pregnant, and neither my brother nor my best friends were speaking to me, so I didn't have one."

"Well, that's unacceptable." He claps. "We'll just have a double bachelor party."

"But I'm not a bachelor."

He tilts his head. "Well . . . technically . . ."

"I'm a divorcé, not a bachelor. Oh, and also, I don't want a bachelor party."

"All right, then we'll have a divorce party."

I watch him with a less-than-patient glare. "Kyle, Logan doesn't want a party. I don't want a party. It's his wedding, so how about we figure out something he'd enjoy? Like a . . . silent retreat in the forest?"

"Boring. The both of you. The boring Coleman brothers."

I ignore him, dropping onto a log. Bachelor party or not, I'm not going to find someone who'll distract me from Charlotte. Hell, I don't even want to be distracted. I want her—*more* of her.

He settles on a different log, and for a while, we just sit there, the air smelling like pine and fresh-cut wood.

"So, another redhead, huh?" he says after a while. "Subconsciously trying to replace your ex-wife?"

"Jesus. I didn't hold out auditions, Kyle."

"I'm just saying it's a recessive gene. Most people never get to date a redhead, and you're two for two."

"Can we talk about something else?"

"Sure, sure." He leans back. "So about the strip club . . ."

CHAPTER 18

A Plate Too Full

T he scent of roasted vegetables and garlic wafts through the house as Sadie and I step inside, the low hum of conversation trickling out from the kitchen. My mom's voice—warm, familiar—mingles with Primrose's gentle laughter, Logan's voice, and the occasional fussy coo from the twins. It's the first family dinner we've had since the twins were born six months ago, and it'd be almost peaceful, if it weren't for the troubling pile of secrets and tension threatening to bury us all.

Sadie tugs at my hand, leading me into the kitchen where Mom stands at the counter, preparing a salad. She looks up when I enter, and only briefly smiles before dragging Sadie into a tight hug.

Should she even be standing up after she twisted her ankle?

Primrose, holding one of the babies, grins. "Oh, good, you're here!"

Sadie darts toward the twins with a delighted squeal. "Can I hold them?"

"Are your hands clean?" Logan asks.

Sadie huffs but marches to the bathroom without complaint.

After watching her go, Logan finally looks at me and nods a half-hearted greeting.

Conversation flows easily enough as I settle at the table, though my responses are stilted. I don't know what to say to Mom that doesn't circle back to the one thing we're not talking about. I don't know how to sit at this table knowing she's making me lie to Logan. And I'm definitely out of ideas when it comes to getting him to open up.

My phone buzzes in my pocket. I slide it out under the table, not unlocking it, just glancing at the screen. There's a voice message from Charlotte, along with the preview banner of three separate texts.

> Thinking about you tonight.

> Don't play this in front of Sadie.

> Or anyone else you're not okay sharing me with.

I stare at my lock screen a beat too long, fighting a growing smile, before shoving the phone back into my pocket. I can't *wait* to listen.

Primrose launches into a story about the twins' latest milestone, and Logan chimes in with a correction, and Mom asks questions. It's all deceptively normal, until I see from the corner of my eye Mom's hands shaking as she tries to twist a jar of olives open. She grits her teeth, twisting harder.

Without thinking, I push back my chair and stand. "Here, let me—"

"Do you think I need help opening a jar, Aaron?" she asks, voice too loud, silencing the room as her head snaps up.

"I just—" I try, heat crawling up my neck.

"I *don't*," she barks, slamming the jar onto the counter.

"Daddy?"

Sadie, back from the restroom, looks up at me with wide and

worried eyes, so I sink back into my chair like nothing happened. "Took you a while, sweetheart. All good?"

"Y-yeah, I was talking to Grandpa." She walks closer, clinging to me and throwing a disgruntled look at her grandma. She's not the only one who noticed, unfortunately, because as I meet my brother's gaze, I see the silent question in his eyes.

"Oh, everyone is here already!" Darren says, interrupting the awkward silence as he steps into the kitchen. Sadie settles into her chair, her tiny arms carefully cradling one of the twins with a face of pure concentration as she supports the baby's head just like Primrose shows her. Logan watches her like a hawk, but when she doesn't drop his kid, he snaps his fingers.

"Aaron, help me grab the fold-up cribs from the car."

I know a bullshit excuse when I hear one, especially since my brother could probably carry the whole car inside the house. But I follow him obediently into the evening cool air.

He heads for the trunk, lifting it open before giving me a look. "What did you do?"

"What?"

He crosses his arms, leaning against the bumper. "Mom flipping out like that? You must've done something."

Of course he'd assume *I* did something.

"We had a bit of a spat," I admit. "But it's fine."

"A spat, huh? Does it have anything to do with her visit to the hospital the other night?" When I hesitate, wondering how much he knows, he shrugs. "Is that why you told me not to come?"

"What? No, I—"

"Take a second to really *think* about what you want to say right now, Aaron."

I scoff, watching his jaw tighten. "What, you're going to punch me like you did two years ago?" I point at the house. "Should I call my daughter so she can witness it this time? Your children? Our parents?"

"What are you hiding, Aaron?"

I look away, teeth grinding. I really need Mom to tell him about her diagnosis, because the last thing the two of us need is *more* reasons not to trust each other. "Nothing, I told you. We just had a spat."

He doesn't look convinced, but doesn't push it. Instead, he studies me for a beat too long. "You had a spat with Amelie too?"

For a moment, I'm too stunned to speak—her name was the last thing I expected out of his mouth. "What?"

"She called." He pulls the first crib from the trunk and sets it on the ground. "Said she hadn't heard from you in a while. Apparently, you've been ignoring her texts."

I focus on the crib, on anything but the weight of his judgmental stare. I haven't answered because she's the last person I want to lie to. And I *will* have to lie about everything that's happened with Charlotte. About what I've done with her every day this week.

"I'm not ignoring her," I say flatly, grabbing the second crib. "I've just been busy."

Logan watches me for a second longer before nodding. "Aaron, if you're in some kind of trouble . . ."

"I'm not." The response comes too fast, but I don't care. "Everything is fine."

He lets out a deep breath through his nose, the kind that usually means he's barely holding on to his patience. "Really? 'Cause you're acting cagey. And the last time you were acting cagey, you were fucking my girlfriend."

My fingers tighten around the crib frame, knuckles aching. I've wanted to talk about this for years, but now that the moment is here—brought up with all the grace of a sledgehammer—I want to shove it back into the dark corner we've both been pretending doesn't exist.

"Oh, so we're going there?"

Logan's expression hardens. "What's that supposed to mean?"

"Just that you've avoided having more than a surface-level

conversation with me for years. I wasn't sure we were *allowed* to discuss Josie."

He glares. "If you wanna talk, just talk."

I tug out my phone. "You know what? I'll text Amelie right now. Just to prove it's nothing, okay? Get off my back."

I unlock the screen, but instead of hitting Amelie's contact, Charlotte's voice message blasts through my speakerphone.

"Mmm . . . oh, fuck . . . I'm thinking about your tongue, Chef . . ."

Holy shit!

My hand flails for the screen like I'm swatting a bee. I miss. Miss again. The audio continues, lewd and unmistakable, echoing off the damn driveway like it's surround sound. I finally manage to slam the volume down, but not before a low whimper squeaks through.

When I look up at Logan, he's staring at me like I just kicked a puppy.

"I—sorry, I—" I clear my throat and try to summon a lie. Any lie. "I was just watching . . . porn today. Yeah. I love . . . porn."

He blinks.

"Audio porn," I clarify, because apparently I'm not done ruining my life. "It's . . . more immersive, you know? You get to picture yourself . . . and it's more family-friendly, right?" *Huh?!* "And, uh . . ."

There's a beat of silence so long I wonder if I've entered a different plane of existence. "Are you sleeping with Amelie?"

"*What?*" The air is sucked from my lungs so fast it leaves me lightheaded, my chest twisting violently enough that I *physically* clench.

His eyes are sharp, assessing my reaction. "Because I might not like Ian, but I will kick your ass in his place."

The idea of him even *thinking* that makes the blood boil in my veins. Is that how he sees me? As some asshole who goes after other men's wives? That Josie wasn't just an isolated incident, but a pattern?

I step forward before I can think better of it, closing the space between us. "Are you fucking *kidding* me? You think I would do that? After everything?"

His expression doesn't change. "You tell me. Did *she* send you that?"

"No! I told you, it's—"

"You know, it's not very reassuring that you'd rather me thinking you listen to family-friendly audio porn—whatever the fuck *that's* supposed to be—than just tell me who you're seeing."

I laugh, but it's humorless, jagged. "I'm not *sleeping* with Amelie. She's a friend."

He smacks his lips. "So was Josie, before you slept with her."

Wow.

"So that's it?" I ask. "I'll forever be the guy you can't trust around your wife? The guy who's just one step away from fucking someone else's woman? I make one mistake, one misstep, and that's all I am?"

"Why won't you just tell me why you're avoiding her, huh? Just tell me who *that* was."

I pause, mind wandering.

Maybe Logan has a point. Sure, Charlotte is single, but she's also the last person I should be involved with. Is he right? Am I just a step away from shoving my dick somewhere I shouldn't?

Instead of saying any of that, I lean closer to his face. "It's none of your fucking business."

Logan bends down and grabs the crib. "Fine."

My heart is still hammering, but the moment is over. I should be relieved as he walks back into the house, ready for another evening of polite, empty chatter.

I'm not.

"WHY DON'T you let her sleep here?" Mom says as she closes the door behind Logan, Primrose, and the girls, then makes her way back into the kitchen. She's talking about Sadie, who's currently napping on Darren's shoulder in front of the fireplace.

"Hm? No, that's okay."

"You look like you're not getting much sleep. Is she still having nightmares?"

I nod, watching her struggle to walk. "Yeah. But Miss Delaney, her teacher, says she's doing better. I'm worried about Mother's Day, but . . . she'll get through it. We both will."

Mom settles onto the chair next to mine in the silence that wraps around us. She pats my hand and asks, "You and your brother had a fight?"

Of course. She's always been perceptive, which didn't often work in my and Logan's favor when we lived at home. "Yup. Just the usual, don't worry."

"Was it about me? About . . ." She looks down at her hand, clenches it, then tucks it away.

"No," I lie. "He accused me of sleeping with a friend."

She blinks, like she doesn't understand the problem with that.

"A married friend," I clarify.

For a moment, her lips form a small circle. Then: "Are you?"

For fuck's sake. "Mom!"

"Oh, Aaron." She cups my cheek. "You carry so much on your shoulders. All this guilt and pain, all these impossible standards you set for yourself, the responsibilities you feel like you have to face alone . . . You know what happens when gas inside a bottle builds up?"

"The cap pops off?"

She nods, smiling wide. "So who is she?"

I open my mouth. Close it. I should say no one and move on—brush it off like I've done with everyone else prying into my life lately. But it's Mom, and I'm scared shitless of all the things I *won't* get to share with her.

"Her name's Charlotte."

"Charlotte," she repeats, like she's weighing it on her tongue. "What does she do?"

"She's . . ." I think of her profile on TOP and clear my throat. "She models."

Mom narrows her eyes. "Oh, Aaron. Are you making up girlfriends again?"

I roll my eyes. "No, Mom. I'm not fourteen. And she's not my girlfriend, but she *is* a model. She likes designing clothes too."

"A model *and* designer." Her eyes brighten. "She must be smart and beautiful. Can I see her?"

Her TOP profile flashes through my mind again—Charlotte, sprawled out and bent like a pretzel, wearing next to nothing, watching the camera like she'll fuck you then fuck you over.

"I don't have any pictures."

Mom hums a disappointed sound. "Well, is she single?"

"*Yes*, she is."

"So what's the problem?"

That's the million-dollar question, isn't it? "There's several. First of all, I have no idea what we *are*. She's not exactly looking to settle down."

"Are you?"

I open my mouth, then close it. "I guess that's the second problem."

"And the third?"

"She's, um . . . young."

Mom's posture stiffens slightly. "Not *inappropriately* young, right?"

"She's twenty-three."

Mom lets out a low whistle, shaking her head. "Aaron, honey, that's . . . quite the gap."

"I know."

She studies me for a long moment, tilting her head slightly. "You *like* her."

"I—" I start, but she gives me a look. The kind only a mother can give, that says *Don't even think about lying to me.*

"Yeah. I do."

She picks up a loose crumb on the table. "And does she like you back?"

I think of Charlotte's teasing smirks, how she gets under my skin like it's her favorite pastime. How she looks at me when she thinks I'm not paying attention—like I'm something she doesn't want to want, but can't help herself.

"I think she does," I admit quietly. "In her own way."

Mom's fingers find mine. "Then what are you so afraid of?"

Everything.

"Though she *is* single, there are other factors that make it complicated."

"Well, dear, whoever said love is simple wasn't paying attention. People are complicated, therefore so are relationships."

"Yes, but after everything that happened with Josie—"

"That's in the past," she cuts me off.

"But it's not. I've worked so hard to earn back Logan's respect—I still am. If he found out about this, he wouldn't understand."

Her shoulders slump. "Different dads, and my sons are equally stubborn. It oughta be studied."

"Really?" I muse. "You can't find *any* explanation for it?"

She playfully smacks the side of my head. "Don't you use that tone with your mother."

When I raise a hand in defeat—and self-defense—she points a finger at me. "You listen to me, Aaron Coleman. We are a *family.* We don't keep score, or use past mistakes to harm each other. Your brother isn't quite ready to forgive you yet, maybe, but he'll get there. You need to live your life knowing that if you fall, your family will catch you. That here," she says as she holds a hand to her chest, "you'll always find support and love."

I squeeze her hand over the table.

"Thank you, Ma." This is all true when it comes to her or

Darren. But Logan? There's too much hurt for that. Too much history to ignore.

Mom leans back in her chair, tilting her head like she's watching a movie play in her mind. "This reminds me of Mr. Bubbles's death."

I blink. "The goldfish?"

She nods. "You were, what, ten? And you decided it was your fault he died because you forgot to feed him one morning. Never mind that you fed him so much every other day, I'm pretty sure he went into cardiac arrest from overeating. You spent a whole week in mourning."

I nod, vaguely remembering the fish but almost tasting the sense of guilt I felt back then. "What does Mr. Bubbles have to do with anything?"

"You gave him a funeral in the backyard, remember that? You and Logan wore suits, and you made me officiate. And then, instead of flushing him down the toilet like a normal person, you insisted on giving him a Viking funeral in the kiddie pool. Complete with a Popsicle-stick boat and a candle."

I stare at her. "Let me guess. I almost set the farm on fire?"

She grins. "Oh no, honey. You *tried* to set a fire. The boat just kind of . . . sank immediately. And you cried harder because now you thought you'd drowned Mr. Bubbles."

Right, right. I believe the term being thrown around was "re-murdered."

"You have always, *always* held on to guilt like it's a full-time job. But the point is," she says, patting my hand, "that life isn't a fish funeral, Aaron."

"*That's* the point?"

"You were a kid who made a dumb mistake. Just like now, you're a man who made a human one. You messed up with Logan. We all know that. But it's time to stop living like you need to earn your place back in his life. Like you're on some lifelong quest for redemption."

I swallow hard, her words sinking deep.

"You've said you're sorry. You've shown it in every way a person can. And if that's still not enough for him, that's *his* burden to carry. Not yours."

I look down at the table, our hands still linked. "I just . . . I want to be better. For him. For Sadie. For—"

"Be better for you," she interrupts gently. "Not because you owe it to anyone. Not because you're afraid of messing up again. Do it because you love yourself enough to believe you deserve good things, too."

A lump rises in my throat. I nod, because it's all I can manage.

She leans in and kisses the top of my head. "And for the record, my eulogy was perfect. If anybody had cared about that fish beside you, there wouldn't have been a dry eye on the farm."

I squeeze her arms, eyes stinging.

"Thanks, Ma."

"Anytime, sweetheart." She lets out a yawn. "I think it's time for me to get to bed."

I glance at the clock. It's not even that late, and Mom always used to be the last to turn in. Is she just aging, or is it the disease? "Yeah, go. I'll wake Darren up," I offer.

She pats my arm as she stands, wincing slightly as she shifts her weight onto her bad ankle and limps toward the hallway. "Thank you, sweetheart."

"Mom?" I call as she's shuffling away. "I'm not the only one who shouldn't shoulder every single problem alone, you know."

Her smile wavers. "You and Logan are my sons. You're not supposed to take care of me—*I'm* supposed to take care of you."

"Maybe this whole thing works better if we all take care of each other."

She looks out through the patio door in thought. When she turns back to me again, she grins. "After the wedding. Let Logan enjoy his big day, then I'll tell him."

CHAPTER 19
Simmer Down, Chef

I park in front of Beatrice and Charlotte's apartment complex, an unsettling feeling crawling up my spine.

When Beatrice texted this morning, she didn't say what the issue was. Just that she was sorry to bother me on a Sunday, that something in the kitchen broke down and she needed me to come over at my earliest convenience. It could mean a million things, but I have a sinking feeling I already know.

The damn microwave.

I should've just told her I broke it. Should've come up with some bullshit excuse instead of getting it fixed myself. But if it's still not working, if she found out, if she's pissed—

I push that thought down as I walk past the usher and take the elevator. I ring the doorbell, and Beatrice opens it a moment later, standing there in her usual pristine way—straight-backed, expression unreadable, not a silver hair out of place. She doesn't invite me in, just steps aside like she expects me to know better than to linger.

"Chef Coleman." Her tone is all business. "Thank you for coming."

"No problem. What's wrong?"

"It's the—" She waves a hand toward the kitchen as she walks ahead. "The stupid burner. It won't turn on."

Relief floods through me, and the tension that had been gripping my shoulders falls away. "Oh. Let me take a look."

I enter the open space and throw a glance at Charlotte, who's sitting at the table. Headphones on, she's drawing on her sketchpad, but her gaze meets mine, and she smirks. Trouble. She's trouble in a sexy blue minidress.

I lower to my haunches, checking the gas valve, then turn the knob and press it until the burner clicks to life. Beatrice watches, unimpressed.

" . . . Seriously?"

"Maybe the ignition was being fussy. It happens."

I glance at the fridge, the sink, the half-prepped ingredients on the counter. It looks like she was in the middle of cooking before the burner stopped working. Or like a hurricane recently hit her kitchen. A citrus juicer is out, sticky with orange pulp. There's a small saucepan with caramelized sugar cooling near the back, and beside it, a duck breast, skin scored, waiting to be seared.

"I can take care of lunch," I offer. "Since I'm already here."

Beatrice's sharp gaze cuts to me. "Please, I already feel silly for calling you over. You're not supposed to work for us on weekends."

"I don't mind, really," I say.

She glances toward the counter, and when she speaks, her voice is cooler than before. "No. You do enough for us. How about you stay for lunch?"

I start to shake my head but she turns toward the fridge, already dismissing me.

"I insist," she says over her shoulder. "Sit down, relax."

I hesitate, then glance back at Charlotte. This is atypical, isn't it? Beatrice asking me to stay over for lunch? She's barely interacted with me for weeks, but I'm now supposed to buy that the woman who made me restart an omelette four times doesn't want to inconvenience me?

Weird, but I get to sit with Charlotte for a while, so I'll take it.

There's that same mischievous glint in her eyes as I walk over, then pull out the chair next to her. With a glance at the drawing of a gown she's working on, I sit.

"Charlotte."

"Chef," she says in acknowledgment.

Nothing else, but I think she sees it in my eyes. That I've missed her, that I've been thinking about her non-stop. That I'm starting to dislike weekends, because I don't get to hear her voice and bury my face between her legs.

Beatrice works in silence for a while, and the scent of onions and shallots sautéing in duck fat fills the air, sharp and savory. She deglazes the pan with orange juice and Grand Marnier, her movements precise. There's no sense that she actually enjoys cooking—it's just something to be done—but she definitely knows her way around the kitchen.

"I'm sure this won't be anywhere near as good as what you're used to," she says.

"I'm not that picky."

"That's kind of you to say. But I assume your standards are higher than most." She stirs the sauce in the pan, its amber sheen catching the light. "Where'd you learn? Cooking school?"

Charlotte is still holding her pencil but she's no longer sketching. Annoyance flickers across her face, quick but noticeable. Is she bothered that I'm interacting with her mom?

I meet her gaze, trying to silently reassure her that everything's fine, then say, "Amelie Preston taught me most of what I know, actually."

Charlotte's jaw tenses. Not a flinch, exactly—but something cold and unreadable flashes through her eyes.

"Really?" Beatrice hums, spooning some of the sauce onto a tasting dish and blowing on it delicately. "Daisy's chef." She glances at me. "She's mentioned in every cooking magazine possible."

Charlotte shifts beside me, still pretending to be absorbed in her sketchbook, and just as I open my mouth to tell Beatrice just how special Amelie's cooking is, her hand lands on my thigh.

I throw her a panicked glance, but she ignores me, eyes stuck to the paper. Her fingers flex and dig into the muscle just above my knee.

Fuck, her touch sends a jolt straight to my groin.

I try to subtly shift away, but her hand follows, sliding higher, grazing my inner thigh.

Beatrice is now reducing the sauce, her back to us. She's oblivious to what's happening here, but if I want to keep it that way, I need to say something.

"Her late father was an internationally renowned chef, and she's pretty much blowing him out of the park. It's quite—" Charlotte's hand slides further up. I can't breathe. "Im-impressive."

"Yeah. 'Impressive' is a way to describe that man."

Sensing the disdain in her voice, I ask, "Did you know him?"

"Not personally, no. I saw him on TV more than I cared to though." She smacks her lips. "Distasteful man, I always thought."

"Sometimes," I agree, thinking of the way he often blew up at the contestants of The Silver Spoon. "But duck à l'orange? That's *his* recipe."

She turns around, shoulders stiff. "Excuse me?"

"That's, uh . . . that's what you're doing, right? Duck à l'orange?" For a moment, I'm afraid she'll throw a knife at me. "You used Grand Marnier—that was one of his staples."

Charlotte makes an amused "hm" sound, and just when I think Beatrice will walk over and shove a duck breast down my throat, she grins. "I had no idea."

"I'm not surprised. It's in most recipe books about French cuisine."

"I'm really looking forward to eating at Daisy," Beatrice says, her voice casual. "But not until Amelie's back. I refuse to eat anything from a backup chef."

Charlotte's fingers are inching closer to the danger zone, massaging and caressing, and all I can fucking think about is her hand—how her thumb is pressing into the flesh of my leg, how her nails are just barely scratching at my jeans.

"Yeah, no, you should definitely wait," I manage to grind out. Fuck, she's so close to my dick now I can feel the heat radiating from her palm. My balls tighten, and I bite the inside of my cheek to keep from groaning. "There's no one quite like her."

"Mm. Well, I can tell you've been trained by someone exceptional. Your food speaks for itself."

"Thanks. Really." I try to move Charlotte's hand away, but her grip tightens. Fuck, she's killing me. "I was—lucky," I choke out.

Beatrice's eyes linger on me for a moment too long before she turns back to the stove.

Charlotte takes that as her cue to go full throttle. Her hand moves again, and this time her fingers are right there, cupping my dick through my jeans, her palm pressing into the length of it.

She's not even fucking touching me directly, but after five days of eating her out, it's enough to make me want to explode.

Beatrice's phone buzzes loudly, cutting through the silence. She wipes her hands on a dish towel before pulling it from her pocket.

"Oh, damn it." She gives her silver hair a quick fluff. "I forgot about this meeting. It'll probably be fifteen minutes," she says, tapping to accept the call. She turns off the burner. "Lunch is ready. Serve yourselves if you're hungry, all right?"

She steps away, voice dropping as she answers, her words trailing off as a door shuts somewhere in the penthouse. The second she's gone, I turn to Charlotte, my hand snapping to her wrist to remove it from my leg.

"What the hell are you doing?" I hiss. "Your mom is right *there*."

Before I can react, she swings a leg over mine, straddling my lap with the kind of confidence that makes my cock throb. Her weight settles over me, her pussy pressing on me through our clothes. Fuck—she's warm. Soft. *So* soft. "She said fifteen minutes."

My hands fly to her waist in an attempt to push her off, but she just grins down at me, her lips curling into a devilish smile.

"What's the problem?" She says into my ear, her fingers trailing up my chest. "I thought you could handle a little *pressure*."

She rolls her hips against mine and I choke back a groan. My erection is trapped between us, aching and desperate, and when she rocks forward again, I can't stop the sound that escapes me—a low, guttural noise as her teeth sink into the side of my neck.

"Charlotte," I breathe. "Beatrice could walk back in any second."

"Then we better enjoy it while we can." Her hands slide up my chest, her fingers splaying across my pecs as she grinds down on me again. "Or would you rather think about how *amazing* Amelie is?"

Amelie? Is that why she's doing this?

I thought she was annoyed her mom was talking to me, that this was just another act of rebellion and I was caught in the cross-fire. Is she jealous? Is that the problem? Because she's never reacted that way to Josie, but this isn't the first time she's seemed annoyed at Amelie.

The friction is maddening, the heat of her pussy burning through the thin fabric of her panties. My hands tighten on her sides, but the fight in me is melting faster than ice cream in a heat-wave as I pant hard and fast.

"You feel so tense. Does this help?"

"Fuck, Charlotte." Unable to hold back, I press my lips to her neck. I feel the pleasure building, crawling up my spine, mixing with the taste of her skin, with the sound of her little gasps as she works herself up. "Amelie is just a friend. You know that."

"Stop thinking about her then."

"Your mom—"

"Stop thinking about her too."

"We can talk, you know. Me and you," I say as she tugs at my hair. I try to focus, to picture anything but her expression every time I make her orgasm. "About your feelings? You don't need to do this."

Through her chuckle, she rasps, "Feelings? Afraid that's not part of the deal, Chef." Her tongue licks up my neck. "But *this* is."

"Wait, Charlotte—"

It's too much. Too. Much.

My hand tightens at her waist, hard enough that she'll wear the proof of it tomorrow. I grind her down over my lap, thrusting up to meet her, desperate friction sparking through every layer between us. The other hand slides into her hair, twisting, forcing her to look at me.

"Don't look away," I growl.

Her lashes flutter. The next time her thighs clench around mine, the tension snaps. An orgasm crashes over me in waves so intense I can't stop it. It's been too fucking long and she's been teasing me too mercilessly.

A ragged groan rips from my throat as I bury my face in her shoulder and hold her flush against me. My cock jerks, spilling hot and helpless into my jeans, the damp heat spreading as she strokes my back.

Shit.

Shit, I just came inside my pants.

Did she notice? She definitely noticed. This is fucking embarrassing. What if Beatrice comes back now? What if it's visible through my jeans?

Charlotte strokes my hair, and though my ears are ringing, I can hear her mom talking on the phone in the other room. I look up at her and meet her gaze. It doesn't look mocking—maybe she didn't notice after all.

"Of course," she says sweetly, one hand cupping my face. "I should have known."

Known? "What?" I force out.

"That you'd look so pretty when you come . . ." Her smile widens. "Cole."

CHAPTER 20
Honey, Don't Hurt Me

E very day last week, Charlotte texted me in the morning. The same message, like clockwork. "Come over." Every day, I left my house early and came here. She took my hand at the entrance, then led me to her room, where she stripped off her panties and told me to get on my knees.

And every day, I did.

But since the awkward lunch we shared with her mom yesterday—when she returned to the kitchen and we ate in uncomfortable silence, my briefs wet and sticky—I haven't heard a peep from her, and there was no message this morning.

What's going on is no mystery. She knows I'm Cole—that I've outright lied to her when she asked me if we'd ever been on a live. And I don't know how she figured it out or when, but she must be livid. Too pissed off to want me around, apparently. Maybe too angry to ever want my mouth on her again.

I told myself to stay home, to take the silence as a sign. But my feet carried me here anyway, my body too used to the routine she's carved into my mornings. I came early, the same as always, hoping to find her waiting. To feel her fingers curl into my shirt and pull me in. To hear her exhale, sharp and wanting, when I touch her.

But she isn't here.

I drop my bag onto the counter and hesitate. Should I go to her room? This is clearly a message, and the silence means I should walk away, let this thing fizzle out before it ends in disaster. Before I'm left wanting more than we could possibly have.

Maybe this is what's happening—she's setting me free. Except it feels like being chained to the ground after learning how to fly.

I'm considering leaving when I hear a noise from deeper in the penthouse. Guttural. Pained.

Shit.

She's sick. My body moves until I knock on the second door—the bathroom. "Charlotte?"

There's a pause. Then a hoarse, "Aaron?"

"Are you okay?"

The toilet flushes, then the sink runs. A few seconds later, the door swings open and she steps out, her skin pale, her lips pressed together like she's annoyed to find me standing there. Her cheeks are flushed, her hair messy.

"Why are you here?"

I hesitate. "Uh, I—"

"I didn't text you."

"I know." Yeah, she definitely hates me. "I was worried."

She glares like I'm being ridiculous, then moves past me, retreating to her room. She doesn't close the door, so I take it as permission to follow, stopping just inside the threshold.

"Can I make you tea or something?"

"I'm fine."

She doesn't look fine. She looks exhausted, like she barely has the energy to stand. But I know better than to push, so I nod, shifting on my feet.

"I was going to make mushroom risotto for lunch, but if you—"

"I'm not hungry."

"Okay." Her voice feels final, like a door slamming shut. I

should leave it at that, but I need to say something. "Do you want to talk about it?"

She doesn't look up from her phone. "About what? Nausea?"

"No, not that. About what happened yesterday."

Her eyes narrow. "Yesterday?"

"Yes. The . . ." How do I phrase it? "The whole . . . *Cole* situation."

She hisses through her teeth. "Yeah, Aaron, that's not really a *yesterday* thing." Her finger traces a circle around her face. "What's the one game you should never play?"

"Poker," I mumble on auto-pilot. Wait, does that mean . . . "You *knew*?"

"The moment your eyes went all deer-in-headlights when Beatrice introduced us."

Oh, for crying out loud. She's been playing me this whole time —probably laughing at my expense when I tried to hide the fact that I have a cat, or when I slipped up and told her about the art equipment in her room.

I should be mad, but I deserve it after lying to her.

"So you're not . . . angry?"

"About you not wanting to share with your client's daughter that you're the guy who burst into tears after she gave you an orgasm?" Her nose wrinkles, but she's clearly amused. "Nah, I kind of get it."

"Not exactly my proudest moment."

"I know you think so." She drops onto her bed. "But it was what you needed. I'm just glad I could provide."

Okay, so that's . . . sorted, I guess. But if that's not the reason she didn't text this morning, then there's gotta be something else. Is it because she feels sick? That doesn't explain her bad mood.

"What's going on?" I ask, blanking on something better.

"Nothing's going on." She still keeps her nose buried in her phone, avoiding my gaze. "I'm on my period, cramps are killing me, and you heard what just happened in the bathroom."

So that's why she didn't text. She didn't need me. Simple as that.

A bitter taste fills my mouth. What did I expect? That she'd call me just to talk? That she'd ask me to hold her, to stay? She was clear about what this is—she told me yesterday, before she made me spill into my briefs. Feelings aren't part of the deal.

"A heads-up wouldn't have hurt," I say before I can stop myself.

She looks up sharply. "I need to explain myself for not wanting to have sex with you?"

"Sex?" I bark a laugh. "We don't have *sex*."

"Really? What's with the attitude, Chef?"

Unbelievable. "We don't have sex, Charlotte. You use me—not even all of me, just my mouth. My lap, if you want to piss off your mom. And when you're done, you toss me aside."

She lets out a sharp, mirthless chuckle. "And what do you do with me on TOP? You watch me. You use me. And then you leave." Her gaze is razor-sharp. "Why should I act any different?"

My chest tightens. I don't even know what we're talking about anymore. Is she mad because she thinks I've been watching her on TOP? She's always known I'm Cole, so she *must* know I haven't. Not since that night we talked for hours.

"I'm not . . . I haven't been on TOP."

She tilts her chin slightly, studying me from beneath her lashes. "That's right. *You're* not on top." She glares. "*I* am."

The words land like a slap, cold and cutting.

"What did you think, huh? That because we've been fooling around, I now owe you something? I *don't*. You don't even know me, Aaron. You don't know the first thing about me, and if you did, you wouldn't be here. If you knew the real reason—"

She cuts herself off, but I *want* to know. "The real reason . . . for what?"

"Forget it."

"No, Charlotte, I—"

"I said forget it." Her gaze holds mine. "Just do me a favor, all right? Don't pretend this is something it isn't, and don't leave the door open on your way out."

I watch her for a beat, then, with a tight jaw, I turn and walk away.

She wanted to hurt me, and she fucking managed.

My phone rings, and holding back a curse, I pull it from my pocket, my pulse kicking up when I see Sadie's school's contact flashing on the screen.

"Hello?" I say into the phone, scrambling to answer.

"Hi, Aaron. It's Penny."

"Yes, hi. Is everything okay?"

"I—yes! Oh, I'm so sorry I worried you. Sadie is perfectly fine. Currently giving Thomas a lecture on waiting for his turn. Between the two of us, he needs it."

I nod even though she can't see me. "Oh. Good." I wait for her to say something else, and when the silence stretches, I prompt, "What can I do for you?"

"We've hit a last-minute snag with the Mother's Day event." There's hesitation in her voice, like she's worried I'll shut her down. "I'm sure you have a lot going on, but—"

"That's okay. What's wrong?"

"Well, you're a cook, right? Sorry—a chef?"

I lean against the counter. "Had issues with catering or something?"

"Something. A mom offered to cook, but she's sick, and . . ."

"I could take care of that." Cooking, I can do. It's the easiest thing to control in my life these days.

"Really?" Relief floods her voice. "You're *amazing*. Seriously. I couldn't ask any of the moms, and I'm not—I mean, I can cook, but I'm not a chef."

"Happy to be of service."

"Great. Great. Should I meet you at your place? Maybe tomorrow?"

"You want to meet?"

Movement catches my eye, and I glance up just as Charlotte steps into the room. Her gaze flicks to me, then away as she opens the fridge. Even though I know she's listening, I turn slightly.

Penny continues. "Yeah. I'm not going to let you do all of it by yourself, with how busy you are. I can help you come up with a menu, at least."

"Right." Clearing my throat, I grip the phone a little tighter. "Sure, you can come over. Say, eight p.m. tomorrow?"

"Yeah, that's perfect. I'll bring a bottle of wine."

I blink. "You want to drink?"

"Oh! Not—not for *us*. Just as a thank-you."

I switch the phone to the other ear. "No thank-you necessary, really. It's my pleasure."

"Well, I'll see you then."

"Sure. Bye, Miss Delaney."

"Penny."

"Right. Bye, Penny," I say, ending the call.

When I look up, Charlotte is still standing by the fridge, one hand braced against the door, her eyes fixed on the near-empty shelves like there's an actual choice to be made.

Then, without turning, she says, "Date?"

Oh, for fuck's sake.

"It's not like you care either way, right?" I say, knowing I shouldn't. I can't beat her at her own game, and besides, I don't want to. I don't know what's wrong, but something happened. Just like something happened yesterday, when her mom started chatting me up.

I can't make Charlotte talk, but I don't want to fight her either.

She moves, closing the fridge door with a sharp click before turning to face me.

"Sadie's teacher needs help with Mother's Day," I explain, folding under her watchful gaze. "The mom in charge of it bailed."

"Sure they did." I wait for her to say more as she steps closer, arms folding across her chest. "You're a newly single father. Hand-some and well-mannered. Sweet, with a decent job and a beautiful daughter."

"And?"

"And you can't be that naive."

I stare at her, irritation bubbling up. I suspect Penny is inter-ested, but Charlotte has no right to act jealous. Not after the way she just treated me.

She lifts a shoulder. "Who knows. Maybe you are."

"So what if she's into me? Nobody else is."

She scoffs. "If you expect me to beg—"

"*Beg?* How about you just *talk* to me? How about you accept for once that someone cares about you? And maybe, just *maybe*, don't push me away?"

"Oh, you *care* about me?" She sputters a laugh. "You're unbe-lievable, you know that?"

"Am I?"

"You called me a mistake, didn't you? So why should I bother letting you in? What can *you* offer *me*?" she asks in a shrill voice. "Not a relationship. Not a future. Not any sort of long-lasting feel-ing." She grimaces. "Just your tongue."

I roll my jaw.

She's right—it's undeniable. I'm asking someone who's excep-tionally closed up to do the opposite so that I can break her heart by inevitably disappointing her expectations.

But it fucking hurts anyway.

"Maybe Penny sees more in me than my tongue."

"Yeah, maybe." She pushes off the counter, and just when I think she's done, she reaches for a piece of paper at the corner and slides it toward me. "New instructions, chef. Risotto won't do."

Her fingers brush mine as she lets go, and her ponytail swings behind her as she walks out of the kitchen without another word.

I look down at the paper, reading the words scribbled on it.

Charlotte has gained weight. Whether that's because you didn't follow my instructions or she didn't, I don't know, but these are the amendments to her diet. Make sure they're respected to the letter. See you at lunch.

No more oil, I read. Only lemon and vinegar allowed. No carbs, no fruit. The only thing that's left is vegetables and lean meats.

"Fuck," I breathe.

So that's what's going on.

If I know Beatrice like I think I do, Charlotte has been through hell in the last twenty-four hours. I can almost see it all playing out in my mind. Beatrice must have weighed her, seen that she's gained half a pound. She must have demanded answers—answers that Charlotte couldn't give her. The pizza, the corn dog. The salt I put in her food. All of it must have piled up after years of barely eating.

She saved my ass—my job. But as I stare down at the paper, its stark, cruel instructions burning into my mind, it's clear that the price she's paying is far too steep.

This isn't just a diet. This is a punishment.

You know what's a bad, bad idea? Logging in to TOP when just this morning, Charlotte accused me of using her on here. Doing it after she's ignored my texts—probably an even worse idea. On top of that, this is the first time we'll interact on here since she told me she knows I'm Cole.

But I didn't get a second alone with her while I cooked dinner, and I'm out of good ideas, so this'll have to do.

I search her name then wait for her profile to buffer. My

stomach is a tangled mess of anxiety, my heart hammering against my ribs. When her homepage finally loads, I loosen a breath.

A red dot blinks in the corner of the screen. She's live.

I would have much rather had a private call with her, but she wouldn't have accepted it anyway. This? This is my only shot. And, hey, at least she hasn't blocked me.

I click to join the live, my mouth dry. The feed appears, and then—there she is.

Charlotte is lounging on her bed, her delicate frame loosely covered by a black silk robe. Her long red hair is cascading over her shoulder in loose waves, and her lips, glossy and full, curl into a playful smirk as she speaks to the chat.

"You bet, Mateo," she says in a syrupy-sweet voice—probably responding to some goddamn viewer. But then, as soon as the notification flashes on the chat box—*Chief.728 joined the live*—she falters, just a fraction.

I see the moment when she registers that I'm watching. And then, just as quickly, she masks it.

"I think it's time we played a game. Don't you?" She tips her head back and hums, trailing a finger down her sun-kissed collarbone. "How about you tell me every single spot you'd like to dump your load on me, and I'll drip this on it?"

She holds up a squeeze bottle of clear honey, her manicured nails pressing against the plastic.

Jesus Christ.

The chat explodes with messages, flooding the screen with obscene requests, each more depraved than the last. Then, the unmistakable *ka-ching* of an old-fashioned cash register overlays the feed. Donations. Big ones.

$50 FROM AFK.TOFUCK

$150 FROM BALLS_DEEP

$350 FROM BEGMEFORMORE

A visceral, ugly jealousy coils in my gut, twisting tighter with every chime.

"Aww, you guys! You're so sweet," Charlotte purrs, tilting her head. She shrugs the robe off, and in a set of white lingerie, she lifts the bottle and squeezes, letting the golden liquid drip onto her tongue. Some of it she swallows, but the rest trails down her chin, thick and glistening, pooling in the valley between her breasts.

I glance at the chat again.

JOHNFORLOVE

Bet you suck dick so well, Cherry.

Fucking hell, my head is going to explode.

I tear my gaze away, pressing my lips together as I click on the fourth button—*Choose your own*. My fingers hover over the keyboard, then I type.

CAN WE TALK?

I hit send.

Charlotte barely glances at the screen. "Ohh. You want to come on my stomach, Luke?"

She tips the bottle, letting honey trickle over her navel, then spreads it with two fingers. "Just like this, sexy?"

A red notification pops up.

REQUEST DENIED.

Fuck.

"My ass? All right." She turns on all fours, arching her back. Honey drips down the curve of her ass before she drags her fingers through it, smearing it down her thighs

My hands are sweating, my heartbeat an erratic drum. I type again.

JUST GIVE ME ONE MINUTE OF YOUR TIME. PLEASE.

Seconds pass. Then—another red notification.

REQUEST DENIED.

She's punishing me. I know she is.

I run a hand through my hair. "Fuck!"

Charlotte hums, tilting her head. "My face, huh? Who wants to see my face drenched in cum?"

The chat erupts, and the *ka-ching*s ring out like a slot machine. My patience snaps as I rush to type another custom request.

I UNDERSTAND YOU'RE ANGRY, OKAY? I'M SORRY. BUT I'M NOT GOING TO DO WHAT BEATRI—

Damn. Out of characters. I send it anyway, then start typing again.

BEATRICE ASKED ME TO. IT'S TOO FUCKED UP, AND I'M QUITTING. I'M REALLY SORRY AB—

"Fucking stupid characters!"

Her eyes flick to the screen, mid-drizzle of honey. Her expression falters, the sultry mask she wears cracking.

"Sorry, everyone, but I have to go. Connect at the usual time tonight or tomorrow morning, and we'll continue our game."

No anger in the chat. No protests. Just a few understanding comments before the screen buffers, then goes dark.

I run a hand through my hair, my mind racing. Should I call? Should I text again? What should I do?

Then—a chime.

A private call request from Cherry.

Without hesitating, I click to accept, barely reading the disclaimer about the call being free of charge.

The screen lights up, and there she is. Her makeup is smudged, remnants of honey still glistening on her skin. She's holding a wet towel, moving it over her belly with absent strokes.

"Hey," I say quietly.

She pouts. "What do you mean you're quitting?"

"I mean I'm quitting—on Monday. I've already told Ian to call me in the morning. I'll tell him everything Beatrice is doing, and then I'm out."

Charlotte's face hardens, the bright glow of the screen catching the tremble in her jaw. She continues to drag the towel over her stomach, the tension in her shoulders tightening like a bowstring. "Ian?"

"My boss. He'll want to know why I'm flaking out. I'll have to explain it to Amelie too."

Her lips press together, a muscle in her cheek twitching. "You can't tell them."

"Why not?"

Her eyes flick up to meet the camera. "Because it's my life, and I don't want you to."

I sink back in my chair, chest heavy. She's right. It's not my place to expose her, no matter how much I want to fix this for her. No matter how much it kills me to watch her go through it alone.

"Okay, then . . . then I'll tell them about us," I say, my throat tightening around the words. "That we're involved, and I can't continue working for your mom. Either way, I'm not doing this anymore."

Though I expect her to be relieved, her lips twist. "So you're abandoning me."

"What? No, I—"

"You won't come over anymore."

"No, but once I'm not employed by your mom, we can just . . ." My mouth stays open, but the words don't come. We can just do what? Date? Be normal? Pretend we aren't tangled in a mess of complications? She's a cam girl. A twenty-three-year-old firecracker who doesn't belong to anyone. A model who travels the world.

And I'm . . . me.

"What?" she mocks, setting the towel down. "You'll come to my shows? I'll watch *Willy Wonka* with your daughter?"

I swallow hard. The idea isn't absurd to me. It's terrifying, sure. Uncertain, improbable, but it's not bad. If anything, it almost feels like an unattainable dream.

Her expression shifts, something breaking behind her eyes. "You're leaving me with her."

My brows knit together. "Charlotte—"

"You won't be there to put salt in my lunch, to sneak me extra food, to make my days better, and I'll just—" Her lips wobble, voice cracking. "I'll starve. I'll disappear. I'll once again be nothing but my body."

The words cause physical ache, like my ribs are caving in. She's not just talking about food. She's talking about *me*. How I make her feel and have her back.

"But you won't have this on your conscience, right?" She wipes at her face with the back of her hand, even as fresh tears spill over. "So, who cares? Who cares if we never meet again? If you never touch me again?"

Her face crumples, and suddenly, I feel smaller than a coin. Insignificant.

She's right.

What did I think? That just because I quit, Beatrice would stop? That just because I stepped back, Charlotte would be okay? She won't. Nothing will change. The only difference is I won't be there to see it.

"I'm sorry." I want to reach through the screen, pull her into my arms, and promise her that she's not alone. That I'll fix it. That it'll be better. But all I can do is sit here, helpless. "I won't quit, okay?" The words rush out, desperate, pleading. "I won't. I'm not going anywhere."

A sob wracks through her, and she buries her face in her hands. She looks so small like this, nearly naked, her body so thin I can see the sharp angles of her hip bone, the faint ridges of her ribs.

I need to know something. I need to ask her the one thing that's gone through my mind since I heard her being sick, since I read her mom's list. And I really don't want to do it now, when she's already so vulnerable, but I'm afraid it can't wait.

"Charlotte, this morning, did you . . ."

She sniffles. "Did I what?"

"Did you vomit . . ." I glance at the screen, afraid she'll end the call on the spot but dragging the words out anyway. " . . . on purpose?"

Her shoulders stiffen just a tad before she swipes at her cheek. "It's not a big deal."

Fuck, it feels like dying. Like she just ran a knife through my heart, and with every quick intake of breath, it causes more blood to spurt out into my chest cavity.

"You—it's a *huge* deal, Charlotte."

"No, it's not. I'm not bulimic or anything. It's just something I do when I've eaten a little too much and Beatrice will weigh me. I hadn't done it in years, but lately, I mean . . ."

But lately, she's been eating more. Because of me.

God, this is so fucked up, whichever way you look at it.

"Charlotte, listen to me," I say, leaning closer to the laptop. "You have to promise me you'll never do it again."

"Chef, I—"

"*Promise.* If you want me to stay, if you want me to keep feeding you, then you have to swear it'll never happen again. No matter what."

"I promise." She sniffles, then pulls her hair back over one shoulder. "I want to see you, but I'm not allowed to go out . . . not since I gained that weight."

I unclench my jaw. "I left something for you today."

"You did? Where?"

"Behind the baking equipment—figured Beatrice would never touch that. Can you go get it?"

She quickly jumps up, and I wait for the noise of the door opening as she comes back, holding the jar filled with folded pieces of paper. Her eyes shimmer, and her voice is barely a whisper. "You made me a jar of stars?"

"I did," I say. "I wanted you to have something, just in case. A reminder that there's so much more to you than your body. That someone sees it. Sees *you*."

"Aaron, I . . ."

"Whenever you need the reminder, just . . . open the jar, okay?"

Her lips wobble, and after pressing a key on her laptop, she says, "I just allowed you to turn your camera on. Can I see you?"

I search the bottom part of the screen, frowning. I didn't even know that was an option. "How do I turn it on?"

"Seriously, Grandpa?" A weak, teary smile tugs at her lips. "The camera symbol."

"Which one?"

"Come on, Aaron. It looks like a camera."

"Well, I don't see it."

"The third one!"

"Oh." I press the button, and after a few seconds of buffering, my own face appears in the bottom right corner of the screen. "Hey."

"Hi." She swallows hard, her lips trembling again. "Do you still want me?"

The absurd question has me frowning. "What makes you think I ever stopped?"

She wipes the tear tracks on her cheeks. "I'm so sorry."

"About what, baby?"

"About today. And . . . every day. I treat you so bad all the time."

"No, you don't."

"Yes, I do," she insists. "I'm just so . . . angry. Constantly, from the time I wake up until I go to sleep. I'm so angry, I want to . . ." She buries her face in her hands, her shoulders shaking.

"Of course you're angry, Charlotte." There's an ache in my chest so deep I almost can't stand it. "You're hungry. You're constantly starving, and not just for food, but for freedom, recognition, love. That'll make anyone go crazy."

She heaves out a sob, her shoulders curling inward. She looks so fucking tired. Like she's been fighting a battle no one sees, and she's losing.

And I swear, right now, I'll be her armor. I'll be her sword, her shield.

I'll be whatever she needs until she wins the war.

CHAPTER 21

Sticky Fingers

AMELIE

So you're alive! I thought you'd fallen on a burner and caught fire.

AARON

Alive and well. Just busy with Sadie and work.

AMELIE

Is that all you're busy with?

Picture a winky face. My phone's bugging and emojis don't work.

I swallow the thickness in my throat. "Picture a winky face?" What's the fucking winky face for? There's no way she knows about Charlotte, is there? It can't be. Please, tell me she doesn't know.

My fingers hover over the keys, but the screen shifts to an incoming call, and I stare at Charlotte's name flashing on it for a long moment before I pick it up.

"Hello?"

"'You exist with your whole heart. It's beautiful to see.'"

Warmth unfurls in my chest. She's read one of the notes I left for her.

"Did something happen to make you need the reminder?"

"You're crazy if you think I have the kind of self-control needed for a jar of stars."

"You opened them all?"

"Last night. Then I folded them all back up and opened one today."

I grin, shaking my head lightly. "Of course. Well . . . I can make more. I think I could make an infinite amount, in fact."

She chuckles, then after a long pause, she says, "You know I'm not *using* you, right?"

"Yeah?" I settle on the couch, lowering the volume of the TV. We haven't really talked about our fight besides yesterday's video call since Beatrice was around all day today, but I thought we'd cleared things up. "When I said that . . . I was just upset, Charlotte."

"And it was my fault. But I want you to know . . ." For a moment, there's only silence. Then, her voice comes back, quieter. "You matter to me, Chef."

I let my head drop against the back of the couch.

"You're not just some guy I use for pleasure." She pauses, like she's searching for the right words. "You're . . . steady. Patient. *Good.* I don't know if you realize how rare that is."

I grip the phone a little tighter.

"I don't do this," she admits. "Not just the whole . . . being with one person thing, but *this*—talking. Letting people get close. I don't know how to be what people expect. And I think some-times . . ." She lets out a laugh, like she's still trying to make sense of it herself. "Sometimes I'm the worst version of myself to see if you'll stick around. And you always do."

A lump rises in my throat. "You'll have to try harder than that."

"Wait, I'm not done." Her voice is firmer now, but there's something nervous underneath it. "I just need to say this, okay?"

I stay quiet.

"At some point, you won't stick around," she says finally. "I'll do the one thing that's . . . too much. That would break even someone like you. Don't say it's not true, because you don't *know*. You don't know . . . a lot of things."

I really want to interject, to reassure her, to ask her what *things* she's talking about, but I respect her wishes and keep my mouth shut.

"So I need you to know now, when things are good, that you're not just some guy. You're *the* guy. The guy I'll compare everyone else to, the one who set the standard, who'll make it even harder for me to settle. Because when I'm with you . . . I feel perfect. I feel *right*. And I've never felt like that before."

For a second, I can't speak.

Charlotte, who never lets anyone in. Charlotte, who keeps the world at arm's length and acts like it doesn't bother her. She's giving me this.

I close my eyes, let the words settle, let myself feel the emotions trapped in them. The pain, the hope masked as certainty of failure, the fear. Then I say the only thing I know is true.

"You *are* perfect." I draw an imaginary pattern on my jeans. "In fact, I'd go as far as to say that you're the exception to the 'nobody's perfect' rule."

She laughs, the sound like cherry blossoms sprouting in my chest.

"Well, I'll travel out of town for a shoot this week, so if you want to get some of this *perfect* on you . . . how about we hang out Friday night? I have a show in the afternoon, but you could come see me. We could spend the night at your place, watch another movie with Sadie."

"Ye—" I immediately blurt, stopping once I realize Friday won't work. "Fuck. I've got my brother's bachelor party."

"You do?"

"He's getting married in a week and a half."

"If you're looking for a plus-one, you should know I'm in quite high demand. You better book fast."

I hum, reveling in the fantasy of bringing her to my brother's wedding. Of kissing her in front of my friends and family—hell, of kissing her at all. I wonder if she'd let me. Of dancing with her, getting her a second serving of cake, watching her win over everyone so fast they wouldn't even notice it. "I don't know, Charlotte. You might end up falling madly in love with me, and I've got a strict no-refund policy."

Listening to her giggles, I feel my shoulders relax. I want to stay here all day, talking to her and making her laugh. Pouring our feelings out to each other one moment, then playing around the next.

"You know you can tell me anything, right?"

A beat of silence, then, "What do you mean?"

"Just . . . you keep talking about this *secret* I don't know. These *things*, these *reasons*. You don't have to tell me anything, but if you want to, you can."

"You'll run away, Aaron."

"No, I won't. I—" The doorbell rings, and I glance at the time on my phone. Miss Delaney.

"You have to go, don't you?"

"Yeah. There's . . ."

"Penny," Charlotte chimes in.

"Yes, Penny. She's here to help me figure out the menu for the Mother's Day recital."

"Uh-huh."

Is she annoyed? She sounds annoyed.

"You're not jealous, are you?"

I don't even have the *energy* to put my mouth on another woman, let alone the will to do so.

"No, of course not."

"Okay." Her voice still sounds clipped. "'Cause you know, I—"

"Relax, Chef. We're good." She clears her throat. "I'll see you tomorrow, yeah?"

I'm about to suggest I could call her later, but she's hung up already.

"So, what are we thinking in terms of menu?" I ask Miss Delaney —right, *Penny*—as she takes the first sip of a cup of coffee. After some awkward chatter about Sadie, who's currently at her grandma's, we set up in the kitchen.

She's wearing makeup—a heavier application than what she usually has on at school. Her lips are glossy, and there's a touch of eyeliner that makes her eyes pop. She's not in her usual overalls either. Instead, she's wearing a blue sweater and a pair of fitted jeans.

Did she dress up for this?

"We'd originally planned some finger food. Mini sandwiches, fruit skewers, cheese cubes for the kids, and then crostinis and stuffed mushrooms for the parents. We expect about forty moms and forty kids."

"Piece of cake," I say before taking a sip from my cup.

"Great. We just need to make sure we avoid these ingredients," she says, holding a piece of paper out. "Allergies, intolerances."

We're silent for a few moments as I read through the list, though I can see her fidgeting in my peripheral vision.

"It looks—" I start at the same time she says, "I was—"

We both fall silent, and I gesture toward her. "Sorry, go on."

"No, I . . ." She swallows. "Do you want to get coffee? With me?" She looks down at her mug with wide eyes. "I mean as a date. Like, outside. Or here, just not . . . oh, I'm messing this up."

I look up at her—this pretty, slightly awkward woman who

loves my daughter dearly. She's exactly my type too, and she's obviously into me. Nervous just to be around me.

Why doesn't that do anything for me?

Because *Charlotte*.

She's not Charlotte.

Nobody is.

"I'm flattered, Penny. Really. But I'm already seeing someone, and—" A knock comes at my front door, and she avoids my gaze as I stand from my stool. "Excuse me."

I walk over and open it, my jaw almost hitting the floor when I see Charlotte standing on the other side, wrapped in an oversized burgundy sweater and a plaid mini skirt that swishes around her thighs as she shifts her weight.

"What—"

She quickly steps in, then grips my hand and pulls me toward the stairs.

"Wait," I whisper, eyes running down her long bare legs, all the way to the white knee-high socks and vintage brown heels. I thought she couldn't leave the house—I'd already given up on seeing her until tomorrow. "Penny's here."

"Uh-huh." She tugs at my hand but I stand my ground, so she purrs, "Tell her you'll be back soon."

"What—why?"

I throw a worried look at the kitchen, and once I turn back to her, she steps closer until her forehead is pressed against mine. "Because it turns out I *am* jealous."

Seriously? I hesitate, but who am I kidding? She left me starving for days, and now she's serving herself to me on a silver platter.

I won't be able to say no.

"Penny, uh, help yourself to another coffee. I'll be right back," I call. Once she says it's no problem, I follow Charlotte upstairs and guide her into my bedroom.

My heartbeat is through the roof, and I briefly wonder again how much of this is self-destructive behavior, because I'm hard the second the door closes behind us.

I guide her toward the bed, but instead she pushes me against my door, my back hitting it with a thump.

She leans forward, her lips hovering so close to mine that her breath—hot and teasing—washes over my skin like a promise. My cock twitches in anticipation, already straining against my briefs.

I don't want to get my hopes up again, but is she going to kiss me? Am I the exception to her rules?

"Did she already do it?"

"Do what?" I breathe. "Who?"

"*Penny*," she says, as if her name alone is insulting. "Did she ask you out?"

"Yeah," I breathe as her long, lethal fingers find my belt, and the sound of it unbuckling is obscenely loud in the silence. I pant, and my cock throbs in agreement, desperate for her touch.

"Did you tell her that you belong to me?"

Her hand slides to my zipper, tugging it down with agonizing slowness, the rasp of metal against metal sending a jolt of electricity straight to my balls.

God, she's killing me.

"Yes."

Her fingers hook into the waistband of my briefs, and I let out a strangled noise as she pulls them down, letting my cock spring free, already leaking pre-cum at the tip. The cool air brushes against my feverish skin, but it's nothing compared to the heat of her gaze as she steps back, her eyes locked on my dick.

I have no idea what's about to happen, but I might explode before I find out.

"Who do you belong to, Chef?"

"Y-you." I can't breathe. I can't think. All I can do is watch as she reaches for the hem of her skirt, her fingers gliding up her smooth thighs to hook into the waistband of her panties. She's wearing red silk—fuck, I love her in red—and as she slides them down her legs, I'm struck dumb by the sight of her bare cunt, glistening with arousal, so pink and tempting I want to drop to my knees and bury my face in her right fucking now.

Before I can move, her skirt is pulled back down, and with her panties in one hand, she steps closer. Her lips brush against the pulse point of my neck as she says, "These are my favorite panties, Chef." Her voice drips with sin. "Paint them with your cum."

Oh *fuck*. She wraps the silk around my cock, her grip tight and perfect, and I let out a ragged sound. The fabric is smooth, almost *too* smooth, but I'm so fucking sensitive that even that feels like heaven. Her hand starts moving, sliding up and down my shaft with a rhythm that leaves me aching for more. The silk clings to my skin, trapping every drop that leaks from me, and the sensation is maddening.

"*Charlotte*," I beg, reaching forward and squeezing her hip.

She tightens her grip, her other hand roaming across my chest, her nails digging into my flesh just enough to make me hiss.

I can't believe how good this feels—how dirty, how wrong, how perfect.

Her free hand slides lower, cupping my balls gently as the strokes of her other hand turn rapid and sharp. She rolls them in her palm, her touch electrifying.

Fuck. It's the first time she's *truly* touched me, and it's so little, but I gasp for air as my hips buck involuntarily, seeking more of that exquisite pressure.

"You're so heavy," she murmurs, her fingers exploring, caressing.

More.

More. Now.

She traces the seam with her fingertips, sending shivers up my spine. "So full. You've been saving this load for me, haven't you?"

More, more, more.

I can only grunt in response, my ability to form coherent words long gone. She chuckles, a low, throaty sound that vibrates through me. Her fingers dance across my sac, alternating between light touches and firm squeezes that make my toes curl.

"That's it," she praises, her lips brushing against my ear as she speeds up her movements, twisting her hand around the head of my cock until I see stars. "I'll remember how hard you came into my panties every time I wear them."

Fuck. Her words send me spiraling, pressure building low in my stomach and my hips snapping forward as I chase my release.

Once her teeth graze the side of my neck, I'm done for. With a guttural groan, I come hard, thick ropes of cum erupting from my cock and soaking into the red silk still wrapped around me. It's messy, it's filthy, and it's the best handjob I've ever had.

She doesn't stop until I've emptied myself completely, her hand squeezing every last drop from me until I'm trembling and spent. Then, with a wicked smile, she pulls the panties away from my cock, holding them up to the light like a trophy. They're drenched, the silk clinging to itself in sticky strands, so obscenely hot that my dick twitches weakly, as if it can't fucking believe what just happened either.

She leans in again, her lips brushing against mine for the first time. "Good boy," she says. "Wash them and return them tomorrow."

I'm still catching my breath when she shoves the panties in my hand and walks out the door. Dizzy and flustered, I drop them on my nightstand and follow her out as I adjust my pants.

This must mean something, right? If she's jealous about another woman asking me out—so jealous she came here to give me the best handjob of my life—then she must feel some type of way about me.

I follow her, fully planning to ask her what this means, and more importantly, if she's really going to take an Uber with no underwear on, but she's out the front door before I take the last step down the stairs. I turn around, only to find myself face-to-face with a horrified Penny.

Holy shit.

I'm certain my face is that of a man who just got jerked off. Flushed and in fucking heaven.

"Wow. She's . . . beautiful."

I clear my voice, so embarrassed that it feels like my skin is melting off my skull. "Th-thanks." I close the door, then point my thumb at it. "As I was saying, I'm . . . seeing someone."

"No kidding."

I watch her frown as she turns around and walks to the kitchen.

That's *one* way to make it official.

CHAPTER 22
Cherry Lips

I enter the nightclub, relieved when I confirm there are no strippers in sight. Just a dark, pulsing room, tables pushed to the edges, and a dance floor packed with bodies swaying to the deep bass of some song I don't recognize. The air is thick—sweat, perfume, and alcohol blending into an intoxicating haze.

It's been a decade since I stepped foot in a place like this, and judging by the fresh faces around me, I probably should have stayed away. But Logan's wedding is just over a week away, and on this fateful Friday, everyone's been forced out of the comfort of their homes and dragged here.

Some of us had much better plans. Like accepting a spunky red-head's invitation to go see her show, then spend the night at my place. Charlotte's been gone for a shoot for the last two days, and I miss her more than I thought possible. More than I find bearable.

She's texted a couple of times, but it's not enough. Not after the last time I saw her, when I returned the panties she used to jerk me off.

Kyle, the ringleader in this situation, waves me over from a table to my right, his expression already loose with alcohol. Next to

244

him, Logan glares at his beer like it personally offended him, while Shane sits stiffly, clearly wishing he were anywhere else.

This should be interesting.

"Hey," I say, sliding into the seat next to Shane. Kyle immediately grabs the pitcher and fills my glass, shoving it toward me like he's on a mission. "How's it going?"

He grimaces. "No one is nearly drunk enough."

I take a sip, the bitter taste of the beer washing off a little of my nerves. Logan and I haven't talked since our fight last Sunday, so I'm not sure what to expect. But as he gives me a curt nod, I realize that maybe I should expect nothing, because things will continue to be exactly like they have been.

Kyle is shouting something about his culture of pumpkins over the thumping music, and Shane and Logan lean in, intrigued.

Not exactly what I pictured for the night, not that I'm complaining.

"For the record," someone says behind me, right before a firm slap lands on the back of my head. "My wife doesn't have a bad side."

I wince and turn. "Ian?" I say, rubbing the spot that stings. "*What?* I didn't know you were coming."

He smirks. "Yeah, well. I figured Logan would be even more displeased with the surprise."

I glance at Logan, who just lifts his glass and takes a long-suffering sip. Fair enough.

I pat his shoulder. "How's Amelie?"

Ian brings a hand to his chest. "Yes, I *am* great. Thank you for asking." Then his grin widens. "Amelie's kicking ass. They already asked her to come back for the next four seasons. Of course, you'd know all of this if you bothered to answer her messages."

Oh, so she told him about that, huh?

"I, uh . . . I've been really busy, and—"

"Don't." He motions behind me. "You can tell her yourself."

My head snaps up. "Wait, what? She's here too?"

"She's at Prim's bachelorette. Right there." As I turn to the direction he's pointing to, he adds, "We're heading back in the morning."

There she is—next to Primrose, Heaven, and a few women I've never seen before. Bright, colorful drinks in their hands, sequins catching the dim lights. They look like they belong here. Like they're having the right kind of fun for a place like this. No mention of pumpkins in that conversation, I'm sure.

"Wait," I say. "Both parties are here?"

Ian shrugs. "Kyle says it was the only way to convince Logan to come."

Yeah, that checks out.

"Well, I'll go—" I begin, but Ian's hand clamps around my arm before I can rise from my stool.

"Not so fast, cowboy." His grip is firm, almost amused. "No boys allowed."

Oh. I sink back into my seat, mildly annoyed. I'd never really thought about it before Kyle said it, but Amelie *has* become my best friend. After spending so much time together over the last year, not seeing her in weeks—not even talking, though that's my own fault—has made me miss her.

"I figured *we* could talk instead." I study Ian, who's watching me with a rare seriousness. "If you don't mind."

I shift in my chair, bracing for his words. I have a feeling I know where this is going.

He's going to ask about me and Amelie. Probably wants reassurance that I'm not out to get his wife or something. It's to be expected, I guess, since these guys all know about Josie.

"What's up?" I ask, forcing casualness into my tone.

"I wanted to thank you."

I blink. "For what?"

"For your friendship with Amelie, of course."

"Oh. Well, I'm the one who's grateful."

He glances past me, toward his wife. "I think it was cathartic for her—passing her knowledge on to someone else the way her dad did with her. You know there were a lot of unresolved issues between them when he died, and she's been struggling to face the fact that she won't get the chance to solve them."

"She's been going through a lot."

"And you made it better."

I look down at my glass, running my finger along the condensation. "I thought . . . I thought you'd warn me that—you know."

He cocks his head. "What? That I'd be jealous of how close you two got?"

"Maybe, yeah."

Ian laughs, loud and unapologetic. "Dude. I mess with you, but . . . I'm just fucking around. I hope you know that."

"It's not because of you," I cut in quickly. "It's . . ."

"Oh. *Oh*, your—" He gestures vaguely at Logan before tucking his hand away. "Right, right. Well, look, my wife was engaged to another man when I met her. I'm hardly going to judge you." He snorts. "Of course, her fiancé wasn't my *brother*."

"Still not judging?"

He beams. "Not even a little."

I hold his gaze for a beat. "As long as you know that Amelie and I . . ."

"You're like a brother to her."

"She's like a sister to me."

Ian squeezes my shoulder. "And I want her to live a life surrounded by amazing people who love her, so . . . we're cool. Really."

I nod, raising my glass slightly. I didn't even know how much I needed to hear this, but now that I have, I feel ten pounds lighter. "Thanks, man."

"Unless you hurt her, that is." He takes a sip of beer, then winks. "Then we're *not* cool."

"Okay, uh . . . the bouncer," Logan says with a smirk.

"Not the bouncer!" Kyle cries.

The whole group erupts into laughter as Logan points toward the entrance, where the large, angry-looking man is standing.

Kyle hesitates, then saunters toward the big guy. Though the music is too loud for any of us to hear a word, we wait.

"Ten dollars says he smacks him," I wager.

Shane tsks. "Are you kidding? Twenty that he gives him his number."

We all watch, breath held, as the bouncer smirks and actually takes Kyle's phone, tapping something on the screen. Kyle returns to the table, triumphant, waving his phone like a trophy.

"*Oooh!*" I slap a twenty-dollar bill in Shane's hand, and he passes it to the waitress as he orders another round of shots. There's been a lot of those.

Kyle plops back into his seat, shooting back his drink. "Well, there you go. He said I should give him a call if I ever feel like switching sides. Whose turn is it?"

"I believe it's mine," Ian says, but before he can make a move, Amelie plops onto his lap, and Primrose does the same with Logan. Heaven follows suit, nestling onto Shane's thighs.

"You guys look like you're having fun," Primrose teases, her tone light. She doesn't sound drunk at all, probably because she's still breastfeeding.

"*Boo!*" Kyle half-heartedly shoves her shoulder. "I agreed to this embarrassing bachelorette-slash-bachelor party, but the deal was everyone would stick to their own guests."

"Sorry, I wanted to kiss my fiancé."

I turn to Amelie, her eyes dancing with warmth, and just like that, I realize she missed me as much as I missed her. "You're here."

"I am."

"Couldn't stay away from your kitchen, could you?"

She shrugs. "Well, I'm happy to see it, that's for sure."

"I hear you're also in a rush to leave."

"Yeah." She frowns for a moment, then she points at me, eyes twinkling. "But I'll be back next week—just on Thursday. Barbara needs to be home and since I have the day off, I'll work the dinner service at the restaurant. But before that, you and me, my place. I have to show you this *unbelievable* recipe. You're going to love it."

"Hell yes." I meet Ian's gaze, and there's no tension. "Can't wait."

"Seriously, you're a bunch of losers," Kyle complains, pouting as he crosses his arms. "We were playing a game."

Primrose kisses the tip of Logan's nose. "Then keep playing!"

"*Ugh.* Fine. Ignore the girls. Whose turn was it?"

Ian starts to say something about skipping his turn, but I hardly hear him as I grab a shot from the table and down it. When I look up, all eyes are on me.

"What?"

"It's your turn."

Oh. "All right." After making Logan dance on a raised platform in the middle of the dance floor and forcing Kyle to ask for the bouncer's number, I know I'm in for it.

"Maybe we should set him up with someone," Heaven suggests.

"Excuse me, but you're not part of the game," I playfully scold. "The guys have to decide."

Shane raises his hand. "I vote for the setting up thing."

The table nods, their faces lit with amusement.

Great. "Whatever. Who am I being set up with?"

"Who looks good?" Amelie asks.

I scan the room, my brain clouded by the mix of vodka, rum, and beer. I'm not even looking for someone attractive—just someone to get this over with. Until red catches my eye.

Is that . . . it can't be. It *cannot* be her. I didn't tell her I'd be here—I didn't know the name of the place until I texted Kyle for the address two hours ago. But as I take in the backless, deep emerald dress hugging curves I know too well, my heartbeat skips. It looks like her.

"Oooh. Winner winner, chicken dinner," Ian calls from beside me.

"*Another* redhead? You have a problem," Kyle chimes in, immediately looking away when I glare.

"Yeah, she's cute, but . . . not her."

Amelie smacks my arm. "Cute? Look at that body."

"Maybe a bit young," Shane muses.

I barely process Primrose questioning how Shane can tell from her back alone as Kyle declares, "Bachelor's decision."

After a careful look at me, Logan raises his thumb like a Roman emperor at an execution.

Well, *shit*.

A chorus of "Come on," and "Get up!" pushes me forward as Amelie says I should only come back a winner. I stand and move, unable to look away from her backless dress. It's her. It's gotta be her.

I step closer and her friend notices me first, gesturing that someone is behind her before walking away. She turns, and my breath catches in my throat as dark green eyes lock onto mine.

"Chef?"

"Charlotte."

She turns fully, and the sight of her knocks the air from my lungs. The dress clings to her, the fabric flowing down her frame and the neckline plunging just enough to be devastating. She's holding a vibrant cocktail with a maraschino cherry floating at the top.

She looks stunning, unreal, like these few days apart only made her more irresistible, and for a moment, my brain is absolute *mush*.

I swallow hard. "You look . . . incredible."

"Thank you." Her fingers toy with the hem of her dress, the material shifting beneath her touch and skimming over her curves.

"It's one of yours, isn't it? The dress?"

"A new one." She pulls slightly, smoothing it over her hip. "I was thinking about you when I made it."

Green, my favorite color. The same deep, rich green as her eyes.

"What are you doing here?" she asks, tilting her head in curiosity. "Oh, wait. The bachelor party, right?"

"With a splash of divorce celebrations."

She hums. "Sounds interesting."

"Trust me, it is." I take a breath, inhaling the faint scent of her perfume—floral, devastating. *How* is she here? I still can't believe it.

"What?"

"Nothing, just . . . I'm surprised you're here."

She must catch on to what I'm thinking, because her eyes roll. "I'm not *stalking* you, Chef. I came with some of the people from the show."

"I wouldn't mind you stalking me," I say, enjoying the smile that blooms on her lips. Her poker face has been slipping more and more.

"So . . . where *is* your party?" she asks, looking around.

"They sent me on a mission. I'm supposed to, you know, hit on you."

"Oh?" Her lips curve in amusement as she hooks one arm around my neck, pulling me a fraction closer. "On me, really?"

My hands find their way to her waist, fingers slipping under her dress and grazing the curve of her hip. "I guess they caught me staring at you."

She tilts her head as her gaze flickers to my lips. "I told you, Chef. You have no poker face."

Maybe I don't *want* a poker face when I look at her. What if I want her to see everything? Everything I feel, everything I want? What if I want her to know that the moment she steps into a room, the air itself rearranges to make space for her? That she's the gravity pulling me in, the only thing my eyes search for, the only thought that has mattered since the second I first saw her?

"So what does my face tell you right now?" I ask, stroking her side.

She giggles, her breath warm against my cheek. "That you're drunk."

"What else?"

"That you really want to kiss me."

Fuck yes.

"Will you let me?"

She breathes out a laugh, shaking her head slightly. "You're drunk, Chef."

"Will you let me kiss you?" I say again, my grip tightening.

Her eyes flicker, and she bites her bottom lip. She's thinking about it. I give her my most sincere smile, hoping it'll tip her decision toward the answer I'm desperate for.

"The moment we kiss, this will stop being about the fun of sneaking around," she says, her voice lower now, serious. "The thrill of danger."

"I think we're past that already, aren't we?"

"Not until we *kiss.*"

"What will it be about then?" I ask.

She leans into my touch like it's the most natural thing in the world. "I guess that depends on how the kiss goes."

Well, I want to find out. Us kissing—it would be everything. I *know* it. I can feel it in my bones. The taste of her, the heat of her body against mine. I want to kiss her until my head spins, until my hands memorize the curves of her body. Until nothing else exists but her and me.

"Let's do it," I say, leaning forward.

She tilts back, giggling. Her glass shifts in her hand, the cherry bobbing in the liquid, and my chuckle vibrates against her skin as I kiss the delicate spot just below her jaw. The sound she makes—a breathy sigh—sends heat curling through my veins.

"You're *drunk,*" she reminds again.

"Stop saying that."

"But you are!"

"Who cares?" My fingers press into her lower back. "I've wanted to kiss you for weeks, Charlotte. Since you were just Cherry to me."

She studies me, her fingers grazing the nape of my neck, tracing deliberate circles. "And you want to do it in front of your friends?"

I shrug. "They told me to. Amelie said that I should *only* come back a winner."

"Amelie?" Her joy dims slightly. "I thought you said it was a bachelor party. Why is *she* here?"

I frown. Again with this? "It's a bachelor-slash-bachelorette party—and she's married. All the women with us are taken."

Before I can reassure her further, she grabs my hand and pulls me with her.

The dance floor is packed, bodies swaying and colliding under the pulsing strobe lights. The music pounds in my ears, the bass thrumming through my chest. She stops in the middle of the crowd, the press of people forming a barrier around us. It feels like another world in here—dark, hazy, intimate.

Why did we just run away from . . . Amelie, apparently?

"Isn't she married to your *boss*?" Charlotte asks, eyes widening like I'm missing something obvious.

"*Oh.*" She's worried about the two of us being seen together. "He's here too, but everyone's drunk, Charlotte. And in this darkness, I doubt they'd recognize you if they saw you again."

My hands find her waist, pulling her closer, and with her body flush against mine, I trace the length of her neck with my fingers, down the slope of her shoulder. I press a kiss on her skin, then another, then another, rising up her neck. I love the way being drunk around her makes me daring. Because fuck, do I want to dare.

"We should kiss, baby," I say into her ear. When she watches me, eyes hooded, I continue. "It won't change a thing about how we feel."

She seems irked. "Really?"

"Really. You're the most complicated, impossible thing that's ever happened to me. Not a mistake, not a regret, not something I can walk away from and pretend it never happened. You've wrapped yourself around every part of me, and I don't know how to untangle it. So, *really*, kissing you won't change a thing."

Her sharp inhale is lost in the music, but I feel her breath against my lips, like I've just unraveled something inside her. Her hand slides up, fingers threading through my hair, nails scraping just enough to make me shudder.

"That was good," she says, her lips curving, but I see her throat bob, betraying her.

I smirk. "I have my moments."

She hesitates, her gaze flickering between me and the half-empty glass in her hand. Then, she leans back slightly. "But you know I have my rule against kissing. I'm afraid I can't say yes."

Oh. I nod, trying to keep my expression neutral. The last thing I want is for her to feel pressured, but I'm pretty sure she can see the disappointment flicker across my face. I *really* thought that things were different between us. That I'd be her exception.

She lifts her glass to her lips and finishes the rest of her drink in one smooth motion. "So I guess if you want this *Cherry*, you'll just have to come and get it."

With that, she flashes a smile at me, the maraschino cherry from her drink trapped between her front teeth.

I burst out laughing, a sound I couldn't have held back even if I tried. She joins in, the joyful noise spilling into the air and making her shoulders shake.

She's so fucking amazing.

The playful challenge in her eyes shifts to something darker as the space between us disappears entirely. She tugs me down, pressing her lips to mine, testing at first, a slow drag of warmth. But the moment I respond, her fingers tighten in my hair, her body molding against mine. She tastes like sweet, tart cherry, and the music, the crowd, the flashing lights—they all fade into the background. It's just her, the way she tilts her head to deepen the kiss, her tongue brushing against mine until she's stolen the last of my restraint.

I grip her waist, fingers sliding beneath the fabric of her dress, tracing the dip of her back. Her tongue pushes the cherry in my mouth, and with a grunt, I swallow it, the taste as intoxicating as hers.

When my hand presses her closer so she can feel what she's doing to me, she gasps against my mouth.

"I knew it." She nips my bottom lip. "I knew you'd kiss me like this, Chef."

I press my forehead to hers, catching my breath. "I'm not done kissing you yet."

Her fingers toy with the hem of my shirt. "Then don't stop."

CHAPTER 23

She's a Knockout

My hand slides down to cup her ass, and finding nothing but bare skin, I pull back from our kiss. "No underwear?" Her lipstick is smeared, a tantalizing stain on her swollen lips—proof of how long we've been tangled up, devouring one another through the pulse of several songs. "Is it to torture me?"

Her dark eyes gleam with mischief. "This dress requires full nude. I told you I was thinking about you when I made it. You're just lucky you get to see me wearing it for the first time."

Jesus fucking Christ.

I claim her mouth again, kissing her harder, deeper, like I might be able to drown in the taste of her. "Let's get out of here."

She hums against my lips. "You're at your brother's bachelor party."

Right. "Let's go to the bathroom then."

With a chuckle, she pulls back just enough to search my face. "I have been in that bathroom. Trust me, that's not a good idea."

Fuck, fuck, fuck.

My whole body is on fire. Every nerve ending is attuned to her, every ounce of restraint hanging by a thread. I need to know if these desperate, all-consuming kisses have her as wrecked as I feel.

If she's as wet as I imagine. If her body is just as strung out with desire.

My gaze flicks around the room, just a cursory glance to ensure no one is watching too closely, before I let my hand drift lower, sliding down the front of her dress. The second I make contact with slick skin, she stills, her green eyes going wide. Then she bites her lip and subtly parts her legs just enough to let me in.

That's a green light.

And green is my favorite fucking color.

My fingers graze her heat, and I nearly drop to my knees when I discover how soaked she is. "Jesus, baby." I speak into her ear, letting my fingers tease along her folds, dragging the slickness up, circling her clit once—just enough to make her shudder. "This all for me?"

She gives a shaky moan, her hands clutching at my shirt before she pulls me down for another breathless kiss.

I press a finger inside her, swallowing her gasp as she clenches around me, her walls tight and molten-hot. "Shit," she whimpers, dropping her forehead against my shoulder, her nails biting into my skin through the fabric of my shirt.

Around us, the bass thrums through the floor, the low lighting flickering over bodies swaying too close to notice what's happening. The crowd pushes in like a perfect shield.

I slide my finger out before thrusting back in. "So sensitive." I press a kiss to the shell of her ear. "You know how fucking crazy you drive me? Squirming in this little dress, soaking wet, desperate for me to make it better?"

Her her hips rock forward, seeking more. "Make it better. *Please.*"

I add another finger, stretching her open, relishing the way she takes me, how she tightens.

"Keep going. Oh, fuck—*please!*"

Oh, I'll keep going.

Mouth on hers now, I curl my fingers just right and stroke over that spot that makes her whole body tense, makes her grip on my shoulders turn bruising. I love making her come almost as much as I love knowing exactly how to do it. "Right there, baby?" I coax.

Her hips roll forward in a desperate attempt to chase the friction. "Yes, yes, yes . . ."

Fuck, this *feeling*. Knowing that I'm the one making her tremble. That we're in the middle of this crowded dance floor, surrounded by oblivious people, and I've got her coming apart in my arms. It's intoxicating.

I speed up my fingers, pumping into her harder, pressing one finger against her clit in tight circles. Her entire body shudders, her thighs clamping around my hand as she fights to keep herself standing.

"That's it. Don't stop," she pleads, her breath hot and desperate against my neck.

Like I ever could.

I curl my fingers again, just a little sharper this time, and that's all it takes. She comes with a shuddering moan, her lips an inch from mine. Her entire body shakes, her walls fluttering around my fingers in the most addictive way as I hold her through it.

When she finally sags in my arms, she lets out a breathless "Fuuuck."

Fuck indeed.

I want to start all over again.

"You okay?" I say into her ear, my clean hand stroking her back soothingly.

She nods, then lifts her head to look at me. Her eyes are dark, a flush high on her cheeks. "More than okay."

Her tongue slides against mine, and I'm more drunk on her than I am on alcohol. I reach for the side of her face, but before I can, I'm yanked backward, the force so abrupt that I stumble into the solid mass of people dancing behind me.

What the fuck?

Everything's a blur of flashing lights and disoriented movement as I regain my footing, my heart slamming against my ribs. When I see the culprit, he grabs a fistful of my shirt.

"What the fuck are you doing, kissing my date?"

I study the polished and familiar blond man in front of me, and the words register, but they don't make sense. My brain lags, still hazy with the lingering taste of Charlotte on my tongue, with how I had her body melting against mine only seconds ago.

"What?" My voice comes out uneven, caught somewhere between disbelief and confusion. "I'm not—"

"Peter, let him go! Are you serious?" Charlotte shouts.

Peter? The tight knot in my gut twists harder. Of course— that's the guy who wanted me to get Charlotte drunk so he could take advantage of her. Did she come here with *him*? Was she on a fucking date while she was letting me finger her?

I shake the thought away and refocus on Peter, who's still got a death grip on my shirt.

"Wait—I know you, don't I?"

I swallow, now actually nervous. Last time, he said he'd get me fired, and I just handed him ammunition. He just saw me kissing Charlotte.

"Yeah. Yeah—you're the chef, aren't you?"

"Look," I say, raising both hands in the hope of placating him, "I didn't know she was here with you, okay?"

He shoves me again, the force jarring. "Fucking prick—get out of my goddamn face."

I try to unclench my jaw. Charlotte's face is still flushed, her lips parted, her breath coming in quick, uneven bursts, and my mind flashes back to why she looks like that.

Something dark and possessive coils in my chest, and I meet Peter's glare again. No matter how much trouble it'll get me into, I won't leave her here with this predator. "I don't think so, all right?"

His eyes narrow. "Oh, you don't think so?"

Jesus. Shoulders squared, fists flexing at his sides . . . this guy is spoiling for a fight.

"Not unless Charlotte comes with me."

Peter's lips curl like I just told the dumbest joke in the world. "Do I look like a fucking asshole?"

Yes, though it's probably best I keep that to myself.

I glance around, hoping to spot one of my friends, but they're nowhere to be found. Not that any of them would throw themselves into a fight. We're grown-ass men, for fuck's sake. What the hell am I doing?

"Charlotte," I say, looking past him to where she's still standing. "Let's go."

Before she can respond, Peter's back in my space, chest brushing mine. "Excuse me?" He sneers before he shoves me a third time.

My first instinct is to swing, to push him back just as hard, to plant my knuckles into his stupid, arrogant face. But I force myself to breathe and push the anger down.

All I want is for Charlotte to come with me and get out of this place.

I look him dead in the eye, keeping my voice steady. "I'm not going to fight you, man. Okay?"

"Oh, you won't?" He grins, like he's been waiting for that answer, like he's thrilled by the fact that I won't hit him first. "You're done, asshole. You can kiss your job goodbye."

I don't see it coming. One second I'm standing there, trying to keep my temper in check. The next, there's a sharp, blinding crack as his fist slams into my eye.

The world tilts, pain exploding through my skull, white-hot and immediate, and my vision bursts with stars. My knees buckle, and then . . .

Nothing.

I SHIFT the ice pack over my swollen eye, the cold biting into my skin. My fingers press lightly against the bruised flesh, testing the ache, before I lean back against the cinderblock wall of the holding cell.

The dim lighting does nothing to soften the harsh reality of where I am. A fucking *jail cell*.

On the bench opposite me, a couple of guys are sprawled out, one snoring lightly, the other slumped forward, his arms crossed as if he just gave up on the idea of staying awake. For a second, I almost envy their ability to sleep through this. My own nerves are buzzing too much to even consider closing my eyes.

The drive here sobered me up quickly, but my memory of what happened before that is patchy at best. Peter hit me—that part I remember clearly. A punch to the face, a blur of movement, Charlotte's voice—but the rest? A hazy mess.

Charlotte.

Where is she?

Last I saw her, she was being handcuffed and led to a different police cruiser.

Fucking hell. Why did I drink so many shots?

My stomach twists, an uncomfortable, sickening churn. Is she okay? What happens when Beatrice hears about this? Because she will. That asshole will tell her we were there together. And Josie's cop friends will tell her everything—about the fight, about Charlotte. The fallout will be brutal.

"Aaron?"

I jerk my head up as Max, Josie's partner, appears on the other side of the bars. Relief slams into me me as I push off the bench and hurry over. "Max, thank fuck. You have no idea how glad I am to see you."

He studies me, eyebrows drawn tight. "Shit. It's really you. What the fuck happened?"

"Bachelor party gone wrong," I say, wincing as I shift the ice pack. "I, uh . . . might have been with someone who . . . was there with someone else, apparently."

"Yeah? Let me guess—her boyfriend didn't take too kindly to it?"

"Something like that."

"You seem to be into that sort of thing." He adjusts his belt. "Who threw the first punch?"

Ignoring the comment, I say, "He did. I didn't hit him back."

His chin jerks back. "You didn't?"

"No."

"But he has a broken nose. Pretty bad-looking."

I blink. A broken nose? That makes no sense.

"I didn't touch him." He squints, as if he's not sure he believes me, but I need one less worry in my mind, so I ask, "Where's Charlotte? Charlotte Arnault? She was brought here with me."

"She's in holding. Looks fine, except for her . . ." He pauses, eyes widening. "Her hand. Wait—*she* punched him?"

Charlotte. She's the one who broke his nose.

Holy shit.

I'm not sure if I'm impressed or worried, but a strangled sound escapes me as I squeeze the bar harder. "I need to see her. Now." My heart is hammering. If he touched her—if he so much as laid a finger on her—I'll end up in a real cell, one I won't be walking out of anytime soon.

Max eyes me carefully. "So, you and her . . ."

"Uhhh . . ." Of course he'd put it together. He probably knows how young she is too. "Yeah."

"Huh. Come on, let's go," he says, moving to unlock the cell. I step out, my muscles aching with every movement. "I'll just need to fill in some paperwork, then you can go."

"What about Charlotte?"

As we walk toward the front desk, Max avoids my gaze entirely. "I can talk to the other guy. See if I can convince him to drop the charges against her with the leverage that you won't press any against him."

"And if he agrees?"

"Everyone walks."

I nod. "Do it."

He studies me for a long moment, then, "All right. Be right back."

"Max?" I call as soon as he takes a step. "Can I talk to him myself?"

"No." He crosses his arms. "Why?"

"Well . . . Charlotte—if her mom found out she was with me, she . . . wouldn't be pleased."

He shakes his head, as if he's just been proven right about me. "I'm not doing this for you, all right? Only for Josie, because she doesn't need any more of your drama." He turns around and mumbles, "I'll tell him to keep his mouth shut."

I watch him walk away then drop onto one of the plastic chairs in the waiting area, resting my elbows on my knees, my head in my hands.

How could Charlotte do this?

Why the hell would she let things go that far if she was there with someone else? And why was she on a date with Peter, of all people?

But just as quickly as the anger rises, it deflates, swallowed by the worry clawing at my insides.

Is she okay? Did he hurt her? Her hand must be killing her if she hit him hard enough to break his nose. And what about Beatrice? Will she find out about this?

I squeeze my eyes shut, but it does nothing to ease the pounding in my skull. Between the hangover, the pain in my face, and the mess I've landed myself in, I'm getting a migraine.

"Aaron?"

My breath catches at the sound of her voice. A voice that once meant *home*.

I lift my head, and there she is.

Josie.

What the fuck is she doing here?

She's standing in front of me, red hair pulled back into a tight bun, piercing green eyes staring me down like I'm some criminal she's about to book. My stomach twists as I notice her uniform, the way she's looking at me—judgmental, disappointed, like I'm the one who's let her down.

"What the hell happened?" she demands, stepping closer. "I was out on a call when a colleague phoned me. Were you arrested? For a *bar fight*?"

She spits out the words like they taste rotten in her mouth, like she can't even fathom that I, of all people, would be sitting here in the drunk tank of her police station, but I barely hear her, my eyes locked on her uniform.

She's working. She's *back at work.*

And I had no idea.

I force myself to stand, my eye throbbing with every beat of my pulse. "What—why are you here?"

Her expression flickers, just for a second. "I'm . . ." She glances away. "I'm back at work."

Something inside me cracks.

"But you didn't say anything. You didn't come home."

Her lips press together. "I'm staying at my parents'."

At her parents'.

Not with Sadie.

Anger and betrayal flood my veins so fast they nearly knock me sideways. I thought she was still in rehab. I thought she was still trying to get better. She kept her promise and called Sadie every day, and I thought she'd show up when she was ready.

But she's back, and she hasn't even come to see our daughter.

"You owe me an explanation, Aaron. I leave Sadie with you, then I get a call saying you were arrested? Are you *kidding* me?"

I can't believe what I'm hearing. *I* owe her an explanation?

The door to the holding cells buzzes, and my head snaps up just as Max steps through, leading Charlotte into the waiting room.

She's still in that green mini dress, the hem scandalously short. Her heels click against the tile floor, and her makeup is smudged, black streaks of mascara ghosting beneath her eyes. Even with her lipstick faded and kissed away, and her hair a red mess of strands ruffled and tangled from the chaos of the night, she looks radiant —and then she *smiles*.

A small, lopsided curve of her lips. Tired, but unapologetic. A little amused, even, like she can't believe we've actually ended up here.

Like it's just another adventure to her.

I should be pissed. I should be so fucking pissed. But instead, the tightness in my chest eases just seeing her standing there, in one piece.

I close the distance between us in an instant. "Are you okay?"

"Yeah." Her eyes skim over my face, landing on the bruise around my eye. Her fingers lift, brushing the swelling so lightly it's barely a touch. "Are you?"

"Jesus." I catch her hand, turning it over. The skin over her knuckles is dark purple, swollen. She really *did* hit him. "He didn't hit back, did he?"

"No, he started crying about his face and Instagram." She scoffs. "Pathetic."

"I can't believe you fucking *punched* him."

She smirks, her fingertips ghosting over my bruised cheek again. "I'll punch anyone for you."

I press a kiss to her knuckles. "I'll bail you out every single time."

Her grin lights up her face, and *god help me*. She's never prettier than when she smiles like this. Genuinely, with her heart.

"Who the hell *is* this, Aaron?" Josie's voice slices through the moment like a blade. "What is going on?"

I don't have to check to know she's glaring at Charlotte. I can feel the judgment radiating off of her.

I groan. "Josie—"

"Holy crap." Her eyes dart between Charlotte and me, widening. Her voice drops to a furious whisper. "Is she . . . *underage*?"

Charlotte stiffens beside me. "No, *she's* not underage," she bites out. "And *she's* right here if you have any questions."

Josie ignores her. "Getting into fights, Aaron? You've obviously lost your damn mind. Did you take her home? Introduce her to Sadie? Please tell me you didn't." When I just keep glaring, she mumbles, "Oh, you're unbelievable."

I have a sense that her next words will be against Charlotte, and I'll be fucking damned if I let Josie make tonight even more difficult.

"You know what?" I say, raising a hand. "Just . . . *stop*."

She crosses her arms, eyes daring me to say that again. "Excuse me?"

"You have no right—absolutely *no* right—to be here screaming at me."

"Oh really?" she spits. "Because—"

"*You're here*, Josie." My voice rises, my anger roaring past my ability to control it. "You're standing right here, and you couldn't be bothered to see your own child."

Her mouth opens. Closes.

"You deserted your daughter." The words feel like fire in my throat, like acid in my veins. "You've been gone for months, mostly without calling or checking in. You canceled on her when she was supposed to come see you. Fuck, Josie, she was so excited, and you didn't think about anyone but yourself. And now—now you want to come at me over who I choose to spend my time with? Over who I bring home?"

Her face crumples, her lips wobbling.

"You don't get to pass judgment until you come home and hug your daughter. Until you prove you're here to stay. You don't get to show up when it's convenient for you and pretend you still have a say in my life. In Sadie's life."

I take a shaky breath, my hands trembling.

"*You* don't get to say a single damn word to me," I finish, voice hoarse, "until you stop making excuses and start fixing what you broke."

Silence.

The whole precinct is staring at us now. Officers. Civilians. The guy at the front desk who was half asleep two minutes ago. Until Josie's tears finally spill over, and she walks past us in a flurry.

The door buzzes again as she disappears through it, leaving me standing there, my chest heaving.

A hand lands on my shoulder and I turn, locking eyes with Max.

"I think you should go now," he says quietly. "Both of you."

I let out a shaky breath, then nod.

I made a scene. A huge fucking scene.

Charlotte is still beside me, silent, eyes downcast. She gives Max a small wave, then grabs my hand and drags me toward the exit.

I follow her, no questions asked.

No wondering.

No looking back.

CHAPTER 24

Rinse and Repeat

I open the door to the house and hang my head, the weight of the night settling on my shoulders like a heavy coat. I found texts from everyone once I finally checked my phone—they assumed I struck gold and left with the hot redhead, which in a way, I did.

I guess they don't need to know I was handcuffed and in the back of a police car.

The whole place is empty, silent, and I wish Sadie weren't at my mom's place tonight. Wish she were home so I could tiptoe upstairs, tuck her blankets under her chin, and press a kiss to her forehead.

Just seeing her, hearing her breathing, would be enough. She has this magic, this inexplicable power to make all my bad moods disappear.

But tonight, the house is just a house. Cold. Quiet. Hollow.

Charlotte steps in behind me, closing the door with a click, then her gaze sweeps over the darkness like she's feeling the same emptiness.

"I need a shower," she says, voice hushed but certain. "Do you need a shower?" Without waiting for an answer, she laces her fingers with mine, tugging me gently up the stairs. I follow, flicking the light on when we make it to the top. The golden glow spills into the hallway, illuminating the moment she reaches for the zipper of her dress. With a single fluid motion, it slides off her shoulders and pools at her feet.

My breath stalls.

Okay. Seeing Charlotte naked performs miracles on my bad mood too.

She steps closer, a knowing smirk playing on her lips as I try to keep my eyes on her face and fail spectacularly. When I jerk my chin up in a pathetic attempt to be noble, she tilts it right back down with a teasing finger.

"Don't look away *now*," she murmurs.

She strips me of my shirt, then my jeans, her fingers brushing over my skin like she's memorizing every inch. Without a word, I turn the shower faucet on and step into it behind her, the roar of the water drowning out everything for a blissful moment.

She's spreading soap over my chest when I finally say it. "I went too far, didn't I?"

Her hands pause for just a second before she looks up. "I might've punched her if my hand wasn't already in bad shape. *That* would have been too far. What you said was just . . . what she deserved. A long time coming."

Water beats down on my back. "But it's her workplace. I went too far."

She resumes moving, gliding her hands up my shoulders, then down my arms, her touch firm but soothing. The tension starts to bleed from my muscles, and for a moment, I wonder—would she let me kiss her again? Would that help?

"She should have told you she was back," Charlotte says.

Yeah, she should have.

I close my eyes as she works lower: my hip, my groin. The second she reaches my cock, my body reacts.

"I honestly don't understand how you can be horny right now," she says with a laugh.

I crack an eye open. "You're here."

Simple as that. My body doesn't care that I'm pissed off. It doesn't care about right or wrong, or that my night descended into madness. It just knows that Charlotte is here, and that does something to me.

She positions me under the jet of water, then rinses the soap from my skin with her hands. "At least tonight was fun until the screaming match."

"Yeah?" I shoot her a look. "Getting arrested was fun?"

"Not my first time."

That makes me tilt my head. "Oh?"

She shrugs like it's nothing. "A couple of years ago, I kicked some guy in the nuts."

"Damn." I brush some hair off her face. "What did he do?"

"He was in charge of talent for a shoot, and he . . ." She taps her chin. "Got handsy. I had to correct his misconceptions—it was my *duty*, in fact."

Her fingers return to my chest. "Does that happen a lot?"

"Men being gross? Yes."

"No, I mean . . . people in positions of power around you trying to . . ." I swallow, the thought alone making my skin crawl. "Making things unprofessional?"

"No." Her hand presses on the side of my neck. "Sometimes. It's part of the gig, I guess."

I trace the bruise on her hand. "And this was fun too?"

"The punch was a first." She pauses, looking down at her knuckles with a proud smile. "And I low-key always wanted to do it."

"Really?"

"Have you ever?"

"Not since I was a kid. Got punched a couple of years ago though. By my brother."

"Aww," she says with exaggerated pity, lifting the shampoo again with her busted hand. "Always getting hit because of a girl, are you?"

I stop her before she can tilt the bottle.

"Hey," I say quietly, taking it from her. "Let me."

There's a protest in her eyes, but I point my chin toward her hand. "You can barely close your fingers. Just . . . let me take care of you for once."

She hesitates, then lets her arms drop to her sides and leans back slightly under the spray of the shower, granting me access.

I pour the shampoo into my palm and step closer, close enough that I feel the warmth of her breath as I reach up and gently massage her scalp. My fingers move through her thick, wet hair, slow and careful, like she's something precious, because she is.

She closes her eyes, and it's quiet for a beat—just the water and the sound of my hands working through her hair.

I can't stop thinking about it.

She's letting me touch her. We're here talking about men who touched her without consent, and she's letting *me* in. Letting me do this.

I rinse the soap from her hair and her body sways toward mine. "This feels nice."

"Guess it's another of those dating things, huh? Showering together?" I say, meeting her gaze through dripping strands of hair. She gives me a content smile, and before I can stop it, the question slips out. "Were you on a date with him tonight?"

She rolls her eyes. "No."

I arch a brow.

"I wasn't!" she insists. "He was the photographer at the show, and the whole group went out for a night at the club."

Oh. So it wasn't a *date*.

"When I saw you . . ." Her hands glide over my shoulders as she leans in. "Trust me, I didn't even remember, let alone care, who I showed up with."

I slide my hands down her sides until I grip her hips, holding her there.

"You let me kiss you tonight."

She doesn't look away. "I let you finger me on the dance floor too."

"Yes." I don't think I'll *ever* forget that. "But you let me *kiss* you."

Her lips part, her breath fanning over my damp skin. "I did."

"You *like* me." I grin as joy takes over her face. "You've got a big ol' crush on me, baby."

"Shut up. You're so corny."

I step forward, forcing her back until her spine meets the wall. I cage her in, my arms braced on either side of her, my body so close that all I'd have to do is tilt my head and I'd be kissing her again.

When she looks up at me, lips kiss-bruised and glistening, I swallow hard. I could take her right here, make her fall apart all over again.

"But do *you* have a crush on *me*?" she asks, fingers toying with my hair.

I jerk back slightly as I notice the self-doubt in her eyes, then I pinch her chin and tilt her head up. "What's that mean?"

"Nothing. It's stupid."

"No, it's not, Charlotte. None of your fears or doubts or *thoughts*, even, are stupid. And if you share them with me, then I'll know how to reassure you. How to make you feel safe again." I hold my thumb on her chin. "Let's not do this, okay? Shoving fears down and letting them fester."

"It's not a big deal. I just couldn't help but notice . . ." She tries for a teasing voice. "Your ex-wife and I look a lot alike."

"Oh. And you're worried my attraction to you might not be about *you*?"

"Maybe?" She laughs at herself. "I told you it's stupid. You just have a type—it's normal."

"*Not* stupid. *Never* stupid," I reprimand, cupping her cheek. "And to answer your question, though you're not the first person to point out the similarities between you and my ex, I have to say I just don't . . . see it."

"You don't *see* it?" Eyes wide, she points at her face. "We both have red hair, green eyes. We're leggy, skinny, tall women."

"You have *ginger* red hair. Hers is auburn. And her eyes are light green, but yours are . . ." I study them carefully, unable to give that color a name. "Muted green. Deep green. Like staring into a clear mountain lake at dusk."

"Oh yeah?"

"Yeah." I tuck some wet hair behind her ear, the water hitting our shoulders. "And you have a little skip in your step. Like you own the space around you without even trying."

Her eyes soften.

"And when you talk," I continue, "there's always an edge, a purpose. You don't just fill silence for the sake of it—you speak because you have something worth saying." I only pause to breathe. "You throw your head back when you laugh and let it take over. You scribble in the margins of your sketchbook, like your brain moves faster than your hand. You tap your fingers on your thigh when you're drawing." I brush my thumb over her lip. "You hum under your breath when you're comfortable—when you're focused, or happy, or tired, like your body can't help but create sound."

For a long moment, she just stares at me. Like she's processing, maybe trying to find the right response. Did I freak her out? How many times can this woman remind me about having a poker face before I start listening?

"And besides, Josie avoids conflict at all costs, and you're the most confrontational person I've ever met." I grin, trying to break the tension. "You keep me on my toes."

Her grin is subdued now. "So I'm a challenge? Like a fun puzzle?"

"No, it's not that." I press my forehead against hers. Why do even her insecurities make me like her more? "It's that when you choose me, it's real. When you say yes, it's because you *want* to." Charlotte wouldn't marry me because her family told her to. She wouldn't agree to be mine if she wasn't sure of it. She wouldn't accept my love without giving it back. "You want me in spite of the difficulties, not because it's the easy thing to do." I swallow. "So no, I don't think you two are similar at all."

She looks like she's not sure if she wants to tease me or kiss me senseless, so I make the choice for her.

Sliding my hand to the back of her neck, I tug her just enough for her to understand what I want. And when she doesn't resist, when she leans in, I close the space between us.

My lips brush against hers, tender at first, like I'm waiting for her to stop me. But she doesn't, her arm curling around my neck, pulling me closer.

And just like that, I'm drowning.

Kissing Charlotte isn't like kissing anyone else. It's not just heat or softness or the rush of something new. It's the sharp inhale before a storm. It's the pulse-pounding moment before you jump off a cliff, knowing you'll never be the same once you hit the water.

When we finally part, I rest my forehead against hers. "Still think I have a type?"

"Yeah." She laughs, breathless. "*Me.*" She stares at me for a long moment, then, instead of speaking, she lifts our joined hands and presses my palm flat against her chest. "You feel that?"

I nod, barely breathing, her heart pounding hard against my fingers.

"That's what you do to me, Chef."

CHAPTER 25
A Pinch of Magic

Most of tomorrow's refreshments for Mother's Day are ready, the smell of food wafting through the house as I throw another look at Sadie, sitting next to me on the couch. "How about some ice cream?"

"I ate pizza at Grandma's," she says in a small voice.

"That's okay. You can have ice cream too."

She nods but avoids my gaze completely, instead stroking Mollie like it's her job.

She's been like this since I picked her up, and Josie's mom said she barely spoke a word the whole afternoon, which must mean something happened at school. But what?

I can almost hear Josie's voice telling me to give Sadie time, that I can't press her into speaking to me. That it's never too early to give her space to process her emotions. I always thought it was a load of bullshit—always had more of a protective "let me fix it for you" attitude. But since Josie's been gone, I've had time to rethink everything.

"Do you want to watch cartoons? Or talk?"

"There's *Bluey* on Monday night," she says, already reaching for the remote.

The TV flickers to life, filling the room with cheerful noise that feels at odds with the tension in her small shoulders. I bite back the questions crowding my throat and bend to pick up her backpack, abandoned in the corner.

But before I can move toward the hooks by the door, the Paw Patrol bag is yanked from my hands.

"It's mine," Sadie snaps, clutching it tight.

I freeze, my hands still midair where the backpack used to be.

That was . . . abrupt.

She hugs the bag, her little fingers curled tight around the straps, but she doesn't even look at me—just turns on her heel and hurries toward the couch.

Something's in there.

She scoops up Mollie, the backpack still clutched tight against her chest. I don't like it. Not the tension in her tiny frame, nor the way she averts her eyes. But I don't push it—not yet. Instead, I head to the kitchen and call, "I'll get some ice cream."

She doesn't answer, but I hear the familiar jingle of some cartoon theme song. Good. At least she's doing something normal.

I get two bowls and add a scoop of chocolate ice cream, then a scoop of strawberry. Normally, she'd be right next to me, chattering about her day, sneaking a spoon when she thought I wasn't looking. Not today.

Once I finish, I grab the bowls and head back into the living room. She's curled into the corner of the couch, Mollie sprawled across her lap. She strokes the cat absently, but the moment I sit down beside her, she nudges Mollie away and reaches for the backpack.

Not even a second of hesitation.

I settle in, draping an arm along the back of the couch, making sure to keep my voice light. "You really needed that, huh?"

She nods, pulling it closer.

I offer her the bowl. "Here. Nothing better than ice cream and *Bluey*."

She takes it, fidgeting with the spoon, but doesn't eat it.

I keep my eyes on the screen and gently ask, "What's in the backpack?"

She stiffens beside me. Doesn't answer.

"It's okay, you know. Whatever it is."

"It's nothing."

I hum, nodding like I believe her. "Must be pretty special for you to keep it so close."

She tugs her lip between her teeth, a tiny crease forming over the bridge of her nose. She's thinking about it.

"Sadie," I say, dipping my head slightly to meet her gaze. "You don't have to tell me. But if something's wrong . . . you know you can, right?"

She hesitates, then nods.

I reach out, running a hand over her hair, smoothing down the strands. "Okay."

"I'm sorry, Daddy." The second she lets go of the backpack, I pull her onto my lap and set our bowls on the coffee table, holding her close.

"You're sorry?" I whisper. "Sorry for what, baby?"

"You told me n-not to take it to school, b-but I wanted everyone to see it."

My heart squeezes at the guilt in her voice. I tilt my head, trying to meet her tear-streaked gaze. "That's okay, love. What did you take to school?"

She hesitates, then pulls away just enough to reach for the backpack. Her fingers tremble as she unzips it, her breathing shallow. When she finally takes it out, I don't understand what I'm looking at—not at first.

But as she unfolds it, everything in me tightens.

It's her dress, the one I bought her for the recital. But the once shiny, pale blue fabric is now smeared with dirt. The hem is torn, a jagged rip running up one side. Faint stains—something dark, maybe paint—mar the front, and the delicate lace along the collar is frayed, barely hanging on.

"Sadie," I murmur, too stunned to say more.

She rubs her eyes with the heel of her palm. "I just wanted to show Monica and S-Selene, I-I'm sorry, Daddy."

Oh, sweetheart.

I cup her cheek, guiding her face up so she has to look at me. Her big, watery eyes blink up at mine, her lip trembling. "Can you tell me what happened?"

Her fingers grip the ruined fabric like it might disappear if she lets go. "It was an accident," she rushes out. "I didn't mean—"

"Hey, hey." I stroke her hair again, keeping my voice steady. "I'm not mad, princess."

Her face crumples, fresh tears spilling over. "But it's ruined, and now I don't have a dress for tomorrow."

I pull her back against my chest, wrapping her up tight, and press my cheek to the top of her head. "That's okay. We'll find another dress."

She cries harder, fisting my shirt. "I don't want you to be mad."

"I'm not mad at you, love. Never at you. How about we put this away now?"

"I won't have a pretty dress for Mommy's Day."

She looks so fucking sad. I hope someone at school can explain what the hell happened, because I'll be asking.

"Are you kidding?" I blow out a raspberry, hoping to coax even the smallest smile from her. "You've got plenty of beautiful dresses. The orange one with the flowers? Or—oh! The purple one with the big skirt? You know that's my favorite."

She shifts, her little shoulders sagging. "But they're not new. I told Mom I'd wear a *new* dress."

The breath I take is measured, because suddenly, I'm realizing this dress might be the least of my problems.

Does Sadie think Josie is coming to the recital? Is that why she was so excited to participate? I'd wondered if Sadie had brought it up to her mom during one of their phone calls, but Josie never said a word. *Will* she come? She's not in rehab anymore—she could. But after the way I talked to her . . . Fuck, did I just ruin every chance of her showing up?

When Sadie looks up at me, eyes wide and searching, I know I need to say something. Something to comfort her, to soften the blow.

But I can't think of a single damn thing.

She sniffles. "I can wear the purple one. Don't be sad, Daddy."

I press my lips together to keep my frustration in check. What I really want to do is bury my face in my hands and scream into the void, but I can't do that. Not in front of her.

Then it hits me.

"You know what?" I sit up straighter. "Daddy is going to fix this."

"But the purple dress . . . the purple dress is okay."

"No, it's not," I say gently, reaching for the ruined fabric she's still clutching. "Because *this* is your dress. The one you were excited about. The one you picked out." I press my thumb over a torn edge. "And I think we can save it."

Her eyes widen. "We can?"

"Uh-huh. We'll clean it, fix the rips, maybe even make it *better* than before. Add some extra sparkles, a few bows—" I pause, lowering my voice like I'm letting her in on a secret. "Maybe even a little magic."

She sniffles, but there's the tiniest spark of hope in her eyes. "Magic?"

"Of course." I grin. "We'll make it good as new. Better than new. Because you see, Daddy knows someone who can make magic with clothes."

"Like a fairy?" she asks, lips parted.

"Better than a fairy." I pull my phone out of my pocket and hold it up. "Shall we call her?"

When Sadie nods, the light has returned to her face.

And you know what? *That's* fucking magic.

I BITE my nail as Charlotte paces back and forth, surveying the pale blue dress—or rather, what's left of it—spread across the living room table. She brings a hand to her chin, humming thoughtfully.

I've missed her so much all weekend, but Beatrice wouldn't let her out. She wasn't at home all day today either, and I cooked only for Beatrice. Through her absence, I kept thinking about Friday. After the shower, I rubbed the towel all over her, then dried her hair. And then . . . then we spent all night doing everything but *that*. We kissed for hours, gave each other some pretty unforgettable orgasms, and eventually fell asleep in each other's arms.

I thought I knew happiness, but then I woke up to her sleepy face and she wished me good morning from the pillow beside mine.

Sadie, crouched beside the dress, covers her face with both hands and watches Charlotte through the gaps between her fingers. "Can you fix it?"

Charlotte turns to me, and the second I see her face, I know the answer.

No, she can't.

Fuck.

"Okay, here's the thing." She lowers herself to her knees, her elbow nearly touching Sadie's, and leans in to whisper conspiratorially. "I didn't want to say anything in front of your dad, because he got it for you, but this dress?"

She scrunches her nose.

Sadie's gaze drops to the tattered fabric. "You don't like it?"

"Oh, it's beautiful, don't get me wrong." Charlotte waves a

hand. "It's just . . . you know your dad. He doesn't know the first thing about dresses."

Sadie nods, hanging on to her every word.

"And this color?" Charlotte brings a hand to her chest. "It's all wrong for Mother's Day."

"It is?!" Sadie's jaw drops.

"Absolutely. Pale blue? For a recital in the *morning*? Pfft." She clicks her tongue as if the thought is simply ridiculous.

Sadie nibbles her lip, her face twisting with worry, and I warn, "Charlotte."

What the hell is she doing? I called her to *help*, and I get that the dress might be unsalvageable, but this sure isn't helping.

When she shushes me with a flick of her fingers, Sadie says, "Daddy said I should wear the purple one with the big skirt."

Charlotte gasps. "A *big* skirt? Do we want everyone to see your underpants every time you twirl?"

Sadie's eyes widen in horror. "No!"

"Exactly." Charlotte nods.

"What about the orange one with the flowers?"

"No, no." Charlotte takes Sadie's hand and leads her to the armchair, where she's dumped rolls of fabric and four tote bags overflowing with supplies. "This is an important recital. You're going to need a *new* dress."

Sadie's eyes dart between the bags and Charlotte's face. "But where will we get it?"

"We will *make* it."

Sadie's hands fly to her cheeks, her entire body practically vibrating with excitement. "*Really?*"

"Absolutely. You pick the fabric and I'll do the rest while your dad makes us hot chocolates." She tosses me a wink. "Your dad's better in the kitchen than he is with fashion anyway."

Very funny.

But I don't even have time to react before Sadie's bouncing on her toes, her face radiant. "Daddy! Did you *hear*?" She whirls around, her fists up in the air. "Charlotte is going to make me a new dress!"

She spins back to the armchair, already reaching for the fabric rolls. She brushes her hand over a shimmering lilac one, then another with tiny silver flowers. "Look at this one!" she squeals, holding up a deep red fabric that glows under the light. "It's *sparkly*!"

Charlotte grins. "You like sparkles, huh?"

Sadie nods emphatically. "Oh! But this one has flowers! And this one is pink! Charlotte, how do I choose?"

Charlotte laughs, plopping down onto the armchair. "Well, you take your time, and—"

Now holding a royal blue fabric, Sadie gasps. "This one! This one's *perfect*."

"Then perfect it is," Charlotte says before wrapping the fabric around her like a cloak. "*This* is queen material."

I watch Charlotte take out her scissors, and once I'm sure she has it all under control, I head into the kitchen, sneaking one last glance at Sadie. She's standing tall, her eyes bright, completely enchanted by the fabric Charlotte's working with.

An hour ago, she was curled up in misery, clutching a ruined dress to her chest. Now, she looks like she's ready to take on the world.

And it's all because of Charlotte.

Funny, because that's exactly how she makes *me* feel too. Like with her, I'm not just existing—I'm *living*. Like every step with her leads straight to the top.

CHAPTER 26

The Taste Test

Charlotte is gathering her things, her hands moving too quickly, and I hate how familiar this feels. Borrowed time. Always borrowed time.

Sadie just fell asleep, so I should have two to three hours before one of her nightmares wakes her up. The house is quiet. For once, there's no chaos demanding my attention. Just her, and I'm not ready to let that go.

"Are you sure you have to leave right now?" I ask, knowing I sound pathetic but too far gone to care. "You wouldn't believe how much I fucking missed you."

"Well, I've taken the measurements and cut the dress. There isn't much more I can do without my machine, and Sadie needs her dress in the morning."

And she's already doing this as a favor—I really can't ask her to stay longer.

"Maybe another half hour?" I try, shamelessly. I don't want her to go. Not yet. Not when the house is quiet and I finally have her all to myself.

"Half an hour, huh? Do you have any plans for it?"

My hands settle on her hips. I'd be happy to spend the next

thirty minutes just kissing her. It feels like I could do that forever. Just kiss her, feed her, let her sleep. Take care of her the way she needs.

But I don't want her thinking I'm trying to get her out of her clothes, so I offer the safe option.

"Wanna eat something?"

"Eat? That's what you want to do?" She steps back, chuckling as she gives me a look. "You really are on a mission to fatten me up, huh?"

"I gotta make sure you're taken care of when you go back to . . ." The words catch, twisting in my mouth. I hate the idea of her leaving. Of going back to that harpy, to a life that's not large enough for her.

Her smile dims, like she feels it too, but then, in true Charlotte fashion, she flicks the mood away with a smirk, fingers tugging playfully at the tape measure draped around her neck like it's some kind of warning.

"I think I'd like to..." she drawls, "take your measurements."

"Take my what?"

"I'm creating a portfolio." She waves a hand around. "You know, just in case."

In case? In case she decides to pursue her design career instead of modeling and camming? "That's . . . that's amazing, Charlotte." I straighten my arms at my sides. "Go ahead. Take measurements —whatever you want."

Her eyes glint playfully. "Stand still, Chef."

Her fingers brush the back of my neck as she loops the tape around it, her breath fanning against my jaw as she leans in. I swallow hard, my entire body locking tight.

Get your head out of the gutter for five minutes, Aaron.

"Relax," she murmurs, the word rolling off her tongue.

I try to keep my body in check as she moves lower, measuring my shoulders, her knuckles grazing the fabric of my shirt. Then she hums, her lips quirking up at the corner as her eyes flick up to mine.

"Shirt off, please."

Fuck.

I hesitate. This is about to be either very flattering for her or extremely embarrassing for me, because the moment her fingers graze my skin, I won't be able to pretend that her touch doesn't burn, that I don't crave her the way a flower needs sunshine.

Still, I yank the shirt over my head and let it drop.

Her gaze skims over my chest, and when her tongue darts out to wet her lips, my dick twitches in response.

She loops the tape around my torso. The cool fabric barely registers, but her fingers dragging along my stomach steal all of my attention.

"Chest," she says to herself. She pulls the tape a little tighter, her knuckles pressing against my abs, and I have to keep myself from making any sound.

"You good?" she asks.

No. No, I am absolutely not fucking good.

"Yeah," I rasp.

Her fingers linger a second too long, then she moves lower. Waist. Hips. I don't know much about taking measurements, but this feels like a hell of a lot of touching.

She kneels in front of me, the tape slipping around my waist. I guess this part is necessary, but my brain doesn't care, because she's on her knees looking up at me, eyes dark and mischievous. Because her breath is warm against my stomach.

"Almost done?" I ask.

She hums. "Do you not like me down here?"

Oh, fuck. She's playing me.

Measurements, *my ass*.

"No, you look great down there. Perfect. Like you belong on your knees for me."

She smirks—fuck, that smirk—as her fingers hook into the

waistband of my jeans, and then the sound of my zipper being pulled down mixes with my heartbeat.

"Seven point one inches," I offer, tucking some hair behind her ear.

"Hmm?"

"I took those measurements in the eighth grade."

She presses a kiss to my stomach, then, holding the measuring tape to her cheek, she muses, "On a good day, I can take about . . . four in here."

It's like a dirty math problem. If I'd known this was one of its applications, I might've tried a lot harder in high school algebra.

My briefs are slowly pulled down, and, oh *fuck*. She's going to touch me. Not just touch me—she's going to suck me off. The thought makes my head spin like a carnival ride.

"I think I'll have to handle the rest with my fist."

Shit, I might come from the promise alone.

"You're shaking," she rasps. Her fingers finally brush against my cock and my hips jerk forward, desperate for more. "Nervous, Chef?"

"Bewitched," I huff out.

She grins, then her hand wraps around my shaft, and I fucking choke on a breath as her fingers squeeze just right.

The second her mouth envelops me, the sound of keys rattling against the doorknob sends a jolt of panic straight to my chest.

Shit. Who the fuck is entering my house?

Charlotte freezes, her eyes widening as everything shifts from buzzing anticipation to a full-blown scramble. Her hand jerks back as I pull my briefs up, but it's too late, because the door swings open and Logan steps inside, a look of mild confusion on his face.

"Oh, you're . . . awake," Logan says, looking at me. I see the moment he registers the bruise on my eye, then his gaze flicks to Charlotte, on her knees.

"Y-yeah. Hey," I say. "What's up?"

He hesitates. "Prim lost her keys last night and she's got to leave early in the morning, so I came to grab the spare we left here."

I gulp down air, zipping up my jeans as Charlotte stands, head tilted down to hide her chuckle.

"Oh, yeah." I can feel my heart pounding in my throat as I cross then uncross my arms. "They're in there. Top drawer to the right," I say, pointing at the walk-in closet.

His eyes narrow ever so slightly, but he doesn't comment before he walks to the closet and disappears inside.

I meet Charlotte's amused gaze and mouth *Fuck*, but she just giggles into her hand, completely unfazed. But she knows this is a problem. My brother finding us like this? He's going to have questions I won't be able to answer. Not honestly, at least.

"Got it," he says, coming out of the closet with the keys. "Sorry about this."

Sweat drips down my back. "No, no problem."

Logan crosses his arms, eyes finally settling on Charlotte. "So . . . you're *young*."

"Thanks?" Charlotte's lips twitch. "I'm twenty-three."

Logan hums. "Inappropriately young, but technically okay." He turns his glare back to me. "So why are you keeping her a secret?"

"I . . ." I look anywhere but at him. "I didn't really want this to be public."

"That must be nice to hear," Logan says dryly.

Charlotte shrugs. "I'm not here for the boyfriend experience."

Logan nods, his suspicion not budging an inch. He sticks out his hand. "Well, I'm Logan. Nice to meet you . . ."

"Cherry," I interject.

The second the word leaves my mouth, I feel Charlotte's glare on me and know I will pay for this. And she's got every fucking reason to be mad too—I have no right to use her alias to hide my sins.

Charlotte takes it, shaking firmly. "Nice to meet you too."

"Cherry." Logan takes in her outfit—her miniskirt, a low-cut top that can barely be called that held up by thin straps, and the high, strappy heels. Then, with all the casual brutality of an interrogator, he says, "You must be the reason my brother smiles at his phone then?"

Charlotte shrugs, though I see the pride in her eyes.

"And the reason his phone moans back at him, I assume." When neither of us says a word, Logan's eyes narrow. "So what's with you, huh? Are you married? Sugar baby? Mob wife? Cult leader?"

"Seriously?" I say flatly. "You left out murderer on the run and prostitute."

"Right." Logan grins at Charlotte. "So which one is it?"

Charlotte doesn't even flinch, eyes pinned on him. "I can be whatever you want," she says smoothly. "How much are you paying?"

Oh my god.

Logan's stare slices through me like a blade.

"She's *not* a prostitute," I rush out, horrified. "Or—any of that. I can't *believe* you, Logan."

"Can't you?"

I don't even know why I'm surprised after all this time. I don't know how I still let his poorly veiled opinions of me hurt me. Yet I do.

"You know what—I'm tired of this, Logan. Yes, I fucked up—*seven years* ago. How long is my punishment going to last, huh? When will I have paid enough?" I bark. "Or does one mistake grant you the irrevocable right to come into my house and insult me and my—"

Logan's brows pull together.

"My *guest,*" I say, Charlotte rolling her eyes beside me.

"Right. Well, I didn't mean to insult you, Cherry." He breathes sharply through his nose, refocusing on me. "I'll see you."

He vaguely gestures at me and Charlotte. "Enjoy . . . whatever this is."

Of course. When things get hard, Logan skedaddles. Some things never change, do they?

"You know, Josie *should* have chosen you," I say as he turns his back on us. He flips around, lips twisted in a grimace. "'Cause you're both so fucking good at leaving."

He hesitates for a long moment before moving closer. "Fine. You wanna talk? Let's talk about how it's been seven *fucking* years, and you still think any of this is about Josie."

"I know it's not."

"Yeah, you know it's not," he echoes, his voice eerily calm. "What the fuck do you want me to say, Aaron? I still can't look at you without seeing the guy who slept with my girlfriend and then *married* her. You were my best friend and you betrayed me, and I don't know how to get over it. And you know the worst part? Every time I try to trust you, you go and prove why I shouldn't."

"What the fuck does that mean?"

Logan gestures vaguely in Charlotte's direction. "This." His eyes are sharp, accusatory. "You sneaking around, lying. Hiding whatever *this* is."

My chin jerks forward. "This has *nothing* to do with you."

"The hell it doesn't," he snaps. "You're my brother, Aaron. You're my daughters' uncle and my mother's son. You work for my friends, for Christ's sake. And I know you. I know that when you keep secrets, it's because you're doing something you *know* is wrong." His eyes flick to Charlotte again. "Or maybe just something you're ashamed of."

When I step forward, shoulders tensing, Charlotte places a calming hand on my chest and purrs, "Careful, Logan. I don't like people talking about me like I'm not in the room."

Logan, eyes on me, nods. "Then maybe you shouldn't be involved with someone who's too much of a coward to acknowledge you."

Coward.

I feel it in my bones, in their marrow, in the places I don't let anyone see. It's not just an insult—it's the truth. Because Logan isn't wrong, is he? If he were, I would've come clean about Charlotte already. If he were, I wouldn't be standing here, watching her take the hit for my decision.

Shame curdles in my gut, hot and corrosive. It climbs up my throat, twisting around my tongue, making me feel like I might choke on the weight of it.

I don't look at Charlotte. I can't. Because what if she's looking at me differently now? What if she *sees* it too—the same thing Logan does? The same thing I do?

I swallow hard, forcing myself to stand my ground, to keep my face neutral. But inside, everything caves in.

Logan holds the keys up, then turns and heads for the door.

But I've got one more thing to say.

"I've been apologizing, trying to mend things, trying to get close to you for years. Again and again, I've proven myself as a good father, son, friend, and brother. So if you still have a problem with me, then it's *your* fucking problem, Logan. I'm out."

He hesitates, then leaves without another word, the door clicking behind him. In the silence, I don't know what to say.

Charlotte shifts beside me, adjusting the strap of her top, and the sound of it—a quiet snap against her shoulder—somehow makes the moment even heavier.

She clears her throat. "I should probably go."

"No, Charlotte, I—" I reach for her, gently coaxing her closer. "I have so much to apologize for, I don't even know where to start."

She waves me off, but the gesture is stiff, detached. She's not even looking at me, chin tilted down. "Don't worry about it."

I do though.

"I shouldn't have called you Cherry," I insist. "That's your alias. I had no right to use it without your permission."

Her lips twitch. "I get why you did it."

"I'm also sorry I said I didn't want this to be public."

That earns me a real reaction—a humorless laugh as she finally looking up at me. "You might be sorry for *saying* it, but it's not like it isn't true."

"It's *not*—" I start, but she's right. I'm actively trying to keep this a secret from everyone. "I'm not ashamed of you, Charlotte. Shit—you're so far out of my league I'd need a spaceship to get to your level. You know that, right? That this has nothing to do with you?"

She nods then. "Yes, Chef. I know."

Shame makes me feel small and insignificant again. "He's right, isn't he?" I turn to the door. "I'm a coward."

She doesn't answer right away, but eventually, she cups my cheek. "It's fine, Aaron. We're just . . . hooking up—we don't need announcements in the paper for that."

Just hooking up.

It's bullshit. We both know it is. She might not know how to ask for it, I might not know how to give it to her, but we both want more than that. *I* do. I want to get out of this mess with her, want to reassure her that I'll come clean with everyone and will face whatever consequences I deserve, because I'm *not* a coward.

Because she's worth being fearless for.

I don't say it though. I let the lie settle between us as she moves toward the door, grabbing her purse. "I need to finish Sadie's dress."

I nod. I don't want her to go, but I don't have any right to ask her to stay. So I let her leave, standing there in my too-quiet house, alone.

Like a fucking coward.

CHAPTER 27

Cha-Cha-Cha(rlotte)

C harlotte's front door opens before I even knock. She's barefoot, wearing one of those oversized T-shirts that hits mid-thigh and turns my brain to mush. Her hair's a mess, eyes rimmed with fatigue. She looks like she hasn't slept, but perfect nonetheless.

I spent all night thinking about what I wanted to say. Rehearsed it a dozen times. But now that she's standing in front of me, none of it feels like enough. Still, I have to try, so I say, "Hey, gorgeous. About last night—"

She grabs my wrist and tugs me inside. "Forget about last night. Bedroom."

"Wait, no, I—" I close the door behind me and stop walking, resisting the pull just enough to make her glance back. I see it—the fear in her eyes. The need to bury it all under something fast and physical, to outrun the feelings clawing their way up.

"I want to do *that*. Always," I assure her. "But I also want to talk. Can we?"

Frustration flashes across her face like a storm cloud. When she pivots and heads for the kitchen, I follow, watching as she pulls a water from the fridge.

"Want some?"

"No, thank you." She brings the glass to her lips. "Look, about yesterday—"

"I know this thing between us has to stay a secret, okay?" Her voice is sharp. "I'm not—this isn't news. You have nothing to apologize for."

"Okay," I say soothingly.

"I'm not asking you to make it public. In fact, I don't want you to. I want this—exactly this."

Does she really? Or is that what she's telling herself so it doesn't hurt as much?

"Okay," I say again, even though it's the last thing I want to agree to. But she's overwhelmed. Scared. Scarred. So I step closer, hands hovering at her waist.

"Can I?"

She nods.

I wrap my arms around her, resting my hands on the small of her back. When she loops her arms around my neck, I start swaying.

"What's happening?"

"We're slow-dancing in the kitchen."

"With no music?"

I shrug. "Do you want music?"

She studies me, like she's trying to decode me. "Why are we slow-dancing in the kitchen?"

"Because I think you need someone to hold you more than you need someone to eat you out."

She doesn't pull away, doesn't speak, either. Her fingers twitch against the back of my neck, and as she rests her forehead against my shoulder, I feel the tension ease from her like a long-held breath. Her arms stay around my neck, loose but holding.

"I'm sorry." I slide my hands up and down her back in easy, grounding strokes. "For last night." She doesn't tense up, so I continue. "I'm sorry for how Logan spoke to you. I should've defended you. Should have told him about us. I didn't want the fight to escalate, but you deserved better."

She pulls back a little, just enough to look up at me. Her face isn't guarded or angry. It's just . . . open. Raw. "I'm used to worse," she says quietly.

"I know," I say, tension building in my jaw. "And I hate that. I hate that you think the only way to keep someone around is to ask for nothing."

She bites her lip and looks down. "Aaron . . ."

I tip her chin up with two fingers.

"You're allowed to want things. From me. From this. You don't have to pretend you don't." She looks like she might cry, but she's trying as hard as she can not to. So I add, "And you don't have to tell me right now. But if you ever want more—if you ever want *anything*—I'm listening."

For a second, I think she's going to argue. Tell me not to get attached, that this isn't real and nothing happened last night and we're fine. But she leans back in and rests her head on my shoulder again. "I want you to stay."

That's it. She deserves so much more than a guy who just *stays*. But I get it. After everything she's been through—everything *I've* been through too—all we want is each other's presence.

All we want is to slow-dance in the kitchen.

"I will," I say. "As long as you'll have me."

We stay like that for a while. No music. No words. Just two people swaying through the silence, holding on to the wreckage like it's something worth saving.

"I dropped Sadie's dress off at school this morning. Even left her a little encouraging note with a Bluey doodle. I hope she'll love it," she says after a while, interrupting the peaceful silence.

"I'm sure she will." I swallow past the sludge in my throat at the mention of today. "I can't stop worrying that she'll be there alone. She didn't want me there, didn't want her aunt either. I told her she didn't need to go—that we'd spend the day together, go to the movies. But she wanted to participate, and she's still . . . hopeful. What if Josie doesn't show up?"

Charlotte stops swaying. I pull back and watch her face, expecting worry, maybe even pity, but finding something entirely different.

Anger.

"Why wouldn't Josie be there?"

"Well, after our fight, the other day—"

"That has *nothing* to do with Sadie!"

"I'm aware," I say, somewhat defensively. Is she mad at me? "But I don't know for a fact that she'll be there."

She moves fast, running into the corridor and disappearing behind the corner.

I blink. "What's happening?"

She's back after a second, pulling down the sides of an obscenely short pink dress. "Come on," she says, waving me over. "Let's go."

"Wh-where?"

"To Sadie's school." Her voice is firm, no room for argument. "The show starts at eleven, right? We can still make it."

We? *We* can still make it?

I stare at her, my pulse hammering.

"Jesus, Aaron. Come on," she says before stepping closer, pushing me forward with both hands.

I stumble a little as I follow her. "What about lunch?"

"You'll have to make something that doesn't take eleven hours."

I glance at the clock. Beatrice will be here in three hours, and I need at least two for the poached seabass. It's just not possible.

"But your mom—the menu she approved—"

"We'll say there was no seabass at the supermarket!" she calls over her shoulder as she snatches her purse. "Or that I found out I'm allergic, or that you're sick or—" She whirls back, eyes wild. "I don't know, okay? We'll figure it out. Let's go."

I hesitate for half a second—long enough for her to grab my wrist and yank me out the door—then the hallway blurs as I jog to keep up. She presses the elevator button and steps in, pulling me the rest of the way in before the doors fully open.

This'll get me in trouble. Beatrice will be pissed, and the other moms at school will talk, whisper about Charlotte and me showing up together. They'll assume things, ask questions.

But none of it matters right now.

None of it remotely dampens my enthusiasm as I grin back at her.

Because my daughter is *not* performing for Mother's Day with no one to cheer her on.

"WHAT ARE we going to tell the parents? The teachers?" she asks as I thrust my car into the first parking spot available. I ended up texting Beatrice that I'd need a sick day, and though all she answered back was "Okay," I *know* she's displeased.

In a flurry, we remove our seat belts and step out, and I meet Charlotte's gaze over the hood. "What do you mean?"

"About me. *Us.* Being here together, you know?"

We break into a run toward the school entrance, and the sound of children singing drifts through the air. Fuck. It's started already.

"Oh, who cares," I mumble, not breaking my stride. I'm the villain either way, aren't I? "Let everyone think whatever they want."

"Is that how it is?" She throws me a wink. "I like this Aaron. But stop looking at me like that. Remember? Poker face?"

"Pretty sure this *is* my poker face."

"Then we're screwed," she quips, flashing a grin as she pulls open the door.

We rush through the corridors until we reach the one that leads to the gym, where a small crowd of parents turns our way, heads swiveling. They're familiar faces. Jenny's mom—Linette. David's mom, whatever her name is. The second their gazes land on Charlotte, their expressions flicker with barely concealed shock. They try to mask it, to their credit, but they fail miserably.

"Hello, everyone. Is the show . . ." I gesture vaguely toward the door.

"It's starting in ten minutes," Linette says, eyeing Charlotte's short dress with unmistakable curiosity. "The other class ran late."

"Oh, great. I thought we'd missed the beginning."

Linette turns her attention to Charlotte. "So nice to meet you, uh . . ." She extends a hand.

Charlotte barely shakes it. "Yeah, nice to meet you."

"And you are . . ." Linette probes, eyes roaming down the short dress clinging to her curves.

Great, I'll be the main topic of gossip for the next year.

"More thirsty than I've ever been." Charlotte turns to me, completely unfazed. "I need a glass of water to keep down last night's vodka. The run kinda shook the whole mix."

Every mother within earshot stiffens, eyes snapping to us like we just set the gym on fire.

"Yeah. Yes." I clear my throat. "We'll . . . um . . . we'll be back."

I grab Charlotte's wrist and steer her toward the hallway before the judgmental stares can melt my skin off. The moment we turn the corner she bursts out laughing, the sound full and unrestrained.

"Jesus Christ, Charlotte." I press a hand to my forehead, trying to will my heartbeat back to normal. "You just love to get me in trouble, don't you?"

"I love to get *us* in trouble." She steps into my space, beaming. "And besides, *you* said 'who cares,' and I certainly don't."

I beam back. *Us.* "I like getting in trouble with you."

I like everything with her.

Her eyes soften. "You know what's really hot?" When I tilt my head, she pulls a lock of my hair back. It's the most tender gesture. "Someone who never asks you to be *less*."

"Less? Less of what?"

"I don't know." She looks down at her bright pink mini-dress. "The way I dress, my flirting, hell—everything about me. Some people would say, and in fact *have said*, that it's too much."

Too much? "I can't get enough."

It's the same as last night, the same as every time—this invisible pull, this stupid, reckless gravity. It never lets up. Not even now, in the dim hallway of my daughter's school, with parents just around the corner and whispers waiting to follow us.

I need to say something about last night. Anything—actually, I need to tell her everything. How I'm scared of losing my brother and my friends. How my job brings me happiness like nothing ever has before, and I'm terrified of not having a purpose again. How last time I blew up my whole life for a woman, I ended up with nothing. How I feel like if I do it again, I'm a heartless, selfish prick, and if I don't, I'm a coward.

And how through it all, I need her even more than I want her.

But a sharp burst of applause echoes from the gym, snapping me back.

"We should go in," she says, a comforting look in her eyes as she tugs at my hand.

We walk over, and the auditorium is packed with moms. The stage is lined with pastel-colored decorations—paper flowers taped to the curtain, cut-out hearts with each child's name in glitter.

I scan the crowd for Josie, and I'm pretty sure I see Charlotte doing the same, but she's nowhere to be seen. Whenever I think I've got no more space left for disappointment, she manages to carve it in.

I adjust my cuffs for the third time, but my knee won't stop bouncing once we take a seat. Charlotte notices, because of course she does, and without a word, she reaches over and slides her fingers over mine, squeezing.

The lights dim, and a hush settles over the crowd.

One by one, the kids take the stage, each stepping into the spotlight for their turn. The first is a boy in suspenders and a bow tie, stomping his feet in a tap routine that's more enthusiasm than rhythm. The audience claps along, and he grins, waving wildly at his mom as he skips offstage. Next, a little girl in a pink tutu does a series of careful twirls. Another girl comes out adjusting a tiara on her head, giving the audience a royal wave before attempting a wobbly cartwheel that sends her tiara flying across the stage.

Some kids beam under the attention, others freeze for a second before launching into their moves, and one boy in a superhero cape gets so caught up in posing that Miss Delaney has to gently usher him offstage.

Then it's Sadie's turn.

She steps out hesitantly, small fingers tugging at the fabric of her dress before letting go. It's royal blue, sleek in a way that stands out from the fluffier outfits around her. The square neckline and puffed sleeves give it a regal feel, and the way the fabric flows as she moves makes her look like a tiny queen stepping onto her dais.

My throat tightens as I squeeze Charlotte's hand tighter.

She *made* that. She sat at her machine all night, stitching together something perfect for my daughter. Not just any dress— something to make her feel special.

Sadie clasps her hands in front of her, shifting her weight from foot to foot as she scans the crowd. When her lips press together, my chest tightens. Is she looking for Josie? Did she see me?

The music starts, and she hesitates, her fingers twitching at her sides. When her gaze locks onto mine, I recognize her crying face.

I sit up straighter. "It's okay, sweetheart." She can't hear me from the stage, but I grip the back of the seat in front of me and nod. "You got this."

Charlotte tenses next to me. "Aaron—"

Sadie's bottom lip trembles, then her whole face crumples.

Shit.

When the first sob escapes her lips, I rise to my feet.

"Daddy?" Her voice is small, broken, carrying through the room.

I'm already moving, and it's when I reach the makeshift stage that I realize Charlotte is right beside me. Sadie stumbles forward, practically flinging herself into my arms.

I catch her, lifting her up easily as she clings to me, her face buried against my shoulder.

"Mommy isn't here," she cries. Her chest shakes against mine as I soothingly comb through her hair, the auditorium so silent, we'd hear a pin falling on the floor.

"*I'm* right here, okay? And I'll make a video for Mom, so she doesn't miss a thing."

"I didn't think you would come," she hiccups between sobs.

My throat goes tight as I turn to Charlotte, who smiles with misty eyes. I can't believe I almost *didn't* come. I should have known better, trusted my instincts the way Charlotte did.

"Of course I came, baby." I kiss the top of her head, holding her closer. "I wouldn't have missed it for the world."

She sniffles, then tilts her head up over my shoulder.

"Charlotte?" she asks, voice wobbly.

Charlotte pinches her cheek "Hi, kiddo. You look beautiful."

Sadie blinks at her for a long moment. Then without warning, she untangles one arm from around me and reaches for her.

Charlotte stills.

I look at her, and she at me—like she's asking for permission. It's almost laughable—I wouldn't be here for my crying daughter if it weren't for her.

When I pull her to me, she steps forward and wraps an arm around both of us, and just like that, we're all tangled together.

There's no better feeling in the world.

"Thank you for my dress, Charlotte," Sadie whispers.

"You're so welcome, sweetie."

I shut my eyes, pressing my lips to her hair, then doing the same with Charlotte. Fuck whoever's watching. For the first time in a long time, it feels like nothing is missing.

Sadie pulls back after a few seconds, rubbing at her face with the back of her hand. "Daddy, I wanna do my dance."

I brush a curl behind her ear. "We can't wait to see it."

Her big brown eyes flick between us. "Will you and Charlotte dance with me?"

Before I can think of a way to get out of this without hurting Sadie's feelings, she's nodding. "Sure we'll dance with you."

Say what now?

"Charlotte," I hiss through gritted teeth, but she widens her eyes at me as if to say I don't really have a choice.

"What! We were just dancing at home. This is the same."

How is this the same? I look back at the moms, at Miss Delaney watching Charlotte with a frown, and groan inwardly.

I guess I'm dancing.

The audience claps as I help Sadie back to her spot. Charlotte quickly joins her side, then watches me expectantly until I pull myself up on the stage and join them.

The teachers restart the music and this time, Sadie dances—with me and Charlotte right beside her, following along, fumbling our steps, completely out of sync but laughing through it.

And when the final note plays, and Sadie throws her arms up in the air, beaming at the crowd—Charlotte and I do the same, mirroring her movements, grinning just as wide.

The applause is deafening, but all I hear is Sadie's giggle, and all I feel is Charlotte's hand in mine, squeezing tight. I playfully pull her closer, her shoulder bumping against mine as her eyes widen in surprise.

"We're not just hooking up, Charlotte," I say, low enough that only she can hear. She gives me a look—a look like she doesn't want to burn my life down to ashes—but I've made my decision. "I'm turning this spark into a wildfire."

Play

CHAPTER 28
A Family Feast

Charlotte's phone buzzes again on the table.

It's been lighting up since we walked in the door, vibrating angrily. I glance over as she flips it facedown for the third time. It's Beatrice, isn't it?

"You okay?" I ask as Sadie chatters between bites of pizza, her legs swinging under the table. "I can take you home if you need to go."

Charlotte brushes a strand of hair behind her ear. "Nah. I'll come up with a lie. I always do."

I study her for a second longer. "You sure?"

The last thing I want is to get her into *more* trouble.

"I'm fine," she says then adds with a little shrug, "Half of these are just notifications from TOP anyway."

My muscles tense at the mention. "Really?" I ask, aiming for a casual tone. "How come?"

"Guess my fans are worried about my prolonged absence."

Prolonged? How long has it been? And will it be permanent?

She spent years under her mom's control, and I'm not about to be the guy who tells her to quit camming, but if we're going to

304

keep seeing each other, we'll have to talk about it eventually. Set some boundaries. Figure out what makes sense for both of us.

She turns to Sadie, who's barely stopped talking since we got home—first about the performance, then about the ice cream we got after, then about the park, where she made Charlotte push her on the swings *way* higher than I ever would have.

Charlotte, for her part, played along like a pro. She cheered at every trick, gasped at every daring move, and let Sadie cling to her the entire walk home. And now, even as we sit around the table, she's still giving Sadie her full attention, nodding along as if this is the most fascinating story she's ever heard.

"And then I did *two* spins on the bars," Sadie says around a mouthful of cheese, beaming. "Did you see?"

"I did," Charlotte says solemnly. "I don't know how you didn't get dizzy. That was some Olympic-level stuff."

Sadie giggles, and I just sit back, watching them together.

"Lucy's mom says you're dating my daddy," she says out of nowhere.

Charlotte, mid-sip of water, chokes so hard she nearly spits it out. Her eyes widen and she thumps a fist against her chest as if trying to force the water down.

"Shit," she gasps, dropping her slice of pizza onto her plate.

"Daddy, she said a—"

"I know, sweetheart." I shoot Charlotte a look, a mix of amusement and warning, before turning back to Sadie. "Charlotte and I are friends, just like the two of you."

Sadie frowns, as if dissecting my words. Then she shifts her gaze to Charlotte. "We're friends?"

Charlotte dabs at her lips. "Sure we are. I let you pick the biggest slice."

Sadie lifts her chin. "I need it more than you! I'm still growing."

Charlotte laughs, a full, warm sound that seeps under my skin and settles there. She watches me as she bites into her slice, eyes bright and happy.

"So are you having dinner with us again?" Sadie asks between chews.

"Would that be okay with you?" Charlotte asks.

"Yes! Daddy smiles more."

I grin, ruffling her hair before meeting Charlotte's gaze. She playfully widens her eyes. "Hear that? Even your daughter thinks you have no poker face."

"Ha-ha."

"Daddy, can we watch *Bluey* after dinner?"

"Sure, sweetheart."

Sadie picks up her crust and chews absentmindedly. I'm so proud of her, even though she dragged me onto a stage to embarrass myself. Today was hard for us, but Amelie was right. We made it. "Are you happy, love?"

She nods and points at the biggest slice of pizza still in the carton. "Dibs!"

Charlotte sets the slice on her plate as I say, "Last one. We don't want you to get a tummy ache, huh?"

The doorbell rings just as I take a sip of my drink, so I set my glass down and push back my chair, then walk to the door.

The moment I open it, my breath catches in my throat.

Josie.

For a beat, I just stare at her. I should probably be annoyed she showed up here without warning, but all I feel is relief. She's here. *Finally*, she's going to see her daughter.

Before I can even find the words, Josie brings a finger to her lips, her eyes flicking past me toward the house. She gestures for me to step outside.

I hesitate, glancing over my shoulder, then step out and pull the door almost shut behind me.

She shifts on her feet, arms crossing over her chest like she's bracing herself. "Hi. I . . . want to talk to you."

If she wants to talk out here, it means Sadie's not supposed to hear. Is it bad news? I don't think I can take her saying she's going back to rehab again. "Okay."

"First of all, sorry for the ambush." She takes a breath, looking down for a moment before meeting my gaze again. "But, uh . . . there's a lot more I need to apologize for. Starting with what I said at the station."

"Oh." The memory of that argument is still fresh, but it's the *last* thing I want her to apologize for. "Thank you, but—"

"No, let me say it." She holds up a hand. "I have no right to tell you how to live your life. How to parent Sadie, when I wasn't around to do it." A single tear spills over. "I never thanked you. Not *once*. You took care of our daughter when I couldn't, and I never bothered to tell you how grateful I am for it."

A lump forms in my throat. "You don't need to thank me, Josie. She's Sadie. She's the person I love the most in the world."

"I never thanked you for that either." She presses her eyes closed for a moment. "For being such an amazing, present dad." She looks at her hands, then back up at me. "I know you didn't do it for me, but . . . Sadie is the person I love the most too."

We stand in silence, and I swear I can almost feel the grief. Can almost taste the regret, the loss. Maybe one day, seeing her won't be such an ugly reminder, but right now, it's devastating.

"I appreciate that, Josie. I do."

She offers a tight, almost hesitant smile. "It's not enough, but—"

"No, it's not nearly enough, because the problem isn't whether you thanked me or you're sorry for what you said. The issue is that you vanished from your daughter's life for months. That I had to *beg you* to call her. That you came back without saying a word and missed her Mother's Day recital."

"I *was* there, actually."

"What?"

"Yes." Her lips wobble. "Sadie didn't see me. I was going to

her, but then, you and . . ." She huffs out a puff of air. "Charlotte . . . you hugged, danced. I . . ."

Oh, damn.

I can't imagine that would've felt nice.

"It's fine," she says, wiping at her cheeks furiously. "I figured I
didn't deserve that moment, that you and Charlotte did."

"Why didn't you tell me you were back, Josie? Why didn't you
come to see Sadie?"

She sniffles. "I needed time."

"*Time*? Time for what? Because if you're out of the rehab, I
assume you've got your problem under control. Right?"

"Yes, I do."

"Then what do you need time for? What's more important
than Sadie?"

Josie flinches, wrapping her arms around herself. "I needed
time to be okay. To not just be sober, but to be someone Sadie can
rely on. I've relapsed so many times that . . . I was scared, Aaron."

"Scared of your own daughter?"

"You don't get it, do you?" she snaps. "I love her so much it
hurts. And I was a *bad* mom to her. I was a *drunk*. The thought of
doing it again, of screwing her up . . . I couldn't take it. I thought
—" She chokes out a gasp. "I thought maybe it was better for her if
I wasn't in the picture at all. If I never came back. If I didn't *exist*.
Even a dead mom is better than a deadbeat."

I blink, caught off guard.

She doesn't mean that, does she?

"Every single day, I convinced myself I was doing the right
thing. That Sadie was better off with you and not me." She sniffles.
"I told myself that as long as she had you, she'd be okay. That she
wouldn't need me."

My anger wars with something dangerously close to understanding. "No, Josie—"

Her face twists in anguish, and when she speaks again, her
voice is barely a whisper. "What if I ruin everything again?"

I scrape my teeth over my bottom lip. "You're wrong. There is no scenario where Sadie doesn't need you. She *always* will."

Josie presses her fingers to her lips, her shoulders shaking. "I'm so sorry."

I look down, nodding.

Of course I'm pissed at her. I don't trust her, and I'm as worried as she is that she'll mess things up again. For a moment, the words burn on my tongue. *This is your last chance.* But I don't say them, because she's Sadie's mom, and she's a human being who's not perfect and will eventually make mistakes.

Because forgiveness doesn't come with demands.

"I don't want to run anymore." She looks at me, her light green eyes red-rimmed. "I want to be her mom."

Silence stretches between us. "You *are* her mom. You've always been her mom, whether you were here or not."

She steps closer, arms tentatively open. "C-can I give you a hug?"

I wrap my arms around the top of her back. She drops her face against my shoulder, crying, and I wait for her to feel better, because I don't want Sadie to see her like this.

"I missed you, you know?" When I tense up, she quickly adds, "Not—not that way. Just . . . you."

I let her go. "I missed you too."

She clicks her tongue. "And I missed your pancakes."

"Pancakes for breakfast tomorrow then."

"Breakfast?"

I shrug. "You're crazy if you think Sadie will let you go back to your parents' place after she sees you."

"And you're okay with that?"

Oh, *I'm* fine with that, but I'm pretty sure the woman who made me spill into her panties because Penny asked me out might not be. "I'll take the couch or sleep at my parents'."

With a grateful smile, she points at the door. "Let's go?"

"Wait, before we—" I begin, wanting to warn her about Charlotte, when the front door opens and Sadie's big eyes meet Josie.

"Mom?"

Josie sucks in a sharp breath. "Hi, baby."

For a moment, Sadie doesn't move. Then, like something snaps inside her, she launches forward. "Mommy!"

Josie drops to her knees just in time to catch her, and Sadie crashes into her chest, her arms wrapping tight around Josie's neck. "Oh, my sweet girl," she sobs, rocking her back and forth. "I missed you so much."

Sadie squeezes her tighter, and her voice is muffled against her mom's shirt as she says, "You left."

Josie pulls back just enough to cup Sadie's face in her hands. "I know, baby. And I'm so, *so* sorry. But I'm here now." She brushes a tear from Sadie's cheek. "If you want me to be."

"I do, I do, I do!"

I step back, giving them space, my throat tightening at the sight of them together. Charlotte, leaning against the wall near the hallway, she shifts and crosses her arms with a light smile.

What is she thinking? Is she jealous? Worried? Upset?

Josie kisses Sadie's forehead and pulls back. "She got taller."

I ruffle her hair. "Yeah. She does that."

Josie's expression falters when she notices Charlotte. "Oh. Hello. Charlotte, right?"

"Yes." Charlotte straightens but doesn't step closer. "Nice to officially meet you."

"You too." Josie studies her for a beat. "Thanks for looking after them."

"I didn't—" Charlotte cuts herself off. "You're welcome."

It's quiet for a moment, until Sadie pulls at Josie's sleeve. "Mom, are you staying?"

"If that's okay with you."

Sadie beams. "Can we watch *Bluey*? Can I sleep with you tonight?" Without waiting for an answer, she grabs Josie's hand

and tugs her toward the couch. "You can see all my new drawings! And my new books! And I got a gold star at school last week—"

Josie lets herself be pulled away, throwing one last look over her shoulder before disappearing into the house.

"Well," Charlotte says as she takes a step forward. "That's certainly something."

"You okay?" I ask.

She lifts a shoulder. "Yeah. I'm just happy for Sadie."

So am I.

She begins moving. "Guess I should go."

"What? No." I lace my fingers with hers. "They need time together. We can both go."

"No, you *all* need time together. As a family."

As if on cue, Sadie calls my name. I guess Charlotte is right. Sadie needs to see that things are okay between her parents too. That we're still a family, albeit not the one she's used to.

"It's okay." She squeezes my hand. "I'll see you tomorrow."

She steps away, but just as her fingers slip from mine, I tug her back to me. "Please, don't go."

Her eyes fill with something as sweet as sugar. "Aaron . . ."

"*Please*. I need you here, and more importantly, I want you here. You're part of my family too."

When she hesitates, Sadie turns to us over the couch. "Charlotte?"

"Yes, sweetie?"

"Didn't I tell you that you and my mom look the same?"

Oh, for fuck's sake.

Charlotte tilts her head at me, her bottom lip trapped between her teeth. "You think so?" she asks before entering the house again. "I really don't see it."

CHAPTER 29

Soft Serve Conversations

"Y ou," Amelie says the second she opens the door to her apartment, "are going to love this."

"I am?" I ask, shutting the door behind me and toeing off my shoes.

She's already strutting toward the kitchen. "Ooh, yes. Yes, you absolutely will."

The kitchen lights glow warm, reflecting off the polished countertops. Several pots simmer on the stove, the air thick with sugar and something fruity.

"Don't worry, I didn't start without you—just prepping."

I watch her move from one pot to the other. It's good to have her back, even only for the day.

"Hey, where did you end up last Friday?"

Shit, the bachelor-slash-bachelorette party. I figured she'd assumed like everyone else that I left with Charlotte. I drop onto a stool next to the island. "Oh . . . just, with that woman. Took her home."

A loud snort. "No you didn't."

What . . . "Yeah, I did." Hell, for once I'm not lying.

"I'm sure she sucker-punched you too, huh?" she says, pointing at my eye.

"I was a little too drunk and walked into a door."

Lies, lies, lies. I fucking hate this.

"Uh-huh."

Eager to change the topic, I ask, "You're leaving tomorrow?"

"So early it's basically tonight." She stirs one of the pots, releasing a cloud of steam that smells like ripe strawberries and vanilla. "I'm shooting again tomorrow, but I'll be back this weekend for the wedding."

"All right," I say, pushing to my feet and making my way to her side. If this is the only moment we get just the two of us, we'll make the best out of it. "What are we making?"

She smirks at me, eyes alight. "Only the most universally beloved dessert in history."

I scan the counter—heavy cream, vanilla, milk, sugar. A few scattered eggs, a bowl of melted chocolate, a bottle of something dark and syrupy.

"Ice cream?" I guess.

"Ice cream," she confirms with a victorious nod.

"You're not usually a dessert person."

She tosses a spoon into the sink. "True. And I know what you're thinking. Ice cream is hard to get just right. If you nail it, people will say 'Big deal, you know how to make ice cream,' but if you screw it up . . ." She gives me a look of mock pity. "'You can't even make *ice cream*?'"

"Oh, yeah. That's exactly what I was thinking."

She wags a spatula at me. "But wait till you try this. I swear you've never had ice cream this good before. And no machine needed, though . . ." She glances toward the corner of the kitchen, where her sleek, high-end ice cream maker sits, gleaming under the light. "It's better if you *do* have one."

She turns back to the stove, stirring another pot. The scent of dark chocolate blooms through the air, rich and bittersweet.

"Where did you learn it?"

"One of the contestants. And he's a kid, Aaron. Twenty-one. Can you believe? An incredible chef—I one hundred percent want to hire him after the show ends."

A grin tugs at my lips. "So I take it you're glad you said yes to this gig then?"

She dips a spoon into the pot and lifts it to her lips. "Very much. I'm learning a lot about my dad too." Her face is shadowed with nostalgia. "One of his old chef friends told me he once went to Italy, tried this pineapple cake—*Torta Mimosa*—and completely fell in love with it. He insisted on having it for his wedding cake, careless of the fact that my mom was allergic to pineapple." She shakes her head, amused. "Apparently, someone reminded him a week before the wedding, and he recreated the entire recipe using kiwi instead. Spent every waking second perfecting it."

I let out a low whistle. "Sounds like *food* was the love of his life."

"It really was." Her eyes settle on the saucepans. "Tell me about you. What's new?"

"Actually, Josie's back."

Her eyes go comically wide. "She is? Since when?"

"A couple of days."

"Aaron, that's . . . that's amazing!"

"I hope so," I say. I'm feeling positive, but I'm not naive. "She's staying at the house right now, so we'll have to talk. Find a solution." I shrug. "But Sadie's mom is back. That's all that matters for now."

Amelie walks closer and squeezes my hand over the island before rushing back to the stove. "And how's your first gig going?"

The scent of the fourth pot curls into the air.

Cherries.

Deep, syrupy cherries.

Delicious, addictive cherries.

A roar of heat works through my chest. "It's . . . It's going well."

Amelie freezes mid-stir. "Uh-oh. Is it?"

Shit. *Poker* goddamn *face, Aaron.* "Yes. The client is . . . *something.* But being paid to cook is a great feeling."

"Not regretting your career path yet, then?"

"Hell nah. I'm at home."

We exchange a smile, one charged with silent understanding. Cooking is home. The smells, the sounds, the way ingredients transform under careful hands—it's the only thing that always feels certain.

"Well," she says, snapping her fingers, "let's get to work. We have ice cream to make."

I join her, and we quickly fall into an easy rhythm—whisking, stirring, tasting. Amelie guides me through the steps, explaining how cooking the fruit intensifies the flavor, how a splash of balsamic makes the cherries sing.

The kitchen fills with the scent of sugar and cream, the churn of the ice cream maker humming in the background. When it's finally ready, she lifts a spoonful to my mouth.

And holy shit, it's heaven—rich, creamy, bursting with flavor.

I groan, licking my lips.

"Told you," Amelie leans against the counter, pleased.

"This is insane." I let my arms hang loosely at my sides, at a loss for words.

"It's totally going on the menu at Daisy. Maybe with a nice crumble."

I point my spoon at her. "And a soft brioche."

"Like my—"

"—blueberry one!" We say it at the same time, voices overlapping.

She huffs out an exhilarated laugh, eyes bright. "You might be the only person who gets this."

"I *do* get it." This ice cream isn't just dessert. It's something more. A poem of flavors, each bite a little piece of happiness that lingers after it melts.

Amelie grabs two bowls and fills them, sliding one across the island toward me. We sit, comfortable in the silence, letting the sweet coldness dissolve on our tongues.

"So, you want me to tell you how I know you're lying?"

I tense. "Wh-what?"

"About the bachelor party?" she teases. "You leaving with that woman?"

It feels like I'm on my way to a heart attack, but I nod, casual. "Uh-huh."

"Because I hear there's a new woman in your life, and I think you're pretty monogamous."

I choke on my spoonful, nearly inhaling the ice cream. Grabbing the closest napkin, I cough into it, eyes watering.

How the hell does she know about Charlotte?

Kyle and Logan are the only people *she* knows who've seen her. Well, besides Sadie, and it's not like my daughter has been gossiping with Amelie. Logan might have mentioned something, but I seriously doubt he would.

It's gotta be him.

"Kyle?" I ask, voice still rough.

"The new woman in your life is Kyle?"

I give her a deadpan look. "You know what I mean."

"No one told me," she says, smirking. "But thank you for confirming."

Jesus, *seriously?* That's a preschooler trick.

"You're lucky your naiveness is endearing." She smacks her lips. "I guess this explains why you didn't have time to answer your friend's texts."

I glance down, embarrassed. "Sorry about that. I—"

"I'll forgive you if you tell me about her."

There's nothing I'd love more, but I can't tell her anything before I make sure Charlotte's on board. This is as much my secret as it is hers. And, yes, I'm *also* scared shitless. I know this only goes one direction: with me out of her life. Out of a job, and possibly a brother too. So I bite the inside of my cheek, hating the lie as it comes out. "We're still figuring it out. Nothing much to say."

"Mmhmm."

"We're keeping it under wraps."

"Because of Sadie?"

"No, actually, Sadie met her."

Her spoon pauses halfway to her mouth. "She did?"

"Yeah. It wasn't planned. It just happened."

Amelie leans in slightly, studying me. "And?"

And of course, she's amazing with her.

I shrug. "Sadie's Sadie. She gets along with everyone."

"So why the secrecy?"

Eyes stuck to the ice cream, I hesitate. "Like I said, it's casual."

"Oh. *Sure.* Okay."

I narrow my eyes. "What?"

"Nothing."

"*Amelie.*"

"It's not my place." She takes another bite, all innocence.

"Just say it."

She grins. "Well . . . people who are having a casual thing certainly find the time to answer their friends' texts."

"That's not—" I huff. "I've just been busy."

She masks a chuckle with her hand. "Busy with a very *non-casual* woman," she teases.

"We haven't even been on a single date," I insist, trying to convince her.

She gasps. "And you're already this into her?"

When I glare, she raises her hands.

"Okay, okay. I'm letting it go."

"Thank you." I scrape the bottom of my bowl. "So what other flavors did you try?"

Amelie taps her spoon on her bottom lip. "Let me just say one thing."

Oh boy. Here we go.

"You came into my life at the right moment." Caught by surprise at the shift in her tone, I listen. "After my dad died, all I wanted to do was throw myself into cooking. Not the restaurant, not Ian's business—just cooking. Rediscovering it from the basics, like I did with my dad when I was a kid."

She beams. "And as much as I love my *perfect* husband, he doesn't get this the way you do." She exhales a chuckle, but there's nothing dismissive about it. "He tries, really, but . . . to him, food is just ingredients mixed together." Her smile lingers, then fades. "Anyway, my point is . . . during the last year, you let me confide in you more than once. You told me about the loss of your father when you were a child. You made me feel better about my grief."

"It's the least I could do."

She watches me closely. "Well, the least I can do now is tell you that if you need space, time . . . you got it, Aaron. But when you're ready to talk to about this totally *casual* woman you blush over, I'd be happy to lend an ear."

I'm a piece of shit, aren't I?

Here she is, telling me how much she values our friendship, and I'm putting it on the line like she doesn't mean a thing to me. I'm putting *her husband's* business in danger.

I swallow hard. "Hammond was your dad on top of everything else, but . . . you understand that gratitude, that respect you feel for the person who taught you everything you know about cooking."

She nods, eyes crinkling at the sides.

"Then you know how I feel about you."

She reaches out, squeezing my arm before she shifts back into the familiar, confident Amelie. "So you approve? Artisanal ice cream is going on the menu?"

"Hell yes."

"Great." She grins, grabbing my empty bowl and setting it in the sink with hers. "Maybe you'd be open to teaching the cooks?"

Me? Teaching Daisy's professional chefs? "You know I'd do anything for you, but—"

"Then it's settled." She presses her lips together, clearly deciding whether to say more. Finally, a barely concealed squeal escapes her. "Okay, okay. There's something else I need to tell you."

I arch a brow. "All right."

"You know Rhett?"

Her sous-chef? Yeah, of course.

"He's quitting. His wife got a job in Mayfield, and he's going to work for a friend of mine."

"Oh, wow," I say, narrowing my eyes.

"Yes, I had a meltdown for a while. But then I figured . . . maybe it's for the best, because there's this guy I know who'd be perfect for the job."

I blink. *Me*? Amelie's sous-chef?

She bites her bottom lip. "What do you think?"

"I . . ." I think it's insane. I don't have the experience for a role like that. Hell, I've been professionally cooking for a handful of weeks. "I thought you said a restaurant kitchen is like a dance, and I didn't know the steps. I don't want to mess up your choreography."

She grins. "I did say that. Then I sent you to take that course. Aaron, I've always known you have incredible talent, you only lacked the basics. But you don't anymore. And honestly, you're wasted as a private chef. You'd probably be wasted at Daisy too, because you could land far bigger jobs."

"I don't care about that."

"Which is why I can't pass up the chance to have someone like you in my kitchen." For a moment, she looks nervous. *Really* nervous. "Tell me you'll think about it."

"Of course I will."

I'd be crazy not to.

"AARON!"

Primrose's voice rings out as soon as I step out of the car. She moves down the porch steps with an easy grace, her blonde and pink hair pulled into a loose ponytail, strands escaping to frame her face. Despite the exhaustion she must be battling, she still radiates warmth.

"Hey, Prim." I meet her halfway, pulling her into a firm hug. She smells like wild strawberries, a scent that always lingers around their house. "You look good."

"I feel good—tired, but good," she says as she pulls back. "Let me tell you, twins are no joke."

"Oh, I bet."

When my gaze flicks toward the house, her shoulders roll back. "I hope you're not here to see the girls. Your mom just got them to fall asleep, and if you wake them up, I'll have to kill you."

I make a *pfft* sound. "Show up without warning? I'm a parent too, you know."

"Right, right." She clicks her tongue. "Oh, Logan isn't here. He's . . ." She waves a hand. "Dealing with some stubborn peppers, whatever that means."

"That's fine. I'll just try his phone."

She nods but doesn't walk away. Instead, she keeps watching me, her expression expectant.

"What?"

"Are you here to say yes?"

My brows knit. "I think Logan already proposed to you."

She waves me off. "To being his best man."

Oh. Heat pricks at the back of my neck. He wants me to be his best man?

Primrose doesn't seem to notice my hesitation and barrels on.

"I mean, I know the wedding is just in a few days, but it won't be a big deal. All you'd have to do is show up on the day and, you know, have fun."

I swallow, my throat suddenly dry.

"We're having it here," she continues when I'm silent. "And I'm not even wearing white. He's probably going to be in his boots —god knows I can't get him to wear anything else—and—"

She cuts herself off as realization dawns. "Oh no. He didn't ask yet, did he?"

"Uh . . . no. Not really."

She tilts her head back to the late afternoon sky as if praying for patience. "I thought—ugh, I'm so sorry. It's the sleep deprivation. I'm not even sure I'm awake right now."

I shake my head. "No, it's fine."

"Yeah? You look . . ." She squints, searching for the right word before finally giving up with a shrug.

"I'm just surprised. I figured he'd ask Kyle, or—"

"You're his brother," she says, like it's the simplest thing in the world.

But it's *not*.

I'm his brother, and I betrayed him. I hurt him. And he's been hurting me ever since.

Our relationship has never been as bad as it is now, and the last real conversation we had ended with me telling him I was out. He called me a coward—someone he can't trust. And now he wants me to be his best man? It makes no sense.

Her gaze turns warm. "You know I wasn't your biggest fan for a while back there," she admits. "But I also don't think you should carry all this blame. So you fucked up. Big deal. Everyone fucks up once in a while. And Josie was there too, you know? She gets half the blame. Everyone keeps acting like you stole her from Logan, but she let herself be stolen. I dare you to do it with me and see what happens."

"I'd much rather prefer he didn't," Logan's voice cuts in.

He strides toward us, his assessing eyes locked onto mine. He moves behind Primrose, looping an arm around her waist and pressing a loud, exaggerated kiss to her cheek until she giggles. "Are you absolving my brother of his sins, Barbie?"

"Hm-mm. You should have done it already." She taps his chest, then with one last look at me, disappears inside the house.

Logan leans against my car, crossing his arms. "So," he says, voice measured. "What brings you into this neck of the woods?"

I shift my weight from foot to foot. "Mom asked me to bring these over."

He grabs the cufflinks, smirking. He probably figured out just like I did that Mom used this cufflinks excuse to get us together. I guess that's what I deserve for checking on her.

"Thanks." He watches me with that piercing stare, the one that makes me feel like he's peeling back layers, like he can see straight through me and all the tangled-up mess inside.

Maybe this was a mistake.

Maybe I should have told Mom to bring him the cufflinks instead.

"Amelie offered me a job," comes out in a breath.

He looks impressed. "Is she trying to poach you from her husband?"

"Oh, I think Ian's been made aware. He's physically incapable of saying no to his woman anyway."

A hint of a smile on his lips. "That I get."

Yeah, me too.

"So what's the job?"

"Sous-chef."

"Wow, that's . . . that's like the head chef's right hand, isn't it?"

I nod. "Yes, I'd work right beside Amelie. She says I'm talented. Really believes it too."

He shuffles his feet. "Well, congratulations. I'm happy for you."

"Thanks." When he doesn't add anything, I step back. "I'll see you at the wedding then."

"Aaron?"

I turn to him. "Yeah?"

He rolls his sleeves up. "I wanted to . . . I guess I have to find a —" He cuts himself off with a groan. "The wedding is in three days, and—"

"You want me to be your best man?"

"Uh, yeah."

Me? *Really?* Maybe he's doing it for Mom. Or to maintain appearances. But whatever is his reason, I'd do it anyway. "You got it."

For a moment, he just stares at me, like he doesn't quite believe it's that simple. Then, awkwardly, he nods and looks away. "All right. Cool."

I round the car, but his voice halts me once again. "Will you take it? The job?"

Oh, I don't think that matters. Once I come clean about Charlotte, Amelie will take her offer back, possibly smack me, and I won't work for her *nor* her husband. It's either that or losing Charlotte.

There's no winning either way—it's just about deciding what I want to lose. What will break a smaller piece of me.

"Wow, that's a record pause."

"I'm still thinking about it, I guess."

"Well, you take your time." He scratches the side of his neck. "I'm sure whatever you choose will be the right thing. I, uh . . . trust you."

I tilt my head. "You do?"

"Yes."

"Since when?"

"Since *now*." He glares, but I'm going to need a little more information about his sudden change of heart. "You're right. You've done everything you can to prove yourself. You're the best father Sadie could ask for, you're there for Mom, for me. For everyone."

"But you still can't forgive me," I conclude in his place.

He kicks some dirt with his boot. "I realized I won't be able to forgive you until I actually try."

I swallow. "And what does trying look like?"

"I don't know yet." He shoves his hands into his pockets. "But I know that just pretending nothing happened . . . it's not working. For me. For us. And for our kids."

Something sharp twists in my chest.

"They deserve better," he continues. "They deserve what we had. A big family, Sunday lunches. They should get the best version of us. I don't want my daughters growing up thinking their dad and uncle barely tolerate each other. That's not the kind of family I want for any of us."

"Me neither."

Eyes on the ground, he continues. "So, I guess this is me saying . . . I don't want to keep doing this. *Being* this." His hand gestures between us. "It's not me forgiving you overnight. It's not us being best friends again, because I don't know if we'll ever get there." A pause, heavy and raw. "But I want to try. You've been trying for years, and it's my turn to trust you now. With your job, with Cherry, with . . . everything. You know what's best for you."

My heart hammers against my ribs. "That's all I've wanted since day one."

Logan scoffs lightly, shaking his head. "Well, I'm not the best at handling emotions."

"You *weren't* the best. You've improved quite a bit."

He lifts his chin. "Thank you. So have you."

My shoulders relax as if I lost the hundred-pound weight pressing on them.

"So . . . dinner next week?"

It's so normal that it knocks the air out of me.

"Yeah," I manage. "Dinner next week."

CHAPTER 30

The Secret Ingredient

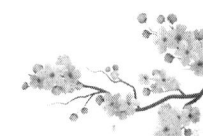

Charlotte's fingers trace lazy patterns across my chest, her body spent and pressing against mine as I tighten my arm around her. "We should go out."

"Out where?"

"Out. Like on a date."

Her fingers pause their movement. "We should?"

I watch her expectant gaze. Though we've talked before about us not just hooking up, we haven't made anything official, have we? Do people her age even *make* things official? Do people *my* age?

"Yes. I'd like to, you know . . . take you out to dinner. Maybe bowling." Noticing the scrunch of her nose, I quickly course correct. "A movie?"

Her fingers continue their path up and down my arm, lazy, absentminded. "I haven't been on a proper date in forever."

I brush my lips over her temple. "What's a proper date?"

"A date you actually care about."

My heart clenches. I press my face into the crook of her neck, overwhelmed by the simple fact that she cares. That she wants this. "I haven't been on *any* date in years."

Charlotte shifts to meet my eyes, warm and teasing. "Are you nervous?"

I give a sheepish laugh. "I'm always a little nervous around you."

"Yeah." She grins, tilting her head like she finds that impossibly endearing. "You are."

No poker face. Never with her.

"Are *you* nervous?"

"No," she says, but her voice wavers, betraying her. "Not about the date."

"About what?"

"Well, what happens when your brother hears about it? Or my mom? Or . . . everyone else?"

"I actually wanted to talk about that." She tenses, chin tilting up. "If you'd like to go on that date—and many others—maybe we should come clean, tell everyone about us."

She pulls back just enough to meet my eyes, curiosity flickering across her face. "Everyone?"

"My brother. Your mom. And . . . my boss. Amelie too." She blinks but doesn't react otherwise, so I continue. "Logan asked me to be his best man. I thought he was just doing it for Mom, but we talked. Really talked. I think things might be looking up between us."

She grins. "Aaron, that's amazing."

"It is. And Amelie offered me a job."

Her smile's gone. "You already have a job."

"A better job. As a chef in her kitchen."

"Oh." She studies me for a long moment, then tilts her head. "So . . . now that everything's going great in your life, you want to smash it with a wrecking ball?"

"No, of course not." I squeeze her hands before releasing them, trailing my own down her arms. "But what's the alternative? Waiting for them to find out in the worst possible way?"

"The alternative is we just keep having fun. Secretly. We don't let anyone else make it complicated, so we can continue to enjoy this. So we don't lose each other."

She's scared. I kiss her forehead, taking a moment. Of course we can't do that, but the thought that she wants to keep me hidden because she's afraid something will come between us speaks to how much she cares about this.

"Are you worried about your mom?"

"No. What is *she* going to do?"

"Then what?"

Her lips part, but nothing comes out for a long time. Eventually, she tucks her head under my chin. "Well, for one, you say you're ready to come clean, but . . . are you sure you're prepared for the consequences?"

"Yes," I say honestly. I can't imagine losing Amelie or Logan, but I can't continue to live my life like a hostage of my own past. If Charlotte is the proof they need to decide I'm an irredeemable fuckup, then so be it. "They'll get over it. Probably. We have a better chance if we come clean, that's for sure. But I'm ready for the alternative."

I barely catch the flicker of something vulnerable in her expression before she sits up and reaches for the sheet to cover herself. "We can tell Logan if you really want, but leave Amelie out of this."

Oh, come on. What's her problem with Amelie? She's fine with Primrose, fine with Josie, with all the women in my life but her—I don't get it. "Why not Amelie?"

"Because I don't know her."

I smirk. "As opposed to the long-standing friendship you share with Logan?"

"At least I've met him."

Yes, and he insulted her, then me. It's not exactly a foundation built on trust.

"Okay, uh . . . I think we need to talk about this."

"There's nothing to talk about." She swings her legs over the side of the bed, and I reach for her. When I try to pull her back, she resists. I feel the tension thrumming beneath her skin, the walls going back up.

I don't know how to break through them.

"Charlotte?" I call, gently pulling her back. "We got better at this, didn't we? At talking about our feelings?"

She bites her bottom lip. "I'm sorry, I just . . . I don't think this is a good idea. It'll ruin everything, and I really don't want to lose you. In fact, I can't *take* losing you—I think it'd actually break me. So, no, I'm not okay with this."

Watching the anguish play on her face, I squeeze her hand in comfort. I don't get it—Charlotte is the most unapologetic and secure person I know. She offered fictional prostitution services to Logan when he offended her. She came out of a jail cell *laughing*. Why is she so afraid of this?

"And besides, what's that going to change? If anything, my mom will just make it harder for us to be together, and we don't want that, right?"

I run my hands along her arms, tracing the warmth of her skin and trying to soothe her. "Maybe we could start working on a version of your life more similar to your fictional town. One where your mom doesn't have this control over you."

"Yeah?" She waves her hand around. "I'll get my own apartment, then? Quit modeling, look for a job as a fashion designer?"

When she looks up at me with a frown, I know she's just masking the questions with snarky remarks. That's what she wants, and this is her asking me if I think she can make it. "That's *exactly* what you do."

She laughs, like it's a fun dream to think about but not one she believes in yet. "I don't even know how to . . ." She shrugs, frustrated. "I don't know. Pay rent? Cook food? Change a lightbulb? Beatrice is right, I'm helpless."

"Well, guess what? I'm a chef, and I've paid rent for"—better not focus on that—"a long time."

"So I'd go from relying on my mom to relying on you."

"No, because I'd teach you, Charlotte. I wouldn't treat you like you're too stupid to learn."

Her face puckers in thought.

"Look, this is a lot to think about. And I'm not saying you should walk away from your life if that's not what you want to do. I'll support you either way. But what we're talking about . . . it's not a pipe dream. We can have it—all of it."

"No, we can't."

"Why not?"

"Because—" She looks away, eyes closing. "Because . . . we've only just met. There's a lot you don't know about me. And some of it may . . ."

Break me? Is that what she's talking about? The thing she'll do that will push me away? I remember that conversation, how she was so adamant about it.

"Charlotte, I don't want you to think like that." I cradle her face in my hands, my thumbs brushing over the wet skin beneath her eyes. "There's nothing you can do to push me away."

She looks down. "Aaron—"

"I won't leave, and that's the end of it. It's just not going to happen." I bring our foreheads together. "I never wanted perfect, okay? Just someone who tries as hard as I do."

Charlotte's eyes shine, her lips trembling like she wants to speak, but I don't let her. I kiss her instead. I pour everything into it, every bit of longing, every ounce of certainty, hoping she can feel what I mean.

When she pulls back, she's shaking.

"Aaron, there's something . . . something you should know. About me. And I want to tell you, but I'm so . . . *so* afraid." Her teary gaze meets mine as I pull back slightly, and I can taste her terror.

Whatever this is, it's big.

"Okay, let's hear it."

"But you have to *promise*—"

The front door opens and slams closed, a thunderous echo that shatters the bubble we've been wrapped in. Instantly, the warmth is gone. The affection. I feel Charlotte stiffen before I even fully register the sound.

In a blink, it's sheer, unfiltered panic.

"Charlotte?" Beatrice's voice carries from the corridor, clipped and expectant.

Shit. Shit. Shit. What is she doing here? According to her schedule, she should be out on a Friday afternoon.

Charlotte jolts upright, scrambling to put some clothes on, her hands moving so fast they fumble with the fabric. My pulse pounds through my skull, an urgent drumbeat of *get up, get out, get the fuck out.*

The handle rattles.

"Open this door, Charlotte."

My body locks up. I take a step back, then another, as if putting distance between myself and the door will somehow erase the fact that I am very much here. In Charlotte's bedroom. Smelling like her.

She turns to me, wide-eyed, her breath coming fast. "Just a second!" she calls out, and then she's grabbing my wrist and tugging me toward the closet.

Seriously? Am I *seriously* hiding in her closet?

There's no time to argue. The handle rattles again, more insistent this time.

I've barely stumbled into the closet before the door is yanked shut behind me. The space is cramped, filled with the scent of her perfume, her clothes brushing against my bare skin. My heart hammers against my ribs as I listen to her footsteps hurry back across the room.

"What the hell are you doing in here?" Beatrice asks, her tone sharp as she bursts inside. Through the gap in the closet's door, I see her enter the room and look around with a grimace.

"What? I was on the phone."

Beatrice's eyes narrow. "Were you recording one of your *videos*?"

Holy . . . fucking . . . shit. Is she talking about what I think?

Charlotte hesitates, lips parting. "What—videos?"

"Don't play dumb, Charlotte. Peter told me everything. About 'Cherry.' About your little peep show."

Charlotte goes rigid, her fingers tightening in the hem of the oversized sweater she threw on. "Oh, that."

That asshole! How the hell did he find out?

This is revenge over what happened at the club, isn't it? I sent a cop to tell him to keep his mouth shut about us, so he threw Charlotte under the bus.

"I always knew you acted like a whore"—Beatrice steps closer, her voice dripping with disdain—"but I didn't know you made a *job* out of it."

I wish I could burst out of here to shout in her fucking face that if she calls Charlotte a whore one more time, I'll . . . I don't know, put cheese in her food. Or poison.

Charlotte doesn't flinch, but her throat bobs.

"Where's the money?" Beatrice presses, crossing her arms. "I assume you don't do it for free?"

Charlotte shifts her weight. "I spent it."

Beatrice barks out a deranged laugh. "Yeah? On clothes? Makeup? Or is this some sad attempt at independence?"

Charlotte's jaw tenses. "It's my money, and it's gone."

Ohhh, no it's not. I can see it in her face. She has the money, which means that no matter what her mom does, she has a way out of here without needing anyone's help. I'm so proud of her, the urge to jump out of here is even stronger.

"How much, huh? What's sex with you worth?"

"I didn't have *sex* with anyone."

"Fifty thousand? Sixty? Maybe . . . eighty-four thousand dollars?"

Charlotte blanches.

"I have to commend you on something. You haven't spent a *dime*."

"Did you take my money?" Charlotte whispers.

"You mean *my* money?"

"How is it—"

"Because your body? *My* diet made it. The bed you use to sell your body? *I* bought it." She points around. "Everything in here is mine, and so is that money."

Fuck. My. Life.

She took her fucking money.

"And we'll need it, won't we? Especially if this comes out. Your career will be over. You think brands will want to work with a model who takes her clothes off for strangers online? You think they wouldn't drop you the second they found out? You've worked your entire life for this, Charlotte, and you're just going to throw it away for . . . what? Tips from desperate men?"

"Maybe I don't want to do this your way anymore."

Beatrice slams her hand against the nightstand, making me flinch. "You don't get a choice. You will delete that account immediately. You will do whatever it takes to clean up this mess. And you will focus on your real career."

Silence stretches between them, taut and suffocating.

Then, quietly, Charlotte says, "I want my money back."

Beatrice's nostrils flare. "Excuse me?"

Charlotte's gaze flickers toward the closet, where I am pressed against the back wall, barely breathing. There's desperation in her expression.

She wants out.

She's going to tell her mom.

"I'm done modeling." She swallows hard. "It's not what I want to do for the rest of my life, and neither is camming."

Beatrice's chin jerks back, lips parting slightly as if she's just been struck. "What?"

Charlotte's throat bobs. "You know I like making clothes. I want to—"

"Oh, you want to be a stylist now."

Charlotte lifts her chin. "So what if I do?"

Beatrice taps her heel against the floor. "Charlotte, you're so beautiful."

"It doesn't matter," Charlotte barks. "I'm much more than beautiful."

"That's where you're wrong." Beatrice steps forward and takes her daughter's hand, her grip deceptively gentle. "You're beautiful, and you're lucky you are, because you're not much else."

My stomach turns to lead, and I press my fist against my mouth to keep from making a sound.

Charlotte flinches. Just barely. Just enough that if I hadn't been watching her so closely, I might have missed it.

"If it wasn't for me, you wouldn't be a model," Beatrice continues, voice smooth. "If it wasn't for my work, my help, my diet, my money, you'd be a college drop-out with no prospects. Do you get that?"

I can see the war in Charlotte's eyes—the battle between the truth she wants to believe and the version of herself her mother has spent years shoving down her throat.

"So what, because you like drawing cute little outfits for yourself, sewing them up, and putting them on, you think you'll be the next Vera Wang?" She scoffs, folding her arms at her hips. "You have no formal training. Who's going to hire you? Are you going to make coffee for actual designers in hopes that someone recognizes your talent? Is this your Devil Wears Prada fantasy playing out?"

"I—" Tears coat Charlotte's lashes. "I don't know."

"No, you *don't* know." Beatrice releases her hand, shaking her head with an air of finality. "And luckily for you, you don't *need* to know. You just need to make sure you do what *I* say."

Charlotte perches on the edge of the mattress, breathing heavily, her whole body rigid as if locking herself in place is the only thing keeping her from crumbling.

And me? I press my back harder against the closet wall, biting my tongue, fighting the urge to burst out and tell her what I already know.

She's more than beautiful.

She's everything.

She can do whatever the fuck she sets her mind to.

Charlotte doesn't say a word, just stares down at her lap as silent tears spill onto her bare thighs. She doesn't fight. Doesn't argue. Just sits there, defeated.

Once Beatrice leaves and the door clicks shut, I step out of the closet.

Charlotte is still crying quietly as the front door slams—the kind of crying that comes when you've been broken so many times that the fight in you has just worn thin. And god, I want to make her feel better, want to gather her in my arms and tell her she doesn't have to put up with this, that she doesn't have to live like this.

Something falls from the closet behind me as I come out, the dull *thunk* startling me. I lean down to grab it, but when my fingers close around the cool edge of a silver frame, I hesitate.

It's a picture. A child, maybe four or five years old, grinning at the camera. But it's not Charlotte. It *can't* be, because her hair is dark brown, a shade deeper than her eyes. Yet she looks . . . familiar in a way that sends a cold rush through my veins.

I've seen this face before.

That smile. Those sharp, knowing eyes.

The realization slams into me like a freight train. "Is this . . ."

Charlotte doesn't look at me. She doesn't move, except for the trembling rise and fall of her shoulders. Then, finally, she says, "Amelie."

The name lingers in the air between us.

Amelie.

I drag my gaze away from the picture and look at Charlotte. She wipes at her cheeks, but fresh tears keep slipping free. I don't even know where to start. Why does she have this. Why does she look so guilty.

Why, in this picture, is Amelie the spitting image of her mother.

My mind is racing, leaping ahead faster than I can catch up. The pieces are all there, just waiting to be put together, but I don't *want* to put them together. Because if I do, it'll mean—

"Beatrice didn't *lose* her daughter." Charlotte's voice cracks, her hands curling into the sheets. "She might feel like she did, but she abandoned her. She left her behind."

The words slice through my ribs like glass. "What?"

Charlotte squeezes her eyes shut, pressing the heels of her palms against them. "That's why we're here. She wants to reconnect with her, but Amelie wouldn't agree to meet her, so . . ."

So she's tricking her. How? Doesn't Ian know who Beatrice is? He's never met her in person, but they did talk on the phone.

"She gave them my father's name. Arnault."

Oh god. That's why she didn't introduce herself as Beatrice Montgomery. I can barely breathe.

Amelie is Beatrice's daughter.

The picture frame presses into my palm. Beatrice specifically asked for Amelie to come cook for her. She didn't even try to hide how pissed she was when I showed up instead. She invited me here for lunch and asked about her. And every single time I mentioned her name, Charlotte was so annoyed. I blamed it on jealousy, but that's not it, is it?

A sickening thought snakes its way from the back of my mind. It lasts but a second before I shove it away, but the damage is done —the doubt is planted, and it spreads quicker than I can rationalize it.

"This isn't why I'm here, is it?" My voice is hollow. I already know the answer but need to hear it anyway, and for every second she doesn't say a word, the crater in my chest keeps expanding. "Did your mom make you . . . seduce me?"

Charlotte's head jerks up, her wet eyes wide. "Would you believe me if I told you she didn't?"

"Yes." I just need her to tell me, and I'll believe her. I really fucking will. I'll believe anything rather than this disgusting, twisted version of the truth.

"She didn't, I swear."

I hear her, but it's like my body doesn't. My muscles are stiff, wound so tight I might snap. I don't know if I want to run or scream or demand answers.

I need to get out of here.

Charlotte scrambles closer the moment I take a step toward the door, reaching for me, her fingers barely grazing my wrist before I pull back. She flinches like I struck her, and it makes something in my chest crack, but I can't bring myself to move to her.

I don't know what to say.

I don't know what to do with any of this.

"I'm sorry, okay?" She breathes hard, like there's not enough oxygen coming in. "I didn't know Amelie was your friend until you first mentioned her name. Beatrice played me exactly like she did with you."

I force myself to look at her. Her face is flushed, her eyes glossy and desperate.

Her hands tremble as she grips the fabric of her sweater. "I swear," she whispers. "I didn't know when we started . . . I *didn't*."

I believe her, but I have to go.

"No, no, please." She clings to me when I try to step past her, burying her crying face into my chest. "You said you wouldn't. Just a minute ago, you said—"

"A minute ago I didn't know you were keeping *this* from me. That you're my best friend's sister. Does she even *know* about you? Does she even—" I'm getting a headache. "This is a fucking mess."

"Can't you just scream at me and be done with it?"

I don't think I could even if I wanted to, and I struggle to picture a scenario in which I'd *want* to scream at Charlotte. Even if she lied and kept this secret from me.

"No, I won't raise my voice at you."

"You can!" She waves me on. "Come on. Tell me I'm a liar. A bitch. That you wish you'd never met me, that I ruined your life."

My brow furrows. That's not "screaming" at her. That's verbal abuse.

"I don't think any of that. I just—"

"It doesn't matter," she scolds like *I'm* the one missing the point. "You don't have to mean every single thing—just say it so you'll feel better." She doesn't let me speak and insists, "Seriously, I can take it. I know I'm a bad person, Aaron. I told you from the start that I'd ruin everything. And I'm irresponsible. I should have kept away from you, but you showed me kindness, and I was selfish—"

My chest tightens. "Charlotte—"

"Tell me that I don't deserve your time or your patience. That you're sick of me, that I've pushed too far, that I exhaust you." Her voice wavers, but she powers through, chin lifting like she's bracing for a blow. "That you'd rather never see me again than deal with this shit one more time."

She's not just throwing words out, is she? That's how her mother talks to her. Maybe how people at work do. Maybe men before me. "Charlotte, stop."

"It's okay, seriously." Tears leak out of the corner of her eyes. "I just . . . please don't leave. Please, don't let this be the thing that breaks you." Her shoulders drop an inch. "Please, I'm beg—"

I wrap my arms around her and pull her to me.

She stiffens for half a second, like she doesn't believe I'm really holding her, then she melts, her arms looping around my neck, her fingers fisting in the back of my shirt. Her breath is shaky against my shoulder, her body convulsing in my arms.

She's wrong—about all of it. About what she deserves. About what I think of her. About how this ends.

"None of that is right, Charlotte. None of it is even remotely true, okay? Yes, I'm . . . hurt, I guess. Shocked too. But I will *never*, for any reason, talk to you like that. Ever, you hear me?"

"But—"

"But nothing. You don't *ever* need to beg me to stay."

She nods, sniffling against my chest, when my phone vibrates inside my back pocket. I take it out and look at the caller ID.

Amelie, of course.

"I, uh . . ."

Charlotte nods, taking a moment to dry her tears. "Take it. It's fine."

"Hello?" I say, bringing the phone to my ear without letting go of Charlotte.

"Aaron?" Amelie says in a frantic voice. "Ian said he'll send Robbie to your client tonight—I need your help."

"O-okay." I don't think I can take more thrills today. "What's up?"

"Remember I told you Barb had to leave yesterday? Well, her youngest is sick, and—everything's okay, but she couldn't come back to Roseberg. *Of course*, I missed her calls because I was shoot-ing, and now—"

"Woah, woah, okay." She must be talking about Barbara Wilkow, the chef who's taken her place at Daisy. "What do you need me to do?"

"Head to Daisy. Prep for dinner service is going to start soon, and they need a head chef."

Wait, what?

CHAPTER 31
Sweet & Sour

Dinner service is finally over.

After four hours of constant shouting, the metallic clanging of pans, and heat pressing in from all sides like a damn furnace, I'm done. My take? Cooking in a restaurant is completely different from being a private chef. There's no time to think, no space to breathe, just a relentless rush, one plate after another.

It's nothing like the calm of cooking at your own pace, putting love and care into every plate, knowing exactly how the person you're cooking for likes their food.

This was more like . . . being a cog in the machine. Or like being stranded at sea, and I spent the entire night treading water.

And yet, somehow, I fucking did it.

"Thanks for a great service, Chef," Oliver says, smacking my shoulder playfully, his helmet dangling from his other hand. "You still owe me that beer."

"Yeah. Next time."

The door swings shut behind him, and as soon as the restaurant is silent, the adrenaline that's been propelling me all night drains from my body like someone pulled the plug.

I set my chef's hat on the counter and stretch my neck.

My body aches—the sharp sting of burns on my fingers, the dull throb in my legs, the buzzing exhaustion in my skull.

I fish out my phone. I should text Amelie, let her know everything went well—not that she needs me to. She probably had spies reporting every detail.

Just as I tap on our conversation, the scuff of footsteps echoes behind me. I turn, expecting to see one of the busboys or a lingering chef. Instead, I'm met with fire-red hair, a constellation of freckles, and green eyes that make my skin burn hotter than the kitchen did.

"Charlotte?"

"Hey, Chef. Or should I call you . . . Head Chef?"

"Pro Tempore Head Chef at best, but I guess that's a bit of a mouthful." I set my phone down, forgotten. "What are you doing here?"

"I missed you," she says, like she's not rewriting my entire day with just three words.

I step closer. I hate that I had to leave her like that this afternoon. She couldn't stop crying no matter how many times I reassured her we were fine. That we'd talk about this, and that we were not over.

And though I haven't had time to think about any of it, seeing her feels good. Understanding her better feels great. I can see the parts of her personality she shares with her sister—her determination, her confidence, her insecurities.

I just wish she'd told me sooner.

"And I wanted to see how tonight went."

I press my tongue against my molars. "It was . . . a lot, honestly. I'm wiped, but I think I did a pretty decent job."

"I'm sure you did more than that."

Her body presses against mine. Instinctively, I wrap my arms around her, my nose sinking into her hair. The scent of her shampoo—fresh, a little sweet—makes my exhaustion recede, even if just for a moment.

"Are we okay?" she asks against my chest. "I didn't break you?"

"No." Closing my eyes, I breathe in her smell. "I'm right here."

When she looks up at me, she seems far more relaxed.

"But we do need to talk, Charlotte, so here's what we're going to do." She steps back with a nervous glance. "We'll have a conversation, and it might even turn into an argument. What we're not going to do is raise our voices at each other, say hurtful things, or—"

"I'm sorry, Aaron. I'm—I'm the worst."

"I'm not talking about you, baby." I cup her cheek, wishing I could stop the tears already forming in her eyes. "I need you to know that sometimes we'll fight. Sometimes, we'll fuck up. But we're not walking out of here alone, all right? We'll go home together. I need you to know that."

"Promise?"

"I swear."

When she nods, I offer her a light smile. "I think I know why you didn't tell me about Amelie."

"I was afraid you'd end things." She swallows. "Which now I know won't happen."

"No, it won't." I inhale, thinking about the hundreds of questions I have. "Have you ever met her? Amelie?"

"Never."

Okay. "And . . . what do you expect will happen when you do?"

She gives me a once over. "Are you worried she'll break my heart?"

"No, absolutely not. Amelie's—"

"Amelie and Beatrice talk on the phone, you know that?" she interrupts. "Maybe . . . once a month." She turns her attention to the countertop, her fingers pressing into the metal. "Beatrice never told me about it. I only found out last year because I overheard them."

I nod, my hatred for this woman growing with every single word out of Charlotte's mouth.

"I confronted her about it, and you know what she said?" Charlotte's voice is light, like she's telling me about the weather. "She said she didn't want me to be upset about Amelie not wanting to get to know me."

I have no idea how to respond to that. It's a lie—it has to be. I know Amelie. I know her heart. If she was aware she had a sister, she would *demand* to know her. She's starved for family the same way Charlotte is starved for love.

I try to find the right way to approach this, to soften the jagged edges of this conversation without undervaluing the weight of it.

"What?" She fidgets with a dish towel. "Just say it, Aaron."

Fucking emotions playing out on my fucking face.

"Have you ever considered that your mom could be lying?"

Her nose scrunches, and I can see the immediate instinct to dismiss the idea. But she doesn't. Instead, she hesitates. And that hesitation tells me everything.

"Lying?" she repeats.

"About Amelie not wanting to know you. About her even knowing you exist."

She scoffs, shaking her head. "No, I haven't considered it. And I don't want to consider it now."

Though she doesn't say it outright, the problem isn't that she doesn't believe her mom would do this. It's that she doesn't want to let herself hope. She's afraid of getting hurt.

But she has me to rely on now.

"Well, I invite you to think of it this way." I step closer, tucking a lock of her smooth hair behind her ear. "You know me. Do you think I could ever call someone like that my best friend?"

She studies me, searching my face for something. Maybe hope. "I guess you have a point."

"I do," I insist. "Amelie's a wonderful person, and she—"

Charlotte cups my mouth. "But I'd rather not count on it, if you know what I mean."

I nod and she releases me, looking around the kitchen.

"She needs to know, Charlotte. I need to tell her about this. I know you're afraid and you don't want me to, but I *have to*." Forget about how unprofessional what I've done is. Knowing Charlotte is Amelie's sister brings this situation to a whole new level of messy. If she finds out about this before I tell her, she'll be destroyed.

I interject once she opens her mouth. "It's non-negotiable. But we're still not walking out of here alone."

Charlotte's frown turns into a half smile, which is more than what I'd hoped for. "I understand."

That's it? "So . . . you're okay with me talking to her about us? And about . . . you?"

"Are *you* ready for what will happen once you do?"

"Yes, Charlotte. I told you, I'll face whatever consequences—"

"You know what's worse than falling short on your friend's expectations?" I shake my head, and she steps closer. "Her falling short on yours." She takes my hand in hers. "Are you sure you're ready for that possibility?"

I'd be ready to bet my left ball on this. Amelie does not know. "I'm sure."

After a long moment, she sets her eyes on me. "Okay. I'm in."

I stare at her, searching for any trace of hesitation, any sign that she's saying what she thinks I want to hear instead of what she truly feels. But there's none. Just Charlotte, standing in front of me, her green eyes determined, her lips curved in the smallest, most heartbreaking smile.

She's in.

"Really?" A rush of something too big to name swells inside my chest. I know fear is still whispering in her ear that none of this is real. That the second I face Amelie and Logan, the second I feel my entire life shift beneath my feet, I'll regret this. I'll regret her.

I'd like to reassure her, but she's heard too many lies to believe me. I'll just have to prove it to her instead.

She giggles. "Yes, really. I might have been playing with your job, but I'm not playing with this," she says as she taps her finger on my chest.

"Good to know." Her lips mold against mine like they belong there, and tapping her chest back, I say, "I'm not playing with this either."

Another kiss. This time, a little longer. Her tongue just barely skims my bottom lip, and part of the stress inside me melts like sugar over heat. "I think I like fighting with you."

"Oh, yeah." My lips ghost over hers. "We should fight all the time."

Her hands move lower, skimming down my chest, my stomach, until she finds the hard length straining against my jeans.

"Hmm . . ." I pull back, my breath uneven. "What do you think you're doing?"

"What do *you* think I'm doing?" When she presses her palm against me, I nearly lose my grip on sanity.

I chuckle, though it's more of a groan, and wrap my fingers around her wrist. "Something really unhygienic, and in my case, unprofessional."

"I think that ship sailed a while back, sailor."

Yes, but Amelie's kitchen? This place is sacred.

Yet as Charlotte's fingers twitch under my grip, memories of the last time she touched me slam into my mind, and suddenly, every reason I have for resisting seems insignificant in comparison.

"You'll get me in trouble, Charlotte," I warn. "And there isn't a closet to stick me into here."

"The only place I want to stick you into is myself."

Oh, boy. Does she mean what I think? That she wants to break her third rule? *Sleep* together?

She traces the shape of my jaw with her finger, her gaze meeting mine. "Rules are for suckers anyway, right?"

Yeah, I'm fucked.

"Charlotte," I plead, my hands gripping her hips as I attempt to step back, but she follows, pressing herself against me. "We can't. Not *here*."

"Dinner is over and there's no one besides us."

"But there are cameras—"

"That nobody's going to check unless we set the restaurant on fire. Or would you rather go to my place and hide in the closet again? Oh! Shall we join your ex at yours?"

She makes a good point.

"You know, I'm getting tired of you saying no to me." Her lips graze my jaw as her hands fumble with my belt. "I think it's time *you* beg . . . and *I* say no."

My belt comes off and my breath hitches as she brushes against me, her touch devastating every ounce of willpower left in me.

"Fuck," I mutter.

"Shh," she purrs against the shell of my ear. "Just let go."

She unbuttons my jeans, and I should stop her, I really should. But her touch, her scent, the heat rolling off her body—it's too much. I'm fucking exhausted of trying and failing to resist her.

The moment her fingers slip beneath my waistband, my restraint snaps.

With a low growl, I spin us around and guide her back until she's pressed against the counter. She gasps, but it melts into a delighted laugh as I pull her up and settle her on the cold stainless steel.

"You win," I murmur against her lips.

She grins, fingers tangling in my hair. "Of course I do." She runs her fingers from my balls to my cock. "Now beg me, Chef."

Beg her. I don't even know where to start. Beg her to make me come again? Beg her to let me feast on her one more time? Beg her to break her last rule for me?

"Beg me, Aaron," she insists, stroking me fast, then stopping before I can truly enjoy it.

"Please . . ." I whisper, watching her.

Please what?

I look down at her, at the flickering glow catching in the copper and crimson of her hair and setting it ablaze. The freckles dusting her nose and cheeks look like stars scattered across a night sky.

She's so beautiful I feel like I'm falling and I'll never hit the ground, like she's the one thing I want to chase for the rest of my life.

My heart stammers. Maybe it can't take this much beauty all at once. But as I look at her plump, delicious lips, I know exactly what I want to beg her for. "Please . . . let me kiss you again."

She blinks, and there's a moment—the briefest instant—where she doesn't look flirty, or irreverent, or turned on. Where she looks small, and fragile. And I want to tell her I'll take care of her, make her promises I intend to keep.

But her vulnerability flicks away as quickly as it showed up. Instead, her grip on my hair tightens, and she pulls me closer, lips inches away. "Fuck kissing." She uses her other hand to rub the head of my cock against her panties. Her wet—*drenched*—panties. "Ask me what you really want."

Shivers run up my spine and down my arms, making my body shake. I need to feel her around me. Need to sink inside her. Need *her*.

"Let me fuck you."

She smiles wickedly. "*No.*"

"Please." My voice stutters when she keeps dragging my cock up and down her slit. "*Please*, Charlotte. I need you."

She giggles, though it comes out breathy. "No."

Oh fuck, I'm going to lose my mind.

She pulls her panties to one side, and the moment she presses my cock against her wet folds, I drop my head against her chest, biting down on her dress to keep myself from making noise.

She feels like heaven. No, fuck that—she feels like *sin*. Wet and hot, even just against the outside of her. My hips buck forward instinctively, my cock sliding through her slickness, the head brushing against her clit before dragging back down. The sensation is torture and ecstasy all at once, and I moan against her chest, my breaths uneven.

"Do you like that, Chef?" she teases. Her chest rises sharply against my mouth, her nipples pebbling beneath the thin fabric of her dress.

"Fuck," I manage, pressing myself against her again. "You're killing me."

"Bet it'd feel even better inside, wouldn't it?"

"*Please*," I whimper, grinding against her again with a wet noise. "Please, Charlotte, let me fuck you."

"No," she breathes, but her voice is shaky as her nails drag down my arms, leaving faint red trails in their wake.

I'm fucking losing it. There's something wrong with me—something broken and fucked-up—because I love this. I love when she denies me, when she makes me beg. I want her to keep saying no, to keep me on the edge, to keep me desperate and fucking hungry.

But I also can't take one more *second* of it.

"Feels so, hmm . . ." I lock eyes with her. Her pupils are black obsidian, her lips parted as she pants. "You're so fucking wet." My hips snap forward again. "You want me as bad as I want you."

"Maybe," she says, her thighs squeezing me.

I lean forward, my mouth hovering over hers. "Say it," I demand. "Say you want me to fuck you."

She bites her lip, weakly shaking her head. "No."

I moan before capturing her lips in a searing kiss, my tongue plunging into her mouth as my hips move against hers again and again, driving us both closer to the edge.

She pulls away from the kiss and breathes her next words. "Have you been checked recently?"

"Hmm?"

"For STDs. Have you been checked?"

Is she going to let me fuck her? "I—y-yes, but I have a condom."

"I've been tested too, and trust me, I'm better protected than Fort Knox." Her hand moves between us, and she gives my cock a tug before letting the tip sink inside her.

"Ohh . . ." My eyes roll to the back of my head, every single muscle tensing up.

Instinctively, I push forward, but her hand keeps me in place, only the head inside her tight hole. Her walls close around me, squeezing me in the best possible way.

"Please, fuck . . ." I want to push inside her so badly I'd kill for it. I'd set the world on fire just for a taste. I'd do anything—everything. "Charlotte, baby, please, you feel—you fucking . . . god."

Her breathless chuckles vibrate against my lips, then her hand abandons my erection, her arm looping around my neck.

Does that mean . . .

"Fuck me, Chef."

I meet her warm gaze, trying to reach her through the fog of arousal between us. "Are you sure that's what you want?"

The tip of her nose brushes mine. "Fuck. Me. Chef."

God, *yes*. I push into her slowly, watching as her eyes close and her mouth falls open. She's so tight and wet around me—the sensation is almost unbearable.

"Are you okay?" I ask, my voice strained with the effort to maintain control.

Her head tilts back, exposing the delicate curve of her throat, and I can't help but press my lips there. She grips my shoulder, her voice barely a whisper as she says, "More."

I oblige, pushing deeper until I'm fully inside of her, my balls pressed against her slick skin. I take a moment to savor the feeling before I start moving, building up a rhythm that has us both moaning and gasping for air.

"Fuck," I hiss through my teeth as she clenches around me. "You were made for me, Charlotte. I was made for this."

Her response is lost in a moan as I start to move faster, my hips snapping against hers. The scent of her skin, the taste of her lips, the way she gasps my name like it's the only word she knows—it's overwhelming in the best possible way.

"Can't speak, baby?" I muse as I interrupt my rhythm to sink completely into her. It feels so good to see her lose control. "Use your words."

"Hmm . . . 'aron" Her eyes cross even as she tries to find my gaze. She's so fucking stunning, I never want to look at anyone else. I never want to do this with anyone but her.

It hits me when she bites her bottom lip and manages to keep her eyes on me for a couple of seconds.

I think I'm in love with her.

No, I *know* I'm in love with her.

"Mine." I grind against her. "Say it."

"I'm yours, Chef."

Yes, she fucking is.

Her moans turn loud and desperate as I pound into her over and over again. The sound of our bodies slamming together echoes off the kitchen walls, mingling with the slick sound of me sliding in and out of her drenched pussy.

"I'm not stopping until you're shaking," I say, every flutter of her walls around me making me more and more daring. "Until you're wrecked, Charlotte."

She gasps, her nails digging into my shoulders like she's trying to claw her way inside me.

"You're going to take it, aren't you?" I push her legs up, her knees pressed to her chest, and bottom out inside her. The new position is even better, and her back arches off the counter as I hit that sweet spot inside her.

"Y-yes."

"Yes what?"

"Yes, Chef."

So fucking hot. My climax is building, coiling in my stomach as she tightens around me, and I won't last much longer. She said no man has ever made her come this way, but I'm also the only man she kisses, the only one she dates, and I'm nothing if not motivated.

I reach down between us to rub circles on her clit with my thumb, and her eyes widen, her breath caught in her throat at the added stimulation. When her walls clench tightly around me, I can tell she's close too.

"Breathe, baby," I growl. "Breathe while you come all over my cock."

A long exhale that turns into a loud whine. "I'm coming. Aaron—I'm coming, I'm—" she sobs, and once she sucks me in deeper, I'm done for. Watching her come around my cock is pure poetry, a piece of art, a thing of true beauty. I can't stop staring, and the heat feels like it might rip me apart.

My hips thrust erratically, every muscle in my body tensing as I empty myself inside her and grunt out her name again and again.

I collapse on top of her with a long groan, unable to hold myself up any longer.

Fuck.

Fuck, this is it. She is *it*.

I keep my forehead against her chest, lips kissing whatever skin I find in my haze. It's not enough, so I reach up with both hands, tracing my fingers down her arms.

"You good?"

"Uh-huh," she says in a breathy voice.

"Sure?"

"I love you," she says, her hand buried in my hair.

Did she just . . . say she loves me?

I look up and she swallows, her lashes fluttering. "I do. And I don't need you to say it back. I just want you to know that I'm in love with you. You made it really easy, even for me."

Again, my heart stutters.

She said she loves me.

She said it more than once.

I straighten, my cock sliding out of her.

Eyes on mine, she pulls herself up too. "Did I freak you out?"

"N-no, I . . ."

"Aaron."

My heart lurches as I turn toward the kitchen door where Ian stands, arms crossed, jaw clenched tight. His eyes pin me in place.

Holy shit. Why is he here? When did he come back?

"I—Ian."

I'm already shielding Charlotte with my body but I shift anyway, angling myself to better block his view as she frantically yanks down her skirt. My pulse pounds so hard I swear it rattles my ribs.

"My wife is fifteen seconds behind me," he warns, his voice a low, urgent growl. "So I strongly suggest you buckle your pants and get your friend off the counter." His gaze flicks to the floor—Charlotte's underwear, stark against the tile. His nostrils flare. "Right now."

CHAPTER 32
Burnt To a Crisp

S hit. Amelie's here? Shit, shit, *shit*.

I lift Charlotte off the counter, setting her down as gently as I can while every nerve in my body screams at me to move faster. Before I can reach for her panties, her hand clamps around my wrist.

I meet her panicked gaze, her breath coming in quick, uneven bursts.

"It's okay," I reassure her. Fuck the panties—right now, fuck Ian and Amelie too. She's terrified. "It'll be okay, I promise"

I mean it. *She* has nothing to worry about. I, on the other hand, have already made peace with what's about to happen. I'm going to lose my job. Amelie. Logan—everyone who matters. But no part of me regrets what happened between me and Charlotte. No part of me would take it back.

"I can't do it." Her voice breaks, tears pooling in her eyes. "I'm scared."

"Whatever happens, we're walking out of here together." I press a kiss to her forehead, trying to soothe her even as it feels like my heart will squirt out of my ears. "I promise."

And then Amelie's voice rings out from the corridor.

"Hey, did you—" She steps into view with an easy step—until she sees Charlotte. Her expression falters, her confusion morphing into something really, *really* angry. "Charlotte?"

Oh, shit. She *knows* who Charlotte is?

Charlotte stiffens beside me, her fingers tightening around mine. "H-hi, Amelie."

My gaze jerks between them, then to Ian, who looks just as blindsided as I feel—right up until his eyes widen in dawning horror. He knows about her existence too.

"What is she doing here?" Amelie's gaze flicks to me. "With you?"

"She's . . . We . . ." My throat is stuck together. "Her m-mom, Beatrice, is—"

"No," Ian says, stepping back like I've hit him. "She said her name was Beatrice *Arnault*. Not—not—"

"It's my father," Charlotte explains. "She gave you my last name."

Ian drags a hand through his hair before shaking his head like he already knows the answer but can't bring himself to accept it. "Please tell me you're not having sex with your first client's daughter."

And there you have it. The final piece of the puzzle.

"You sent him to work for my *mother*?" Amelie asks, turning to Ian.

"I-I had no idea, Amelie. She never said a word about you. I'm —I don't—"

The silence in the room descends like a heavy fog we can't escape from. Every inch of me is frozen, the weight of everyone's stares pressing down on me harder than I ever thought possible.

Amelie's eyes lock onto mine, wide with shock and betrayal. "*She's* the woman? The one you've been so mysterious about?" she asks, her voice a whisper of disbelief. "And you knew who she was? Who her mom was?"

I can't speak, the words too heavy in my mouth. "Yes. I-I figured it out. I was going to tell you, but . . ."

Amelie's eyes tear away from mine as if she can't bear to look at me any longer. "Oh my god."

This is the end, I realize. The beginning of the end.

And even while my heart breaks in my chest, I feel Charlotte's hand shaking in mine. She's scared, hurt, probably disappointed. Trying to figure out what this means for her, for us. I told her Amelie couldn't possibly know about her existence, yet here we are.

"T-there's a lot I need to explain, and I will. But before then, I . . ." I tug Charlotte closer, then give her an encouraging smile. "I'd like you to meet your sister. Properly. She's very excited to—"

"I'm leaving," Amelie says, voice flat, before turning on her heel.

Her footsteps are quick, echoing down the corridor like gunfire. A door creaks open then slams shut.

Silence.

I turn back to Charlotte; steady tears streaming down her cheeks. Her hand is still wrapped around mine, clinging hard enough to hurt.

I don't understand. Amelie recognized Charlotte immediately —she must have seen pictures of her. She definitely knows she has a sister. And for some reason, she doesn't care.

Beatrice didn't lie.

"Why—" I face Ian. "Why has she never gotten in touch? Why —why did she never say anything about Charlotte? Why keep her a secret?"

"Let me see if I'm getting this right. *You* expect *me* to explain myself?"

Charlotte, beside me, jerks backward, fingers sliding away from mine. "I-I have to . . ." She sobs. "I need to go."

"Baby, wait," I try, but she runs past Ian, and with a glance at him, I move too. "I should . . ." I point at the corridor, and he scoffs.

"Don't let me stop you *now*." His voice drops to an ominous tone. "I'll be in touch."

"IT'S GOING to be okay, I promise," I say into the phone as I approach the back door of Daisy.

"No, it won't," Charlotte counters with a sad voice. "Were you in the same room as I was yesterday? Ian set this meeting up to fire you, Chef."

And there's nothing I can do to change that. I made my decision, and though the last thing I wanted was for Ian and Amelie to find out the way they did, this was going to happen regardless. It just happened in the worst way possible.

I've been repeating this like a mantra since last night, when I caught up with Charlotte outside of the restaurant.

She was hysterical, barely breathing between sobs, her hands shaking so hard she couldn't even get her phone out of her pocket. I had to hold her, had to press my forehead to hers and murmur over and over that I was there, that she wasn't alone.

At least Josie was kind enough to take Sadie to her parents and give us the house for the night. Charlotte barely slept, and I with her.

"How are you doing?"

"I'm okay, seriously," she says. "I didn't have big expectations, so . . . I'm good."

That's not true. She feels like she just got proof, once again, that she isn't worth fighting for, and I can't stand it.

I wish I could see her, but Beatrice has been home the whole day. Hopefully Ian won't talk to her just yet, because the last thing Charlotte needs is more drama right now.

"Are we still on for later?"

"Yes, of course. Beatrice thinks I'm going to Bonnie's. I've got a whole four hours clear."

Great. Or . . . not *great*, but I'll take it.

"I better go in. I'll text you, okay?"

"Yeah. I'm . . ."

"Stop saying you're sorry."

"Okay. But I am."

"It's been noted." This is probably the worst time to bring it up, but her "I love you" has been ringing in my mind since last night, so I say, "We got . . . kind of brutally interrupted yesterday, huh? But about what you said—"

"We can talk about it some other time."

I pause. Is she scared I won't say it back? Hell, maybe she's scared I will too. "Charlotte, I . . ."

"Call me after, please?"

She hangs up before I can protest again, so I make my way inside, then knock on the office door, my heart hammering so hard it shakes my ribs.

I'm about to get fired. Ian has no other choice, I get that. But I still wish I could avoid the inevitable. It reminds me of being a kid, hiding in the cabinet under the sink after I'd fucked up, hoping Mom wouldn't find me.

There's no cabinet big enough to hide this mess, though.

"Come in."

I push open the door and my stomach knots. Ian sits behind his desk, fingers laced together over his mouth, and beside him, Shane stands stiff, his glare sharp enough to slice through bone.

"Hello. Should I wait, or—"

"No," Ian says. "Shane was just on his way out."

Shane doesn't move. He's staring me down like he's got plenty of things to say, and I know him well enough to be thankful that Ian's my boss and not him.

I swallow, keeping my eyes on the floor, waiting for the hit that might come—not physical, but something just as brutal.

"Yo, Mr. Asshole," Ian says.

With a deliberate click of his tongue, Shane walks past me. It's only when the door shuts behind him that I breathe again.

"Sit."

I settle on the chair across from Ian. My hands are cold, but my skin burns hot. I'm a kid, curled up in that cabinet, waiting for my mother's footsteps, for the inevitable fallout of whatever I'd done wrong. Only this time, it's worse. This time, there's no amount of apologies that will fix it.

He watches me in silence, his elbows braced on the desk. "So, Aaron . . . Explain to me why Amelie makes me drop everything and drive all the way from Mayfield on a Friday night to make sure your first dinner service went well, and I find you screwing her sister in her kitchen."

I press the heel of my hand to my temple. "I'm sorry, Ian. Mortified, actually. I wasn't aware of the relationship between Amelie and Charlotte until a few hours before you found us, and—"

"Oh, okay," he cuts in, his voice a blade, his blue eyes cold as ice. "Let's talk about that."

The muscles in my throat tighten.

"Would you have stopped if you'd known?"

I blink, caught off guard. "What—what do you mean?"

"Well, hurting your brother obviously wasn't enough to stop you all those years ago." His tone is eerily calm, but his eyes are anything but. "Would hurting my wife have?"

My response lodges itself somewhere in my chest, twisting.

Ian leans forward. "The woman who gave you a chance? Who tutored you? Who taught you everything she could, and made me give you a job, then offered you a *second* job, and—"

"Trust me, I—"

"Would you have stopped?"

I want to believe I would have. I want to say yes, swear up and down that I would've made the right choice. But the truth is . . . I don't know.

Something that that feels so good can't possibly be a mistake.

"You know I care deeply about Amelie," I say, my voice hoarse.

Ian scoffs. "Yeah, I *do* know. Of course, you don't care about me. My company. My work. And you don't care about your job either."

"No, I do. I—"

"Chef & Tell is a new business, Aaron." He presses his fingers to his forehead. "Do you have any idea what this could do to us? We could lose everything. If Beatrice made this public and people found out one of my chefs was sneaking into her house to fuck her daughter, a woman fourteen years younger than him, I—" He pulls at his hair. "Dozens of people could lose their jobs because of you, myself included."

My chest constricts to the point of pain. "I know."

He snorts. "You *know*. Well, that doesn't help us, does it?"

"Look, I fucked up, okay? There's no excuse. I should have handled this completely differently. I should have quit, which I didn't do because I . . ." I close my eyes for a moment. "Because I love this job so much. I was selfish and irresponsible."

Ian studies me, unimpressed. "Why do I feel like there's a 'but' coming?"

My hands fist on my thighs. "I have feelings for her."

It's the first time I've said it out loud, but it's undeniable. And maybe it doesn't make any of this better, but Ian *knows* what it's like to lose his mind over a woman. He met Amelie when she was engaged to someone else.

His fingers drum once against the desk, then still, a long silence stretching until the door swings open with a sharp crack.

Amelie storms inside, her eyes finding me instantly. The hurt in them is a gut punch.

"Hey, beautiful," Ian tries, but she silences him with a flick of her wrist. She's breathing hard, and I can see the vein in her forehead popping from here.

"Amelie," I say, my throat dry. "I'm so—"

"You're fired."

The words crack through the air, final and absolute.

I roll my lips, bracing myself. I knew it was coming, but hearing it—hearing *her* say it—shatters something inside me.

"Hey, let's just think about this for a second, okay?" Ian stands, placing a calming hand on her arm.

"There's nothing to think about. He's fired, effective immediately, and that's the end of it."

Ian's hands rest on his hips.

That's it. It happened. I'm fired.

I've been trying to convince myself that losing my job isn't the end of the world. But the truth is, this isn't just about a job. It's about losing my purpose. The people who gave it to me, and made my life worth something.

Ian shifts beside her, his lips pressing into a thin line. "He has a young daughter," he reminds her. "Maybe we could—"

"What? Send him to another client? See who he sleeps with there?"

"No, of course not." Ian scratches at the stubble on his jaw.

Amelie crosses her arms, her expression hard. "Because I definitely don't want him in my kitchen. Not when I don't trust him. When I don't even *like* him."

I stare at the floor as my hands begin to shake.

"You can't even look at me, Aaron?" she demands.

I force myself to raise my chin, and the anger in her face twists into something worse. Her jaw quivers, and her eyes—fuck, her eyes—gleam with hurt so raw it almost knocks me back.

"You were my best friend," she says. "I thought I could count on you. I wanted you by my side, wanted you to be my second. I thought you had my back."

"I do," I rasp, voice breaking.

"No, I was wrong." She fights the tremor in her chin. "You're not my best friend. You *know* Beatrice left me, and you couldn't bother to tell me she was here? That you were sleeping with her daughter?"

Her daughter? Doesn't she mean "my sister"?

I squeeze my eyes shut and breathe through my mouth, fighting the overwhelming urge to ask.

"So you're fired," she repeats. "And not that it matters to you, but we're done. I never want to see you again."

My mind scrambles for words, but nothing I could say would be enough to change her mind right now.

"Am I clear?"

I force myself to nod.

"Good. Now get out."

I hesitate for a moment, looking to Ian, my boss, the one with actual authority to fire me. But he's not looking at me—his gaze is locked on Amelie, forehead creased in concern.

He's not thinking about his business, his company. He's thinking about his wife, the woman standing before him who has endured so much pain in her life, and who I've now hurt too.

He finally meets my gaze, and after a long pause, nods. "I'll figure out your papers and be in touch," he says. Then, rolling his shoulders, he adds, "As of now, you're no longer an employee of Chef & Tell."

I stand and turn, and every step toward the door feels like another nail in the coffin of the life I've just lost. Through the open sliver, I see the kitchen, the place where I found purpose, where I became more than just some guy who blew up his whole life. I see the laughter, the late nights with Amelie, the hours of sweat and exhaustion that never felt like work because I loved it so much.

It's all gone.

I grip the handle, heart hammering against my ribs. If this is the last conversation I'll ever have with Amelie, I need to say something. I need to tell her that cooking changed my life. That I'll never forget what she taught me. That she's the best chef I've ever seen at work, and that she shouldn't feel bad about this, because I know she will.

I turn back, meeting her gaze, and see nothing but ice and exhaustion staring back at me. She doesn't want to hear anything I have to say.

So I say the only thing I *really* need to get out.

"She needs your help."

Amelie's brows draw together. "Excuse me?"

"Charlotte," I clarify. "She's not . . . she's not doing well."

"Unbelievable." Her jaw ticks. "I've needed help more times than I can count, and nobody showed up for me."

"So she should suffer the same way you did?" I counter.

She jabs a finger on her chest. "*I* was the one who was left behind, Aaron. Not her."

"And that might have been the biggest blessing of your life, because Beatrice . . . she's not a good person, trust me."

Amelie scoffs. "Really? The woman who abandoned her daughter isn't a saint? You don't say."

"It's more than that. She's—" I struggle to find the right words. "She's the kind of person who makes you believe you're nothing. That you're worthless. That you're only good for what she can take from you."

She hesitates, her mask of anger faltering. I know for a fact she's gotten rid of people like that in her life, and I'm not sure how much of Beatrice she's seen, but she must know there's truth behind what I'm saying.

"No," she says, almost to herself. "No," she repeats more firmly. "You've seen it with Sadie—you know what being left behind by your mother does to you. I can't—" She breathes out as if willing herself not to cry. "I've worked hard to free myself of toxic people, and I'm not letting her destroy everything."

"She's not Beatrice, though. Charlotte is not toxic, Amelie. She's—"

"There's nothing I can do to help her." Her shoulders arch. "I'm sorry."

Oh, come on. This is bullshit, and she's better than that. At least, I think she is. "You're the *only* one who can help her. You're her sister."

"Her *sister*?" Amelie straightens. "I don't even *know* her. My family was my dad, who was a piece of shit but a piece of shit who stayed. And now he's gone, so I made my own family. This man" —she gestures at Ian—"is my family. Heaven and Shane with their kids, Primrose and her family, and you—you were part of my family too."

A sharp ache pierces through me at the past tense, but I don't interrupt.

"Charlotte?" She crosses her arms tightly over her chest. "Charlotte is a stranger. Someone who never once reached out, never even tried. And now she needs me because she has no one else?" Her lips curl, her voice dripping with resentment. "Well, I suggest she figures it out—just like I did."

"Do you know what your mother does to her? She—"

"I can't help her." Her chest rises and falls, her gaze stuck to the floor. "I can't open that chapter again."

Charlotte was right. This hurts more than getting fired. Even more than losing Amelie's friendship.

"I guess we're both disappointed, then," I say, and without waiting for her answer, I walk out the door, then out of the restaurant.

CHAPTER 33
The Perfect Sundae

"Seriously, I'm not hungry," Charlotte says as she joins me in the kitchen. She's been dragging herself around since I told her about my meeting with Ian, even though it's not her fault I got fired.

I take out a few bowls then open the fridge and grab heavy cream, whole milk, sugar, and vanilla extract, setting everything on the counter with a clink. "That's okay. The point is not eating—it's cooking."

"Cooking?"

"Baking, I guess." Scale, spoons, and spatulas are set on the counter too. "You know what's the one thing I don't do while cooking?"

"Based on the last few weeks . . ." She looks up, humming. "Exerting self-control?"

"*Thinking*," I correct, pleased that she's feeling better enough to joke. "I could use a break from that right now, and you could too."

When I gesture at her to step closer, she drags herself to me. "I never asked how you got into it."

"I started back in high school with Mom. When Logan started

dating Josie. Mom knew I liked her, and she wanted to keep me busy. Keep me from thinking about it too much."

Charlotte watches me closely. "Did it help?"

"Not at first, no. I was pissed off all the time, distracted." I weigh our ingredients. "It showed. But then, one night, she made me knead dough for what felt like hours. And, I don't know . . . something about the repetition, the way my hands moved through it—it calmed me down. I didn't stop being angry, but I wasn't up to my neck in it anymore."

Charlotte runs her fingers over the counter, tracing an invisible pattern.

"After that, I kept going. It became . . . safe." I glance at her. "A place where I didn't have to think about anything but the next step."

She's quiet for a long moment before she nods, just once. "Okay. Teach me."

"We're making ice cream."

Charlotte blinks. "From scratch?"

"Well, yes. You thought I was going to pull a pint out of the freezer and call it cooking?" She rolls her eyes as I push a bowl toward her. "First step—egg yolks and sugar. Whisk them together until they're pale and thick."

She picks up the whisk, glancing at me warily. The moment she starts whisking, I watch the tension in her shoulders ease just a little, her focus narrowing to the simple motion of her wrist. I step behind her, reaching around to cover her hand with mine.

"Like this," I murmur, guiding her movements. "You want it smooth, not grainy."

Charlotte melts into my chest and follows my lead.

"Perfect," I press my lips to the side of her neck. "Keep going."

I move to the stove, heating the cream and vanilla in a saucepan. "Once this is warm, we temper the eggs—gently, so they don't scramble."

She watches me intently, arm brushing mine as she whisks. "You're good at this."

"Cooking?"

She traces the veins on my hand with her finger. "Taking care of people."

"It's easy when it's you," I say, enveloping her hand with mine.

Her cheeks turn pink as she stares down at the bowl. There's something different about her now—something softer. The weight of the night isn't gone, but at least it's not crushing her anymore.

I reach for the saucepan, pouring a thin stream of warm cream into the yolks as she stirs. "Careful," I say, watching her movements. "Slow and steady."

"Not my specialty."

"No kidding."

She glares at me, but there's no bite behind it.

Once the mixture is combined, I guide her back to the stove. "Now, we cook it until it thickens."

She watches the custard begin to swirl in the pot. "How long?"

"A few minutes."

She leans against the counter, tapping the whisk against the rim of the pot. Though she's not saying it, she's miserable. Hopeless. I can see it in her eyes.

"Are you in your fictional small town?"

Meeting my gaze, she smirks. "You bet."

Though I was the one who asked, knowing that she's picturing a reality where I'm not part of her life hurts. Even though none of this is about me.

"What would you be doing there at . . ." I check the time. "8 p.m., on a Saturday night?"

Without a second thought, says, "I'd be waiting for the custard to thicken so I can make ice cream with my boyfriend. Then saving some to eat with his daughter tomorrow."

I swear my heart stops beating. Just for a second.

She doesn't seem to realize what she's said. She just keeps stirring, watching the custard as if it holds all the answers.

Boyfriend.

It was probably an accident. A slip of the tongue, something she didn't mean to say out loud. But she doesn't take it back. Doesn't even hesitate.

I wet my lips. "Yeah?"

She hums. "Yeah." Then she glances at me, like she's only just realizing I've gone completely still. "What?"

I run my thumb over my bottom lip. "Nothing. Just . . . I thought you didn't do . . . *boyfriends*. Commitment."

She snorts. "I didn't." Then, quieter, "I do now."

When I step closer, she stops stirring.

I want to know if she meant it. If, in that alternate life she was imagining, the one where she sells flowers by the beach, I'd be there too. I stroke my thumb over her pulse. "I should ask, right? Officially?"

"You want to ask me to be your girlfriend?"

I think so. She deserves to have it spelled out, to know that this isn't just something casual or assumed. "Yeah," I say, shifting her towards me. "I do."

"Okay. Ask me."

My heart does something weird—too fast, too full—but I just lift her hand, press my lips to her knuckles, still slightly bruised, and look straight into her eyes. "Charlotte, can I be your boyfriend?"

I wonder for a moment if she's going to make me sweat, but she exhales and says, "Yes, Chef."

I swear, my whole body exhales with her.

She tugs me down, pressing her mouth to mine, and it's the perfect antidote for what happened today. For the grief, loss, and humiliation. It's so good that I forget where we are, what we're doing. So consuming that I don't even care.

When she pulls back, blinking, she mumbles a breathy "Burned."

My tongue swipes against her bottom lip. "Hmm?"

She gasps when my lips trail along her jaw. "Smells burned."

I look at the custard, smoking and bubbling in a way it definitely shouldn't be. "Shit." I turn the burner off as her giggle melts against my ear. "Well, the next step was to let it cool down."

"The custard or us?"

Good point.

"Sorry. I ruined our ice cream."

"That's fine. Actually, we were going to have to let it cool down for a few hours, so . . ." I walk to the freezer and take out a tub of homemade ice cream. "I'm prepared."

Her smile is bright enough it might just melt the whole tub.

"Vanilla?"

"Of course," I say, scooping some into one of Sadie's novelty ice cream bowls.

She settles on the stool next to me, watching me take out the toppings. Chocolate sauce, a long drizzle. Sprinkles, for a little color. Whipped cream, high and fluffy.

When I'm done, I slide the sundae across the island, setting it between us, and tap on the bowl. "Go on. Try it."

Charlotte grabs the spoon and scoops up a bit of everything—the ice cream, the whipped cream, the chocolate and sprinkles. She pops it into her mouth, her lashes fluttering as she hums in pleasure.

I watch her, my heart a steady thrum. "Good?"

"So good." She swallows, licking a bit of chocolate from her lip.

"Only the best for my girlfriend."

She meets my eyes for a beat, but the warmth fades almost instantly. "I don't think I can do this, Aaron."

I pause mid-squeeze on the chocolate bottle. "Us?" My heart begins pounding. "You can't do us?"

"No, not us," she quickly corrects. "But everything else. I can't move out, can't apply for that job, can't pay bills and cook dinner. I just . . ." Her voice catches, and she swallows hard. "I can't."

I set the bottle down.

"If you want to be with me," she continues, "then you'll have to just . . . take me with all my mess. Living at home with Beatrice, modeling and making clothes in my spare time."

I can't help but notice she hasn't mentioned TOP. She said once that if she ever had a boyfriend, she'd stop camming, and the question burns on my tongue, but I save it for some other time, because it looks like she's waiting for me to disagree. To tell her that she has to change, to be better, to fit into some version of a life she doesn't have the strength for.

Instead, I nod. "I'd take you in any form. With whatever mess comes attached."

"Yeah?" she asks, picking at her nail.

I hate that she's still nervous about this. About me. "Charlotte, you feel like home in a world of strangers. So, yes. I'll take your mess. Any mess."

She smiles briefly. "Then forget about everything else. Amelie, and moving out, and the new job. Just let it go."

I hesitate, wanting to tell her she's more than this fear, more than the exhaustion weighing her down. But I also know she's too raw for that right now. "All right."

She dips her spoon into the sundae but just stirs absentmindedly, watching the ice cream mix into swirls of chocolate and vanilla.

"You know, I didn't suggest it before because, well . . . it's still early, and you're so young, but . . . we could find a place together."

She freezes with her spoon mid-air. "What?"

"I mean, this whole arrangement with Josie . . . it's temporary. At some point, one of us will have to find another place, and I guess it'll be me. So we could . . . find something together. I could help, you know. With whatever you need."

She brings a spoonful of ice cream to her lips. "That's . . . really sweet, Aaron. But I want you to be my boyfriend, not my babysitter."

"No, it wouldn't be like that. I—"

"Would Sadie live with us?"

I shake my head, though it's more of a "I don't know" than a no. Nobody gives you parenting guidelines, but if they did, I'm pretty sure there wouldn't be a how-to for this situation.

"She needs you, Aaron. Sadie and Josie need you to help them through this new situation."

"We could—"

"Just let it go," she insists, voice sure. "Please?"

I nod, though I only intend to give her the night, because I'm hardly done with this.

"As long as you know . . ." My fingers graze her cheek before I let my hand drop back to the counter. "You don't have to imagine some other life where things are different. A world where you're someone else, somewhere else, to find peace."

I stand and walk to the fridge, fish a cherry out of the jar, and place it carefully on the sundae.

When I catch her smile, I beam too. "We'll get it, me and you. Everything you've ever wanted."

"With a cherry on top," she says wistfully.

Yeah. With a cherry on top.

"Well, starting tomorrow, you'll need to stop feeding me this much junk food, or *Cherry* and *TOP* is all I'll have left once they stop booking me for shows."

"Oh, no." I quickly slide the sundae to my side of the island. "We wouldn't want that."

She bursts into wild laughter. "Is someone feeling a little jealous?"

"Me? Never," I mock before walking to her. "Just worried about your career and all."

"Uh-huh."

"Lucky for me, I've got no shows coming up."

"Yeah?" she muses, fingers pulling my hair back.

"Yes. I can eat whatever I want, all night long." I tap the island next to her. "Hop up."

She bites her lip, but does as I ask, hopping onto the cool marble counter. I grab the siphon filled with fresh whipped cream and reach for the zipper of her dress. "May I?"

She nods.

I ease the fabric off her shoulders, letting it glide down her body in slow motion, revealing inch after inch of flawless skin. The dress pools around her hips for a moment before slipping away entirely, leaving her sitting there in nothing but a lacy black thong that makes my head spin.

"You're worthy of worship, Charlotte," I say, my voice thick. "You're art." I give the siphon a shake, the sound of it rattling in the silence. "And tonight, you're dinner."

I press the nozzle and release a perfect spiral of whipped cream over one nipple, then the other. The cold cream hits her skin, making her gasp, her nipples hardening into tight little peaks, begging for my mouth.

My lips are on her in an instant, sucking one peak clean, then moving to the other. She moans, her fingers tangling in my hair.

I trail a line of cream down her stomach, following the curve of her waist, the dip of her navel. She shivers beneath me, her breath coming in short, sharp gasps as I pop a cherry into my mouth, bite gently, and then press the sweet half between her lips.

She takes it, her tongue brushing against mine in a kiss that's so fucking hot it could set the room on fire. The taste of her, cherries, cream . . . it's the most decadent dessert.

I slide her further back on the island, lying her down gently on the cool marble. Her back arches as I lean over her, drizzling cream along her thigh, her hip, the sensitive skin near the crease where her thigh meets her pelvis, licking it all clean within seconds.

"Relax," I whisper when she squirms in my hands. "Let me enjoy my meal."

I sink lower, my lips trailing kisses along the path of cream, my tongue lapping at her skin. My hands grip her thighs, spreading them wider as I move even lower.

Her thong is soaked already, and I can smell her arousal, sweet and heady. I hook my fingers into the lace and pull it aside, exposing her to me completely. She's glistening, pink and swollen, and I can't fucking wait to taste her—but I want to take my time. Make her writhe. Make her *beg*.

"Fuck, Charlotte," I breathe, brushing my lips along the inside of her thigh. "You're dripping for me."

"Please, Chef . . ." She shivers, her hips lifting just slightly off the counter.

I reach over, pluck a cherry by the stem from the bowl, and hold it between my teeth. Her eyes go wide, her lips parting as she watches me lower my mouth to her heat, the cherry dangling between my lips.

Then it touches her.

She gasps as the cool, sticky fruit grazes her clit, the smooth surface sliding over her. I move slow, rolling the cherry over her in small circles, letting it bump and drag against the bundle of nerves until her thighs are trembling and her moans are coming fast and shaky.

"Fuck, Aaron—" she whimpers, her hands clutching the edge of the counter, white-knuckled. "I need you . . ."

I flick the cherry faster, watching her grind against that tiny fruit pressed between my teeth, teasing her until her hips start jerking beneath me.

Then I pull back, pluck the cherry into my mouth, and bite down—her slickness mixing with the juice as it explodes across my tongue.

She stares down at me, flushed and panting, and I chew slowly, swallowing with a low groan. "Fucking delicious. But I know a Cherry that tastes better."

Before she can catch her breath, I press my mouth to her pussy, licking her clit with a long, hot stroke of my tongue. She cries out, her whole body jolting.

I don't let up, my tongue working her clit in tight circles while my fingers slide inside her, fucking her steadily. She's so tight, so fucking wet, and I can feel her walls clenching around my fingers as she gets closer and closer to the edge.

"I want you inside me," she says, reaching for my hair and looking down at me with a crazed expression. "Now."

I don't hesitate. I grab her waist, and once her legs cross over my ass, I steer her toward the living room, my mouth at her ear. "Then get on your knees."

I throw her on the couch, and once she quickly gathers herself, she sits on her heels, naked perfection. I meant the *other* way, so I could fuck her like she requested. But before I can tell her to turn around, she's fumbling with the zipper of my jeans, then taking my cock out.

Her mouth wrap around me, no teasing or dragging it out, and my abs immediately go stiff. Her tongue swirls around the tip, then she sinks lower, her cheeks hollowing as she sucks.

It's like every bone in my body turns into jelly.

"Fuck, baby." I've been craving to feel her sucking me off since my brother cockblocked me, and my hands dive into her hair, gripping tight, guiding her. She hums, sending vibrations down my shaft that make me curse under my breath. "Just like that, shit . . ."

She takes me deeper as her hand works in tandem with her mouth, stroking what she can't fit in while still maintaining a steady rhythm.

I fully intend to finish inside her tight cunt, so I pull back slightly, panting as I try to regain some semblance of control. But, unhappy I've pulled back, she leans forward and takes me again.

Every nerve in my body is on fire, every thrust of her lips, every flick of her tongue sending electric shocks straight to my soul. I'm moaning, *begging* her not to stop, my hips bucking into her mouth as she takes me faster, until I'm right on the fucking edge.

My hands bury into her hair on either side of her head. I resist the impulse of shoving her down, and noticing my hesitation, she looks up. "Take what you need, Aaron. Use me. I can handle it."

Fuck.

With a guttural noise, I tighten my grip on her hair and thrust forward, burying myself deep. She chokes around me, the contraction making my vision blur as I lose myself in the wet heat of her mouth.

I set a brutal pace, my hips snapping forward as I take exactly what she offered. Each thrust is desperate, my cock hitting the back of her throat again and again. She takes it, eyes locked on mine, swallowing me down like she was made for this.

"Charlotte—oh my—take it, fuck yeah, I can't believe—shit, I . . . fuck, fuck, *fuck*!"

Tears prick the corners of her eyes, saliva slicking her chin, but she doesn't pull away. If anything, she urges me on, her fingers digging into my ass like she wants me to fuck her mouth even harder.

"Hold on—wait—" I mumble. My muscles lock and my body shakes as I slam deep one last time, then appeal to every bit of my self-control and pull back.

She licks her glistening lips clean, dark green eyes staring up at me. "What's wrong, Chef? I thought it was my turn to eat?"

I'm at a loss for words with how gorgeous she looks like that. Red-rimmed eyes, tear marks on her cheeks, her hair a mess of ember curls. Disheveled and undone for *me*.

I grip her arm and turn her over, enjoying her squeal when the rough skin of my hand meets her soft ass with a loud clap.

I wait for a reaction to make sure I didn't overstep, and she arches perfectly for me, chest spasming against the couch cushion. I take a second to admire the sight. Her legs spread for me, the red shape of my hand on her asscheek, moisture glistening on her inner thighs.

"Should we move this to the bedroom?" she says, meeting my gaze over her shoulder. "I'm not in the mood for another family reunion."

"You're delusional if you think I'd make it past the stairs."

I strip out of my clothes in record time and run my hands up the backs of her thighs to her hips. I press a kiss to her shoulder blade then line myself up until the head of my cock slides through her slick heat. The scent of her skin—shit, it does something to me. More than desire, more than lust. I *love* her, and I need her to know.

"Stop playing," she hisses, tugging me closer. "If you don't give it to me right now, I—"

Fine. I thrust into her in one slow, steady stroke, and her hands grip the couch tighter as I start to move, my fingers digging into her hips. The sound of our bodies meeting echoes off the walls—wet, filthy, perfect.

"That what you needed?" I grit out, thrusting harder.

"Yes, fuck, yes." She pushes back against me. "This cock—my *God*."

I slide a hand up her back, fisting her hair, pulling her head back to expose the long line of her neck.

"You feel how deep I am, baby?" I whisper against her ear. "No one else's ever going to fuck you like this ever again. No one will make you come like this but me."

"Only you," she moans. "Only you, Aaron."

I reach around and find her clit, rubbing tight circles in reward. Her moans turn into high, broken cries.

"I'm so close," she gasps. "I'm gonna—"

"Come for me," I growl. "Let me feel you lose it."

She falls apart with a sharp cry, her body convulsing, her pussy clenching around me so hard I nearly blackout. I hold her tight, driving into her a few more desperate times before I come with a whimper, spilling inside her.

We collapse together, breathless and shaking, her chest pressed into the cushions, me blanketing her from behind. I press lazy kisses to her spine, her shoulder, her damp skin.

She laughs softly, exhausted and glowing. "Couch sex is underrated."

I smile, trailing my fingers over her hip. "With you, everything is."

The landline rings, bursting our perfect bubble. I exchange a look with her, then slide out and quickly kiss her shoulder. "Be right back, baby." I drag myself away from her and into the kitchen, then pick up the phone. "Hello?"

"Aaron?" Logan's voice is tight, urgent. "Where the fuck is your phone? I've called you seven times."

"I—" A chill runs down my spine. My phone is in the pocket of my jeans, discarded somewhere on the living room floor. "What's wrong?"

"You need to get to the hospital right now. It's Mom."

CHAPTER 34

Breaking Bread Again

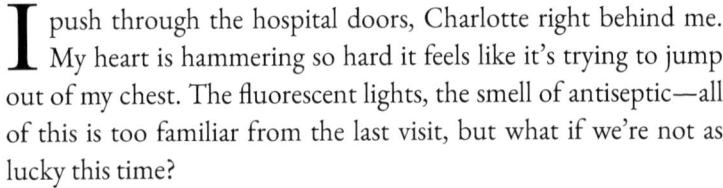

I push through the hospital doors, Charlotte right behind me. My heart is hammering so hard it feels like it's trying to jump out of my chest. The fluorescent lights, the smell of antiseptic—all of this is too familiar from the last visit, but what if we're not as lucky this time?

Where is she? Where's Mom?

My eyes dart around the waiting area until I spot Logan standing near the reception desk. His arms are crossed, shoulders tense, his face drawn tight.

I don't stop moving. "Where is she?"

His head snaps up, relief flashing across his face before something heavier settles in. He jerks his thumb toward the hallway. "They're stitching her up now."

I breathe sharply, trying to push air into my lungs. "What the hell happened?"

Charlotte steps closer, her hand brushing my back in quiet reassurance.

"She and Dad came over to help with a few final things for the wedding. She went to grab a bowl from the cabinet, but she—she must have knocked into a stack of glasses. Everything came down.

It shattered all over her—there was so much blood, Aaron." He swallows hard, eyes flicking away like he's still seeing it. "She cut up her hands, her arms. It wasn't stopping. We had to wrap her up in dish towels until the ambulance came."

Fuck.

My mind races, but my body feels like it's made of stone. I knew something like this would happen eventually, but that doesn't make it any easier to hear.

"I think something's wrong with her," he continues, voice lower now, like he's almost afraid to say it out loud. "You know this isn't the first time, right? She dropped her phone so many times it finally broke last week." He looks at Charlotte, like he's registering her for the first time. He's momentarily stunned before he focuses on me again. "She's been—off. Is she getting confused? She's still *young*. What's happening to her?"

I swallow hard, throat tight.

This is exactly why Mom didn't want me to say anything. She didn't want Logan to worry, not until after the wedding. But he's already worried. He's already looking at me like he knows something isn't right, and I can't lie to him. Not now.

"I . . . I know what's happening," I say.

Out of the corner of my eye, I see Charlotte straighten, like she's bracing for impact.

Logan stiffens. "You do?"

"Yes." I force myself to meet his eyes. "Mom has been diagnosed with Parkinson's."

His expression freezes, his whole body going rigid. Then, quietly, "What?"

"She has Parkinson's." The words taste final, like they're changing everything.

"No." Logan steps back like I just threw a punch. "No, that that doesn't make sense. She's too young. She's—" His voice cracks, and his jaw clenches so tight I can see the muscle twitch.

Beside me, Charlotte squeezes my arm.

I say nothing. What the hell is there to say?

He grips the back of his neck, his chest rising and falling too fast. "I don't . . . understand. How long have you known?"

I hesitate, and that's all he needs. His eyes darken.

"How long, Aaron?"

"A few weeks."

He stares at me like I've just shattered something between us. "Since the last time she ended up here." He scoffs, eyes narrowed. "And you didn't think to tell me?"

"She asked me not to. She didn't want to tell you until after the wedding—didn't want you to worry."

"Well, I *am* worried!" His voice breaks, raw and exposed, and I see it: the fear in his eyes, buried under all that anger. "I'm—I'm fucking terrified."

I breathe through the ache in my chest. "Me too."

"She should've told me. *You* should have."

"Yes," I agree. "But you're her *baby*, Logan—the youngest. You know how she is. She was trying to protect you."

He lets out a shaky breath, pressing his fingers to his temples. "I don't need protecting."

I glance at Charlotte and she meets my gaze, like we both know we *all* need protecting from this.

"Hey," a tentative voice interrupts. We turn to the entrance, where Ian stands awkwardly with a set of car keys in his hand.

'Cause that's what we needed right now. More fucking tension.

He looks . . . uncomfortable. Like he'd rather be anywhere else but here. His gaze flickers between me and Charlotte before settling on Logan, and I see the exact moment he starts reconsidering his life choices.

He holds up the keys. "I brought your pickup."

Logan catches them in the air. "Oh, right. Thank you."

"You got it. How's your mom?"

"They're just stitching her up." Logan's gaze flicks to me, then to Ian, probably noticing we're fully avoiding looking at each other. "What's going on here?"

Ian shifts his weight, scratching the back of his neck. "Look, I'm sorry. I really didn't have a choice. Amelie made me fire him." He points a finger at me. "And I *did* warn you that we'd have a problem if you hurt her."

Logan's face twists in confusion. "Wait, what? You *fired* my brother?"

Ian visibly winces at Logan's anger, shoulders tensing. Probably thanking his lucky stars we're already in a hospital. "I . . . I had no choice, Logan. He slept with a client's daughter."

Holy fucking shit.

"And may I remind you that I'm more useful to you alive, because I'm a wonderful babysitter."

His humor is lost on Logan as he turns to me, nostrils flaring. "You *what*?" His voice is eerily calm, which is never a good sign. Then, louder, "What the *fuck* is wrong with you?"

I could die. Of all the ways I imagined Logan finding out, this wasn't even in my top ten. Or in my top fifty.

I pinch the bridge of my nose. "Don't be mad at Ian. Or Amelie. I deserve it."

"Oh, you *deserve* it?" Logan laughs, and it's the laugh of a man who is two seconds away from throwing hands. "Jesus Christ, Aaron. It's like I don't even know who you are anymore."

"Maybe you don't," I fire back, heat rising in my chest. "You haven't been part of my life in almost a decade. You have *no* fucking clue what the last two years have been like. Parenting alone, no friends, almost no communication with you. No one in my life."

"So you fuck *Cherry*?" he barks.

Ian blinks. "Who's Cherry?"

Logan's eyes widen like he just unlocked a new level of disappointment.

I open my mouth, then close it. Then open it again.

"That's . . . Cherry isn't her name. It's just her . . ." I look at Charlotte, waiting for instructions on what to say.

She twirls a strand of hair around her finger, amused despite the tension. "My alias on TOP."

Ian's face scrunches. "TOP? You mean like the erotic subscription service? That's what you do?"

"That's what I did," Charlotte replies casually. Then, catching my confused look, she adds, "Well, you're my . . ." Her eyes flick toward Logan and Ian.

"Boyfriend," I say, steady and sure. I'm not ashamed of it, and I want her to know that.

"Right. My boyfriend." She grins. "Guess I'm hanging up the thong—for now."

Oh. *Relief.* I didn't even know how much I needed to hear that, but it's clear I did. I don't want to share her, not even if it's just a gig.

Logan turns to me again, looking more and more like he wants to kill me. "*That's* where you met her?"

"Okay, okay. Put your pitchforks down, all right?" I raise both hands. "Let's not do this in a hospital."

Logan storms toward me, his face dark with anger. "You *absolute* fucking idiot," he spits, his voice sharp enough to cut. "Do you ever stop to think? Or do you just act on impulse and deal with the fallout later?"

I stand my ground, but my heart is hammering in my chest. He's *pissed*, and last time I saw him this pissed, I ended up on the floor.

My muscles lock up, instincts screaming at me, and before I can think, my arm moves—shielding Charlotte.

Logan falters.

It's subtle, but I see it. The flicker of understanding in his eyes, the moment something *clicks.* His chest rises and falls, his fists still clenched at his sides, but his jaw tightens like he's swallowing down whatever insult was about to leave his mouth.

"Mr. Coleman?"

A doctor steps into the waiting area, flipping through a chart. The air between us shifts in an instant. Logan tears his glare away from me, but I see the words he doesn't say.

This is *hardly* over.

I DRIFT awake to the sound of Charlotte's voice.

For a moment, I think she's talking to me. But then Logan responds, and it takes me a second to catch up—to remember where I am, why my back aches like I've been run over, why the scent of bleach is thick in the air.

We're still at the hospital. Still waiting.

Mom is okay. The doctor said that the new medicine will help manage her symptoms, but that we need to be prepared for more of this—more accidents, more moments where her body betrays her.

Stage three Parkinson's.

There's a plastic chair squeaking, a shift of movement beside me. I don't open my eyes.

"For what it's worth," Charlotte says, "it's not his fault."

I tense, my pulse kicking up.

"What?" Logan's voice is wary.

"It takes two to tango, but . . . I can be very persuasive, and he *did* try to resist."

"Yeah? How long did he last?"

"Two weeks," she says, and I can hear the amusement in her voice. "Hey—the average man lasts two minutes before their hands are on me."

Logan exhales a slow breath. "Sorry, I just don't find it that impressive."

I keep my eyes shut, but every muscle in my body is coiled

tight. Fuck, I hate that Logan and I are here again after we just turned the corner on Josie. After we agreed to find a balance.

"You don't like me, do you?" she asks out of the blue.

Logan clears his throat, and I can *hear* his discomfort. There's a beat of silence before he finally answers. "You'll break his heart."

She doesn't sound surprised. "You think so?"

"I know so." Another pause, like he doesn't want to say the next part. "You're young and beautiful. You're a . . . a . . ."

"A cam girl?"

I crack one eye open just in time to see Logan give a sharp nod.

"And a model," Charlotte adds, her voice light, almost teasing.

A snort. "Even better. What are you going to do with a dad approaching his forties?" Logan asks. "He can't party. He can't follow you in your private jet around the world. He has responsibilities. A daughter. A sick mother."

Charlotte hums like she's considering his words. "And a brother," she adds. "Is that what you're afraid of? That I'll take him away from you and Sadie?"

Logan doesn't answer right away. "I don't even know what I'm scared of anymore."

"Well, I know what you *shouldn't* be scared of," Charlotte says.

I can picture Logan watching her, trying to decide if he trusts whatever is about to come out of her mouth.

"He will be okay," she continues. "He'll find another job, because he's an exceptional chef. He'll parent Sadie with Josie, and he'll be here for you and your mom like he always has."

Her words make my throat tighten, but I force myself to keep still.

"As for our relationship . . ." She hums, like she's deciding something. "I wouldn't bet against me if I were you."

Logan lets out an amused noise. "Yeah?"

Fuck, how long did that take? And he sounds like he likes her.

My brother doesn't like *anyone*.

I risk opening one eye just a sliver, enough to see Charlotte watching him—calm, confident, unshaken by his earlier hostility.

"I love that little girl," she says simply. "And I love her father."

Wow.

She says it like it isn't something big, something life-altering. But it *is*.

"It's messy, sure. But what isn't?" She gestures at him with a pointed look. "You seem messy enough."

Logan scoffs. "Oh, thanks."

Charlotte lifts a shoulder. "With everything you said and implied about me, I don't think you have the right to be offended."

Logan scratches his jaw, shifting uncomfortably. "Again, I never meant to—"

"And Aaron didn't mean to hurt you," she cuts in. "Or Amelie, or . . . her hot husband. Whatever his name is."

Logan chuckles.

"He's just trying to live his life the best he can. To take whatever joy he comes across. To understand himself, and find love, and be happy." She leans forward slightly, tilting her head. "Can you let him do that? Even if that includes the occasional fuckup?"

I open my eyes fully—just in time to see him smiling at her. Logan. He's *smiling*.

"I think you might turn out to be a good fuckup after all."

Charlotte grins. "Yeah. I think so too."

The doctor walks in and Logan shakes my shoulder, so I stand, pretending I'm just now waking up.

"Everything looks good," the doctor says with a detached expression. "She'll be sore for a while, but we've stitched her up well, so you can take her home now."

He steps to the side and Mom comes in, her hands and arms almost completely covered in bandages. Her eyes crinkle with relief despite the exhaustion. "Oh, you're both here."

"Of course we are. Dad is with Primrose, helping her with the kids."

She cups Logan's cheek, then squeezes my shoulder. "I'm all right, okay? Wipe those annoying expressions off your faces."

Her eyes shift to Charlotte, and for a moment, I swear time stops. Her eyes light up with that warmth that is uniquely my mom's, and when she looks at me for confirmation, I nod.

"Mom, I'd like you to meet Charlotte Arnault. Charlotte, this is Lucy Coleman."

Charlotte walks beside me, a little unsure, but Mom immediately pulls her into a hug.

"Oh, I could cry!" Mom's voice is all joy and surprise. "It's so lovely to finally meet you, despite all this." She pulls back and looks Charlotte up and down only to drag her into another squeezing hug. "I've heard such wonderful things about you. You're even more beautiful than I imagined!"

Charlotte stiffens at first, face scrunching like she's not sure what's happening. Maybe she didn't expect Mom to know about her, maybe she's not used to motherly hugs. She turns to me and once I nod, she tentatively returns the hug. "It's so nice to meet you too."

I feel something loosen inside of me. Relief, warmth, maybe even pride. For the first time, we're not this messy thing everyone's worried about, but something *whole*.

Once Mom releases her, Charlotte steps beside me, holding my hand.

Logan clears his throat. "I'll drive you home, Mom. You need to rest."

"Yes. Thank you, sweetheart."

"Of course." As she walks toward the corridor, Logan stops, his hand resting on the doorframe. He looks back at me and my heart thumps. "I'll see you in a few hours at the wedding, right?"

I blink, momentarily stunned, but I should've known. Charlotte could charm a nun into a strip club and get her a front-row seat.

I nod quickly, my voice a little hoarse. "Yes, of course."

Logan looks at Charlotte then. "Both of you?"

"I'd love to come," she says, smiling brightly for a moment. "But I assume Amelie will be attending?"

"And?"

Oh, right. He doesn't know. "It turns out Charlotte is Amelie's half-sister."

Logan blinks. "She's—" He shakes his head. "Nope, forget it. I don't even want to know."

"And Amelie's not exactly eager to . . ." Charlotte shrugs. "I don't know, reconnect? So I think I should probably sit this one out. The attention should be on the bride, not on my family drama."

Logan scoffs. "Wow. Twenty-three, huh?"

Charlotte raises one shoulder and bats her lashes. "You grow up quickly when you're forced to."

I squeeze her hand. Though I'm proud Logan's impressed by her—let's be real, who wouldn't be?—*this* fucking hurts me.

"Well, if you change your mind . . ."

"Thank you."

Logan turns to walk away, but I can't let him leave without making sure this means what I think it does. "Logan?" I call out.

He stops in his tracks and looks back at me.

"Are we good?"

His gaze shifts to our mom, then back to me. "Mom needs us," he says, his expression pained. "And I sure as fuck need my big brother." He shrugs. "So . . . yeah. We're good."

I swallow hard, heart pounding in my chest.

"You fucked up," he continues, his voice rough but not unkind. "Fix it." He squeezes my shoulder. "I know you can."

I nod, unable to speak for a moment, the weight of everything finally lifting.

It's not perfect. But it's *us*. I'll fucking take it.

Even more importantly, I realize as I squeeze Charlotte's hand in mine, I'll return the favor.

AMELIE OPENS THE DOOR, squinting against the dim hallway light. Her pink pajamas are rumpled, her hair sticking up on one side. "Aaron? What—what time is it?"

Five a.m. But after dropping Charlotte off at home, I knew I couldn't wait any longer. We need to talk about this before the wedding. Before she leaves for Mayfield for her last week.

"Her mom starves her."

Amelie freezes.

"Excuse me?" Her voice is sharper now, a thread of warning woven into her confusion. Behind her, Ian appears, his expression mirroring hers—sleepy, but now tinged with concern.

"She counts her calories—twelve hundred a day—and weighs her. She keeps her fridge empty so as not to tempt her." The words spill out in a rush, tumbling over one another. "She calls her names, and insults her, and tries to shatter her confidence every way she can. She abuses her."

Amelie stiffens, her posture snapping straight like a wire pulled too tight. She turns to Ian, who looks back at her as if telling her they should listen.

Good, because I won't let her shut me out. Not this time.

"I get why you're mad at me, okay?" My voice cracks, but I push forward. "I disappointed you. I betrayed your trust. What I don't get is why your sister has to pay for it."

Amelie's throat works, but she doesn't speak.

"It wasn't her choice to be the one Beatrice kept," I continue, desperation laced through every syllable. "She didn't choose not to have a relationship with you. Hell, she doesn't even get to choose what she eats, or when she can leave the house."

Amelie tucks her hair behind her ears. "Look, Aaron—"

"You said you *chose* your family," I cut in, voice rising. "That she's not part of it. And that's all great, except not everyone gets that luxury. Most people don't get to start over. They don't get to build a new family from scratch. They're stuck with the one they were given. Even when it's rotten."

A lump swells in my throat, but I push through.

"Those people," I rasp, "they suffer abuse that runs so deep, it's embedded in them, wrapped around their bones like a second skeleton. They get sick parents who won't ask for help. Brothers who can't see past their mistakes. Wives who never loved them. And—"A jagged, splintering sound escapes my lips.

I suck in a breath, but it isn't enough.

"And daughters who end up paying the consequences of everyone's mistakes." I take a step back, like distance might soften the ache. "And—and—"

I choke on a sob and wince, as if someone just took a knife and drove it straight through me. It's like the weight of the last month, of the last year and beyond, is finally too heavy to bear.

Everything is dead silent as we all stand there.

"Aaron." Amelie's voice is quiet now. Her eyes glisten as she steps toward me, hand lifting, but I jerk back.

"N-no. This isn't about me. It's about you."

She dips her chin, willing herself to listen.

"Charlotte shouldn't be punished for being lonelier than you, Amelie." My voice steadies, even as I swipe roughly at my damp cheeks. "You walked away from the toxic people in your life, but you didn't do it alone. You had help. You had choices because someone presented them to you."

Amelie's lips part, but she lets me continue.

"You don't get to be selfish with her just because your life is finally on track."

Ian shifts then, stepping forward, his voice a low warning. "Watch yourself, Aaron. You've said enough."

But I can't stop now. I won't.

Ignoring him, I keep my eyes locked on Amelie. "You don't get to be selfish when everyone else in her life is."

Ian moves between us, his presence solid and unmoving. "Did you hear me?" His voice is sharper now. "That's enough."

"I'm done," I say, lifting both hands in surrender. My feet shuffle me backward, distancing myself as my pulse pounds in my ears.

I don't look at them as I turn.

I just walk away.

CHAPTER 35
A Missing Ingredient

The driveway crunches under my tires as I pull up to Logan and Primrose's farmhouse. I'm so nervous, you'd think I wasn't invited to the wedding. The guests aren't here yet, but my mouth feels dry the second I spot *them*. Shane gestures animatedly, his whiskey sloshing dangerously close to the rim of his glass, while Heaven shakes her head at whatever he's saying. Next to them, Ian and Amelie stand side by side, his hand on the back of a chair, hers curled around a wineglass. They look relaxed. Comfortable.

The backyard spreads out behind the house, transformed into something out of a magazine. Twinkling lights hang from the towering oak trees, casting a shimmering glow over the space. Round tables covered in crisp white linens are scattered across the lawn, lanterns line the stone pathways, and a wooden arch wrapped in ivy and blush pink roses stands at the edge of the yard, overlooking the rolling fields. It's beautiful. Romantic. I can see Primrose's entire personality behind it.

I take a breath, adjust my tie, and step out of the car.

Time to face the music.

I step onto the lawn and make my way toward them. The moment Shane spots me, his easy grin falters, the story he was animatedly spinning fizzling into nothing. Heaven follows his gaze, and while her expression doesn't harden like the others, there's still a flicker of uncertainty in her eyes. Ian straightens and Amelie goes completely still, her grip on the stem of her glass turning bone-white.

No one says anything. It's like I walked straight into a brick wall of awkward silence.

I clear my throat. "Hey."

"Hello," Heaven says after a beat, offering me a small, hesitant nod. The only one.

Ian nods stiffly, Shane takes another sip of his drink, and Amelie—well, Amelie just stares at me like she's debating whether or not to dump her wine over my head.

"Look," Heaven finally says, shifting slightly between us. "I get that you guys have your issues, but today is for Primrose and Logan, so can we put all of it behind us? For them?"

Amelie takes a quick sip before answering. "Well, I don't know. Aaron isn't that great at following simple rules. Or *common sense.*"

Shane hums in agreement, while Ian just stares into his drink like he wants to drown in it.

"Yeah," I cut in, giving her a hard look. "And I'm not sure Amelie cares about this wedding all that much. She only chooses to care about a very limited number of people. The rest can eat dirt."

Amelie's head snaps toward me, her eyes flashing. "Excuse me?"

Shane mutters something under his breath, Heaven sighs, and Ian finally looks up, jaw clenched.

Yeah. This is going great.

"Oh, shit, you're here," Kyle stumbles toward me, sweat beading at his forehead, his chest heaving like he just ran a marathon. His shirt is half untucked, and his tie is loosened like he's been yanking at it. "We've got an emergency. A real fucking emergency, and I've been running around—but I just—"

"What's going on?" Shane interrupts.

Kyle swallows, his Adam's apple bobbing. "Logan's gone."

A general gasp lifts from the group.

"Wait, what?" I stare at him. "Gone? What do you mean gone?"

"Gone," Kyle repeats, dragging a hand down his face. "He said he was going to pick up your parents, but they were already here when I arrived."

I glance past the group, my gaze landing on Mom. She's seated next to Darren, a pink shawl wrapped loosely around her shoulders and the ends draped carefully to hide the bandages on her arms, like she's trying to pretend nothing ever happened.

"Did you ask them—"

"He drove them over and then took off," Kyle cuts in, hands flying in exasperation. "Said he had something important to do."

"More important than getting married?" Ian asks in a dubious voice.

"Apparently." Kyle takes a sharp breath, pacing on the grass like standing still might actually kill him. "Primrose just asked about him. Someone needs to go distract her while we find Logan, or—Jesus, what the fuck do we do? The wedding is in two hours."

A beat of silence stretches between us before Heaven steps forward.

"Okay, okay." She holds a hand up. "I'll go keep Primrose company. Text me the moment you find him."

With that, she strides off toward the house, her dress billowing behind her.

Kyle's shoulders relax, like he's been holding his breath for hours. "I still have a couple of places to check out. Shane, go to his parents' place. Aaron and Amelie, take my truck and drive around the farm."

"I can go with Aaron," Ian offers immediately.

"No." Kyle shoves his keys into my hand and turns to Ian. "You need to be here. Mingle and entertain once the guests start arriving if we're not back. Use your dumbassery for good in case people start asking questions."

Ian opens his mouth like he wants to argue, then apparently decides against it.

I roll Kyle's truck keys between my fingers. "I can go alone."

"Yes, you can," Kyle agrees, "but to be honest, the tension between you two is about as pleasant as stale fart stench, and if you don't clear things up right now I swear I will grab you both by the ears and—"

Ian steps closer, cocking a brow.

Kyle shrinks and shifts tactics immediately. "And . . . calmly voice my displeasure."

"Hmm." Ian smirks, pointing at him. "You're lucky I take 'dumbass' as a compliment."

Kyle shoos us forward. "All right, everyone. Go."

THE TRUCK RATTLES down the dirt road, every bump jolting through my spine. The air inside feels thick—thicker than the humid spring breeze slipping through the open windows. Beside me, Amelie sits with her arms crossed, body angled toward the door like she's one sudden movement away from flinging it open and jumping out.

She doesn't speak. Doesn't look at me. Just stares out at the endless stretch of fields rolling past, fingers drumming a tense, erratic rhythm against her arm.

The silence is unbearable.

I shift my grip on the wheel. "So," I say, voice rough, "are we gonna talk, or are we pretending the other doesn't exist?"

Amelie doesn't even blink.

I scoff, adjusting my grip. "Right. Silent treatment. Very mature."

Nothing.

The truck creaks as I steer around a bend, the only sound between us the crunch of tires over gravel and the occasional rustle of trees.

"I'm not giving up on Charlotte. And you know what? I don't care if I'm not part of your family anymore. You're part of mine, and I'm not giving up on you either. I'll never stop trying to fix things between us, just like I never stopped trying with Logan. And I won't stop trying to get you to accept Charlotte. You're not going to just wipe us away."

Her fingers pause their restless drumming. "When I say I *chose* my family, I don't mean that I pick and choose," she finally says. "It's not a membership or something."

"I know."

"My mom left me, Aaron. And my dad—he was the most emotionally unavailable man on the planet."

"Worse than Logan?"

"Please. Logan is a teddy bear in comparison." She turns to me, eyes serious. "I worked really hard to get to the place I'm at now."

I nod. I know that, too.

"And I worked really hard to find my people."

"So you want your sister to work just as hard as you did."

"Yea—" She stops herself, turning back to the road with a huff.

"Or maybe the fact that you had to work this hard means she gets to have it easier," I suggest. "That you get to make it easier for her."

She sinks into the seat. "She never reached out, Aaron."

"She's reaching out now."

"Because she *needs* something."

I swallow my annoyance. "Because Beatrice told her you didn't want to get to know her."

I catch her eyes widening in her window's reflection.

"Which, I guess, isn't so far from the truth."

The truck bounces over another dip in the road, and I scan the fields for Logan, but all I see is green and more green. Where the hell is he? He's not leaving Primrose—that's ridiculous. And he's not the type to get jittery about commitment. He might as well have her name tattooed on his forehead.

"Is her dad in the picture?"

I focus back on Amelie. "No. Wants nothing to do with her, according to Beatrice. Left them behind."

Her fingers start tapping again. "So she has no one except you."

"And I can't be everything for her," I admit. "She's too smart to let me. She knows it wouldn't be healthy, that it wouldn't prioritize Sadie, who's already been through enough. Because your sister is also incredibly empathetic and caring."

"Does she need money to leave then?"

I glare. "No, afraid you won't get out of this with a check. She's got money—her mom stole it, but I intend to get it back. She just needs . . . support. Beatrice kept her sheltered, drilled it into her head that she wouldn't be anything without her. So she needs . . ." I tip my head back against the seat. "She needs to learn how to make lunch. How to pay bills. She needs somewhere safe to be herself and follow her dreams. A family."

Amelie is quiet for a long moment. Then, "What else?"

I blink. "What?"

"What else can you tell me about her?"

I shift my grip on the wheel, thinking. "She's very mature. Impulsive at times, and unpredictable, but . . . you know Josie's staying at our place, right?"

She nods.

"Well, Charlotte is just . . . okay with it. You'd expect a twenty-three-year-old woman to struggle with something like that, but no. And it's not because she's not the jealous type, trust me." I smile. "She just gets it."

"What else?"

"She punched a guy who punched me."

"She *what?* So that's how you got your black eye?"

"Uh-huh. And she broke his nose."

Amelie lets out a startled laugh.

"She makes her own clothes," I add. "She's incredible at it." I turn toward the orchard, still searching for Logan. Nothing. "And she loves ice cream," I continue. "Vanilla. Midnight Reckless—"

"What's—"

"A *terrible* band."

Amelie is watching me now instead of the road. Her expression is friendlier, her body more relaxed. "You love her, don't you?"

I glance at her before refocusing on the road. "I do."

"Did you tell her?"

"Not yet, no. She told me though."

"She told you first?" She lets out a short, amused noise, like that alone might actually make her like Charlotte.

"Yeah. She's . . ." I clear my throat when the words stick there. "She's unlike anyone I've ever met, but in this—in how strong and fierce she is—she reminds me of you. A lot."

Amelie blinks, the joy fading from her voice. "And what is . . . what's this thing about her diet?"

"Her mom—she helped her build a career as a model. I guess she forgot to ask Charlotte if that's what she wanted. And in the name of her career, she starves her."

"But twelve hundred calories? Even for a model, that's . . ."

"Sometimes I think Beatrice just hates her. Other times, that she hates herself for leaving you." I purse my lips. "Either way, she's making Charlotte pay the price."

"Well, what—" She squints out the window, then stiffens. "Aaron? Is that . . ."

My neck stiffens as I follow her gaze.

There, in the middle of the open field, stands Logan beside his truck. But what the fuck is he doing?

As we get closer, and what we're staring at becomes clearer, I blink in shock.

"Holy shit."

CHAPTER 36
Plated & Rescued

Logan?" I call as we approach, but he doesn't react.

The sight in front of us is almost surreal. Logan—dressed in a tuxedo—is hunched over the soil, hands digging furiously into the dirt, his sleeves rolled up to his elbows, and mud streaked across his arms. His hair is a mess, damp with sweat, and his tie hangs loosely around his neck like he gave up on it halfway through. He's completely engrossed in whatever the hell he's doing, muttering under his breath as he sprinkles fertilizer over the base of a massive pumpkin vine.

Amelie reaches my side, her forehead creased in confusion. "What am I looking at?"

"Logan?" I call again, louder this time.

He flinches like he didn't even realize we were standing here. His head snaps up, eyes slightly wild as he takes us in. "Amelie? What are you doing here?" His gaze flicks to me. "Aaron?"

I hesitate, exchanging another uneasy glance with Amelie. "Are you . . . okay?"

"Yeah, I'm fine." He brushes dirt off his hands, not that it helps. "Why?"

Amelie approaches cautiously. "What . . . what exactly are you doing, buddy?"

Logan narrows his eyes, probably catching the wary note in her voice. "I forgot to fertilize the pumpkins. Primrose likes to take a picture sitting on top of the biggest one, and she couldn't even fit a foot on the ones from last fall." He turns back to the soil, resuming his manic digging.

I blink at him. "Does she . . . want that more than she wants to get married?"

Logan freezes for half a second, then shoots me a glare. "What's that supposed to mean?"

Amelie places her hands on her hips. "Logan, you're supposed to get married. Remember?"

"Oh." He shakes his head like we're the ones acting strange. "That's in two hours."

"Yes, fair," she hedges. "But you're covered in mud. And wouldn't you like to, I don't know, drink a beer with your brother? Relax a little before the big moment?"

"Nah, I really need to finish up here."

He keeps working, completely unbothered, and my stomach tightens further. This isn't normal. Logan isn't the kind of guy who runs. He's been working on his anxiety, on his emotional wellbeing.

I take a small step forward. "Logan, you and Primrose are made for each other."

"You also have two newborns together," Amelie snaps.

He tosses a handful of dirt to the side. "What are you two on about?"

"We gotta go back," I insist. "You need to take a shower and calm down from whatever spiral you're on right now because you're getting *married* today."

His shoulders tense. Then, suddenly, he throws the too small gardening tool he was using onto the ground and spins to face me, his face red with frustration.

"I know I'm getting married today. *Look at me.*" He throws out his arms, motioning to himself. "I'm wearing a fucking tuxedo."

I watch him, my brain scrambling for something that will snap him out of whatever this is. "Is that the problem? The tuxedo? Because I'm sure Primrose would let you change. Just don't wear the boots."

His jaw clenches as he rolls his eyes, moving to pick up the tool again.

"Okay, keep the fucking boots, Logan. Just—"

"I need to fertilize these pumpkins, and I need to do it today," he grits out, turning away from me. "So instead of wasting my time, go back to the house, and I'll see you soon."

"Why?" I push, stepping forward. "Why do you need to tend to the fucking vegetables today?"

"Because!" he wails.

I go still.

That wasn't just frustration. That was grief bleeding through the cracks.

"Because Mom really wants to make pumpkin pie next fall, and she—she—"

Oh.

A sharp pain stabs through my ribs.

I think I know the problem.

"She couldn't get in the car this morning," Logan whispers, his back still to me. "She just . . . stopped. Like her body forgot how to move. She kept trying. Told me to give her a second. But it was like —like she wasn't there anymore, just stuck. And her face . . . she knew. She knew what it meant."

"It's a . . ." I roll my wrist, recalling some of the stuff I read online. "A freezing episode."

When he finally turns, his face is twisted in agony, tears cutting wet paths down his dirt-smudged cheeks.

Amelie's breath catches beside me. I see the exact moment it hits, the moment she understands Mom is sick. She brings a hand to her lips like she's trying to physically hold back the emotion. I breathe out too, fighting the same battle.

"Logan . . ." I mumble.

"I don't know how many years of her pumpkin pies we'll get, okay?" His voice is hoarse, almost pleading. "So I need to make sure these pumpkins are perfect." His hands tremble as he picks up the bag of fertilizer, scattering it into the soil like it's the most important thing he'll ever do. The granules hit the dirt, lost among the earth, and he keeps going as if enough effort will hold back the inevitable.

"I need to do this." His voice shatters on the last word, and he rakes a hand through his hair, smearing dirt into the strands. "I have to."

I step forward, my chest aching as I rip the tool from his hands and throw it to the ground. Before he can react, I pull him in, wrapping my arms tightly around his shaking frame.

He stays rigid for half a second, like he's fighting to hold himself together. But then the first sob shudders through him, then another. And another.

His body collapses against mine and I tighten my hold, one hand gripping the back of his neck, the other fisting his shirt. His tears soak into my shoulder, his breath coming in gasping, uneven bursts.

I close my eyes, pressing my chin to the top of his head. "That's enough," I say, sniffling. I pat his back twice, the way Darren used to do when we were kids. "Come on, enough."

It takes a minute, but he eventually straightens, wiping his face roughly with the back of his hand. His eyes are red, his face blotchy, but the manic edge to his expression is gone.

"You know Mom would kick your ass if she saw you now, right?" I say, forcing a smirk, trying to lighten the air. "Crying over this on your wedding day instead of reveling in the fact that you're about to marry the love of your life?"

A tired, barely-there chuckle escapes him. "Yeah."

"Fuck the pumpkins—today," I add quickly when he shoots me a warning glare. "Tomorrow, I'll come fertilize them with you. Six a.m. It's a date."

"I start at five."

"Fine. Five a.m."

When he nods, Amelie brushes past him without a word and walks straight up to me. Before I can react, she throws her arms around my neck, nearly knocking the breath out of me.

"Oof." I stumble back a step but hug her back.

"I'm so . . . so sorry, Aaron," she says against my shoulder.

I close my eyes, my throat burning as I bury my face in her hair. I can't cry. I *can't* cry.

"I really wanted to tell you," I explain, "but Mom insisted she didn't want anyone to know, and—"

"Shh." She sniffles and leans back, her gaze searching mine for something—maybe the fact that we're okay. Whatever it is, she finds it, because her expression shifts, her lips twitching into something determined.

"We need to go get her," she says.

"What?"

"We need to get her out of the house. Right now."

It takes a second to register who she means. "Charlotte? How? I doubt her mom will let her go anywhere."

"It's a good thing I don't care what Beatrice has to say, then."

Logan joins my side, sniffling. "What's happening?"

Amelie, already by the car, answers in my place. "We're going on a rescue mission."

"WHAT'S THE PLAN?" I ask as Amelie and I step into the elevator. The usher almost didn't let us in, but Amelie really has a way with words. Or the usher has a thing for brunettes.

"No plan," she says, arms crossed as she watches the buttons light up as we rise. "We go in, we give Charlotte a choice. That's all we can do."

"Yes, but Beatrice—"

"I'll handle her."

I check the time. The wedding is in one hour, and we'll need half of that to get back. Logan understood the situation, but I can't miss the wedding. I'm the fucking best man.

But I also can't leave this place without Charlotte. We're going to get her out.

"That's the door," I say as we come out of the elevator.

"Ready?" she asks.

No. Terrified, actually. "Yes."

She knocks, and the moments that pass before the door opens are the longest of my life. But then Charlotte is there, her vaguely bored expression turning into surprise as she takes us in. "Aaron? What . . ."

"Hi, Charlotte," Amelie says, stepping forward.

"H-hello." Charlotte looks behind her back, then at us again. "What are you doing here? Beatrice—"

"I'm not afraid of Beatrice." Amelie reassures her. "We're here because we'd like for you to come to the wedding with us."

Charlotte meets my gaze, her brows drawing together as if asking for an explanation, so I step to her, taking her hands in mine. "You okay, baby?"

"Y-yes, just . . ."

"Confused?"

"A little, yes."

"Understandable." I cup the back of her head, fingers skimming through her hair. "Amelie and I talked, and . . . and we want to give you the support you need, the chance you deserve. If you really want to be here, I'll support you, of course. But if it's not . . . we're here to give you a choice. An alternative."

"Charlotte?" Beatrice's voice rings from inside the house. "Who's at the door?"

Here we go.

Beatrice comes out of the living room, her chin jerking back as she sees me, then Amelie.

"Oh—Amelie?" she says, bringing a hand to her chest.

Amelie's unwavering gaze is set on hers, but she crosses her arms, like she's bracing herself against her mother. "Mom."

"I, oh . . . I don't know what to say. You're back."

"Yes, I'm back. You showed up here and hired my husband's services under a different name, all because you wanted to see me. You waited for me to be back from Mayfield. Well, here I am." She raises her chin. "What is it that you want?"

"Well, I want . . ." She walks over and reaches for Amelie, who jerks back. Beatrice's expression sours immediately. "I . . . want to get to know my daughter. To be in your life."

Amelie's shoulders rise and drop. "That's it?"

"Yes, that's it. Of course."

"Oh." Amelie half-giggles. "That's easy then. No thank you."

Beatrice's lips turn into a frown. "Dear, I know I've hurt you, and my methods might have been unorthodox, but—"

"Why did you tell Charlotte I didn't want to get to know her?" Amelie interrupts, and Charlotte shrinks in the corner of my eye. I pull her closer, as if getting her physically away from Beatrice will somehow fix this. "I asked about her every time you called."

I barely resist the impulse of taking Charlotte's face in my hands and saying *See? I told you she's a good person. I told you she wouldn't leave you behind.*

"Well . . ." Beatrice shifts position. "It's not like you've ever wanted to meet her, or—"

"The only memories I have of you prior to you leaving Dad are of a decent mother. Of course, what the hell did I know—I was five. But I get it now, the way Dad always spoke about you. How he called you a *vipère*."

Beatrice's eyes go wide. "Your *father*—"

"My father *stayed*. You left. And when you couldn't leave, when Charlotte's father walked out on you, you . . . what? Decided to make her life miserable?" Amelie's expression is unlike anything I've ever seen. Angry, accusatory, but also leveled, like she's immune to Beatrice's effect. "You're right, I should have asked Charlotte to meet me. I had no idea what she was going through with you. If I had, I wouldn't have let this go on for so long."

"That's . . ." Beatrice scoffs, "I'm starting to see parts of Hammond in you."

Though there's no way Amelie doesn't understand that's an insult, she smiles. "Thank you."

"There's a lot we need to talk about, Amelie, but—"

"Actually, we don't need to talk about a single thing. I'm not here to reconnect. To repair the wrongs and have you in my life. In fact, I don't want you anywhere close to me and my *actual* family. That's all I'm here to tell you."

Beatrice's lips wobble, but she steps back with a tight shake of her head. "Well, then. You heard her, Charlotte. Let's go back in."

Charlotte tenses in my arms, and even though she makes no movement, Amelie holds a hand to her arm like she's scared she will. "That's what I'm here to tell *you*, not Charlotte."

She turns to Charlotte, her demeanor shifting. Patient, affectionate. "Charlotte, I can't make this decision for you, but I *can* give you an option."

"What—what option?"

"Come with us. My husband and I have a beautiful apartment, though probably not as big as this one. You can stay with us as long as you need to. You can find a different job if you want it, or not. You can date Aaron, if that's who you want to be with. You can eat what you want, be who you want, and have . . ." She shrugs. "Me. My family. *Our*," she says as her eyes flick to me, "family."

"I . . . I don't know what to say."

"You don't have to say anything. Just know that you're not

alone in this. You have a choice, and I'm offering you a safe place, no strings attached, no expiration date. But it's your decision, and no one can make it for you."

I squeeze Charlotte's hands, my thumb brushing across her knuckles in an attempt to comfort her, even though it's not enough to erase the fear she's feeling right now. "You don't have to go through this alone. We're here for you."

Beatrice's presence looms behind Charlotte, and I can feel the toxic energy radiating from her like a storm about to break. She crosses her arms, her eyes narrowing with disdain as if she's already decided how this will play out. But Charlotte isn't looking at her anymore. She's looking at me, then at Amelie. She's looking at the people who are offering her a lifeline.

"I . . . I can't just leave, right?" Charlotte says, her voice barely above a whisper. "I can't do anything else, my job is all I have—my only chance to—"

"No," Amelie interrupts, her voice rising just enough to cut through the self-doubt Charlotte is tangled in. "This isn't your only chance. You're not defined by a job or by someone else's expectations of you. You're allowed to choose what makes you happy, Charlotte. What's right for you."

Charlotte swallows hard, her gaze flicking to me.

"You are capable of incredible things," I say, cupping the back of her head. "You've helped Sadie through her trauma, won my brother over. You built a career for yourself—two, even—and you can do it again. You can do anything, Charlotte. And no matter *what* you end up doing, as long as I live, you'll have someone who's proud of you."

She bites her lip and I can see the internal battle playing out in her eyes, but Beatrice's voice cuts through the moment like a whip cracking. "Enough of this nonsense. Charlotte, you don't have the luxury of indecision. This career is the only option you have. Do you understand?"

The second I open my mouth to interject, I see the determination in Charlotte's gaze. Beatrice's word are falling on deaf ears.

"I . . ." Charlotte starts, her voice gaining strength as she turns to her mother, "I'm going to a wedding." She giggles, like her joy has bubbled up and can't be contained any longer. "And I'm eating the amazing food they'll serve. I'm drinking margaritas, dancing, and making out with my boyfriend."

"Charlotte, don't be ridiculous—"

"And that," Charlotte continues, speaking over her, "is all I'm doing today."

Beatrice's face turns ashen, but Charlotte's gaze never wavers. I'm so fucking proud of her, of the courage it took her to stand up and finally choose herself.

"If that's what you want, then don't bother coming back."

Charlotte flinches, lips turned down like some part of her still expected compassion from her mom.

I didn't, but fuck, it hurts anyway.

"She won't need to." Amelie turns to Charlotte. "You made the right choice. I promise."

"Thank you," Charlotte says, a single tear slipping down her cheek as she steps into Amelie's embrace.

I feel the air clearing, the clouds retreating. The storm hasn't passed, but she's taken the first step toward something better.

Beatrice is watching her daughters, lips twisted, and Amelie strikes her with a glare over Charlotte's shoulder. "We'll be back for her stuff."

Quickly, I step forward. "Actually, I'll grab some things now."

I don't trust this woman not to destroy it all.

"What—" Beatrice flinches as I step past her. "You can't be in here. I'll call the police."

"You do that. In fact, give them my name, they know me," I say, walking through the corridor and into Charlotte's room. I grab the first tote I find, then stride over to her desk and fit all the sketchbooks inside. I wish I had time to unstick all these drawings from her corkboard, but I have no doubt Beatrice is actually calling the police, and this technically *is* her property.

I open her wardrobe and take the picture of Amelie, shoving it into a backpack with as many clothes as I can fit. She can just get new stuff, but these are *hers*. She made them. When I can't possibly fit any more in and I've got all sorts of shirts and pants and dresses hanging off my arms, I walk to the desk and grab her sewing machine.

I reach the hall again, and Charlotte's eyes brighten.

I got the right stuff.

"You leave all that here immediately," Beatrice barks, phone in hand. "This is private property, and—"

I turn to her and finally glare the way I've wanted to since she made me waste those first four eggs. "You will give Charlotte her money back—every fucking penny. Or I swear, I will personally finance the lawyers who'll take everything from you. You hear me? Everything."

"You—you're all—"

The second I'm out the door, Charlotte reaches back, grips the handle, and slams the door in Beatrice's stunned face.

"There." She grins wide. "She finally shut up."

CHAPTER 37
The Final Course

"M argaritas are my favorite too," Amelie says as she hands Charlotte her third margarita of the day. I watch Charlotte accept the drink from my spot by the kids' area then glance away, eyes tracking Sadie as she climbs onto a fallen log, while Nevaeh and Marty, Shane and Heaven's kids, are stationed on either side like tiny, overenthusiastic spotters.

"Careful," I call.

I turn back to the reception, soaking in the scene. Primrose, barefoot in a flowing pink dress, practically glows as Logan twirls her on the dance floor, laughter ringing through the night like a melody. The wedding was beautiful—quick, with standard vows, but heartfelt enough that everyone got misty-eyed. Watching the love between Logan and Primrose play out so openly, so unguardedly, felt almost intrusive. Like peeking through a window into something sacred.

Now, the reception is a perfect reflection of them—intimate, warm, threaded with easy joy. People move from table to table, eating from the buffet Shane prepared, swaying on the dance floor, sharing drinks and stories. It's the kind of celebration even my socially anxious brother can enjoy. And he is. For once, Logan looks completely at peace.

So does Charlotte. Like she's shed some immeasurable weight. She's had food, drinks, and she's *laughed*. Danced. Chatted. All the things she should get to do.

I don't realize I've been staring until Ian's voice cuts through my thoughts.

"Have you told her yet?"

"Hmm?" I turn as he steps closer, a beer in each hand.

"That you love her."

I force a neutral expression, but my fingers twitch as I accept the beer. "Oh. No, not yet. Is it that obvious?"

"Only when you look at her," he says, taking a sip. "And when you don't."

I huff out a chuckle, shaking my head. "Just . . . waiting for the right moment, I guess."

"Take it from me, no better moment than a wedding." He smacks his lips. "Or the present. Coincidentally, we're at a—"

"Yes, I get it." I roll my eyes. "So, what, do I just . . . drop it on her? Do I need a speech?"

"You say . . . oh!" His eyes light up like he's struck comedic gold. "You say 'I love you *cherry* much.'"

My nose scrunches. "What?"

"Or . . . 'I *cherry*-sh you'?"

Oh, boy. "She'd laugh in my face."

Ian grins. "Exactly. And then she'd kiss you."

Charlotte is now deep in conversation with Amelie. She's got that little crease in her forehead, the one she gets when she's listening intently, absorbing every word. She's gorgeous. She always is, but tonight, with her easy smile and soft joy, she's something else entirely.

"Looks like things worked out," Ian muses, pointing at the two of them.

I nod, taking a pull from the bottle. "Yeah. In no small part due to your help, I'm sure."

He shrugs. "Eh. This was mostly her." He rolls his beer between his fingers, scratching at the label. "How are you doing?"

"Me? I'm fine."

"Yeah? With your mom and all . . ."

I glance toward Mom, sitting in the far-right corner, chatting with a cousin. "I'm trying to be thankful for the good moments without obsessing over the bad ones that will come."

Ian hums. "Sounds like the Aaron my wife tells me is so great."

I snort. "Hey, about the . . . job and everything else, I want you to know there are no hard feelings on my part. I hope with time, we—"

"We're fine, Aaron." He smacks my shoulder. "I wish you'd handled it differently, but we're fine."

Relief loosens something in my ribs. "Thank you, seriously."

"What are you going to do?"

Job wise? Who the fuck knows. "Maybe, um . . . another private chef opportunity will come along." I rub at the ache forming between my eyes. "I'll figure it out."

Ian shoves my shoulder. "Oh, come on, Aaron."

"What?"

"Amelie obviously wants you to be her sous. Are you going to make her spell it out for you? She was just angry."

"Are you sure she still wants . . . actually, it doesn't matter." A deep breath, a moment to steady myself. "I don't think I want it."

Ian's expression falters, the amusement in his eyes dimming. "You don't?"

My heart pounds as I put words to something I've been afraid to admit even to myself. "I love cooking with Amelie, but working in a restaurant is . . ." I close my eyes briefly. "It's the closest thing to a nightmare I've experienced in a kitchen."

Ian's lips part, but he stays silent, letting me talk.

"I like being a private chef. I don't think I'm cut out for being a chef in a high-stakes restaurant. And I've already disappointed Amelie. She doesn't deserve more hurt, but—"

"Aaron—"

"No, let me finish." I bounce my gaze over to where Sadie is dancing with Darren, then continue. "Charlotte walked out on her abuser, even after everything Beatrice did to her. She did it because she knew she couldn't keep playing a part that wasn't hers. And maybe she'll forever be the villain in her mom's story, but . . . it doesn't matter.

"For the last seven years—hell, maybe longer, I've lived my life for other people. For Josie. Then for Sadie. I've held myself to impossible standards, trying to earn Logan's forgiveness, trying to deserve Amelie's teachings. Then Charlotte came, and . . ." I swallow hard. "I finally did something for myself."

When he smirks, I hold up a finger. "Do *not* make that joke. You're better than Kyle."

"Fine."

"She helped me realize I can't keep being the guy who makes himself unhappy to repair his old mistakes. That I need to forgive myself if I want everyone else to. And that sometimes, I need to be a villain in someone else's story to be a hero in mine."

Ian watches me for a moment like he's considering my words. "So . . . you want to be a private chef."

"Yes." The certainty in my voice surprises me. "No late nights at the restaurant, no sweating in a kitchen as hot as the inner circle of hell, no people screaming left and right while I rush through dishes like a machine. I want to listen to the ingredients. Every sizzle, the sound of the knife hitting the board, the angry bubbling of boiling water. I want to watch them slowly transform, to smell them as they roast, simmer, melt. And I want to take my time with each step. Make sure everything is perfect."

"Okay." He tips his beer toward me. "I'll give you a call once I'm settled in Mayfield. For your briefing."

I blink. "What?"

Like it's nothing, he taps his foot in time with the music. "We have quite the waitlist. You can start with a new client as soon as next week."

I stare at him. "You're—you're offering me my job back?"

He gives me a look like *Who are you kidding?* then says, "We both know if it was up to me, you'd still have your job. I didn't want to fire you. Scold you, sure. Reassign you? Definitely. Tease you until the end of time? Oh, absolutely—by the way, that's still happening. But fire you? No."

"But—"

"Do you want the job?" he presses.

"Yes. Yes, of course," I rush out.

"Cool." He snaps his fingers. "I have the perfect family for you. Sweet married couple, both in finance. Three kids still living at home." He squeezes my shoulder with a smirk. "All boys."

"Funny, boss."

Ian's still cackling as he walks away, his shoulders shaking.

It's not funny. Not funny at all.

But I've got my job back.

"MAY I HAVE THIS DANCE?"

I set my beer down and drape my arms around Charlotte, settling a careful kiss on her lips. I've watched her enjoy herself the whole day but barely got time alone with her, and I miss her. "You may have whatever you want, actually."

"Uuh." She tugs at my hand, guiding me to the middle of the area of the backyard where people are slow-dancing, and loops her arms around my neck. "Everything?"

"Yes, everything."

She hums. "A pony?"

"You got it."

"And a castle."

LETIZIA LORINI

"Yours."

Her lashes flutter. "And you?"

My fingers flex against her waist, the music fading into the background, drowned out by the sound of her breath mingling with mine. "Always."

Her eyes flick across my face, as if seeing me for the first time. As if she doesn't already have me etched into her bones the same way she's burned into mine. Then, she grins. "Well, that's good, because I wasn't planning on letting you go."

My heart swells. "It's cute that you think you could get rid of me."

We sway in sync with the music, the warmth of her body against mine making everything else fade into insignificance. I could stay like this forever, in the glow of string lights and laughter, the distant hum of conversations, Charlotte between my arms.

This feels like a good moment to tell her I love her, right? I don't need a speech, or a grand gesture. Just need to get the words out.

"Charlotte, I . . ."

She brushes the pad of her thumb over my cheekbone.

"You know I . . . cherry-sh you?"

"What?"

"Nothing." I let my hands curve tighter around her waist, then home in on her patient but curious gaze. "I—"

"Charlotte!" Sadie calls, landing against her legs and making her stumble slightly. "Come play with me?"

Swallowing my words back, I watch her lean down and pick Sadie up with an *oof*. "Yes, of course I'll play with—oh, you're all sweaty." She turns to me. "Where's her jacket?"

I really need her to know I love her. "It's—"

"Charlotte?" Sadie squeaks.

That talk about interrupting people can't come soon enough.

"Yes, sweetie?"

"I think my daddy loves you."

Oh, man. I guess that's *a* way to tell her.

Charlotte looks up, eyes wide and a smile threatening to burst, before focusing on my daughter again. "You do?"

When she nods solemnly, I ruffle her hair. "Come on, Sadie," I say in a half scold. "That was *my* line."

Charlotte's smile drops, replaced by a stunned gape. I grin as she sets Sadie down, then gently tell her, "Go play. We'll catch up in a second."

The moment Sadie hops away, I wrap one arm around her waist. "Hi."

"Did you mean that?"

I rub her hip. "I was getting to it, yes."

Her shoulders relax, but her frown is quick to take over. "You're not saying it because I said it, right? Because you don't have to. If you don't feel that way, I—"

"I love you, Charlotte. I love you because you make it easy every time you're difficult. Because it comes as natural as breathing, because it feels like an instinct rather than a choice." I smile on her lips. "I'm saying I love you because I do. And I don't intend to stop any time soon."

"Aaron," she says breathlessly. "I love you too."

Her lips part for me like they always do—trusting, open, with that quiet hum that makes my knees weak. I bury a hand in her hair, the strands familiar between my fingers, and she sinks into me like she knows I'll catch her. We kiss like we've done it a thousand times and still can't get enough.

When we part, I press my lips to her forehead and we continue lightly swaying on the spot.

"So what happens now?"

"Well, we enjoy being boyfriend and girlfriend. You find your footing in the world, with me one step behind you."

"All the way?"

"All the way."

She leans back to look at me. "I'm excited to get to know Amelie. And . . . to decide what to do with my life."

"You've got time for that."

"What are *you* going to do?"

"Actually, I . . . I'm going back to work for Ian."

Her eyes widen. "Not Amelie?"

"Turns out I like a more peaceful cooking environment."

She hums. "I did see you move garnish around a plate for twenty straight minutes once."

"Yeah. Perfectionism."

"Or psychosis," she mumbles.

She kisses me before I can rebut, and when her lips leave mine, I can't remember what I wanted to say anyway. "We'll figure it all out together. Right?"

"Right." Her chest presses against mine. "Unless . . . are you gonna break my heart, Chef?"

"Not even a chance."

She grins, green eyes twinkling. "Looking forward to it."

Epilogue: Cherry On Top

TEN YEARS LATER

I check the time once again, nervously biting my bottom lip. 8.30 p.m. She said she'd *definitely* come, and based on the last few months, I think that means there's an 80 percent chance that she'll actually show up.

Maybe . . . 70.

My texts from this afternoon remain unanswered, which is also not exactly news, but she has to come, right? She wouldn't forget. Probably. Oh, boy. She's standing me up, isn't she?

"I'm here, I'm here," Sadie says as she turns the corner and comes into view. Immediately, I exhale in relief. "Mom says hi."

"How was the cake?"

"Cake was fine," she says as she settles on the step next to me. "Greg, on the other hand, remains the most boring man on earth."

I fight a chuckle. She's got a point, but he's what Josie needs, and I'm happy they found each other.

She motions around us. "You thought I forgot about this, didn't you?"

"Well, you *did* ignore all of my texts."

"That's because you keep sending me those corny GIFs."

"'Have a good day' is a corny GIF?"

"When it's a stuffed bear holding a heart saying it, yes." She points at the beers in my hands. "So how does this work?"

Someone's eager to go out with her friends. Better make it quick. Or not. "Beer? Well, it's made from water, barley, hops, and yeast, which all undergo a fermentation proce—"

"This whole . . . birthday tradition. How does it work?"

"Very simple." I twist the cap off one beer and hand it over, then do the same with the other. I hold mine forward and angle myself slightly to face her. "It's your sixteenth birthday. On mine, I drank my first beer."

"A *million* years ago," she teases.

"Ah-ha. I shared that beer with my best friend, Uncle Logan. And now you're sharing it with yours."

"Oh, *you're* my best friend?"

I gasp. "Am I not?"

"Sure. After Harriet, Thomas, Lindsey—"

"Okay, okay. That's just hurtful."

"Come on, Dad. Wouldn't it be sad if you were my best friend?"

Sad? No, it wouldn't be sad. I've been her best friend her whole life. Her confidant and her biggest fan.

I shrug. "You're *my* best friend."

She shakes her head. "Because you're obsessed with me."

I won't even deny it. "I really am."

She clinks her beer against mine. "Here's to my birthday then."

"And to you, a smart, beautiful young woman who—"

"*Daaad.*"

"Fine. Let's just drink."

We both take a sip, and I watch her reaction as she smacks her lips, then hums. "Tastes like every other beer I've had before."

Every other *what?*

I see her smirk just as the words begin forming on the tip of my tongue. She tilts the beer back, but I hold a hand over the top. "That's enough for you, actually."

"What? One sip?"

"Until you're twenty-one," I say, snatching it back. "Especially since you're going to your first party tonight. You need to be sharp."

"Unbelievable," she mumbles, weakly shaking her head. "You know Finn is driving us, right?"

Oh, *Finn* is driving them. Lucky us.

"Tell your *boyfriend* if I hear he's had even a sip of anything but soda—"

"He doesn't drink." She rolls her big brown eyes. "And stop saying 'boyfriend' like that. It sounds like you don't like him."

I don't. I see the way he looks at her. He has *ideas*.

"Dad, I mean it."

"Hey, I'm still better than uncle Logan."

She cackles. "Finn is terrified of him."

Good. I might have promised her I'd talk to him, and I did, but not to ask him to back off *exactly*.

She smacks her thighs. "Okay, well—"

"You're already leaving?"

"Well, you took my beer!"

"Okay, okay. Wait. I want to talk to you about something." I set both bottles beside me. "You remember the first time I told Charlotte I loved her?"

She looks up at the starry sky. "I don't *remember*, but you've told me the story a million times."

"I was just about to tell her, and you—"

"I waltzed in and said, 'I think my dad loves you.'"

That's right. Little party pooper that she was. "It was kind of perfect. I mean, I was really nervous about saying it, and you . . ."

"Damn, I really *am* your best friend."

"You are."

She smiles, beautiful and happy—the best thing I've ever done with my life, and I've done some pretty great things.

I fit a hand into my pocket and pull it back out. "Maybe you'd like to help me again?"

Eyes flicking to the ring box in my hands, she gasps. "Oh my god—Dad?! Are you propo—"

"*Shhh!*" I swat her arm, then point my thumb at the house.

"Oh my god. Oh my god." She opens the box and gasps again. "Dad, *oh my god.*"

I guess she likes it.

Lips wobbling, she throws her arms around me. "I'm so happy for you. This is—" She chuckles. "The weirdest and most unexpected birthday gift."

"I thought so." I kiss the side of her head. "I also got you the guitar you wanted."

"Of course you did." She pulls back and stares at the ring again. "Dad, she's going to *love* it."

"You think?"

"Are you kidding? You made her wait a *decade.*"

Me? I was ready to marry her two months into our relationship, when she came to my place and changed the bulb of a perfectly working lamp just to show me Amelie had taught her how to.

She was so happy, dancing around the kitchen of my minuscule apartment to the latest Midnight Reckless album, only shorts and a bra on.

I knew I wanted to spend my life with her.

But I didn't ask, because tying herself to someone was the last thing she needed after craving independence for so long. Instead I just stood by her side, watching her spread her wings. Long-distance when she left for college, then no distance when she came back and decided not to move back in with Amelie and Ian.

We've been living together ever since, through her first job, which she hated, and the second one, which had her working sixty hours a week. All the way to something that makes her happy.

"Why now?" Sadie asks, still tilting the box to see every part of the ring.

"It feels like the right moment."

It is, right? She's on her way to being promoted to senior designer. We've moved to a bigger place—with an extra room "just in case." She's been hinting at being ready for the next phase of her life.

And it sounds like she's planning to do it with me.

"Do I have your blessing?"

Though I expect a snarky little comment, her lips twist and she nods frantically. "Of course, Dad." She hugs me again, and I can hear her sniffle against my shoulder. "I'm so happy for you."

"Thank you, sweetheart."

She leans back, and once I wipe away the single tear down her cheek, she peers down at the ring. "So how are we doing this?"

"Well, I—"

"There you are!" Charlotte says as she comes out of the back entrance. From the corner of my eye, I see Sadie close the box and shove it in her pocket. "I came to see if your dad was still waiting for you."

She walks around me, brushing my shoulder, then hugs Sadie. "Happy birthday, kiddo."

"Thank you, Charlotte."

Sadie's widened gaze meets mine over Charlotte's shoulder, and I shrug. I didn't come up with a plan. I figured Sadie and I would talk about it, craft the perfect moment. We'll have to discuss it some other time.

"Is he keeping you here against your will?" Charlotte asks, probably sensing the weird vibe. She holds Sadie's shoulders, then turns to me. "It's her birthday, Aaron. Christmas is for family, birthdays are for friends."

I raise both hands. "She's free to go."

"Hm." Focusing on Sadie again, she says, "Your gift is waiting for you in the living room."

"Is it—"

"Uh-huh. A spectacular red leather dress that will give Finn a headache."

"*Excuse me?*" Did she say leather?

"Because the red is really bright!" Charlotte says. She turns to Sadie, and I'm pretty sure she winks. "Try it on."

"Can I wear it tonight at the party?"

"No," I say without thinking, but I quickly realize she wasn't asking me.

"Yes, if it fits right, it's ready to be worn."

Sadie squeals, then runs off into the house.

I look up at Charlotte, who settles on my lap and takes one of the beers. She drinks a sip, one arm circling the back of my neck. "Sixteen, huh?"

"Don't change the topic. A red *leather*—"

"She was only six when I met her."

Unfair. Nostalgia, today, is an unfair game, and she knows that.

"At Tony's," I murmur.

"And she still has never once eaten a pepperoni pizza."

When her eyes glisten with tears, I squeeze her hand. "You okay?"

"Yeah, just . . ." She laughs through the tears. "She's *sixteen*. You're *so* old, Aaron."

"Jeez," I say, playfully shoving her.

"I look around sometimes, and it's overwhelming." She wets her lips. "Our beautiful house, the little model train I got you on that Switzerland trip, those pots you always whine about—"

"Ceramic is delicate, I—"

"And the tree we planted when we got here, or the sewing room you made for me . . . I look at it all and I just feel *overwhelmed* in the best possible way."

I press my forehead against her jaw. "We're lucky, aren't we?"

"So lucky." More tears escape when she blinks, but her smile is as wide as ever. "She can *drive* now," she says with a more cheerful tone. "Little Sadie with the pigtails can *drive*."

I rub slow circles on her wrists. "I know."

"She's smart, kind, and beautiful. She's a full person. A good kid."

"Yeah." I kiss the shell of her ear. "We did a good job."

She melts into me, her face pressed to the side of my head. "In moments like these, I miss her. I miss sneaking her wine after you and Darren mumbled about her bed time."

Mom. Yeah, I miss her too. In the big moments, and the small ones even more. She became a mom to Charlotte too—a real mother. And she left us when we still needed her so much.

Charlotte must notice the tension in my jaw because she presses a kiss to my forehead. "I love you, you know? You gave me all of this. This life, this *dream*. The most perfect family. And yourself."

"Me? I gave you everything?" I shake my head. "Everything you have, you got yourself. I'm just the lucky man who gets to come home to you. Laugh with you. Build something with you."

She pulls back slightly to study my expression, and she must see something she *really* likes, because she leans forward and kisses my lips.

"Charlotte?"

We both turn, and the horror of seeing Sadie in an incredibly suggestive red leather dress is quickly smothered when I notice she's holding out the ring box.

Charlotte gasps, bringing a hand to her lips.

"I think my dad wants to marry you."

Meeting her gaze, all my confusion dissipates. Of course that's how we should do it. Together. With her stealing my line, just like old times.

It's perfect.

"What—wait. Do you mean that?" she asks Sadie. Without waiting for an answer, she faces me. "Do *you*?"

I grin. "Well, she didn't just happen to find a ring your size."

"Aaron—*Aaron!*"

"Charlotte, will you—"

"Stop it! No, don't stop. I just . . ." She sobs, hands cupping my face. "Do you mean it?"

"Will you marry—"

"Holy shit!"

Sadie chuckles behind us.

"Will you . . . let me speak?"

Charlotte laughs too, nodding, and I gently pull her hair back, hoping to soothe her tremor. "You make the ordinary feel like magic, Charlotte. Every morning next to you, every night falling asleep to the sound of your breath—that's all I've ever needed. All I'll ever want." My thumb brushes over her tears. "So . . . will you do me the honor of being your husband?"

"Y-yes," she stutters. "Yes, of course I will. God, I love you." She surges forward, kissing me in frantic little bursts—my cheeks, my forehead, my nose, my lips, my jaw. Her mouth is everywhere, wet with tears and laughter. "You idiot," she whispers against my skin. "You beautiful, ridiculous, perfect idiot. I can't believe you— you just— I love you so much."

I catch her face in my hands, but she's already moving, wild and weightless like joy has made her float. "Let me see it! I *have* to see the ring!"

She joins Sadie, and as they side-hug, they both study the ring with unfiltered joy.

The sound of muffled footsteps has me turning in time to see Logan and Primrose round the corner with the twins. Mal, last born, follows after his mom, but I'm pretty sure I hear even more people walking up. "Hey! What are you guys up to?"

"It's Sadie's sixteenth birthday," Logan calls back. "What do you think we're doing?"

Amelie and Heaven turn the corner next, followed by Shane,

Ian, and Marty, deep in conversation. Last, Nevaeh scrambles toward us with a six-pack.

"We're here for Sadie's first beer!"

"Too late," she calls as I hold up the bottle.

There's a chorus of disappointed *aww*s, but I'm pretty sure they'll be glad they came anyway.

Charlotte glances at me as if checking for confirmation, and when I nod, she announces, "You guys . . . this happened," then holds the ring box up.

"What?" "Oh my god!" "*Finally!*"

I glare at Ian for that last comment, then stand and accept my brother's hug, watching as Charlotte is squeezed by her sister from over his gigantic shoulder. "Wow. Congratulations, man. Mom would be so happy."

My heart stutters, the echo of her loss still digging craters in my soul like it was yesterday. "Thank you." I cling to him tighter, and he to me for a moment. Then, he pats my back twice and steps back, one hand still on my shoulder. "Great, *great* fuckup."

"Best fuckup of my life."

He clicks his tongue. "Well, give yourself some credit. You'll undoubtedly fuck up again."

Ian is the next one to hug me, then Amelie shrieks so loud into my ear I feel lightheaded, asking how I dared not ask her for Charlotte's hand. But through it all, I watch my beautiful girlfriend—my *fiancée* —glowing with happiness. She said yes, and now she's telling everyone, showing off her ring like it's the most precious thing she owns.

"Charlotte, can I try it on?" Harper asks before Maeve starts jumping on the spot.

"Me too, me too!"

"Girls," Primrose gently scolds. "How about we let Charlotte try it on first?"

All eyes are on me as Charlotte twirls, facing my direction. I didn't know we'd have an audience for this, but I guess it makes sense. The last ten years has been a group assignment, and the only reason we're here is that we did it together.

I'm happy they're here for this too.

I gesture at her to step closer, then ask for the ring back. I swear I see her frowning as she returns it, as if she doesn't know it's just for a second.

I take it out of the box, then gently hold her hand and look into her eyes. I guess I've already delivered my speech, but there's so much more I could say. So much more I want to say. I understand her feeling—it's overwhelming.

"Charlotte, when I met you, I had a very clear picture of what happiness meant to me. Working in a kitchen, being close to my family, having a healthy, happy daughter."

I glance at our friends, watching us in complete silence.

"I was tirelessly working toward those goals when you showed up. And I thought . . ." I shake my head. "I thought you'd wipe all my efforts away like the most beautiful tornado. But it turns out . . . I would have never gotten any of it if it wasn't for you."

Charlotte's fingers trace my jaw. "That's not true, Chef. *You* did it."

"*We* did it." I slide the ring on her finger, her hand immediately clenching around mine. It looks so good I could die. "And it turns out you were what was missing from my plans. What I needed for everything else to make sense."

When she lets out a strangled sob, I kiss the tip of her nose.

"You're the cherry on top."

THE END

Also by Letizia Lorini

.

Acknowledgments

Time for lots of much needed "thank yous."

First, I want to express my deepest gratitude to my incredible beta readers—Erin, Iqra, Amanda, and Leticia. You've helped me shape this book into something I'm truly proud of, and your unhinged reactions gave me *life*.

To Britt, my amazing editor, thank you for giving the book the careful trimming it needed. Every single one of your "unprofessional comments" was thoroughly appreciated.

To my agent, Caitlin, who has been in my corner through both the easy and tough times, thank you for your endless patience.

Thank you, Sam, for another beautiful cover, and to Madison for all her assistance as we prepare for the release.

Elodie and L.H., thank you for being not just beta readers but also confidants, fellow authors, and my closest friends. Your unwavering support means the world to me. You've listened to my endless voice messages, and that takes real character. Respect.

To my friends and family, thank you for always asking about the book, for patiently waiting as the timeline stretched out, and for being there every step of the way.

And finally, to Caroline, my beautiful girlfriend, thank you for still being my girlfriend after all these years and books. That, too, takes character. Respect-times-two.

Thank you to my ARC team, to each and every bookstagrammer and booktoker who helped me make it through another great release.

To the community, which at times is one of the kindest and most supportive spaces I've ever found myself in.

And finally, to you, my reader.

Thank you for taking another wild ride with me. I hope you've loved following the stories of these characters through all their messy turns. And I can't wait for you to read the final installment: it'll be the perfect goodbye to the series.

As I always do, I remind you here of the importance of reviews. If you liked the book (heck, even if you didn't) I'd appreciate you reviewing it on any platform.

Love,
Letizia

About the Author

Letizia Lorini is a USA Today bestselling author who is passionate about heartwarming books with high cackling potential. Originally Italian and currently based in a Scandinavian country, she lives with her partner and their fluffy Japanese Spitz. She also has a degree in sociology and one in criminology, speaks three languages, and drinks the daily recommended dose of coffee before breakfast. Find out more at LetiziaLorini.com.

facebook.com/letizialorini.author

instagram.com/letizialorini.writes

tiktok.com/@letizialorini.author

Printed in Dunstable, United Kingdom